NEW HOUSE 5

How a Dorm Becomes a Home

ANDY BUTLER

Copyright © 2005 Andy Butler

www.newhouse5.com

ISBN: 1469990741
ISBN-13: 978-1469990743

Cover designed by Stephanie Mooney
www.mooneydesigns.net

*Dedicated to New House 5, the fifty-six most inspiring
individuals I have ever had the privilege to know.*

TABLE OF CONTENTS

INTRODUCTION

You've got to start somewhere
Find a reason, get a clue
- For Sara

Everybody wants to make a difference. Once in a while, we get a chance to.

My name is Andy. I was born in Seoul, South Korea. Adopted while I was still in the womb, shipped to the USA when I was a few months old, and American as baseball ever since. In Korea, I received the name Ik Hawn Kim. I couldn't tell you what that means if my life depended on it. Here, my adoptive parents named me Andrew Michael Butler. I've been Andy ever since. I'm twenty years old, a junior at college, and last year, I had one of those rare chances to truly make a difference. I was a resident assistant.

Challenging, exciting, heartbreaking, saddening, nerve-wracking. Being a resident assistant was all of these things, but more than anything else, it was the most rewarding experience of my life. I made some incredible friends, was introduced to new cultures and perspectives, and learned more about the world around me than I can even begin to explain. At some schools, RAs are merely policemen, upperclass students who want nothing to do with their residents and smile only when they're told to. Not at my school. At Ashford University, we're about community. And community is what I tried to build. In the process, stories unfolded and relationships were forged.

The phrase "New House 5" could mean a lot of things. It sounds like it could be a band name, a superhero group, maybe a secret code. But for me, New House 5 means more than you can imagine. New House 5 was my floor. New House was the name of our dorm. It was so new, as we liked to say, that it didn't have a name. I was on was the 5th floor, the top of the building. Hence, New House 5. In August, it was just a floor. By May, it was my home.

The characters in my story have been fictionalized to protect anonymity and some situations have been dramatized, but what you are about to read is all based in truth. And it all took place on one residential floor, in one year. Thinking about it now, I can't believe some of the things that happened, and I feel fortunate that I had a chance to make that difference. I think I made the most of my opportunity, but that's up to you to decide.

The friendships I made with residents on my floor last year are some of the strongest I've made in my life. The people in this story are people I truly connected with, people I truly love, and people I will never forget. This story is for all of them, for everyone who made my experience as a resident assistant for New House 5 the most amazing year of my life. Through all of the tribulations, through all of the drama, through all of the problems, we were always there for each other. We were always a community. That's what this story is about: New House 5, the community.

Now, I'm back at school for my junior year and, sitting in front of my glowing laptop, nothing feels more appropriate than telling you my story. Everything is true, everything is real, everything elicits some kind of emotion in my soul. Writing this will no doubt make me nostalgic about what has happened to me and to the people around me over the last fifteen months. The clock lets me know the time is 12:32 a.m. If I'm going to tell you everything that happened last year, we might be here for a while. So let me go put on my pajamas, make some hot chocolate, and share with you the best story I've ever been a part of.

FALL SEMESTER
2003

A NEW BEGINNING

Summer comes and summer goes
And leaves me in its wake
- Things I Learned Over Summer Break

There's nothing quite like driving seventy miles an hour down the highway with the windows down and the radio cranked up. Even after nineteen years, I still get the same thrill when I stick my hand out the window and into the summer air. The feel of the wind against your fingers, the burning sun turning your skin bronze. I don't think I'll ever get tired of that, not even when I'm eighty years old.

On this particular day, in mid-August of 2003, I was heading back to school for my sophomore year. For me, school is in Pittsburgh, a five-hour drive from my home in rural upstate New York. The windows were down and the factory stereo system in my '96 Lumina was blaring. I love this drive. It's easy, it's refreshing, and it always gives me time to myself. Five hours of privacy has become something to write home about. In a few hours, privacy would be a fantasy. Being a resident assistant is a full-time job.

While I was driving, my excitement began to build. I was more excited than I had ever been in my life. I knew being an RA was a big responsibility. But I also knew if I did things right, I could have a positive impact on a lot of freshmen. My freshman year was an incredible experience. For the first time ever, I was around ambitious people in an ambitious environment. No more breezing through classes, no more slacking off on weekends, no more sitting in the back with my hands neatly folded. I missed Dean's List first semester but I made it the second. I joined groups I hated, found a few I liked. I made some friends I'll keep for the rest of my life, I had my heart broken. The typical freshman year. What a rush.

My freshman experience had such a profound impact on me that I decided to become a resident assistant, or "RA" as the lingo goes. That is to say, I applied to be an RA, and I was lucky enough to be selected. To me, being an RA was about helping people. It's what I love to do, and now, it was my job. I was in charge of an entire floor of freshmen, fifty-six of them in all. Goodbye free time, goodbye privacy. Hello responsibility.

I looked up and saw a sign marked with the words "Grove City." Grove City always sneaks up on me, but I'm glad it exists. It always lets me know I'm about an hour from Pittsburgh. It's like a giant green sign that says, "I hope you enjoyed relaxing. It's time to start working." In just an hour, my peaceful ride would be over. During a five-hour drive, you spend the first half getting into it and the last half anticipating what's ahead. That's what happens when you think too much. Free time isn't really free time; it's just an opportunity for your mind to wander. Sometimes, that's the worst thing you can let your mind do. Me, I always think too much. But maybe that's why I can connect with people like I do.

Passing Grove City was my cue to turn off the radio. Without the music, my brain had a chance to focus on the world around me. And to think about what I was getting myself into. I was coming back early, well before classes started, for RA training and Freshman Orientation. I knew the next two weeks would be the busiest of my year. A million scenarios ran through my head: What if my floor doesn't take me seriously? What if they see me as too much of an authority figure? What if they hate me? By the time I finished going through them all, the Cathedral of Learning was in full view. The University of Pittsburgh claims the Cathedral is the largest academic building in the world. Whether it is or not, I don't care. What matters is that it tells me I'm half a mile from home. If home is where the heart is, then Pittsburgh is my home.

A few minutes later, I pulled into the parking lot behind my dorm, trying to keep my composure. "As much as I worry," I assured myself, "this whole RA thing will be easy. Like cake." During the next two semesters, I was in for quite a reality check.

Walking into my dorm felt more like walking into a Holiday Inn. The lobby was pristine, complete with a big screen TV, live plants, and a trophy case. And in addition to looking like a hotel, it felt like heaven. Air conditioning may be the best invention since pizza delivery. And we were the only freshman dorm to have it.

"New House," as we were called, was just what the name would make you believe. New. This was the first year it would be occupied by residents. It had all the modern amenities you'd want in a place you were going to live. It was one giant house. And it was my job to make it a home.

New House was built between two other dorms on Kensington Avenue, a street just off to the side of our campus. Ashford University had been suffering recently from a housing shortage, so it was time to build a new dorm. New House will be called New House until someone coughs up enough money to change the name. From the outside, it looked like any other new building. The windows were big, letting in plenty of sunshine. The architecture was modern, making the view from the front tasteful and intriguing. On a hot day in August, stepping into the cool air conditioning felt like being cleansed. A fresh start, a clean slate.

Five floors made up New House. On floors two through five, there were fifty-six students. Twenty-eight girls on one side, twenty-eight guys on the other. The first floor was inhabited by twenty-six young men, while the other half of the ground floor was occupied by a state-of-the-art kitchen, a laundry room, a huge lounge, a dining area, a study room, and a recreational room complete with pool and ping pong tables. Every floor had a shared bathroom on each side with enough showers and toilets that no one ever had to wait long to use the facilities. Each wing was also complete with a "main" lounge at each end of the hall as well as a "mini" lounge, halfway between the main lounge and the elevators. With all these amenities, New House was not your typical college dorm, but I wasn't about to complain.

I was the first RA to arrive, as I usually am. First to everything. First kid to class, sitting in the middle row of the lecture hall, not too far away, but not too close. First to volunteer if something needs to be done. First to take the blame if something isn't done right. And now, first to move in. I unloaded my car and stacked my belongings outside my room. I lived on the 5th floor, the top of the building. I figured it would be easier to just get everything inside the building, then move it into my room. The big stuff went first: the TV, the clothes, the stereo. The smaller things came next: the books, the toiletries, the sports equipment. And last of all, the object that occupies all of my free time: my guitar.

Some people name their instruments, but I just call mine "The Guitar." It doesn't really merit more than that. It's a bright red acoustic, made by a company most people don't even know exists. Every time I play it, my fingers hurt. In spite of all that, I love it to death. My number one hobby is watching sports. My number two hobby is writing songs. I had six of them before I became an RA. Now, I have about thirty. I go through spurts, times when I'll write two or three songs in a week. Then I'll go a couple months without even thinking about it. I write the music, the rhythm, and of course, the lyrics. I can't play guitar very well, I sing even worse, but my lyrics mean something, and that's what keeps me going. There's an original song lyric at the beginning of each chapter in this book. All of them relate to my story in some way. I write songs about the people around me, and being an RA gave me a lot to write about.

Once I got the guitar up to my room, I opened up my door for the first time. The first thing that popped into my head is what every college kid thinks when he opens the door: Man, this is empty. So I moved my stuff in and spent the next two hours arranging it all. Some people wait weeks to get their rooms situated, but I have to get mine set as soon as possible. I'm obsessive like that. My bed was lofted, which gave me tons of space underneath it. This was on top of the space I already had because I was living in a single. Having no roommate was going to be nice. I was looking forward to living by myself. But I soon found that the only time my room was occupied by less than two people was when I slept.

I put one of my two small dressers underneath my lofted bed. I then set my television on top of the dresser. I put together the large maroon futon I had just bought and placed it across from my bed, perfect for sitting down after a crazy day of classes and watching some baseball. I liked my futon a lot. I found it comfortable and homey, and as it turned out, I wasn't the only one. That futon got a lot of use over the next year.

My desk was placed right next to the futon, close to the door. This way, when I sat down at my desk, a quick turn of the head would let me see who was walking by. My fridge was placed adjacent to the dresser, a cheap microwave on top of that. I put up posters, everything from *Finding Nemo* to *Field of Dreams* to the 1998 Yankees. After just a couple hours work, it looked like a real dorm room. All I needed to do now was hook up my computer, every college kid's best friend. Just as I turned on my laptop, there was a knock at my door.

"Hey, hey. What's up, Andy?"

It was Elaine, my co-RA on the 5th floor. She was in charge of the twenty-eight girls on the south wing and I was responsible for twenty-eight guys on the north side. But the way we saw it, we were in charge of fifty-six people together.

"I thought I'd be the first one here. It's only two o'clock, man. Nobody else is getting here until seven or eight. Training doesn't even start until Sunday morning."

It was Friday. So maybe I was a little early. But it gave me time to settle in. Elaine lived a few rooms down from me during my freshman year, so she had no problem giving me a hard time. Judging by her smile and enthusiasm, I'd say she might have been almost as excited as I was. Almost.

"Yeah, yeah. I just wanted to get everything under control before training starts. How was your summer?"

"How was your summer?" is every returning college student's favorite question. Over the next couple weeks I asked it a hundred times, and got asked just as many. The thing is, most people don't really care how your summer went, they're just being polite. And most people don't actually say how their summer was. But not Elaine. She's got the southern girl talk-your-ear-off mentality, and she proceeded to tell me about her entire summer spent in Houston, her hometown. I zoned out from time to time, but hey, it was still a more interesting response than your standard "Great, how was yours?"

Elaine and I talked for a while about what we were looking forward to before she left to set up her own room. Elaine and I were in a very exciting position. Unlike the other floors in New House, the 5th floor was going to be an academic housing cluster. That might sound scary, but all it meant was that most of the residents (fifty out of fifty-six, as it turned out) were in the same academic program. The program, called Science and Humanities Scholars (or SHS for short), was comprised of about fifty students per year. They had been identified as top interdisciplinary students who had interests in both the sciences and the humanities. One big draw for the program is that all SHS freshmen are given an opportunity to live in the housing cluster together, which had its benefits and drawbacks. On the down side, it didn't make for a lot of academic diversity within the floor. There were no art majors or engineers on the 5th floor, only students majoring in a natural science, social science, or humanity. But the positives far outweigh the negatives. I know this because I'm in SHS myself, along with Elaine, and we both lived on the SHS floor our freshman year. It allows for a better community, since the students all have similar interests, take similar classes, and plan on pursuing similar careers. Because of this, there was a lot of pressure on Elaine and me to turn the 5th floor into an example for the rest of the campus, but I tried not to think about the pressure too much. I knew I just had to do my part my part and hope for the best.

I spent the rest of the day relaxing, because in less than twenty-four hours, everything would start. RA training, Freshman Orientation, and the academic school year. I knew it would go quickly. This was my last chance to be alone and stress-free. Before becoming an RA, I spent most of my life as sort of a loner. I never had any "best" friends in high school, I always depended on myself. And I let other people depend on me. So while I was counting on my residents relying on me as an RA, I never imagined that I would rely on my floor for some things. It's funny how that works. All I could think about was how excited I was for the freshmen to arrive. I had a billion ideas rushing through my head: how to get them motivated, how to make them feel comfortable, programs, activities, trips, meetings. I wanted to do it all in five minutes, make everyone each other's best friend. All before they even got to Ashford. I needed to calm down. I took a short nap and dreamt of the year to come.

When I woke up from my nap, I went downstairs to the kitchen to see if we had any food. During training, the RAs were told we would be fed, and I hoped the fridge was already stocked. When I went into the kitchen, I was startled to see a large black woman standing in front of the refrigerator. She turned around, apparently just as startled as I was. When we got over our initial surprise, we laughed at each other. It was just Tamira.

Tamira was the housefellow for New House. During the last few years, Ashford has phased in a new way of staffing dorms. As normal, each house has a staff of RAs, but now, they are supervised by a full-time, salaried faculty member who lives off-campus, also known as a housefellow. Tamira was originally from Arkansas, in her mid-twenties and excited about working at Ashford. She was essentially the boss of New House, and any problems with residents were discussed with her. In the kitchen, we exchanged pleasantries and went our separate ways, but I would have more than my fair share of conversations with Tamira before the year ended.

That evening, I got a chance to meet the rest of the New House RA staff. There were ten of us total, one RA for each wing plus one Community

Advisor, or CA. The CA was basically the head RA, the RA for the RAs. He was a friendly, heavyset guy named Jimmy, who I would get to know well as the year progressed. Jimmy struck me as a guy who knew exactly what he wanted to do, a man of incredible maturity. Thankfully, he never let me down.

I had met the rest of the staff during training sessions we had the previous spring, but for the first time, I was seeing all of them in a relaxed, natural state. There was Anisha, an Indian girl from Houston who loved to party and program computers. Jack, from Chicago, was the stereotypical Ashford nerd, complete with bad jokes and a wry sense of humor. Rohan, an often clueless kid who lived in India, loved soccer almost as much as he loved beer. Doug was a big half-Asian guy from Maryland who reminded me of every fun-loving college kid I've ever met. Sara, an incredibly sweet (if sometimes ditzy) blonde girl, was planning her business career after she graduated. Jane, an African-American who laughed more than the rest of us combined, was from New York City. Thurm, who lived in Boston whenever he felt like it, was probably the most eccentric guy I'd ever met. Then there was Elaine and me.

My staff played a huge role in helping me become a better RA throughout the year. I won't talk about them much, because this story is about my floor, not my co-RAs. But on that first night, as we all fooled around and ordered pizza, I realized we all had something in common. Despite our different backgrounds and interests, we all wanted to help people. It's the reason we became RAs. Rarely will you find a group of people as dedicated and selfless as the group of people I ate with that night. Some of us became friends, others talked only at staff meetings, but we all had a connection. And we all respected that.

When we departed to our respective floors for the night, we each took a deep breath. Tomorrow morning, everything would be different. A change was coming, a change to our lives and to everything we thought we knew about the world. Everything we thought we could handle, everything we thought we could be strong about was going to be challenged. When I closed my eyes that night, I accepted the challenge silently, confidently.

FIRST IMPRESSIONS

No clue what to expect
I'm so nervous now
I'm just a wreck
- Keep the Light On

RA training was a blur. Ten days of non-stop motion, non-stop thinking. Seminars, role playing, discussions. We were supposed to think about our strengths and weaknesses, but by the end of the week, I was so burnt out I didn't want to think at all. I slept a few measly hours each night and spent the rest of the day learning how to build a community, how to plan a program, how to build genuine relationships. Ninety percent of what they teach us is pointless, but that ten percent that opens your eyes is worth the whole week. For me, the payoff was realizing how important it was to be myself. Trying to be everyone's best friend, trying to be a policeman, trying to be the perfect RA—it doesn't work. I just had to be myself.

Move-in day was an adrenaline rush. The ten members of our staff had collectively gotten about eight hours of sleep the previous night. Last-minute rushing to make bulletin boards and door decorations didn't help our growing apprehension. But even with the sleep deprivation and physical fatigue, I could not have been more pumped up and excited at eight o'clock that Tuesday morning. Like the rest of my staff, I was wearing a kelly green shirt, distinctly marked with the letters "RA" on the back so everyone would know who we were. We sat in the kitchen, silently eating bagels, mentally preparing ourselves for the most grueling day of the year. My heart was in my throat. In less than an hour, students would begin to pour in. It was our job to move two hundred residents into a dormitory in an eight-hour span, be enthusiastic the whole time, and then lead a floor meeting at the end of the day. We sat and waited. The clock struck 9 a.m. The first cars pulled in. Move-in day was upon us.

After move-in day was over, I wanted nothing more than to sleep for the rest of the week. With help from the myriad of Orientation Counselors (OCs) and fraternity brothers, we helped get everyone and their luggage into the dorm. Each floor is assigned three or four OCs to motivate and encourage the incoming freshmen, and one of their jobs is to help with move-in. The fraternities, on the other hand, use this opportunity to advertise and recruit, wearing their letters and introducing themselves to awestruck freshmen. More than once I've had to kick out frat guys who were hitting on the freshman girls as they unpacked. I guess there are a variety of motivations.

We spent the day directing traffic, lugging suitcases up five flights of stairs when the elevators were full, stacking boxes onto dollies. I was thanked profusely by students and parents who appreciated my help and friendliness, but I was chewed out by just as many for not being careful with baggage or being too intrusive. I introduced myself about a thousand times, to parents, to students, and sometimes accidentally to siblings who I thought were students. Towards the end of the day when I was becoming delirious, I introduced myself to a poor family that I'd already greeted on three previous occasions. My arms felt like jelly, my legs were about to collapse, I was hoarse and thirsty, but I could not imagine a more fun and exhilarating way to spend that sweltering Tuesday.

I don't think I ever explained what my job as a resident assistant actually is. While OCs are just around during Orientation, I actually live on the floor in a single room. I told my residents, "You'll never be able to get rid of me." As I said before, I was in charge of twenty-eight guys, Elaine was in charge of twenty-eight girls, and we were separated by wing. I had four main jobs: an administrator, a crisis responder, a community builder, and a peer counselor. I was there as a resource for the students. If they needed suggestions about classes, had a burnt out light bulb, wanted to complain about janitorial services, or talk about private issues, I was there. If someone needed to go to the hospital, I was the first contact. And more importantly than anything else, I planned events and programs to bring the floor together as a community. I wanted everyone on the floor to feel comfortable with each other. That was my ultimate goal. All for fifty-five hundred dollars a year. But honestly, I would have done it for nothing.

The floor I was in charge of was all freshmen, as I've also said. This makes my job more hands-on than a mixed-class dorm and it can also be much more rewarding. When I wasn't lugging crates, I was on the floor, getting to know my new residents. I met young men and women from New York City, Philadelphia, Washington D.C., Houston, San Jose, Nebraska. City dwellers, rural farmers, rich snobs. Whether or not they wanted to admit it, they all had one thing in common: They were clueless. Most of them were scared as hell, and I sympathized with them because that's exactly how I felt on my move-in day. I assured those who seemed uncertain and awestruck that Orientation would more than prepare them for the start of the school year. And I explained to those who seemed over-confident that Orientation was a learning tool to be taken seriously. Everyone comes in on page one. If you think you're on page twenty, you're in for a surprise.

Early in the afternoon, a tall, lanky kid with dark hair and thick eyebrows called my name. It startled me.

"ANDY! Hey, you told me to yell at you if I needed anything. So my parents and I are trying to figure out where to go eat dinner. Do you have any suggestions?"

"Yeah, there's a bunch of places down towards the University of Pittsburgh that you can walk to."

I spent the next few minutes explaining the pros and cons of such eateries as Fuel and Fuddle, Uncle Sam's Subs, and Joe Mama's. Before he left, he asked me a few more questions about my major, my freshman year, and my views on Ashford. I answered truthfully, pointing out the good and the bad. I think he respected that.

"You know what," I said, "I just realized that I don't know your name. I'm sure I introduced myself to you earlier, but I probably introduced myself to about a hundred people today. I'm really sorry."

"It's okay, I understand. I'm Samuel Dahl."

"Do you go by Samuel?"

"Sam, actually. Samuel sounds too official for me."

Sam told me a little about himself. He was raised Jewish in a liberal part of the Midwest and planned on studying psychology. He mentioned that he still had a lot of uncertainties about Ashford. I got the impression that Sam was confident in himself and his surroundings, but also somewhat of a pessimist.

"I'm majoring in psychology, but I really have no clue what I want to do. I'm a failure at life. The only things I'm really passionate about are photography and guitar."

"Hey, I play guitar, too," I told him. "We'll have to jam sometime."

This caught his attention. "Yeah, that would be cool. I'm not very good but I love to play."

"I'm in the same boat as you, man. And as for figuring out what you want to do, we can talk about that later. You know what you're passionate about, so you're a couple steps ahead of most people."

"Thanks a lot, Andy. I'll see you tonight at the floor meeting."

I waved and watched him walk away. Sam always looked sort of awkward with his tall, thin body that clothes never fit on very well, but he never hesitated to talk to me if he needed to, and that's all I could have asked for: someone open to my help.

As I turned away from Sam, another freshman walked towards me and asked if I had a screwdriver.

"Yeah, I've got one. Follow me to my room," I said.

"Thanks a lot, man. I have to put this stupid bookshelf together."

I chuckled. "What do you think of Ashford so far?"

"Honestly, I'm still in awe. This dorm is amazing. My older sister goes to Georgetown and I figured the dorms would be like hers. But this is overwhelming."

As I handed him my screwdriver I saw something that made me cringe. He was wearing a Boston Red Sox hat.

"Um, there's going to be a problem this year, buddy," I said gravely.

"What's that?"

"I'm a Yankees fan."

"Ooooh." He laughed heartily. "Yeah, there's going to be a serious problem. I'm Rob, by the way."

Rob Chang and I became friends instantaneously. He was a short Chinese kid from Boston who reminded me a lot of myself: quiet, confident, and excited. Initially I thought he was a little reserved, but I'd soon find out just how wrong that was.

We talked baseball for a few minutes, each of us passionately defending our respective teams. Rob had pitched in high school before he threw out his arm. He lost a lot of his physical ability but never his love for a game that most people can't stand. If for no other reason than that, we knew we shared a bond. As Rob walked away with my screwdriver, I couldn't help thinking that this year might not be so bad.

6 p.m. was the calm before the storm. Most of the students were out eating with their parents, saying their goodbyes, making some last-minute purchases. I sat in the study lounge and looked out the windows over the entrance of the building, watching the students part with their families from five stories up. I would often have to remind myself over the next few weeks that for many of these kids, it was the first time they were going to be away from home for longer than a weekend. The freedom excited some students, it scared others to death. Luckily, in the age of the cell phone, Mom and Dad were only ten digits away. As I watched from my comfortable perch above, I saw a lot of hugs, a lot of tears, and a lot of eager freshmen. This is one day when Mom is allowed to cry, son is allowed to say "I love you," and daughter is allowed to hug Dad for more than three seconds. Goodbye meant goodbye for a long time. It was easy to pick out the parents who had other children in college from the first-timers. I smiled at one mother as I walked by the elevator back to my room. She was wiping her eyes, trying to hide the fact that she was crying.

"I feel so dumb. It's not like he's going to die. It's just college." She spoke softly between sniffles.

"Hey, don't worry about it. My mom did the same thing. If you weren't upset about leaving your son for the first time, I'm not sure what that says about you as a parent."

She looked at me and smiled again, a few tears trickling down her face. "Thank you." And with that, she stepped onto the elevator.

"I'll keep your son in line, don't worry," I yelled as the elevator door closed. I had no clue which of my twenty-eight guys her son was, but I meant what I said.

6:45 p.m. rolled around and it was finally time for the first floor meeting. This was the most important hour and a half I would have with my floor. It was the first time the entire floor would be in the same place at the same time, and it would be their first impression of me, an impression that would last for the rest of the year. It was time to put aside all the exhaustion and make the most of the day's last adrenaline rush.

When I walked into the lounge area, the eyes of twenty-eight freshmen turned to me. The furniture had been moved around to allow everyone to sit or stand comfortably. As I looked around at the students, I saw twenty-eight different emotions on twenty-eight different faces. Fear, apprehension, eagerness, uncertainty. In the next ninety minutes, I had to make all of these feelings go away. I started by relating their current state to my own experience.

"Before we start this meeting, I just want to tell you all something. First of all, you're here. You're a freshman at one of the world's most prestigious colleges. You've spent all summer getting ready to come here, you've spent all day moving in, and now you're on your own. Take a second to breathe in deep and think about what you've just accomplished, because it's pretty amazing."

After a short pause, I continued.

"Secondly, I want to let you all know that freshmen on the first day of Orientation generally fall into two distinct categories. Scared as hell or not scared as hell. If you fall into the 'scared as hell' category, it's okay, because most of this room is in the same boat and I can tell you that's how I felt on my first day of Orientation, too. Just relax, try to take everything in, and I can promise you that by the first day of classes, you'll already be a veteran on this campus."

I think that eased the tension a little, and the meeting went on smoothly from there. I explained to everyone what my role was and went over some basic community standards for the building. The Orientation Counselors assigned to my floor—two amazing guys named Matt and Eugene who were more enthusiastic than I could have ever hoped for—talked about the purpose and logistics of Freshmen Orientation.

Elaine and I decided to bring both sides together for this first night, so with fifteen minutes to go, I led the guys over to the girls' side. As all fifty-eight of us took turns introducing ourselves, the mood once again grew quiet and tense. When I introduced myself, I explained that I liked to play guitar. One of the guys across the room said, "Maybe you can teach me."

Laughing, I replied, "I can teach you how to suck."

As soon as I closed my mouth, Rob Chang yelled, "What? I'm telling my mom my RA is teaching me how to suck!"

That single immature comment sent the room up in laughter, and from that moment on, the 5th floor of New House was no longer separated by wing. It was a single entity. All thanks to a lewd remark by Rob Chang. It wouldn't be the last time Rob made a difference on the floor.

Following the first floor meeting, we led everyone to Ashford's football stadium to take part in the school's notorious freshmen initiation, known as Playfair. Playfair is one giant icebreaker involving the entire freshmen class that lasts for two hours. It's one of those events you can never forget, no matter how hard you try. Watching it as an upperclassman did give a very different perspective, though. My freshman year, I thought Playfair was the most pointless activity ever, but as I watched the students, all clad in their black Orientation t-shirts, running around the field, learning hundreds of names, sorting themselves by birthday and major, I couldn't help seeing the purpose. Very few people like Playfair when they're doing it, but when you look back, it's really cool to think that your entire class, all one thousand plus people, were confined to one small area making fools of themselves and not caring one bit. The essence of college. I smiled. When the festivities ended, I walked back to the dorm for some much needed sleep.

The rest of Orientation went smoothly. As the week progressed, residents of the floor grew more comfortable with each other and with me. On the first night, most of the floor went to bed relatively early, but after that, people started hanging out in the lounges at night. On the second evening, I heard music coming from the lounge. I walked in to find two of the guys playing guitar and singing along to a Weezer song.

"We should have a 5th floor band or something," I said.

"We've got enough people for one." The response came from Eric, a tall redhead from Boston. He was athletic, temperamental, and very, very Irish. As it turned out, Eric was the best of several guitar players on our floor.

The other guitarist in the lounge was Gary, a goofy Korean kid from New Jersey who had one of the most distinct personalities on the floor. He was loud, obnoxious, and constantly stoned. The first time I saw Gary in action was that night when he played a song he'd written. In one of the most annoying singing voices I have ever heard, Gary wailed lyrics that included, "I hope he gave you STDs, I hope you die from AIDS." I walked away shaking my head. It would be an interesting year.

I swung over to the girls' side where I ran into several residents I had already met. Rosalyn had gotten to school before the other freshmen for minority student Orientation, Meghan had come early for soccer. I said hello to them and continued down the hall, following the noise I could hear emanating from the lounge. When I arrived, there was a heated debate going.

"The most important quality in a guy is definitely his brains. It's a total turnoff when a guy is stupid. I could date someone who doesn't have a fabulous body, but not an idiot."

"No way, I disagree. It's definitely how whipped you can make him. I want a guy who doesn't know how to say no."

As I walked around the corner, the four girls having the conversation burst into laughter.

"What do you think the most important quality in a guy is, Andy?" one of the girls asked me.

"Definitely his body," I said sarcastically. "I couldn't date a guy without nice pecs."

More laughter told me that I had given a good answer.

"Hey, Andy, can I ask you sort of a strange question? Are you going to be a cool RA?" It was one of the girls with dark brown hair.

"What exactly is a cool RA?" I asked.

"I don't know. Are you going to be, like, a jerk?"

I suppressed a laugh. "No, I can guarantee you I won't. I just want to try to help you guys out. The whole policeman deal, I don't like that stuff. As long as you guys are open with me and respect me and the rules, we'll be cool."

"Sounds good."

The group of girls was a diverse bunch. There was Elyse, a friendly and enthusiastic Virginian who was very interested in religion. Val was an opinionated New Jersey girl who turned out to be a mother figure to several of the residents. Melissa was also from Jersey, an avid worker who thought the three most important things in life were school, service, and sex, in no particular order. She was a big help when our floor did volunteer work. And finally, there was Alicia, the girl who first spoke to me. Alicia was a sweet girl from the Midwest, short and pretty with brown hair and a captivating smile. But I would learn as the semester progressed that Alicia had some confidence issues. She was quickly categorized by the floor as a J.A.P., or Jewish American Princess. She was spoiled, she was beautiful, and she always got what she wanted. Later that night when I was walking around the floor, I saw Alicia staggering down the hall wearing a soaking wet shirt.

"ANDY!" she screamed two inches from my face. Her breath reeked of alcohol. "I was just at one of the frats! The guys are soooo nice. I just went in the dunk tank. It was so much fun. They wanted me to stay but I promised my mom I'd go to bed by one o'clock."

"Hmm, you should probably get to bed then, Alicia."

With that, she stumbled into her room and I made a mental note to keep an eye on her.

The Orientation events were a hodgepodge of sessions about Ashford, campus life, and diversity. There were sex talks (complete with "Condom Man," an upperclass student in a prophylactic costume who threw condoms into the audience), diversity discussions (how to deal with your homosexual roommate, how to deal with your neighbor who doesn't speak a word of English), and tours of Pittsburgh (where to get the best ice cream and cheap food). Orientation was tiring for the freshmen. They were up every morning by eight, ran around all day, and didn't get much free time until well after the sun went down. But as I said, this gave the floor a chance to bond. They were around each other constantly, and by the end of the week, friendships and groups were already beginning to form.

By Friday, I knew everyone's name, where they were from, and some interesting thing about them. Aaron was a Philadelphian who was already eligible for upper-level chemistry classes. Kim was a half-Asian girl from Houston who loved to write and dance. Jeremy was a basketball player from an affluent area of Boston. Hillary was from Detroit, and she lived and died with the Red Wings. Kate was a quiet but good-looking girl from New Jersey who liked to keep to herself. Chad was from the Pittsburgh area, a first generation Italian who loved offending girls almost as much as he loved hitting on them.

I won't be able to talk about every resident on my floor, though I wish I could. Every person has an incredible story behind their past, their future, their desires. I was fortunate to learn many of these stories throughout the year and I only wish I could have learned more. These students taught me more about myself, about life, and about not taking anything for granted than I ever could have expected. Even from the first week of Orientation, I knew this floor would have a profound impact on how I looked at the world. On

Friday night, I said to Elaine, "I've got a feeling that this floor is going change our lives."

"I get that feeling too, Andy. Like we have no clue what we're getting into. But when we're done, we'll be thankful we had the opportunity."

As Orientation came to a close, the floor started getting anxious about classes. Students printed out their schedules and walked around campus, timing how long it would take them to get from class to class. The line to purchase textbooks at the school store was a forty-five minute wait. I was bombarded with questions like "How hard is this class?" and "Is this teacher cool?" and "How do I know what classes I can skip?"

I tried to assure everyone that after the first week of classes, they would get a feel for how the whole school thing worked. "You'll learn what you can and can't get away with, and you'll figure out real quick that you're not in high school anymore. That first 50% on an exam will shock you into shape."

I made a deal with the floor that if they collectively got a 3.5 GPA the first semester, I would dye my hair pink. This excited them immensely, but I was secretly not worried. A 3.5 is tough to get your freshmen year, especially at this school. You're still adjusting to college, you're taking required classes that may not coincide with what you're best at, and you have to figure out how to study. What got you an A-minus in high school will probably get you a D-plus at Ashford, so I figured my hair was probably safe.

The last big event before the start of the school year is a glorified field day we like to call House Wars. The freshmen in each dorm compete against each other in events such as tug-of-war, passing a soapy watermelon, and three-legged races. As ridiculous as it sounds, House Wars is, without question, my favorite part of Orientation. Our floor tie-dyed t-shirts and painted our faces green. We screamed and yelled until we couldn't breathe as we ran around the grassy area in the middle of our campus, taunting other dorms and throwing water balloons. It was a great community-building activity. The freshmen worked together to accomplish their tasks while the Orientation Counselors, Elaine, and I led the cheerleading for our floor. We made a giant flag out of a bed sheet and sprinted across the field with it.

At the end of the night, New House was in one of the top two positions. For the final event, we had to pick our twelve strongest guys to do a winner-take-all tug-of-war with another one of the first-year dorms to determine the ultimate winner. The rope actually broke, but since we were winning when it snapped, New House won the coveted House Wars trophy. To celebrate, some of the kids took the New House flag and hoisted it up the flag pole in the middle of campus. I smiled to Elaine and said, "I'm sure that's illegal in some way, but it sure is cool."

Sunday night marked the last floor meeting of Orientation. By then, the entire floor was very comfortable busting my chops, making fun of me when I misspoke, and giving me a hard time about the Yankees' losing streak. I thanked my great Orientation Counselors, thanked the students for being so enthusiastic, and wished everyone good luck on their first day at school. As the crowd dispersed and the chatter switched to who had what class and when, it gave me a chance to reflect on the hectic week that we had all just been through.

Despite the complaints, the lack of free time, and the bad food, I could tell that everyone had enjoyed Orientation. We'd all made an impression on each other during those first few days. Some first impressions turned out to be right, others changed with time. But this first week got the ball rolling. I saw early signs of the community that would eventually form on New House 5. It's hard to develop strong friendships in a week when you've known your friends back home for eighteen years, but everyone on the floor kept an open mind, and that's the key. An open mind and a little patience will take you a long way. I went to bed that night feeling good about the week and confident that New House 5 would become more than just a place to sleep.

SETTLING IN

Leave your mark and sign your name
We'll mail your fifteen minutes of fame
- Perfect Sense

The first day of classes felt refreshing. It was cool and crisp outside, the type of weather that lets you know autumn is on the way, so enjoy the summer while you can. There's something about walking outside onto a bustling college campus and for just a few seconds, breathing in deep and remembering why being alive is so amazing. After two weeks of nonstop running around, it was finally time to start school. It's easy to forget the main reason you're at college is to get an education, especially during Freshmen Orientation. But I knew once I got to class, the professors would remind me all too well.

The bathroom was the busiest place in the dorm at 8 a.m. Every shower stall was occupied, every sink was being used, and each young man was checking his hair in the mirror. The first day of college doesn't have the same feel as the first day of high school. In college, you feel more independent, more confident, and a hell of a lot older. Fashion takes a back seat to comfort and convenience. Sometimes I go to class in my pajamas. So although the freshmen tried to look nice on the first day, I knew they would soon slip into the habit of forgetting to put on sneakers when they left the dorm.

On my way out, I walked by Rob, who was knocking on someone's door.

"Chad told me to wake him up for class. He said he'd probably sleep through his alarm. But I've been knocking for like five minutes. I think he died."

As Rob spoke, the door creaked open, and there stood Chad, shirtless and half-asleep. He looked around with squinted eyes and opened his mouth to say something, but before it came out, he realized why we were standing there.

"Oh shit! Hang on, let me put some clothes on!"

Rob and I laughed. I walked away and wished him good luck.

For the first time in my life, I was looking forward to my classes. In high school, you don't have much say, and freshman year of college, you're just fulfilling general education requirements and figuring out a major. But now I was finally taking classes more firmly rooted in my interests. I took a look at my schedule. Organic Chemistry, Macroeconomics, Professional Writing, Probability, and Multivariate Analysis. Okay, so maybe it doesn't sound like the most exciting course load ever, but it sure beats Intro to World History and Computer Skills Workshop.

My classes on Monday went as expected. Nothing too exciting, nothing too involved. It was nice to see some of my friends from freshman year. I greeted a few of them, knowing that even though I would see them every day in class, our friendship would never go beyond a wave and a smile. One tough thing about college is that you cannot possibly become close to every person you meet. Often there's some sort of common interest that brings people together, sometimes it's simply proximity.

For me, the latter usually determined my friends since I've never been extremely extroverted. But being an RA helped me shake off some of my inhibitions as I made an effort to become friends with every one of my residents. I quickly learned that this was impossible, even if it was a noble thought. I learned that you don't have to be friends with everyone, just dedicated to the friends you have.

When I returned to the dorm, the halls were abuzz with talk of what classes sucked, which teachers were hot, and who had already been skipping. I asked my residents if they were able to understand their teachers' English (which can be a problem at times) and what they thought about the classes. Everyone had a good first day. It's important to get off on the right foot academically, and the 5th floor seemed to have done that.

As the week progressed, so did the community. At night the common areas were filled with people talking about their life goals and ambitions, and the study lounge was already being put to good use by groups working on physics, economics, and calculus. The mini lounge in each wing became a popular place for people to gather and eat lunch while they discussed the day's gossip. One Friday evening, I walked into the main lounge on the guys' side and saw about twenty of my residents sitting in a circle laughing hysterically.

You may know of the game "Never Have I Ever," a popular college and high school drinking game. In the game, the person next in the circle says "Never have I ever…" and finishes the sentence with something he or she has never done. (For instance, "Never have I ever had sex in a car.") If you have done what that person said, you're supposed to take a shot or sip of alcohol. On this night, they were playing a modified version with water instead of booze, much to my happiness. I arrived as the game was coming to an end. As the crowd dispersed, Eric said, "That was an interesting game. I learned a lot of things about people I wish I really didn't know."

I just laughed, extremely pleased at how comfortable my residents were becoming with each other.

During the first week, a few of the guys asked if we could purchase a TV for the lounge. I told them that if everyone chipped in, we could do it. After a couple e-mails and a six dollar donation from everyone on the floor, we had three hundred bucks. A week later, we had a 32" television in the boys' lounge that would get a lot of use during the year. Sitcoms, sports shows, movies, video games. They got their money's worth. A crazy idea can go a long way when people are willing to work together.

For the first couple weekends, I took the floor on outings to various museums and places of interest in the Pittsburgh area. I was shocked at how many people went. On the first Saturday morning, over half the floor got up at 10 a.m. (an ungodly hour for a college student) to check out a museum full of stuff that some people don't even consider art. It still amazes me.

We took a bus downtown to the Andy Warhol museum, which is just around the corner from PNC Park, where the Pirates play. The bus system is one of those oddities that you get used to when you live in Pittsburgh. Each year, we pay a preset fee to use the public transportation system. All you have to do is flash your student ID to the driver and you can use any bus in the city. Every single time I've gotten on a Pittsburgh bus—and it's been over a hundred times—I've met someone worth telling a story about. But as crazy as the bus system can be, it's an excellent way to get around Pittsburgh quickly and cheaply.

On the way back from the museum, I fell victim to the first of many practical jokes. We began the day with thirty-five people. Being the frantic, paranoid "mother" that I am, I took a head count at least six times during the trip. When we finally boarded a bus to head back to campus, I breathed in deep. I was home free.

Then my phone started vibrating. It was a number I didn't know.

"Who has a 713 area code?" I yelled to anyone who would listen.

I got blank stares. I answered the phone and heard a familiar voice on the other line.

"Hi, Andy. This is Derek. Um, I'm still at the museum. You guys didn't leave, did you?"

I froze. I'd counted six times and somehow I had left someone behind. This was my worst nightmare coming true. I was the worst RA ever, I should be fired, I would be fired, someone kill me.

Derek was from Rochester like me. I didn't even remember seeing him on the trip. I stood up, phone pressed to my ear, frantically looking around the bus. The two old women sitting next to me discreetly moved further away. Everyone on the bus stared as I yelled into the phone. Then, from the back of the bus, I heard an eruption of loud laughter. It was coming through the phone as well.

"Hey, Andy. This is Aaron. Got you!"

I turned bright red. I don't get embarrassed easily, so I had to give Aaron credit. He knew I wouldn't recognize Derek's voice over the phone yet, and since Derek hadn't come in the first place, there was no way I could have found him on the bus. Had I thought about it, I would have realized that Derek's area code should have been the same as mine. 713 was a Houston area code, so Aaron must have borrowed Kim's phone to make the call.

I hung up and the entire bus burst into laughter. "Aaron, don't ever do that to me again."

He grinned. It wouldn't be the last time he was smiling while my face was bright red.

The community was coming together in a variety of ways. For one thing, we signed up for several intramural sports on campus. Intramural sports are a great way to have fun and fit some physical activity into your schedule. Any group of people can sign up, but for the most part, teams are formed by large student organizations or fraternities. Residence halls don't usually have enough unity, but New House 5 had teams in soccer, basketball, volleyball, and softball. We never did very well, but we always had a blast. No one had as much fun losing 15-1 in soccer as New House 5. Because that one goal made us feel like the greatest athletes on the planet.

Embarrassing ourselves was getting to be a pretty popular method of bonding on the 5th floor. There's an exact moment I can point to when I realized how comfortable the floor was with each other. It was Micah's birthday, and the guys wanted to celebrate. They thought of a lot of different things to do, but everything sounded too cliché, too boring. Then Sam came up with an ingenious idea.

"I've got it! How 'bout all of the guys take off their shirts and put on a tie? We can all go to dinner topless, wearing ties."

Micah was known for walking around the floor in only his boxers. Initially, it sounded like one of Sam's ludicrous ideas that most people let go in one ear and out the other. But this time, he caught the attention of everyone in the room. And for a second, it sounded like the greatest idea in the world. And that second was all it took.

When I heard the commotion in the lounge, I pushed through the crowd of giggling girls and guys shaking their heads. Then I saw one of the funniest sights I have ever witnessed. There were twelve of my residents, all topless, all wearing silk ties. They posed for pictures and then, as promised, they all walked across campus just like that to get food. As it turned out, they weren't let into the dining area, but it was certainly one of the most memorable moments of the first semester. And it let the entire floor know that no matter what you wanted to do, no matter how crazy it was, New House 5 would help you accomplish it. No need to hold back, no need to be embarrassed. Find yourself. Then be yourself.

Ashford is known for being academically rigorous. Ashford students are known for studying until they drop. By the second week of classes, almost everyone was a workaholic, reading textbooks, going over notes, preparing for exams three weeks in advance. When freshmen first come to college, especially at an academically renowned institute, they usually start the year strong and motivated. Then, a few weeks into the school year, people begin splitting off into different categories. There are those who decide they want to be all social, hanging out at fraternities all the time, watching television, skipping class, and blowing off work. These students don't do well academically for obvious reasons. But there are also the students who continue to push themselves to the limit, studying for hours a day without any breaks. While some people can do this effectively, it's very rare, and most of these students get burnt out midway through the semester. They have breakdowns, they go crazy, they can't focus, they can't sleep. And when the end of the semester arrives, the time that really matters, they're too fried to do anything and end up with C's and D's when they were used to getting straight A's in high school.

The key is finding a healthy balance between the two: the students who do well are those who can maintain equilibrium between socializing and academics. For some people, a bad grade on an exam will let them know they have to work a little harder. For others, three straight nights with no sleep might tell someone he needs to slow down the studying. Then there's a third type of student, one who already understands he needs to have balance and plans that from the beginning.

I watched as the residents on my floor began shifting into these categories. I was pleased by the number who learned very quickly that they had to find a balance, and kept an eye on those who were still figuring it out.

For most of my freshman year, I fell into the category of too academically minded. Towards the end of second semester, I realized that college was going to suck if I stayed in my room the entire time, so I started going out with my friends and had a blast. Because of this, I sympathized with the students on my floor who were showing signs of burning themselves out academically. One student I was particularly worried about was Taylor.

Taylor was one of the few students on my floor not in the SHS program. He was a business major who lived about three hours outside of Pittsburgh. His roommate Marcus, who was also a business major, had a very social life. Marcus had been heavily recruited to play on the varsity tennis team. He went out on weekends and frequently had friends over. But Taylor was different. He was a nice guy, I knew this from talking to him a few times, but he was very quiet and studied nonstop. I dropped by his room one day to see how he was doing.

"Hey, Taylor, what's up?"

"Hey, Andy, not too much. Just doing a little reading."

"I see that," I said tentatively. "Dude, you're always reading. I never see you out of your room. You ever think about taking a break? You know, just coming out and hanging around on the floor once in a while?"

"Yeah, I don't know, man. I never really got to know any of these people. I mean, I'm not in any of their majors. It seems kind of late in the year to try to work my way onto their good side."

I walked into Taylor's room and shut the door behind me. I sat down in Marcus's chair and noticed a "How to Play Poker" book on Taylor's desk.

"Do you play poker?" I asked.

"Um, yeah. I'm trying to learn some techniques. I play online a little bit, but it's not as fun as playing with real people. I used to play with my friends at home, but I don't have as much time here. I just study all the time."

"You know, a lot of the guys on the floor are into poker, too. They play in the study lounge sometimes. You should join them."

While gambling was technically illegal in the dorm, I didn't mind when the guys played. It was never for more than a few dollars, and it helped bring the community closer through a common interest.

"Really? I didn't know that. I guess I haven't really been out on the floor much. I was sort of overwhelmed during Orientation so I kept to myself. I figured it'd be good for me, though. It gives me more time to study." He laughed. "But my eyes hurt from staring at my computer screen for so long."

"You can't study too much, man. Seriously, you'll burn yourself out. You have to remember that part of college is having a good time, too. Meeting new people, making friends, learning new things. You've already got a common interest with a lot of the guys. I bet if you just sat down and played with them once, you'd find a lot more."

"I just don't feel like I have the time, you know? I'm doing well in school, and I want to keep doing well."

"I think you can still do well even if you take some time out for socializing. Maybe start with a couple hours during the weekend. They always play on Friday nights. Just check it out, man. See what you think. If it's not your thing, it's not."

"Okay, okay. You're right. I actually do see them in there playing sometimes, I just never wanted to stop in. Next time I'll ask if I can play."

"Awesome. Because they do all know who you are, they just don't know much about you."

"Thanks, Andy. I'll let you know how it goes."

That Friday, there were five guys from the floor in the study room playing poker as usual, so I mentioned that Taylor might be stopping by. They graciously invited Taylor to join them, and so began a tradition of New House 5 poker games on Friday nights. Taylor is one of a million examples of a college student who just needed to find some balance in his life. A little studying, a little fun, a little sleep, and you've got a happy college kid. The trick is convincing the college kid of that.

As my residents got settled in to their college lives, the traditional college problems began popping up. The most prevalent of these problems was the notorious "Freshman Fifteen." Everyone wanted to know if it was true and how to avoid it. The Freshman Fifteen does exist, and for a variety of reasons. Most people who played sports in high school stop playing in college, so their level of physical activity goes down. Students eat more snacks and unhealthy food at university dining facilities, which ups the amount of fat and calories they consume each day. And of course, college students drink, and nothing will kill a diet like a beer, or as some like to call it, "liquid bread." Lack of physical activity combined with poor nutrition leads directly and inevitably to the Freshman Fifteen.

As some of the students began to see a little more of themselves in the mirror each morning, a few of them asked me how to avoid it. I said it was very simple: exercise regularly and eat healthy. I could not have been any more vague and generic, but it was the truth, and the people who asked me took it seriously. The biggest complaint was "I don't have time to work out or eat healthy." So I sat down with a few people to plan out a schedule. Maybe running on a treadmill for twenty minutes each morning was the answer. Maybe lifting weights between classes instead of taking a nap. Or maybe jogging outside while you listen to music. There's always time to fit in physical activity.

As for the nutritional problem, the easiest things to eat on the run are usually unhealthy, but that doesn't mean you can't eat healthy when you're in a hurry. Substituting a yogurt for a candy bar, a sandwich for a slice of pizza. I felt like a mother telling people these things, but it helped. I saw people making immediate changes in their habits. Elyse began working out on a daily basis early in the morning. I saw Julie take a banana with her to class everyday instead of a coffee and a doughnut. When people don't want to gain weight and make a conscious effort to stay in shape, they figure something out.

Homesickness was just as common a problem as the Freshman Fifteen, but it was usually rooted in something much deeper than poor nutrition. For a lot of people, homesickness kicked in during low points. At home, Mom may have taken care of a cold and Best Friend might have been consoling about a poor grade, but at college, it's hard to trust people you've only known for a few weeks. A lot of people are eager to make lifelong friendships like they have at home, but that's not something you can rush into. It's impossible to cram an eighteen year friendship into eighteen days, but people try. The best cure for homesickness is a phone call to a good friend back home and a chat with someone close at college who at least understands that you're upset, even if they don't understand why.

And of course there are the long-distance relationships. At least half of my floor came to college with a significant other waiting for them back in their hometown or at another college. By the end of the first semester, only a handful remained. For some people, long-distance relationships work. For others, they can be a disaster. Erin, one of the girls on the 4th floor who hung out in the 5th floor lounge occasionally, broke up with her boyfriend of four years in October. She went on a rampage. She had previously only had sex with her ex-boyfriend, but in the next two weeks, she slept with three different guys. She started dating someone she barely knew, all with the intent of getting over her ex. Every case isn't this extreme, but it happens. The first thing someone wants to do when they go through a break-up is find someone else. I tried to keep an eye out for these situations, but most of the time, long-distance relationships would break off without anyone but a roommate and a close friend knowing.

These are problems students encounter at every college, and it was no different on my floor. What was different was how people dealt with them. I always wondered exactly how a community formed on a residential floor, and I was seeing it in action. If someone was stressed about gaining weight, someone else would give that person tips on how to stop it, maybe go work out with them for a few days. If a guy was feeling homesick, a few of his pals took him out to see a movie. And if a girl had just broken up with the love of her life, some of the other girls would take her out to drown her sorrows in ice cream. The point is, on New House 5, no problem went unnoticed. Everyone was looking out for everyone else, everyone was willing to help because they knew that someday, they could be in the same position. I was already seeing the development of a different kind of floor, a floor that seemed more like a home than a place to sleep. New House 5 was becoming a place you knew you could count on.

PICTURES AND POETRY

Conversation never felt so perfect
- Whispers

Greatest inventions of the last three thousand years: the clock, the printing press, Friday. At college, sometimes thinking of Friday is the only thing that gets you through the week.

This particular Friday was even better than most. It was early in September, the second weekend of the school year. Pittsburgh hadn't turned cold yet, so campus was filled with students playing frisbee, soccer, and touch football. As the year progresses, less and less people come out on Friday afternoons. The temperature drops, the work picks up, and the laziness that lurks in every college student takes over. But not on this day. I walked outside wearing a white Fruit of the Loom t-shirt and mesh shorts, letting the soft breeze surround me, immerse me. In fact, I rarely wear anything besides white t-shirts. When people see an Asian guy wearing a red cap and a white t-shirt walking in front of them, they automatically yell my name. And on days like today, those white t-shirts feel like the best thing in the world.

I love our campus on days like this. It's small, serene, and beautiful. Sometimes I forget we're only three miles from downtown Pittsburgh. If Forbes Avenue, one of Pittsburgh's main streets, didn't go right through our campus, I might forget altogether that I went to school in a big city. Standing on the highway and looking south gives one of the most detailed views of our school. A large grassy area we like to call "The Cut" runs through the middle, bordered by academic buildings and libraries. On days like this one, students utilize The Cut to play sports, hand out pamphlets, or rehearse scenes for an upcoming play. On days like this one, I really feel like a college student, and it really feels awesome.

I spent most of the evening by myself. Half a mile from our school is the University of Pittsburgh, a public school that has four times as many undergraduates as we do. This means that half a mile from my campus, in the area called Oakland, the streets are lined with restaurants, novelty shops, and other businesses targeting college-aged students. I love walking around Oakland at night. The sidewalks are filled with people going every direction, hurrying to find a friend, get to a party, make a reservation. Clips of stories ring in my ears, glimpses of beautiful girls last for only a few seconds. Everyone is rushing past. Sometimes it's nice to not rush. Sometimes it's nice to watch everyone else rush. It puts your own life in perspective.

When I got back to the dorm at around 10 p.m., the hallways were buzzing. The second weekend of the school year meant the fraternities were all having rush parties, and everyone was going. The term "rushing" refers to checking out different fraternities to see which one suits you the best. So while the guys wanted to see which fraternity, if any, they fit in, the girls wanted to check out some real college parties. Dancing, socializing, drinking, sex—this is what college is supposed to be about. Most of our fraternities are housed in a quadrangle across from my dorm. This can be annoying at times when you're trying to study for an exam and every fraternity has its stereo system cranked up to full volume, but you get used to it, and it's never that bad.

Alcohol is always a concern in college, particularly for an RA on a floor full of freshmen. And rush was the first chance for most people to drink at school. I never worry about the kids who drank in high school, the ones who know their limits already. I worry about the sheltered students who are drinking for the first time, the guys and girls who don't have good friends to keep an eye on them, the ones who wouldn't necessarily know when to stop. They're the kids who end up in the hospital. When everyone headed out to the frats, I reminded them to be safe. When I went back to my room, one of the girls was standing there holding a large, flat plastic object. It was Meghan.

"Hey, Andy, I'm trying to hang this giant picture frame on my wall, but I can't find anything that will hold it up. Do you know if anything will work?"

"Actually I think I have some mounting tape. Let's try that out." I grabbed the tape from my drawer and followed Meghan to her room.

Meghan lived three doors down from me. She was from just outside of Dallas. The first time I talked to her was when she arrived almost a week before all the other freshmen for soccer. She struck me as a very nice girl, sort of shy, sort of reserved. It turns out she was highly recruited as a midfielder. She could have gone to Rice, Dartmouth, or Princeton, but she chose Ashford. And I'm glad she did.

Meghan appeared to be the prototypical All-American girl. Tall, athletic build, cute face, great smile, brown hair up in a ponytail, and Texas pride oozing out of her ears. I saw her a few times during Orientation but never got a chance to really talk to her. She came out to eat with a group of us one Friday night but for the most part, she kept to herself. Soccer consumed most of her life during the beginning of the school year, but I noticed that she was beginning to spend more time hanging out in the floor lounges. And she was obviously comfortable enough with me to ask for my help decorating.

The giant picture frame was actually a bunch of smaller ones glued together in an oddly shaped pattern. It was the largest picture frame I had ever seen. I applied the mounting tape in appropriate spots and tried to hang it up where Meghan indicated. It stuck, so I spent the next few minutes getting it straight. As I did this, I took a close look at some of the pictures. Many of them were simply of her hanging out with her friends at various places. The beach, someone's living room, school, soccer fields. One picture was of Meghan dressed in prom attire, presumably with her date.

The picture frame hung over Meghan's dresser, which was right beside her lofted bed. On top of her dresser was a pile of pillows and sheets. I asked why she had them there.

"Watch," she said. She hopped up onto the dresser and sat down, leaning back against the wall, just beneath where we had hung the frame. A homemade chair.

I sat down on the ground beside her. "So since I helped you put it up, do I get to know what all those pictures are of?"

This question was probably a little intrusive. I still didn't know Meghan well at all, but I figured this was a good way to start. One person at a time, one picture frame at a time.

Meghan smirked at me. She turned her head and began explaining the pictures. As I expected, most of the dozen or so pictures were simply of her friends hanging out in Dallas. Meghan went to a well-known high school in the Dallas area, and I found out just how big soccer was in her community.

"My team won states a couple times. We were really good. It's kind of strange coming here and playing at almost a lower level. Trinity is one of the top teams in Division III. My club team beat Trinity two years ago."

To me, it was fun to meet someone who was good at a sport. Meghan was never going to play for the national team, but there's something to be said about being dedicated to what you do, no matter what level you're at.

I pointed to the picture in the center of frame, the prom picture. Meghan had her hair done up in typical formal dance fashion, her blue dress glistened in the light. Her date was a few inches taller than her, with clean cut dark hair and a sinister face.

"Is that from your senior prom?"

"Oh geeze, I forgot that was still up there."

Meghan removed the picture from the case like it was burning a hole in the wall. She looked flustered. She rolled her eyes. Whether it was at me or the situation, I'm still not sure.

"Bad question?"

"Haha, um, yeah actually. That's Rick. He was my boyfriend for two years in high school. We've actually been best friends for a long time. Well, we had been. We had a pretty bad falling out. We don't talk anymore."

She spoke almost nonchalantly, in sing-songy voice, like she was trying to downplay Rick's importance.

"I call him 'Jackass,' so if you ever hear me refer to Jackass, it's Rick."

I dropped the subject for now. It wasn't the last I would hear about Rick that night. In fact, I would learn quite a bit about Rick as the year progressed.

I turned my attention to the picture Meghan had replaced Rick with. It was another young man, with scruffy hair, hunched over and smiling.

"Who's that?"

"Thaaaat is Arnie. He's sort of my stalker. He's one of my best friends, but he's a little overwhelming sometimes. I always know he'll be there, whether I want him to be or not. I take him for granted sometimes."

Meghan's phone rang. Since everyone at college has a cell phone, no one uses the traditional ring. People download songs and jingles to use instead, everything from Beethoven to hip-hop. Meghan's phone rang to the beat of "Beautiful Day" by U2. I approved.

"That's Arnie right now actually. I've already talked to him today. If it's important he'll leave a message."

Meghan paused for a moment in deep thought. She hopped down from her perch on the dresser and grabbed a bottle of orange juice from her mini-fridge. I noticed the side of her mesh shorts read "Hogg High School," just like the hooded sweatshirt she wore. When she climbed back on her seat, I asked her about it.

"How big was your high school?"

"Hogg was pretty big. We had eight hundred people in my graduating class. It made it hard to find a group of friends. I hung out with the soccer girls my first couple years of high school. I still did towards the end of school, but I also got really into debate and started hanging out with those kids. I loved debate, and I was good at it, but those weren't the best kids in the world to hang out with. That's where I met Rick and Andrew."

"Who's Andrew?"

"Yeah, I usually forget to mention Andrew." She said it in a matter-of-fact tone, like it was embarrassing.

"Andrew is Rick's twin brother. Before I dated Rick, I dated Andrew. Yes, I dated twins, and yes, it was the worst decision of my life. I don't talk to either one of them anymore. I heard from friends that they both started drinking." She rolled her eyes. "I think drinking is so gross and pointless. I don't know why anyone would do it. It shows how much they've changed."

I could tell there was a lot to this story, just like I could tell Meghan wasn't yet comfortable telling a guy she had only gotten to know in the last half hour all the details. I respected that. I later found out that Meghan rarely told anyone about her relationships with the twins beyond the fact that she dated them. "I don't like to tell the world about my past, I always feel like I'm being egotistic when I do that," Meghan once told me. "And I'm trying to shake that mindset, but it's hard." I felt bad for her. So much was floating around her mind that she wanted to let out, but was too afraid to tell anyone.

"One Christmas, my friend got me two identical pairs of socks. She said, 'These socks are twins. Once you've stomped all over one of them, you can throw them away and stomp all over the others.'" Meghan smiled faintly.

I did everything in my power to keep from laughing hysterically. Now that's wit. Meghan saw I was trying to contain my amusement and giggled a little as well.

"Okay, it was pretty clever."

Then she paused and bit her lip. Clearly, Meghan didn't think it was as clever as she said it was. Meghan changed the subject quickly.

"Hey," she said, "do you have a copy of your song lyrics that I can read?"

When Meghan came out to eat with a bunch of us earlier in the year, I told her briefly about my songwriting endeavors. Her eyes had lit up. She made me promise to let her see my lyrics sometime. It's not that I forgot, it's more like I'm always a little embarrassed to show my song lyrics to other people. I've gotten over that, but I still can't perform publicly. To this day, not a single person has ever seen or heard me perform one of my own songs.

"Yeah, I'll print a copy out for you later tonight, promise. Why are you so interested in them?"

"I don't know, I just love that stuff. I love words. I think song lyrics and novels can be so touching and important. I try to find writing that's relevant to me."

"That's really cool. Do you write at all?"

"A little bit, nothing too big. I try writing lyrics. That's what I love the most. I love those verses that stick with you, that float around in your head for days. I always have some sort of song lyrics or inspirational writing in my online profile."

The term "online profile" will be used frequently. A product of the information age is instant messenger, an internet service that allows you to constantly be connected to anyone else in the world with the same software. America Online has a monopoly on the industry. You can sign on to your computer and chat online with one hundred of your closest friends, whether they are down the hall or twelve states away. It allows people to stay close, to become close, and to waste time.

Another voyeuristic benefit of AOL Instant Messenger (or AIM as it is often called) is that you can make a profile for yourself. The service gives you a certain amount of space to quote your favorite songs, tell people your contact information, or express how you're currently feeling. It's all just a mouse click away so you can stalk people even without talking to them. Many college students keep their instant messengers logged on all the time. This lets people leave messages on your computer, so you can return a couple hours later and read at your leisure.

At college, AIM is a way of life. People have gotten in fights over each other profiles. People stay up until five o'clock in the morning talking to six different friends. People ask others out, break up, and make up, all without having to actually say a single word. It's getting to the point where you don't ask if someone got a phone number, you ask if they got a screen name. Welcome to the 21st century.

"I usually keep song lyrics that express my current mood in my profile," I said. "What do you have in there right now?"

"I have a quote from *The Pastures of Heaven* by Steinbeck," Meghan said excitedly. "John Steinbeck is my favorite author ever. I could seriously live off just reading everything he's ever written. I love his writing style. It's so simple, ironic, and thoughtful. Let me show you."

Meghan ran to her cluttered desk. She swept away crumpled papers, Caramello wrappers, and old sticky notes. The excitement in her eyes and her voice when she spoke of Steinbeck was clear. Everyone needs to be passionate about something, and Meghan was clearly passionate about John Steinbeck. Finally, she pulled from the rubble a thick paperback book that looked worn with age and use.

"This is my Bible. It's the John Steinbeck companion book. They took some of his best work—chapters from books, essays, even full novels—and stuffed it all between two covers. If I ever lost this I don't know what I'd do with myself."

She smiled widely as she thumbed through the book. The pages were marked with pencil and highlighter, miniature Post-Its noted various passages. She finally came to a stop and handed me the book, pointing to a spot halfway down the page.

"This is what I have in my profile now. It's my single favorite Steinbeck line ever."

> *After the bare requisites of living and reproducing, man wants most to leave some record of himself, a proof, perhaps, that he has really existed. He leaves his proof on wood, on stone, or on the lives of other people. This deep desire exists in everyone, from the boy who scribbles on a wall to the Buddha who etches his image in the race mind. Life is so unreal. I think that we seriously doubt that we exist and go about trying to prove that we do.*

"You're really into this stuff, huh?"

"Totally."

"I think that's so cool. Most of the people I know still view reading as nerdy. I never got a chance to read any Steinbeck in high school. Maybe I should start."

"You definitely should. Rick was a huge Steinbeck fan, too. He sort of got me into Steinbeck. He got me into music, too." She looked ashamed when she said this.

"He seems to have had a big impact on you."

"More than I'd like to admit. I guess in the back of my mind, I still can't believe we don't talk anymore. Sometimes I wish I could just call him up and ask him how he's doing. Things change, but they shouldn't have to. I've changed."

"You should call him."

"It's not that easy. We'll leave it at that."

I did leave it at that, for the night anyway. I looked at my watch. It was midnight. I didn't realize how long I'd been talking to Meghan. Even though our conversation was awkward at times, due partly to us not knowing each other and partly to our reserved personalities, talking to her felt very natural to me. Meghan was never the most vocal or outgoing person on the floor last year, but she turned into one of my best friends. It took me so long to get to know her because I assumed she didn't want to get to know me. You should never assume what someone else is thinking, you can never guess another person's personality. Sometimes just saying, "Hi, my name is Andy," can show you what a person is really like. In this case, all it took was a picture frame.

"I should get back to my room and do a little work before I go to bed," I said.

"Yeah, me too actually." Meghan yawned. "We're huge nerds, doing homework at midnight on Friday. I love it."

"Me too. I'll see you around."

"Yeah, definitely. Thanks for helping me with the picture frame. It looks like it's going to hold."

As I left Meghan's room, I had a good feeling that this would not be my last long conversation with her. I returned to her door an hour later. The lights were off. She had gone to bed as I expected. I slid a copy of my song lyrics underneath her door. There's nothing like keeping a promise.

❧❧

Kate was an intriguing girl. I never had a chance to talk to her very much because for the most part, she stayed in her room and kept to herself. But unlike some of the other girls who kept to themselves, Kate wasn't constantly on the phone with a boyfriend from back home or typing away on instant messenger. She was a loner, in every sense of the word. From what I could tell, she wasn't involved in any campus organizations or clubs. She just did her homework and sat in her room. Occasionally she kept her door open, and I would walk by to see her sitting on her bed, curled up with a book. She had a black fleece blanket that I had never seen her without. And one day when I walked by her room, I decided to stop in and talk.

Kate's room seemed more spacious than the other rooms I had been in. Everything was neat and organized. Her roommate, Allison, was rarely there. Allison was the opposite of Kate, involved in every school activity she could fit into her schedule. Different people find different ways to stay occupied.

When I knocked, Kate smiled and asked me to come in. She was from northern New Jersey, just a short drive from New York City. Her walls were covered with pictures of the city. Very few of the photos had other people in them. Kate was a creative writing major who wrote about as often as she breathed. What exactly she wrote, I have no clue. But when I did see her walking around the floor, it was always with that black fleece blanket wrapped around her, notebook in hand. And Kate was beautiful. Not the typical hot college girl who showed off her body and made up her face, but strikingly beautiful. One of those girls who you know would have been worshipped as a beauty no matter where she lived, no matter what time period.

I walked in and sat on her desk chair. She was on her bed as usual, sitting Indian-style and hunched over a book. Her long brown hair drooped down over the pages. Every few seconds she had to place a fallen strand behind her ear. I waited patiently for a few minutes, letting her finish her page or chapter or whatever she needed to finish. When she was done, she looked up at me.

"What's up, Andy?"

"Well, I'm glad you know my name," I said jokingly. "I never see you around."

She smirked sarcastically, as if to say, "No shit, there's a reason for that."

"Yeah, I pretty much keep to myself," she said. "I keep busy with my work and my hobbies."

"What hobbies?"

"Mainly reading and writing. I love to read, anything I can get my hands on. I used to read two or three books a week in high school. But my high school was a joke, so I had more time. Here, my studies keep me pretty busy. I put my schoolwork first."

"That's good. What kind of stuff do you read?"

"You're really pressing here." She said it jokingly, but there was a hint of seriousness in her voice. "What's with the sudden interest in me? Are you going to be quizzed or something? Are you supposed to know the favorite color and animal of everyone who lives on your floor?"

Now she was serious, and she was mildly upset. I couldn't help smiling as I answered.

"No, actually. I'll tell you why I'm in here now, talking to you, asking you questions that you think I don't care about. It's because you strike me as a very interesting person. Honestly. And I wanted to get to know more about you. But since you're not volunteering much information, I guess I have to pry a little bit more."

"Nothing against you, but I'm not big on forced friendships."

"Okay, I'll make a deal with you: I get an answer to two more questions and then I'll leave you alone."

She thought about it for a second. Realizing it was the only way to get me to leave, she agreed.

"So what kind of books do you read?" I asked.

"Poetry. Some classic fiction, but I love poetry. I could read it all day. Sometimes, I'll go into a bookstore and stay there all day, just reading through the different poetry books. I've written entire poems on my arm before in ballpoint pen, just so I don't forget them." She paused, realizing that she had begun to ramble. "But yeah, poetry. Next question."

"What do you write?"

"Same thing. Poetry. I probably have a thousand poems. They're stored on my laptop, in boxes full of journals at home. I carry around this little journal with me." She picked up a ragged looking book. It used to be orange, but the cover was faded and peeling. "If I think of an idea, I'll jot it down. Then I'll go back to it and write. I've started to write more in the last three or four years. I don't read as much, because writing is much more fun. It's one of the few things I really enjoy doing. It takes me away from reality for a moment and lets me be, well, sort of alone in my own little world."

She sighed deeply and stared out the window. She looked depressed. And not the whining college student kind of depressed. She looked like she was really lost in the world.

"So I have to leave now?" I asked.

"Well, that was the deal we made. But I don't care. You can stay if you want to."

"Do you have any friends here?"

"What's that supposed to mean?"

"I was just curious. I never really see you hanging around with anyone."

"No, not really. I talk to Allison sometimes, but that's just because we live together. I didn't plan on making any friends when I got to college. I have a few friends back home, but no really good friends. People suck, so I just keep to myself."

"Oh, come on. Not all people suck. That's a crappy way to live, hating people."

She glared at me. "How much do they pay you to say that?"

"Listen, Kate. I'll leave soon because you obviously don't want me here. But just because I'm your RA doesn't mean I'm the biggest fake the world has to offer. No one else comes in here because no one else cares. And maybe you don't think I care, but you can at least admit that I was curious enough to ask. I understand you don't want to talk to people, that's cool. I don't know why, and it's none of my business. But I have issues trusting other people sometimes too, so it's cool, and I understand."

Kate's head popped up. "Why don't *you* trust people?"

"Well, I don't distrust everyone, but I am hesitant about what I tell other people about myself. And who I give confidential information to. I'm not sure what it comes from, actually."

"I'm sort of the same way, but I don't trust people at all. The only people I've ever really trusted were my ex-boyfriend Jared and my parents. And they all let me down. In so many ways."

"How so?"

She just shook her head.

"What do your parents do for a living?"

"My dad is a doctor at a local hospital. He's like the town hero." She rolled her eyes as she said this. "Everyone loves him. I can't walk anywhere without someone saying, 'Your dad this, your dad that.' My mom is a housewife, but I don't call her that. She's a bitch who has made it her goal to ruin my life."

I tried to keep my surprise at Kate's comment to myself. "How's that?"

"I'm an only child, so she only has one thing to worry about since she doesn't work. And that's me. When I was little, she used to go out everyday and do her own thing. I never even knew what she did. But when she was around, it was all about nagging me. What do your parents do?"

This question caught me off guard. Not because it was a strange question, but because it was the first question Kate had posed to me. I'm used to asking other people about themselves, so when someone asks me about myself, I'm always underprepared. I paused for a second before responding.

"My dad works at Kodak, like every other father in the Rochester area. Most people have about a dozen friends or relatives who either work for Kodak or got laid off by them. My mom is a physical therapist. I guess I have sort of a strange relationship with my parents, too. I've always been pretty independent so my parents have just kind of sent me on my way and said, 'Good luck.' I have a younger brother who is in seventh grade and a sister who's a senior in high school. They both need much more attention than I do, so my parents focus on them and assume I'm doing okay. We're more like acquaintances than family almost. I talk to them about once a month."

"I can't imagine that. I think it would be so nice for a little while to not have my parents wondering about everything I do. I'm at college, I make good decisions, but they always assume something is going on. They can be ridiculous sometimes. Whenever I left the house with a male friend, my dad would say to me 'Kate, what are guys?' The proper response would be, 'Guys are evil.'"

I laughed out loud at this. I always imagine that I would be an overprotective parent. I tell people that if I have a daughter, I'm putting up barbed wire around the house as soon as she is old enough to walk.

"That's amazing. That sounds like something I would say. Your dad is the man."

Kate glared at me again.

"Don't say that." She laughed nervously. "They do all kinds of irrational stuff like that. It just gets so tedious and annoying after a while. One time my dad got really mad at me for coming in late and threw my computer out the window. It shattered on the sidewalk. That kind of thing happens a lot. He always buys me something to replace it, though. It really sickens me that people with money think they can buy friendship and forgiveness. Money can't buy a lot of things. I learned that at a very young age. Like I said, they really look out for me, but I don't know, sometimes I just wonder."

"What about this guy Jared you were talking about?"

"This is a quiz."

"I'm just asking."

"I dated him my junior and senior years. I was really quiet in high school, too. Guys used to try hitting on me, but I never responded. It got to the point where they would just say really gross and rude things to me to get a laugh.

But Jared was different. As much as I can't forgive him now for what he did to me, he really was different. He stood up for me. I started hanging out with him a lot my sophomore year because I had no other friends. He understood me. He understood everything going on in my life."

"And what happened?"

"It all just sort of fell apart my senior year. I stopped talking to him and spent the entire year in my bedroom. Thinking and writing. It kept me sane. That's why I love to write so much."

"Well, listen, I can see why you might not be open to being friends with everyone, but you just seem sort of miserable in here. Maybe it wouldn't be the worst thing if you hung out on the floor a little bit and made a few friends. Some of them are probably not your type, but there are fifty-six people on this floor. You live with them. It's worth a shot."

"You totally just changed the subject," she said abruptly.

"I was thinking about it, though. What do you think?"

She hesitated for a moment. "I'll give it a shot. Maybe. It is kind of boring in here sometimes. You're not as bad I thought. Thanks for coming over."

"No problem."

I left Kate's room that day as her friend. She did start to come out of her room more often. She hung out in the mini lounge a lot, talking to people about random stuff. I couldn't tell if she was really enjoying it or if she was trying to make herself enjoy it, but she seemed a lot happier. I talked to her more frequently as the weeks went on, and each time, she was more open, more easygoing. Maybe all she'd needed was a little nudge, I thought.

It turned out she needed a little more than that, but I wouldn't find out what until later.

Despite their obvious differences, Meghan and Kate seemed to have something inherently in common. I'm not sure exactly what it was, though. Kate was cut off from the world, while Meghan was a more social, outgoing person. But they both seemed to have cynical outlooks, even if they didn't talk about them in depth. Each had a past that, for whatever reason, haunted and frightened them. With Meghan, it had something to do with Rick. For Kate, it was her parents. Meghan and Kate didn't seem like people who could ever become good friends. I think each saw too much of herself in the other. Funny how similarities act as barriers sometimes. But it's just as funny how those barriers can be broken down with a little effort.

CREATING A COMMUNITY

Grab your suitcase
And bring some spare change
Make your own movie
Live it scene by scene
- Untitled

Over the summer, I had developed a personal goal for myself as an RA. I wanted to form a strong friendship with every individual on my floor. Looking at that goal now, it seems both ridiculous and stupid. It sounds very mechanical, like I was going to develop a concrete method to gain the trust of each person. It just doesn't work like that. You're naturally more compatible with some people than others. I realized early on in the year that this goal was bad for me and bad for my floor. People were beginning to grow tired of me asking how classes and extracurriculars were going every time I saw them. And I was getting tired of asking.

So a few weeks into the school year, I had an epiphany: I needed to be myself. Yeah, yeah, I know. Some epiphany. But it's something I wasn't doing. I was trying to be the perfect RA and in turn, I was being fake and boring. And I wasn't having fun. From that point on, I decided to forget everything I ever thought I should do and just do what felt right, what made me feel good. And from that point on, New House 5 began turning into the community I had envisioned. From that point on, I started loving every minute of being an RA.

While I didn't have an exact idea of what I wanted New House 5 to be at the time, I can see now what I was hoping for. I just wanted a floor full of people who cared about each other. I knew not everyone would talk to me if they had a problem. I certainly didn't run to my RA when I had a problem my freshman year. But everyone on the floor had someone they could talk to, someone they could confide in and trust, and that's all I could have asked for. A community is a place where you can feel comfortable being yourself. It's a place where you know someone's always got your back. A place where you have the confidence to speak your mind. It's hard to believe that this type of atmosphere is possible to have in a dormitory, but it is, and it's what New House 5 was turning into. As I tell people now, New House 5 was not just a floor. It was a way of life.

⟡

It was becoming very evident that a "core" group of students was forming on New House 5. This core group became the students who were easily identified with New House 5. While I thought it was really cool that the campus could easily identify certain students with our floor, it also bothered me that other students who lived on the floor were in some ways being left out. What kind of community is it if some people within its borders are disregarded? I looked into it closer and found that I was wrong.

There were definitely different groups forming. The main one consisted of over half of the floor. These were the people who wore their New House 5 pride on their sleeves, the Robs and Elyses and Aarons of the floor. There was also a small group of Asians that hung out with each other as well. About six of them became very close and were inseparable. Then there were the handful of loners; people who kind of did their own thing, had their own group of friends, and kept to themselves.

But the reality was, no one was being left out. The Asians were close with the core group, so even though they weren't as excited about New House 5 the community, they helped make New House 5 what it was. They hung out in the lounges, played poker on weekends, and participated in intramural sports with us. Even the loners were still involved in the community to some extent. They came to the occasional floor activity, they hung out once in a while, and they enjoyed the general atmosphere of the floor.

I can't control how people react to the floor, but I can help control how the floor reacts to other people. Some were taking advantage of living on New House 5 more than others, but no one was being left behind. And that's all I cared about.

ॐ

As the friendships on the floor grew, so did the concerns. When people got to know each other better, they learned each others fears, desires, and weaknesses. The generic "How are you doing?" would now elicit a thirty-minute response instead of a superficial "I'm fine." As a resident assistant, I always wanted to know everything that happened on the floor, every concern, every deep-rooted problem. That was about as ridiculous as wanting to be everyone's friend. While I definitely found out information that I was probably never supposed to know, I can only imagine some of the things I never heard, the secrets that were divulged between friends during 4 a.m. conversations.

I talked to Elaine a lot about what happened on the floor. Certain people started going exclusively to Elaine if they wanted to talk, some began coming exclusively to me, but we tried to keep each other updated on what was going on. We pushed the "two RA" idea on the floor and overall, it seemed like we were doing a pretty good job so far. All we had to do was keep it up.

Rob was quickly becoming my resource for major concerns on the floor because he was also quickly becoming the guy everyone on the floor went to if they had a problem. I always considered Rob a more approachable version of myself. Even though I tried to be as open and inviting as possible, most people are still uncomfortable talking to their RA about sex and drugs. Rob, though, was an extremely easygoing and sensitive guy. He was smart, funny, considerate, and open, the perfect kind of person to talk to about a serious issue. I liked him because he had a sense of humility, he never acted like he was above anyone else. Rob kept himself grounded in reality and optimism, which attracted the friendship of almost everyone on the floor.

Rob came to my room one day to ask me about a baseball game, but the conversation quickly turned to other matters. He popped his head in while I was reading my e-mail.

"Andy, who's pitching tonight for the Yankees?"

"Um, Tanyon Sturtze. His ERA is like a billion. You guys might take this one tonight."

"Good, we need it. Forget winning the division now, I just want to make sure we get the Wild Card."

"You guys will be fine, man. It'll be a Boston vs. New York American League Championship series. Everybody wants to see it."

"I hope so. Hey, actually, can I talk to you about something quick?"

"Sure, man, have a seat."

He closed the door behind him and plopped down on my futon.

The bright maroon fabric of the futon's mattress has worn down over the past couple of years, fading a little each time a new person relaxes on it, each time a new story is revealed. If it could talk, it would probably tell this story better than I am right now. I learned a lot of things, good and bad, from conversations with people sitting on my futon. It might be a little worn out, but I still have it in my dorm even today. There's something about it that feels like home.

As soon as Rob closed the door, the relaxed feeling I usually had around him died. Rob's face looked solemn. He glanced at me and made a weak smile, as if to say that what we were about to talk about would not be fun, but was definitely necessary.

"Okay," Rob began. "So, I know you know that a lot of people on this floor drink. I do a little bit, a lot of people do a little bit. Actually, what's your take on alcohol?"

"Personally, I don't drink, but I have nothing against it. I don't have a problem with people who drink socially, once in a while. And my policy about alcohol here is, if I don't see it, it doesn't exist."

"Right, right. I agree with you about not having a problem with people socially drinking. The problem is, we've only been at school for three weeks now, and every weekend, there have been parties over at the frats. So like, I've noticed that for a lot of people, it's not a big problem. We all go out in groups, most people will have a couple beers, a couple shots, then that will be it. Once in a while someone will get totally trashed like Luke."

We both laughed. Luke wasn't someone you would ever take home to meet your mother, but I can't think of many people I'd trust more than him. Luke had a medium build, blonde hair cut in the classic skateboarder style, and spoke in a deep, eerie-sounding voice. He'd gone to a German high school where he'd learned some calculus when he wasn't learning how to drink. It was always kind of scary when Luke got drunk and started speaking in German, totally unaware that we couldn't understand him, but aside from his tendency towards drunkenness, he was an incredibly funny and caring guy. Luke would never let anything happen to anybody on our floor when he was out partying, and I respected that.

Two weekends before Rob came to talk to me, Luke had a little too much to drink. He threw up into a plastic trash can for several hours before finally passing out in his bed. I found out the next morning and went to visit him in his room. His breath still reeked of cheap beer and he had one of the worst hangovers I've ever seen. We talked for a few minutes and he told me that was the first time he had thrown up in a long time. I just told him to be careful and he said he would. Luke ended up pledging at a fraternity. Secretly, I was happy that there would be someone to keep an eye the floor when they were at his fraternity. I don't worry about people like Luke, people who drink with some frequency and learned their limits in high school. Every once in a while, someone like Luke will have a bad night, but I knew he could take care of himself or let someone know if he needed help. I worried more about the people Rob was about to discuss with me.

"Yeah, stuff like what happened with Luke is pretty rare," I said.

"So anyway, I'm starting to see a small problem," continued Rob. "Some of the girls who had never drank before wanted to go out and try it. So a bunch of us went over to the frats with them and supervised while they had a couple drinks. It was no big deal. That was a couple weeks ago.

"The problem is, they're starting to get out of hand. The people who normally drink on weekends only are starting to crave alcohol on, like, Tuesday. The very casual drinkers who never drank before they came here want to go out and get trashed every weekend. And the people who never considered drinking are starting to go out and test the waters. It just seems like a downward spiral. I can see it happening, but I don't know what to do about it. It's going to get to the point where no one will ever be sober. It seems like a lot of people are getting corrupted, and against their will. I guess I never saw peer pressure in action until coming to college."

I leaned back in my chair and stared at the ceiling for a moment. This was an issue I had prepared for, but hoped wouldn't come up. But maybe that was a little too optimistic.

"The problem with peer pressure is it's more intense when you don't know the people very well," I said. "A lot of these girls who didn't drink at home were probably comfortable telling their friends they didn't want to drink, and their friends were probably cool with that. They knew that a certain person wouldn't drink and left them alone. At college, there are no best friends yet. If everyone is going out to do something, you don't want to be the only one left out. I have noticed a few of the girls who used to stay in on weekends going out with you guys. How much do you think they're being pressured?"

Rob looked uncomfortable. "Honestly, a lot. And I don't think it's necessarily by people from this floor. I mean, take Julie. She just started drinking a couple weeks ago, but she's already turning into a pretty frequent drinker. I think the problem is that when she goes over to the parties and she wants to meet some guys or talk to some people, she feels like she can't do that unless she's sipping a beer. And it's getting to the point where she doesn't see it as a problem anymore."

"This goes back to the whole 'reasons for drinking' thing, I think. Peer pressure, social lubricant, fitting in. The unfortunate thing is that on a college campus, if you want to go to parties and meet people that way, alcohol is going to be a big part of it."

"I know, I just see it with her specifically as a big problem. She's gotten out of hand a couple times. Luckily we're all there, but what happens if we're not? Some guy could easily rape her. I know that's extreme, but it's a possibility."

"I know, and that's the biggest fear: getting raped, making a bad decision that gets you killed. It's a serious issue. Here's what I think. I would love to talk to Julie about this but I'm the wrong person. This is a huge responsibility, but is there any way you can talk with her about it, even if just in passing? Sometimes, people might not even know that there's someone who cares, someone who sees the problem. She might be well-aware that she's starting to get herself in rough waters but she might also think she's being abnormal because she's afraid. The worst reason for her to be drinking is because she thinks others would disapprove if she didn't. Just letting her know you're concerned might be all it takes."

"Yeah, I was going to talk to her about it at some point anyway. I just don't want to see anything bad happen to her. I mean, I guess even getting drunk a lot isn't horrible if you're into that."

"I agree to a certain extent. There are so many abstainers that look down on alcohol like it's liquid evil and look down on drinkers like they're the most ignorant people in the world. But I think if you drink in moderation, even if you get drunk once in a while, it's not the worst thing as long as you take necessary precautions. I know a lot of people disagree with me on that, but if students want to drink, they're going to drink. What concerns me is when they start looking forward to it on Tuesdays. That can turn into a problem."

"Yeah, yeah. I guess the thing is, on this campus there's a 'work hard, play hard' mentality. And it's cool that you know you can work hard all week then go nuts on the weekend, but it doesn't seem healthy."

"It's not healthy at all," I agreed. "It happened to some people on my floor last year and it was so sad to see. When you look to drinking to relieve all of your stress, you start becoming dependent on it. I think what we have to do at this point, together, is just keep an eye out on what's happening. If we see a change in certain people, we can take a look. It's good because at this point, we know what's normal and what's not normal for certain people. For one person, going out and getting drunk one night might be nothing, for someone else, it might send up a red flag."

"Yeah, that's why I came to talk to you. I'll just keep watching."

"Thanks a lot, dude. And thanks for letting me know this stuff. You know that what you say won't leave this room." I laughed as he walked to the door. "You know, you're like another version of me, except you know a lot more about what goes on here than I do."

"Haha, yeah, I guess so. Thanks to you too, man. I just wasn't sure if I should be doing anything. I'll let you know if anything else comes up."

Rob did end up talking to Julie, and she did think she might be getting a little out of her comfort zone. She didn't stop drinking, but she did ease off a bit and it seemed to work out well for her.

This was the first of many talks Rob and I had regarding our collective concerns about members of the floor. Rob and I respected how much we each cared about New House 5, and it allowed us to be open with each other about our thoughts and opinions. Though he was Chinese, Rob did not break off into the smaller clique of Asian students on my floor. He kept in touch with everyone, from the students who called English their second language to the main group of friends that made up the core of New House 5. I realize now that Rob helped in eventually bringing all the factions of the floor together, something that wouldn't happen until well into the second semester. But his ability to respect and gain the respect of every person on the floor made Rob the go-to man if I was not around.

Rob was slowly becoming not only my source of information, but also my best friend. We had so much in common, in interests and personally traits, that we seemed destined to become close. That night, the Red Sox beat the Yankees 7-2. Most of the time, I would have been irate, but on that night, there was a karmic balance in the world. Rob's team deserved a win because, well, they had Rob as a fan. I almost smiled when Derek Jeter struck out to end the game. Almost.

∽∾

Friendships were blooming all over the floor, growing not only out of similar interests and similar backgrounds, but also out of nowhere. One of the most intriguing things to me was how certain roommates who appeared to have nothing in common found a bond.

For example, Meghan and Kristen in room 518. Meghan was the soccer player, the Texan, the epitome of responsibility and realism. Kristen was a local girl, born and raised less than an hour outside of Pittsburgh. She listened to emo music, loved literature, and liked to drink. Despite all the differences, these two seemingly incompatible people became good friends. What actually brought them together, I never found out and probably never will. Maybe they were talking late at night one evening and hit upon a common thread, maybe a life philosophy or personality quirk. It's usually something like that. All I know is just a few weeks into the year, Meghan and Kristen became inseparable. They ate together, did homework together, and acted like they had known each other for years. Meghan and Kristen had their share of disagreements, many of them in a public forum, but in the end, we all knew it was more like two sisters arguing than two roommates fighting.

Perhaps the most interesting pair of roommates was Kim and Alicia. Talk about polar opposites: Kim, the small half-Asian girl from Houston who loved to write, didn't drink, and made every effort to make new friends. Alicia, the glamorous Jewish girl from the Midwest who partied at the fraternities every weekend, brought home guys, and was more than slightly arrogant. But each of them loved to help other people and, being roommates, the easiest person for them to help was each other. While they never hung out much during the day, many deep and thoughtful conversations took place behind the door of room 521 last year. It was an incredible learning experience for both of them. Kim learned how and why Alicia's lifestyle was important to her, and as a result, became less squeamish about certain types of relationships. And Alicia got a few lessons in morality and humility from Kim. Both of them became good friends of mine and while both had issues living with the other at times, neither one of them would trade the experience for anything.

On the boys' side, I noticed Sam hanging out with Aaron a lot more, though they lived a few rooms apart. You may remember Sam from the first day of Orientation, the tall, thin, mopey guy. Aaron was the chemistry major from Philadelphia who had a very positive, realistic outlook on life. I talked to both of them frequently, and saw a distinct difference in how they viewed life and school. Sam was the typical pessimist, thinking everything around him sucked, constantly questioning his decision to come to Ashford, to leave home, to go to college at all. And he still had no clue what to do with his life, which bothered him a lot. Aaron, on the other hand, was very laidback. He wasn't sure what he wanted to do after he graduated either, but it didn't bother him. I respected that a lot. Most people don't know what they want to do after school, but the important thing is to not worry about it. You have to keep an open mind and keep moving forward. Aaron was one of the most active members of New House 5 when it came to floor activities. He went on all the group trips, participated in all the planned events, constantly hung out on the floor, and was one of the masterminds behind the multitude of practical jokes that I fell victim to.

For Sam and Aaron, the common thread was religion. Both Sam and Aaron were Jewish, so they began going to services together and got involved in Hillel, the Jewish student organization on campus. I think the friendship was beneficial for both of them. Sam was able to incorporate some of Aaron's optimism into his thinking, and Aaron was able to see where Sam's doubt and cynicism stemmed from. A simple thing like organized religion is capable of bringing together all kinds of people. It's about finding someone who's just as passionate about a certain thing as you are.

Soon, the people who began the school year shut away in their rooms started to venture out onto the floor. Every time I walked by one of the lounges, there was someone else sitting there that I wasn't used to seeing. Rosalyn was getting out of her room a little bit. I had never really seen her on the floor before. Eric, the red-haired Bostonian who was seen as sort of a nerd during Orientation, made his presence felt with his strong opinions and sarcastic remarks. Jeremy, one of the basketball players, started hanging out with the guys in the lounge to talk about baseball, Taco Bell, and Harry Potter. One by one, the residents of New House 5 were realizing that there was nothing scary about people they didn't know. College is about meeting new people, and if you couldn't find someone to connect to on New House 5, maybe life just wasn't your thing.

Three of the guys had decided to join a fraternity, each of them choosing a different one. There are a handful of fraternities and sororities on our campus, so students interested in getting involved in Greek life have some options. Avery, a tall athletic guy in Army ROTC, was planning to "pledge," as it's called, at one of the fraternities that a lot of his friends in the Army belonged to. He was a very strong-minded guy who I could see fitting in well in that environment. There was also Luke, who quickly honed in on what was known as the "nerd" fraternity, because he really liked the guys there. And of course, he loved to drink. Then Devon, a social and friendly but sometimes offbeat kid from Georgia, decided to join a fraternity he had picked after looking at all of them first.

All three of them ended up pledging, but each struggled with the decision. A combination of school priorities and uncertainty about fraternity life made each of them hesitant, but in the end, they all decided to take the chance. That's what college is about: taking chances. Not all of them had a wonderful experience, but it's one of those chances that sometimes, you just have to take.

༄༅

A few weeks into the school year, I had an idea to bring the floor together in a different way. I wanted to publicly recognize individuals who made an impact on the floor. And to do that, I enlisted the help of everyone's favorite Walt Disney character: Nemo.

The idea for Nemo popped into my head one day at an RA staff meeting. As I said before, our staff consisted of nine RAs and one community advisor, or CA, who was basically the head resident assistant in the building. My CA, Jimmy, began giving a stuffed Care Bear to one RA at each staff meeting. Whoever had the Care Bear on a given week brought it to the next meeting and gave it to someone else. I thought, "Why can't New House 5 do this?"

After the staff meeting, I caught two of the girls going down the elevator. It was Hillary (the girl from Detroit) and Elyse (from Virginia). I had become closer to many of the girls on the floor in the last week, simply from talking to them about their classes and telling them about some extracurricular activities they might like. They were hyper this afternoon, giggling and jumping up and down while they waited for the elevator.

"Where are you girls going?"

"We're going to the Waterfront. Do you need anything?"

The Waterfront was the nearest shopping plaza. Knowing I wouldn't have an opportunity to go there anytime soon, I jumped at Hillary's offer.

"Actually, I do. Go to Target, and buy me a large, plush Nemo doll."

The moment that followed was priceless. The two girls, who had just been dancing and yelling, stopped dead in their tracks, turned their heads to the side, and stared at me with confused faces.

"Don't ask. I'll explain after you get back."

Finding Nemo, aside from being the number one grossing Disney film of all time, is a universal movie that is difficult to hate. The RA staff had a Care Bear, New House 5 would have Nemo. The girls returned two hours later with exactly what I hoped for: a large, fluffy, soft Nemo doll, the perfect size to carry under your arm. They were still confused but I promised them they would find out what Nemo was for soon enough. I handed fifteen dollars to Hillary, who glared at me again, uncertain what the fate of Nemo would ultimately be. It was the best fifteen dollars I have ever spent.

I decided to go all out. I printed out a decal that said "New House 5 Lucky Fin Award," named for Nemo's handicap in the movie, a "lucky" fin that is slightly smaller than the other. I sewed the decal to the stuffed animal's fin, figuring the award name was appropriate since it would go to someone who was willing to lend a Lucky Fin. When I showed Elaine, she turned away and laughed. "That's so ridiculous that it's awesome."

Then I called a short, unscheduled meeting the following night to introduce Nemo to the floor. I was mildly concerned that they would blow it off as childish or a waste of time. Luckily, I knew my floor better than that.

Everyone gathered in the guys' lounge. Even three weeks into the school year, even after all the participation in floor activities to that point, it still amazed me that over half the floor showed up to an emergency meeting held on a Wednesday evening. People came with backpacks and textbooks. They yawned and checked their watches. But they were there, without being forced, and that meant a lot to me.

Elaine and I stood in front of everyone. I lifted Nemo above my head.

"We'll make this really short, everyone, since I know we've all got stuff to do. Let me introduce Nemo."

The yawning faces stopped yawning. The homework scribblers stopped scribbling. All eyes turned to the large stuffed fish in my hands.

"Nemo is more officially going to be called the New House 5 Lucky Fin Award. Every so often, probably once or twice a week, Nemo will be given to someone for a big accomplishment, an upcoming event, or for making a difference on the floor. What I need from all of you are nominations. If you think someone deserves Nemo, send me an e-mail. To start things off, Nemo is going to Val for her expert care of Luke last weekend."

Val received a thunderous round of applause that I soon realized was not sarcastic, but real congratulations. She accepted her award with a huge smile. I felt like I was handing an Academy Award to a well-deserving actress. I half-expected flash bulbs to go off in the background.

Val, as I said before, quickly became a mother figure on the floor. She was bold, opinionated, and outspoken. She commanded respect and her strong personality attracted many of the girls on the floor to look up to her. And though she was very friendly, caring, and rational, everyone knew that if they upset Val, there would be hell to pay. She told us all a story once about how she got into a fight in high school. She'd ended the fight decisively by running full speed and jumping on the other girl, bringing her tumbling to the ground. Val referred to her move as the "Flying Leap of Death," and from that moment on, the Flying Leap of Death became an everyday part of the New House 5 vocabulary.

Her title as the inaugural recipient of Nemo was well-deserved. The previous weekend when Luke had been throwing up, Val was the one to take charge of the situation. While several people stood around and wondered what to do, Val stepped up as the leader, a position she would take several more times throughout the year. She calmed everyone down, assuring those who had never seen an overly drunk person that Luke would be alright. Luke sat on a couch in the lounge leaning forward into a garbage can while Val sat beside him, comforting him and encouraging him to throw up. The crowd dispersed and Val stayed with Luke until he felt well enough to climb into his bed and get some sleep. After this, she had earned the respect of everyone who was present. Had I asked for nominations, Val would have received plenty.

After the meeting broke, I went to find Val and ask her how she liked Nemo. I found her in the girls lounge, curled up in a ball on the couch. Nemo was tucked underneath her arm.

"Andy," she said, "I never want to give Nemo up. Ever. He's the perfect size to sleep with. I hope you know you're not getting him back."

With that she smiled again and turned over onto her side again. Elyse came out of her room, which was just across from the lounge. She looked at Val holding Nemo close to her body.

"I think Nemo is going to be a hot commodity," she said. "He's so cute and cuddly."

She brought her hands to her face like fins and sucked in her lips to make the classic fish face. We stared at each other blankly for a few seconds before we cracked up together. As we went our separate ways, Val began snoring, Nemo firmly in her grasp.

What Nemo turned into was more than I ever expected. Not only did the floor take him seriously, but finding out who would get Nemo next became a big deal on the floor. I received nominations almost daily. I sifted through the nominations, consulting with Elaine and other members of the floor. When someone was awarded Nemo, there was always a miniature ceremony where the previous winner would pass the fish on to the next. Nemo was always accepted with great pride. He became just as much a part of the floor as any living person. He represented everything good about New House 5: the selflessness of the residents, the strong bond we all shared, the sense of community, and the little bit of goofiness in all of us. Nemo changed hands forty times during the school year, and each time was just as meaningful and important as the next.

Nemo also gained campus-wide fame in a very strange manner. One weekend, the floor decided to give Nemo to Derek for good luck because he was playing an important role in a student-written musical. Derek accepted Nemo graciously, and the first night of the show, sang and performed wonderfully. On the next evening, which was supposed to have the biggest turn out, Derek took Nemo with him to the show. While waiting backstage, one of the directors asked if Nemo could be used a prop. Derek handed him over to the director, and the next thing we knew, Nemo was being caressed in bed by one of the actors following an implied sex scene. In the audience, the floor roared its approval, recognizing their trophy. And from then on, Nemo was known at Ashford as the dirty fish who weaseled his way on stage.

I remember the moment I realized how much our floor had become a true community. It was a brisk October morning, the leaves were beginning to change color and if you looked hard, you could see your breath. You can complain about Pittsburgh weather all you want, but there are few things prettier than Pennsylvania foliage. As I walked to class at 8 a.m., I thought of nothing more than how much I wanted to be in bed. I was hidden in my sweatshirt, my hood up and hands buried in the front pouch. The view of the bright orange and crimson leaves, uninterrupted by harsh daylight and bustling crowds early in the morning, was the only thing that kept me going. I walked past another RA I knew without realizing it. He stopped me as he walked by.

"Sorry Tim, I didn't see you there."

"It's okay, man. I just wanted to say that I was walking down in Oakland the other day when I came across, I don't know, about twenty kids. They were walking in a group, laughing and enjoying themselves. A panhandler went up to one of them and asked for some change. When one of them said no, the panhandler persisted and grabbed the kid on the shoulder. Then the rest of the group turned around and went completely silent. Someone said, 'Yo, if you want to mess with him, you're messing with all of us.' The guy backed off. I guess he thought it wasn't worth his time. After he left, I asked one of the kids where they were from, where they went to school. They said they were from Ashford so I asked them if they were in an organization or something. He said, 'We all live on the same floor. New House 5, man. We're one person.' You could tell he was sort of joking, but sort of being serious at the same time. I don't know what's going on up there, but it's pretty cool."

I took my hands out of my pockets, pulled back my hood, and walked the rest of the way to class with my head held high. The leaves looked more vibrant than normal, and even the cold October air couldn't keep me from smiling.

WHEN IT RAINS, IT POURS

We know those tears fall when the sun goes down
And you think the answer is a ticket out of town
- Train Out of Paradise

On October 17th, I *thought* I knew Rosalyn Morales pretty well. But that day, my perception of what it meant to "know someone" changed drastically. Before October 17th, I didn't know Rosalyn at all.

If I had to describe Rosalyn in one word before our conversation that day, it would have been "quiet." She was from a medium-sized town in the northeast corner of Pennsylvania. We had an immediate connection because she had a Wegmans in her hometown. Wegmans, for those of you who don't know, is the Mecca of supermarkets. In Rochester, it's a way of life. You can tell a person's social status by which Wegmans they shop at in my hometown. After a few successful years in Rochester, the chain was beginning to branch out into Pennsylvania and other parts of upstate New York. So the most intriguing thing we had in common was that we went to the same grocery chain, but hey, you have to start somewhere.

Rosalyn was one of the girls I made small talk with on the elevator and said hi to in the dorm. She stayed in her room for the most part, talking on her phone and typing away on her computer. I started off on good terms with Rosalyn, as well as her mom. Rosalyn is half-Hispanic, half-African American, so she arrived a couple days before the rest of the freshmen for minority student orientation. When I walked over to introduce myself, the two women were in a bit of a predicament.

"Hello," said Mrs. Morales. "We're trying to figure out how to get my daughter's refrigerator upstairs."

"Most of them aren't that heavy," I responded. "I could probably carry it up for you as long as I have someone walking behind me so I don't fall."

I carried Rosalyn's refrigerator (which was a lot heavier than I expected) from her car to her room, and we had an unspoken friendship from that point on. Her mother, on the other hand, was much more vocal, making sure to praise me at least twelve more times before she left.

I remember that Rosalyn looked so overwhelmed that day, more so than any of the other freshmen that moved in early. She turned her head in confusion, craned her neck in awe. The yellow blouse she wore still had that "fresh from the store" smell. Her hands clutched her Orientation packet close to her body, like a high school student who's too scared to find her locker. She was by herself in a brand new place. Looking back, I should have tried to be more helpful at that point. It may have helped her settle in. But I didn't have another real conversation with her until almost two months later. Things worked out eventually, though. They always do.

ॐ

The term "halfie" at our school generally refers to someone who is half-Asian, half-Caucasian. But Rosalyn qualified as a halfie as well, though Hispanic/African Americans are not nearly as common at Ashford. I thought Rosalyn's ethnicity made her interesting, but I got the feeling she didn't see it as an advantage or a fault. It was just who she was.

From talking to her and the people who took classes with her, I was able to gather small pieces of information. She had a boyfriend who went to Penn State, a three-hour drive from Pittsburgh. She studied hard and strove for good grades. She planned on majoring in Biology. She spoke fluent Spanish. And the weekend prior to October 17th, she went to visit her boyfriend at Penn State. That's all the information I had to arm myself with when she knocked on my door Monday afternoon.

I was checking my e-mail, as I do about a hundred times a day when I'm at school. Outside, the sky was gray and overcast, unsure if it wanted to spew raindrops onto the sidewalks, or just leave us wondering. You can tell when October comes around in Pittsburgh because every good college student wears a hooded sweatshirt no matter what it's doing outside. It's all-occasion apparel, no student should be without a closet full of them. As I looked out the window just in time to see the first drops of water splash against the glass, Rosalyn knocked on my open door tentatively and produced a weak smile.

"Can I come in and, um, talk to you for a second?"

Rosalyn had never come to my room, not even to borrow the vacuum cleaner. Something was up. Even before she finished her sentence, I could tell she was a mess. Her dark hair looked like it hadn't been washed in a week; her eyes sagged, begging for sleep. The t-shirt she wore was wrinkled and dirty. Her countenance was melancholy, her movements erratic.

"Definitely, come on in. What's up?"

The look on Rosalyn's face was an expression of shame, of humor, of apprehension. I could only imagine all the emotions going through her mind, and I had no idea what she was about to tell me. She wiped her dark brown eyes of the tears she has been trying to fight. With a deep breathe, she gained control of herself and spoke again.

"Can we close the door actually?"

I closed my door slowly. When I turned back around, more tears were forming in Rosalyn's eyes. She was silent for a few more moments, willing herself to be calm.

"I'm sorry, you probably think I'm crazy or something," she said.

"It's okay, take your time."

She sighed. "So you know I have a boyfriend, Shane, who goes to Penn State, right?"

"Yeah, you went to visit him this weekend, right?"

I went over scenarios in my head. This could have been something as serious as rape or pregnancy, or something as simple as an irrational fight. Not that a fight with your significant other is minor, but it's a hell of a lot easier to approach than rape. I'd never dealt with anything like that before. But I was getting way ahead of myself, and her. I thought of a direct question to get to the bottom of it quickly.

"What did he do to you?" I asked abruptly.

Rosalyn stared at me, completely taken aback by the question. This was the first of many learning experiences I had on dealing with serious issues. I had assumed Rosalyn had a problem with her boyfriend. My assumption was wrong. From then on, I never asked such a direct question without getting a feel for the situation first. Rosalyn could have been so offended and embarrassed that she walked out of the room and never talked to me again. Some people would have. Luckily, she gave me the benefit of the doubt.

"No, no, no. He actually probably saved my life. Shane isn't that kind of guy." She laughed uneasily. "I mean, I know every girl probably says that, but he really isn't. He'll come down to visit soon. You can meet him. I honestly don't know what I'd do without him."

It was my turn to feel embarrassed.

"I'm sorry," I said, keeping my composure. "Let's forget I said that. Better yet, let's start over from the top."

I got up from my chair and opened the door. After taking a peek outside, I shut it again, sat down, and said, "What's up?"

Rosalyn smiled. A real smile. Thirty seconds ago, we were in totally separate worlds, not connected on any level. But that smile put us back on track. It's crazy how something as simple as a misunderstanding can make two people feel like they are galaxies apart. But it's just as crazy how something as simple as a smile can cure it in an instant.

By now it was raining hard and the steady beat on my window was soothing. Rosalyn started again.

"Okay. So I went to this party with Shane. He was watching me but I kind of ran off to another room. I was having a little bit to drink."

She looked up at me, hoping I wouldn't judge her for this. I never tell people that I don't drink, but somehow everyone knows. And at the same time, everyone assumes that I look down on people who do drink. That part isn't true. All of my friends in New York drink socially, and most of my friends at school do as well. I just choose not to.

It doesn't bother me that Rosalyn was afraid of talking to me about drinking. Even though I was only a year older than her, I did hold some sort of authority position. No one ever wants to tell someone with a title when they've done something stupid. What does bother me is that my reputation as a non-drinker likely stopped certain people from talking to me about alcohol-related issues. Once it got around that I didn't look down on people who drank, my residents were more open to talking to me about drinking, but it was frustrating to know that for the most part, people assumed I wouldn't be able to understand. One girl told me she sat in her room and cried for an entire day after she had gone out drinking and hooked up with someone at a fraternity. She said she considered coming to talk to me about it, but figured I would just add to her misery. I never thought being a non-drinker would negatively effect being a resident assistant. But then again, it positively affected me in ways you'll hear about later.

Despite her initial hesitation, Rosalyn was the first person to seriously talk to me about an alcohol-related issue, and looking back now, I'm thankful someone broke the seal. Her guilty look lasted only a few seconds. I gave her a smile, and she continued her story.

"I took a drink from some guy I didn't know. I was so stupid. They tell you never to take a drink you didn't see poured, but nobody thinks about that when they're at a party. The next thing I remember is waking up in the emergency room."

There was a short, silent lull in the conversation. What do you say to that? I fidgeted in my chair while I thought of how to respond.

"Did you figure out how you got there?"

"Roofies." She said it bluntly, with no emotion. "Someone put roofies in the drink."

Rohypnol, better known as "roofies." A prescription-only sedative that has become the date rape drug of choice in America. Normally used as a pre-operation anesthetic, larger doses can bring on amnesia. Roofies are ten times stronger than Valium and the effects can start happening in as little as ten minutes. They're easy to obtain, with a street price of two to four dollars a tablet in the United States. The pills can be ground into a powder, which is then poured in to an unsuspecting person's glass or bottle. You black out, get raped, wake up the next morning in an alley somewhere, and you have no clue what happened. Scary stuff.

"When I woke up in the hospital bed, the nurses told me. I was so embarrassed. They were so sweet, though. They kept saying how horrible the whole thing was. They said it wasn't my fault to make me feel better, but I was the dumbass who took the drink in the first place."

"Do you have any idea what happened when you were blacked out?"

"Sort of. I mean, nothing happened. Shane found me practically dying with a couple guys around me. He took me outside and I guess I was pretty out of it. I probably drank a ton more than I realized. He said he took me home on Penn State's public transportation system and that I threw up out of the window. I guess I caused quite a scene."

She smiled faintly. I smiled faintly back at her. She was feeling more comfortable with talking about it, and she was clearly feeling better that she was able to talk about it at all.

"After that, I passed out. Shane called 911 and an ambulance took me to the hospital. They had to pump my stomach. How horrible is that? I must have had so much to drink. They gave me oxygen and checked for alcohol poisoning and stuff. Then I woke up."

"You're sure nothing else happened?"

"Yeah, I'm pretty sure. I mean, they checked me for signs of rape and stuff, but they didn't see anything and they're going to call me in a few days to let me know if the tests showed anything. On top of all of that, I got a ticket for underage drinking. My mom is going to kill me. One, for drinking, and two, for being stupid enough to let this happen to me. This whole weekend just sucked."

"So where do you go from here?"

"Tomorrow the Penn State police chief is going to call me. I talked to him before I left. He was really nice actually. He understood the whole roofies deal, but he still had to give me the citation. After I left the hospital, I went back to Shane's dorm room and slept. I missed my train back, so I just got back a couple hours ago."

She let out a frustrated sigh and curled up in a ball on my futon. She reminded me of an earthworm; I'm sure she felt like it too. Cold, slimy, and weak, wriggling around, trying to find a comfortable position. She took her glasses off to wipe the tears that were beginning to fall down her cheeks again. I disagree with people who say crying shows weakness and immaturity. I think at times, it shows more maturity than anything else I can imagine. She wiped her face with her t-shirt, leaving stains of saline in blotches on the sleeve. After she put her glasses back on, she went on.

"I mean, I know it isn't even that bad. It could have been so much worse. I could have been raped or even died or something. But I just wanted to go relax for a weekend with my boyfriend. Instead I got all this shit. I shouldn't feel bad, I don't know why I'm crying."

"Dude, of course you should feel bad. We hear about date rape drugs and stuff all the time, but it doesn't happen to everyone. It happens to a small minority of people who go to parties. Yes, you're lucky that nothing worse happened, but it would be a little strange if you weren't upset about it. I mean, most people wouldn't be like, 'I just woke up in a hospital after getting my stomach pumped. It was so exciting, let's do it again.'"

She laughed a little between sniffles.

"I called my mom and told her what happened," she said. "She was pretty pissed off, but mostly she was glad that I'm alright. Now I have a record in

Pennsylvania. I just feel horrible. Ugh, I do not want to talk to this police chief tomorrow."

I sat silently, watching the Windows logo dance on my laptop screen. It was now pouring outside and the steady beat had turned into an irregular clatter.

"What should I do?" she asked.

That's quite a question. It puts a lot of pressure on the person answering. But Rosalyn wasn't trying to put any pressure on me, she just wanted a little guidance. I wish I could have given her better advice than I did.

"Honestly, I think you've done what you've needed to do so far. You made sure nothing serious happened while you were blacked out. You called your mom to tell her. You're going to talk to the police chief. I don't think there are any other direct actions you need to take."

"Do you think I should press charges?"

"I didn't even think of that. Why wouldn't you?"

"I don't feel like having to go down there again and testify and stuff. I mean, it was a huge party, there would be no way of figuring out who did it."

"I guess so."

"I can think about it, I guess." She stood for a moment and stretched her arms. "Wow, I feel so much better. I really needed to talk to someone."

Rosalyn would later tell me that she came to me for the simple reason that she had no one else to go to. All of her friends were back at home, a good six hours away. I was just two doors down. Rosalyn didn't come with specific questions to ask me, she didn't come seeking certain advice. She just needed someone to tell her story to, someone to listen. That's one thing I can always do.

Rosalyn looked a lot better now than she did when she first came into my room. I thought it would be a good time to change the subject, talk about something else for a little while to take her mind off the situation.

"So when did you say your boyfriend is going to come down here?"

"Oh, I'm not sure exactly. He has a car so he'll probably come down a bunch of times to see me. He's like family, he always takes care of me. He has three brothers and they all treat me like their sister, it's really cool. Hey, you watch football right?"

"Yeah, I follow it pretty closely. Why?"

"Shane's brother played for Penn State last year. He was really good actually. He got drafted by the Jets in the first round."

"LeRoy Painter?"

"YEAH! Yay, someone knows who he is!"

I still don't know why this sounded so crazy to me, but I found myself overwhelmed with joy that Rosalyn was dating LeRoy Painter's brother. I knew a lot about him. I had researched him while I was watching the NFL draft on TV because everyone thought the Bills were going to take him. Then he got drafted before we had the chance. One of the cool things about college that you never read in brochures is meeting people who know famous people. Seriously.

"You know him!" she yelled excitedly. "Yeah, the Eagles are my favorite NFL team because I live close to them, but I'll have to be a Jets fan this year. LeRoy told me I can come visit him sometime and stay in his new house in New Jersey."

Rosalyn was excited that I knew what she was talking about. I was excited that she was talking about it at all. It was awesome. Not only did I know someone who was friends with an NFL player, I had somebody to talk to about football. I never thought that would be a problem at college, but at such an academically minded school, it hasn't been easy.

We spent the next few minutes talking about football. Unlike the first part of our conversation when both of us were a little unsure about what to say, now we didn't hold back at all. We argued back and forth and yelped in excitement when we agreed on something. Any uncertainties we had about each other were being chipped away. Talking about football isn't the most heart-to-heart topic, but football is the reason Rosalyn and I knew our friendship had evolved. Rosalyn came out of her curled-up ball, and I was at the edge of my chair, gesturing with my hand and laughing out loud.

As the conversation waned, I asked another question I was curious about. But talking football didn't prepare me for the answer.

"You said you called your mom. So did you talk to your dad too?"

You know when you get the feeling that you've just said the worst possible thing you could say? The look on Rosalyn's face gave me that feeling. I don't think Rosalyn would have even tried to answer this question ten minutes earlier. But she felt comfortable enough around me after our football talk that she began to explain her situation with her father, a situation I didn't fully understand on October 17th, a situation I will never truly understand.

As some of the color returned to Rosalyn's face, she said, "I don't talk to my dad."

Simple, straight, pointed.

"Oh," I said. "Sorry."

"It's alright. I was basically raised by my mom. My dad was abusive. He hurt my mom, my sister, me. They finally split up, my mom and him. I was pretty young when it happened, but I remember how happy I was, how happy my mom was. He doesn't help pay for anything, not college, not food. Sometimes my sister calls me when she's visiting him. I don't know how he still has visitation rights. The authorities like turning their heads on this stuff if no one is getting killed. My sister will be crying into the phone that Dad is hurting her, and I can't do anything about it. It's a helpless feeling."

Silence. The wind picked up as the rain came down harder.

"He lost his temper so easily. I remember being afraid after I broke something by accident that he would literally kill me. Living in fear around your own family is such a crappy way to go through your childhood. If we hadn't gotten away from him when we did, I think we all would have either killed ourselves or been killed by him."

"You never talk to him at all?"

"I refuse to go visit him. I guess technically my sister doesn't have to either, but she does. He's horrible. He still bothers me sometimes. He tries to contact me, but I do everything I can to avoid him. I don't even want to think about what would happen if I saw him on the street. I'd probably run at him screaming and try to strangle him. Or I'd just break down and start crying. He hurt my mom and sister so much. It makes me sick sometimes to know that I have his genes."

"I can't even imagine that," I said quietly. It was true. I couldn't.

"It's okay. I don't talk to many people about my dad. I'd rather just forget he exists. But he does, and I'm given a reminder about it every once in a while. Even if I don't see him, his genes are always inside me." She sighed again. "See, I have a blood problem. I don't have enough oxygen or iron in my blood."

"Like anemia?"

"It's a little different. I have to get transfusions pretty frequently. That sucks, too, that I depend on other people's blood to survive. I feel like a parasite. I got that from him. It's hereditary. He gave me his bad temper, his violent tendencies, and his blood diseases." She shook her head. "Wow, I don't even know why I'm telling you all of this. I don't think anyone here knows these things about me."

With that she folded her arms and leaned back hard on the futon, causing the steel rods holding it together to vibrate. It sent a chilling, metallic ring through the room. I had never seen the violent tendencies and temper she spoke of at this point, but I would before the year was over. And I would hear a lot more about Rosalyn's father.

"I don't think you can feel like a parasite just because you get transfusions. I mean, that's what people donate blood for. It's a medical advancement and you're proof of how it can be effective."

She groaned. "No one understands. Not even my friends at home. I depend on technology to survive. It's like when people are vegetables and just 'living' in technical terms."

"I think it's a little different than that."

"It is, but it isn't. I depend on other people to live. I'm a parasite and all I ever hear is 'Oh, but you're so lucky.'"

A rift was beginning to grow between us. I thought about what she said, and it made sense. Everyone is so eager to give the "right" answer. Few people take the time to wonder what they would think in the same situation. The old "putting yourself in someone else's shoes" theory. It works.

"I'll say this. I can see your point. It would be strange if you didn't get upset about it. Anyone would. If it didn't frustrate you, there's something wrong with you. But you have to remember both sides. It's there, you're lucky it's there, and you're using it to be a healthy person. There are worse things."

"Yeah, I know."

With that "Yeah, I know," Rosalyn acknowledged that we had each considered the other person's side, and realized we each had a point.

"I guess I should go do some work now," she mumbled, "since I didn't get any done this weekend. Thanks so much for talking to me, seriously."

Sometimes when people say "seriously," it's not a real "seriously." I could tell that this time it was. After an hour of hard rain, the clouds were beginning to break. It was still sprinkling outside, but the sun broke through for a peek at the world.

"Anytime. Seriously."

That was a real "seriously" as well.

"Let me know what you decide to do with the drug thing. After you talk to the police chief and stuff."

"I will. I hope it turns out okay."

"I think it will."

"Me too. I'll see you later."

In less than two hours, I'd learned more about Rosalyn than I ever thought I would. I still wasn't used to the abuse piece. I grew up in a very loving, easygoing home. Coming to college opened my eyes to what goes on in the world, even in upper-class suburban homes. This wouldn't be my last encounter with family abuse, nor would it be the last time I talked to Rosalyn about it. But slowly, I was beginning to learn that sometimes the surface is just a mirror. You look at someone and see a reflection of yourself, you see what you expect to see, what you want to see. Breaking that mirror requires a little effort, and a little luck. From that point on, I made sure never to take anyone at face value. Nineteen is quite an old age to learn that lesson, but better late than never.

Rosalyn's conversation with the police chief went smoothly. She decided not to press charges and after that, the whole ordeal became a bad memory in her past, a bad memory she would certainly learn from.

Rosalyn shut the door behind her. I smiled to myself. Leaning back in my chair, I stared at the *Finding Nemo* poster above my desk. "Small Fish, Big Reef," it said. It certainly was a big reef. And I had a lot of exploring to do. But before I got to that, I went back to my laptop and looked up statistics on LeRoy Painter.

ELAINE

And all that we've created
Was never meant to last
- Paper Houses

There's one person in all of this who I haven't given due credit: Elaine. Everything New House 5 was becoming was because of the dynamic between the floor, Elaine, and me. During Orientation, Elaine and I made a pact that we would do everything we could to help the floor become the best it could be. "Best" in this case is a very objective word, but I think we both had a similar vision. Elaine planned half the events, I planned the other half. And as I said before, some people were more comfortable with Elaine, some were more comfortable with me. For the students of New House 5, there were two RAs for the floor, not one for each wing.

The number of activities we did as a floor and the amount of time we spent planning them caused Elaine and I to become very close. As freshmen, we had lived about ten rooms down from each other so I didn't get to know her as well as I would have liked. Also, Elaine was incredibly active in the campus community. By her sophomore year, she was the president of several campus organizations and knew just about everyone with a title at Ashford. Her myriad of activities sometimes prevented her from being on the floor as much as I was, but it was good to have two different kinds of RAs on the 5th floor. Elaine was the always-on-the-run mother figure, I was the stay-at-home dad. It worked out well for everyone, and the floor got used to it.

My freshmen year, I talked to Elaine on occasion and she came off as a very optimistic, involved, opinionated person. She made a point to befriend everyone on my floor during freshmen year. After we both got hired to be

RAs, we started to hang out a little more and talk about what we wanted to do in New House. During these conversations, I learned about Connor.

Elaine was a very religious girl. She held fast to her beliefs and defended them to the death against anyone who questioned her. While I respected the fact that Elaine was dedicated to her religion—she was a Christian, what denomination I'm not positive—I was turned off by the fact that she felt the need to preach about it to everyone she knew. I also was turned off by how closed-minded she was to other points of view. Everyone is allowed their opinion. Not everyone has to agree, but we should at least respect what other people think. One of Elaine's strong beliefs, based partly on religion and partly on morals, was that you should never get physically or intimately involved with someone you wouldn't consider marrying. At college, this concept is fairly ludicrous. While it's not as crazy as television might suggest, few people expect to marry people they date in college, and most people would be scared simply by the thought of it. But Elaine held fast to her belief, and during our freshmen year, she had many conversations about it with some of the other girls on our floor who tended to be more promiscuous.

Towards the end of the second semester, however, Elaine met a guy. Not just any guy, but someone she really connected with on a deep level. It turns out that Elaine had never really had a boyfriend in high school, and as a result, her interest quickly turned into a serious infatuation. I don't fault her at all, because the same thing happened to me during my freshmen year. If you go through high school without a boyfriend or girlfriend, it's easy to fall for the first person you click with at college and think you've found your true love. A vast majority of the time, it doesn't work out like that. Nonetheless, Elaine and Connor, who she met through a social student organization, began hanging out on a daily basis.

From what I could tell, Connor seemed like a nice guy, and he was definitely into Elaine as much as she was into him. From the conversations I had with Elaine at the end of our freshmen year, I was able to gather that they did date for a few weeks. Elaine thought she had found the love of her life, Connor thought he had found someone to care about. They were together all the time for those few weeks and generally appeared to be the perfect happy college couple. Then, for a reason unbeknownst to me, it just ended. One day they were together, the next they refused to talk to each other. While this situation sounded eerily like a high school crush gone awry, I couldn't help feeling sorry for Elaine. She still has never explained to me what exactly went wrong, but I know that they stopped talking to each other until sometime during the next fall.

Elaine became more rebellious in many ways during that second semester of our freshman year. She started to drink, just a little, but that was still extremely out of character for her. She'd always been one to openly criticize alcohol, but now she was the one getting yelled at. From the outside, it looked like Elaine was losing herself. She wasn't sure what was going on in her life or the world around her, so she was experimenting with all the things she never considered before to find her niche. It was hard for me to gauge exactly what was bugging Elaine until I really got to know her.

During RA training, Elaine was always the one who made things interesting. She was not afraid to call out people who contradicted themselves, stand up to faculty who she disagreed with, or do something utterly stupid to give us all a laugh. With her flamboyance and humor, she quickly became the most visible person on our RA staff. This was the Elaine I knew the first semester of my freshman year. But as training started to get longer, Elaine began to fade into different moods. At times she would be very antsy and scratch at my arm like a bored cat during seminars. Occasionally, she would get pissed off at the world and not talk to any of us. And sometimes, she would be so opinionated and angry that no one would dare tell her to calm down. Still, as much as Elaine changed her moods and opinions, she was always nice to me and I always liked her. Whatever aura she gave off, I knew she was dedicated to helping out the new students who would be coming soon.

When the freshmen finally did arrive, Elaine seemed burnt out. From training, from life. I still wasn't close enough to her to delve into the problem, but I wanted to help her in some way. For the first couple weeks of the school year, Elaine was her old, enthusiastic self again, probably working off adrenaline and her responsibility as an RA. But I could tell that she wasn't all there, that her heart wasn't in it like I knew it could be. It's not my place to say she should have been more dedicated to being an RA, but I knew she wanted to, and she was having a difficult time doing it. The girls on the floor loved her, the guys respected her, and from the outside looking in, Elaine and I were doing an ideal job bringing our floor together. But on weekends, Elaine would go to house parties and drink, sometimes not returning until the next morning. It was getting to the point where I knew I should ask her what was wrong, but it turns out I didn't need to. She came to me first.

On a Thursday night, right before I was about to wash up for bed, Elaine walked into my room, exuberant as ever. Elaine often stopped by for a few minutes to chat and ask about my day, but our talks never went beyond a superficial level. She sat down on the futon and sprawled out, letting out a deep sigh.

"Hey, can you close the door, Andyman?"

I was surprised, but I didn't say anything. I noticed she was dressed for bed as well, in an old t-shirt and gym shorts. Her hair was still wet from the shower.

"I can't deal with this anymore," she said frustrated.

"What's up, dude? You sound beat."

"I've been beat since this summer. Like, I love this floor and I love my friends and stuff, but my head isn't all there. Sometimes I just want to leave this school forever, never come back again. It makes my head spin."

"I've sort of noticed you haven't been all there sometimes. I was going to ask you about it. What's it from? Why are you so bummed out?"

"It's not that I'm bummed out so much as my head is always in a different place. I can't focus on anything, it's bad. This is going to sound stupid, but do you remember Connor? I know I didn't really tell you that much about him last year, but I really thought he was someone special. I felt more strongly about him than anyone else besides my family. It's all so ridiculous because I only knew him for a couple months before we started dating. But I thought it was perfect, I thought it would work out. Then after we started dating—like what, a couple weeks—it just ended. It left a sour taste in my mouth. I figured it would sting for a while, and it certainly has."

I leaned back in my chair. This didn't sound so bad at all. People have problems getting over crushes all the time. I still couldn't imagine how Connor could affect everything Elaine had been doing.

"It's still stinging," she continued, "and I don't know why. This entire summer, I thought about it and worried about it and second-guessed myself. Every day my head was filled with Connor and it was really frustrating. I thought coming back to school would help, and it has a little bit, but sometimes it just makes it worse. When I see him, it makes it a lot worse. We're sort of on speaking terms again, but I'd rather not even talk to him."

"Elaine, I don't want to seem like I'm being insensitive here, but it seems a little strange that you're getting so caught up in this. I mean, you guys did only date for a couple weeks. It doesn't seem like it can be that traumatic."

Even as these words flowed out of mouth, I couldn't believe I was saying them. This was about as hostile as I had ever been to someone about a relationship problem. I didn't think, I just spoke, which is never a good thing to do. I just felt Connor couldn't be the real problem, that maybe there was a deeper issue.

"Yeah, dude, I know what you're saying." She was getting upset at this point, partly with me, partly with the situation. "This is how I get sometimes. I have no problem helping other people with their issues, but when it comes to my own, I'm lost. Everything I do, I question. I wonder if it was a mistake or if I could have done something different. I never had a boyfriend in high school, so how can I know if hooking up with Connor was a good thing? Did I jump into it too quickly? Did I do something wrong? Could it have worked out if we did something differently? I don't know. It's easier for me to put my own problems on the shelf and do something else."

When Elaine said this, it opened up my eyes to what Elaine's real problem might be. It was time to delve a little deeper. And since it was me who was delving, there was no telling how it would turn out.

"Elaine, now that you say that, it makes me think that you worry too much about your place in the world."

"What do you mean? I don't understand." Elaine was puzzled, but she was intrigued.

"Well, it sounds to me like you're just unsure of yourself. Not unsure of your capabilities, but about what you're supposed to be doing, about the decisions you should be making. Like, you're involved in tons of stuff. All the student organizations, the seminars, being an RA. It's a lot of work. You complain about it sometimes, but I know you enjoy it.

"And maybe you're also doing all of these things because they allow you to take your mind off what's going on in your own head. So you're not really into being an RA or being part of a certain organization because while you're doing it, you're subconsciously in another place. I don't think you can ever truly enjoy something if you're using it to cover something else up, and it seems to me like that's exactly what you're doing."

"Dude, I'm not 'not into' being an RA."

I knew saying that would test Elaine's pride, but I wanted her to know my honest opinion.

"I know, Elaine. I'm not saying you aren't. I'm just saying it might not be as fun or enjoyable for you if you've always got something else looming in the back of your mind."

"I'm just trying to find my place in the world, dude. We all are."

"I know, but you have to let it come to you. You were saying you have no clue what you want to do with the rest of your life. I don't either. None of us do. But you can't force it, you can't force a niche or a personality. It'll come."

In my mind, things were certainly starting to come together. Elaine was notorious for changing her mind about what she wanted to do after she graduated, and being vehement about it. First, she wanted to be a doctor. At one point, she wanted to enlist in AmeriCorps to give back to the community. Recently, she'd wanted to plan mission trips to Mexico, which is close to her home in Houston, to help rebuild houses and aid the needy. Each time she found a new idea, she talked about it like it was her life's calling. I believed her the first time. Not the second and third. Elaine was simply impatient about figuring out what she wanted to do and because of it, she made some poor decisions to speed up the process. But she wasn't unlike most college students in that regard. Connor was looking more and more like one of these poor decisions. He wasn't the basis of the problems at all, simply a manifestation of them.

"You know what, Elaine? Here's what I think. I think it's natural to second-guess yourself, especially in this kind of situation, but you can't let it affect your everyday life this much. You said yourself it's making you miserable."

"I know, it is. I'm even considering transferring."

"Elaine, come on. That's just dumb. What do you think you can do to put things like Connor in the past? To be able to learn from them and not dwell on them?"

"I wish I knew." She laughed at herself.

I honestly didn't know either. I was confident that we had identified the root of the problem: Elaine's uncertainty with herself and her decisions. But that's not an easy thing to fix. Especially since it was dictating how she lived her life. Elaine lay there on the futon, seeming more vulnerable than ever. She had always come off as such a strong person, and it wasn't until this point that I realized how much she had been hiding from the world. The Elaine that everyone saw wasn't the real Elaine at all.

"Look, dude, I don't know how you can solve this. And I shouldn't, because only you can figure out how to make this go away. But at least now we kind of know what the problem is. It's up to you to take it from here. Just be yourself, man. I know it'll make things different, but if you can try not to put on a mask, maybe things will get easier. At this point, no one can get in to help you because no one knows what's up, and you're not allowing yourself to get out. You're trapped, but only because you're making yourself trapped."

She thought about this for a while, probably trying to come up with a snide remark. In the end, she just nodded.

"We'll see what happens," she said. "In the meantime, I have to go to a party tomorrow and see Connor. That's sort of why I'm stressing about it right now. It's a house party one of my friends is having, so I promised I'd stop by, and I know he'll be there. But whatever, I'll go for a few minutes, check on a couple of my friends to make sure they haven't had too much to drink, and then head back."

"As long as you don't stay too long. It probably isn't good for you to be over there with him if his presence is this upsetting to you."

"Yeah, no kidding. I'm not going to drink or anything. Jesse will be over there, though. I want to make sure she's okay."

Jesse was one of our mutual friends from freshman year. She was a nondrinker who had apparently started drinking because of her boyfriend, which Elaine wasn't too keen on. Like I said, for all of her faults, she was still extremely dedicated to her friends and to her residents. I truly admired that. I was lucky to have Elaine as a friend.

"Okay, Andyman, I'm going to bed. I need some sleep, I've got an exam tomorrow morning."

"Good luck. Stop by tomorrow night before you leave. I'm on duty so I'll be around."

Every night of the week, one RA is assigned to be in the building at all times after 7 p.m. The RA for that day walks around the dorm occasionally (to make sure no one is dying) and wears a pager that anyone in the house can call if there's a problem. We call this the "duty" system. The RAs take turns being on duty, and since no one ever wanted to be on duty during the weekend, I took a lot of Friday and Saturday shifts.

While I was walking around the dorm late that Friday night, I ran into Elaine before she left.

"Oh, good, Andy, I was just about to come find you. I think I'm going to head over to the party. It's nine o'clock now, so I should be back by 11 p.m. Call me if anything happens here and you need me. A lot of people might come back drunk because there are a lot of parties."

Elaine knew just about everyone on campus and thus was well-informed about social events. She kept me updated about big party nights to watch out for. It was very useful and appreciated information.

"Thanks for the heads-up. Be careful over there. I'll see you in a while. Call me if you need anything, too, and stop by when you get back, if you want. I'll be up."

"Okay, sounds good. Later, Andy."

The night was pretty quiet. I made my rounds from floor to floor. All of them were peaceful. A couple on the 3rd floor were making out in the lounge, a few guys on the 4th floor were playing poker. The 5th floor was dead, since most people were out at parties or asleep.

11 p.m. rolled around and Elaine wasn't back yet, but I didn't make much of it. Elaine had probably run into a dozen people she knew at the party and was talking someone's ear off about her day. I smiled to myself thinking about it. At around 12:30 a.m., I was in my room reading for history class when my phone started ringing. Anytime my phone rings that late at night, it's usually a bad sign. I looked at the screen. "Incoming Call – Elaine." I hoped it wasn't serious.

It was.

"What's up, Elaine?" I said as I picked up the phone.

"I'm in my room throwing up. Come here, and bring a garbage can."

Click.

Instinctively, I emptied the crumpled paper and empty potato chip bags from my own waste bin onto the floor and ran to Elaine's room. The floor was still silent, most of the residents were still out, and I was thankful that I didn't run into anyone I would have to explain this to. When I got to her room, I knocked hard. A young man I had never seen before opened the door. Elaine was lying on the ground, puking into a garbage can. Her face was dripping sweat and her body was shaking as she sat on the floor.

"Andy, Andy. This is Matt, he's a cool guy. He walked back with me from the party." Her speech was slurred and incoherent. She moaned and whined as she leaned over the garbage can in front of her, dry heaving. I peered into it and saw why I'd needed to bring another one. It was full of bright orange vomit, alcohol mixed with whatever Elaine had eaten for dinner. I had to step away and take a deep breath so I didn't end up throwing up as well.

After I had gathered myself, I switched the two garbage cans and handed Elaine a bottle of water from her fridge.

"Take small sips, Elaine." I looked up at Matt. He was a little tipsy himself, but not nearly as bad as Elaine. He was a tall, good-looking guy. And he was clearly scared to death, shivering and fidgeting with his ID card.

"Matt, how much did she have to drink?"

"Um, geeze, I don't know. A lot. She had a few beers, then a few shots, then some more beer—"

"NO! NO SHOTS!" Elaine interjected, waving her right hand aimlessly in the air. "I don't do shots! NO SHOTS! Beer, lots of beer. And some mixed drinks. No shots."

"Elaine, I thought you weren't going to drink, buddy. How much did you have?"

"I wasn't. I saw Jesse. She was okay. Then Connor. He has a new girlfriend. She's fat, Andy. She's sooo ugly."

Her comments were interrupted by more puking. Connor. Not the real problem, but a problem nonetheless. We'd have to worry about that later. The important thing was making sure Elaine would be alright. And it wasn't looking good at all. After she threw up, she fell onto her back. Matt and I lifted her up and leaned her against the bed. I decided I would need more than a scared drunk guy to help me handle this, so I went to enlist the help of another RA.

"Matt, I'm going to be right back. I have to go grab someone to help me. Do *not* let her fall over, keep her upright and awake."

It may not have been the smartest thing in retrospect, to leave Elaine in the care of another drunk, but he had taken care of her up to that point and it was my only choice. I had dealt with vomiting drunk people before, but Elaine looked worse than anyone I had ever seen. My legs were shaking and my breathing quickened. Leaving Elaine and Matt, I ran downstairs to the 4th floor and knocked on Sara's door. Sara, another RA, was a senior who had dealt with her share of drunks, and she was the first person who popped into my head. With her bouncy, whimsical personality, she may not have seemed like the ideal person to deal with an alcohol situation, but at that moment, I trusted her more than anyone. When I knocked on her door, she opened up, rubbing her eyes. She had clearly been sleeping. Her hair was a mess and she squinted to see me.

"Andy? What's up?"

As I talked, I realized how frantic I seemed. I tried to slow down. Surprisingly, I was calm inside, but I didn't do a good job of exhibiting that to Sara.

"I'm really sorry, Sara, but it's Elaine. She came back from a party, she's throwing up in her room right now, and I didn't know who else to get. It's not a normal puking thing. She's been dry heaving, and I just want to see what you think."

"I'll be right there. Hang on." She closed the door. When she came back out ten seconds later, she had thrown on a fleece and some sneakers. We ran upstairs to Elaine's room.

I had done one smart thing and one stupid thing right then. The stupid thing was not calling campus police as soon as I started to worry about Elaine's health. At the time, I wanted to get someone else who was sober in the room with me, but I should have called without hesitation. The smart thing I did was getting Sara. Often times, the smartest people and the best leaders are those who don't hesitate to get help when they need it. I knew I needed it.

When we arrived at Elaine's room, she was still heaving into the garbage can. Matt sat beside her.

"This is Matt," I said to Sara. "He came back with Elaine from the party. We don't know exactly how much she had to drink besides 'a lot.'"

Sara walked over to Elaine and knelt down beside her. She put her hand gently on Elaine's shoulder. At that moment, Sara appeared more mature to me than anyone else in the world. I was still shaking a little, fumbling with my words. Sara was the epitome of calm.

"Hey, sweetie. Are you okay?"

"He was with another girl, so fat, so ugly. Ugh, I feel really sick. I'm throwing up."

"I know, hon. What I need you to do is sip some of this water for me." She handed Elaine the water bottle, which had been tipped over in my absence. It was only half-full now. "How much did you have to drink?"

"Some beers, more beer, mixed drinks, but no shots. NO SHOTS! I don't do shots."

Sara looked at me. We couldn't help it. We laughed a little under our breaths. Even in a situation this serious, we couldn't help it. Elaine leaned over her garbage can to throw up again.

"Okay, no shots. How much have you thrown up?"

We never got an answer. As soon as Elaine pulled away from the garbage can, she fell backwards. We tried pushing her up, propping her against the bed, but each time she stayed awake for little more than ten seconds before falling over again. Sometimes on her side, sometimes on her back, always breathing hard. At this point we started to get scared. I was reaching for my phone when Elaine did one of the scariest things I've ever seen.

When she fell over this time, she began convulsing. Her entire body shook, like she was having a seizure. Her eyes were closed, her breathing was very irregular, and her limbs shook up and down. Sara gasped. I bent down, not knowing what to do. Before I could touch her, she stopped. It had lasted less than fifteen seconds.

Sara and I looked at each other. Matt sat on Elaine's bed, curled up and rocking back and forth. Then Elaine went into another convulsing fit, and I called emergency medical services.

"Ashford campus police, can I help you?" The sound of the operator's voice was the most beautiful thing I had heard in a long time.

"Yes, my name is Andy Butler. I'm an RA at New House. One of my friends is convulsing and throwing up from alcohol. We need EMS over here, like, right now. We're in New House, room 527. Please hurry."

After the second convulsion, Elaine woke up. We propped her against the bed again and told her EMS was coming.

"No, no EMS. No, bad. I don't want them."

"Elaine, you don't have a choice." I was calmer now that Elaine was conscious again. "Listen, until they get here, every few seconds, I'm going to say 'Elaine, are you with me?' and I want you to raise your hand to let me know you're still awake. Okay?"

She nodded and gave a thumbs up. EMS arrived quickly. They were two undergraduate students who I knew from classes. I said hello to them and moved out of their way. For about ten minutes, Sara, Matt, and I stood back while EMS did their work. They asked the same questions we'd asked. They put an oxygen mask on her and kept her awake. Campus police arrived to get our names and other information. One of the EMS guys came out of the room.

"Hey, do you know if she's on any medication?"

How stupid could I be? That should have been the first question I asked. Alcohol mixed with certain prescription and over-the-counter drugs can cause severe, sometimes deadly reactions. I knew Elaine was on birth control and an antidepressant.

"Shit, she's on birth control and some anti-anxiety medication. I'm not sure what it's called. It might be on her desk."

We checked and sure enough, there it was in a tall plastic bottle. Paxil.

"Yep," the EMS worker said. "This will definitely make the affects of the alcohol on her system a little stronger. Maybe a lot."

After a few more minutes of waiting, the head EMS member approached Sara and I.

"We've called an ambulance, they should be here any minute. We're taking her to Presbyterian Hospital. It's a good thing you guys called, she was in rough shape. Those convulsions you were talking about are rare, and they're never a good sign. We got some oxygen in her and she's doing better now, but we're going to take her in for observation, do some tests and make sure it's not alcohol poisoning or anything. You may have saved her life, though. She'll thank you tomorrow morning."

I can't explain how that felt. What if I hadn't called when I did? I don't even like to think about it. I did call, though, and I never again hesitated to call EMS if I thought someone had a serious health issue.

Sara and I decided to accompany Elaine to the hospital. We told Matt to go home, we'd tell Elaine to call him tomorrow. He was much calmer now. He thanked us and left for his dorm across campus. By the time the ambulance arrived, a few residents who heard the commotion had come out of their rooms to see what was going on.

"Andy, what's going on? Is Elaine okay?"

It was Elyse, in her pajamas and obviously a little confused.

"She'll be fine. Sara and I are going to the hospital with her. Do me a favor actually and don't talk about this. Thanks a lot."

Content with my answer, Elyse went back to her room. I trusted her to keep things under control if people started to ask questions.

Elaine was hoisted onto a cart and taken down the elevator. They loaded her into the back of the ambulance while Sara and I rode in the campus policeman's car. Sara grabbed my arm with both hands. The adrenaline hadn't worn off yet. But through all the frantic breathing and sick feelings in our chests, we were both just happy that Elaine was going to be okay.

At the hospital, we waited in the lobby for several hours. Sara and I talked to pass the time, but both of us were too spooked to take our minds off Elaine. We called Tamira, since one of her responsibilities as a housefellow was to respond whenever one of her residents went to the hospital in the middle of the night. That was one aspect of her job that I didn't envy at all. Finally, at around 5 a.m., we were allowed to see Elaine.

She was dressed in white hospital garb, lying down in room 22. On her left was a trauma patient who had just been in a car accident. On her right, an elderly man who suffered a stroke. And there was Elaine, half-awake, trying to wave to us as we came in. She later told me she would have preferred it if we never saw her like that, but seeing her then, seeing her breathing on her own, smiling, gave me a great feeling.

"How are you feeling, dude?"

"I'm okay. A little tired, and my stomach still hurts a little. But I'll be okay. Doctor says I can go home in a couple hours. They're just keeping an eye on me."

Sara chimed in. "You had us worried, Miss Elaine. It was a little scary."

"I am so sorry, you guys. Thanks for coming. You too, Tamira. Ugh, this is horrible. I still feel like shit."

"Understandably so," I said. "We'll go soon, let you get some sleep."

Tamira told Sara and me that she'd wait for Elaine to get discharged. In the meantime, we should go home and rest. As much as I wanted to stay with Elaine, I knew she was in good hands with Tamira, and after twenty-two hours on my feet, sleep sounded pretty good. Sara and I hitched a ride back to campus from a police escort, and soon I was in the comfort of my futon, getting some much needed rest.

ജ◦ള

Later that morning, Sara woke me up. "Just returning the favor," she said. We went to check on Elaine, who was supposed to have returned at 7 a.m. It was noon, and when we got to Elaine's room, her door was open. She was sitting on her bed, talking on the phone. She waved at us to come in.

"Okay, thanks again. I'll talk to you later. Bye." She turned to face us. "Hey, guys, what's up?"

"Not much," I said. "How are you feeling?"

"A little tired, a little hung-over still, but a lot better than I felt a few hours ago. What even happened? No one actually told me. The last thing I remember is waking up at the hospital with a horrible pain in my stomach. Waking up in the hospital and not knowing how you got there isn't fun."

We explained Elaine's night to her as best we could. The throwing up, the convulsing, the EMS. She listened in awe.

"Yeah, they told me it's a good thing you called or I could have been in really bad shape," she said. "But they didn't tell me about the convulsing. I guess I should call Matt and let him know I'm okay. I've called everyone else today. Oh man, my parents did *not* take this one well. It'll be an interesting next few days."

I was happy to see that Elaine was taking the situation as lightly as she could. It's not that she wasn't taking it seriously—she knew the implications of what happened. But whining and crying about it would have done no good. Elaine was trying to stay optimistic about the situation.

Sara looked at her watch and gasped. "Hey, guys, I have to take off. I'm late for a study group. I'm so glad you're feeling better, Elaine."

"Thanks again, Sara. I don't know what I'd do without you guys."

When Sara left, I brought up Connor. When I told Elaine what she'd said the night before, she sighed.

"Yeah, I remember that, too, unfortunately. You know, that really is why I drank. I admit it. I saw him kissing the other girl, and I froze. Then I asked one of his friends and he was like, 'Yeah, it's Connor's new girl.' I couldn't handle that, man. I probably had a dozen drinks in like half an hour. Then after that, I can't remember anything before the hospital."

"I think this is a sign that you might want to take some action to figure this out. 'Cause it's not just Connor, it's a lot more than that."

"I know. I will. I'll talk to Tamira and see what she suggests, but yeah, if nothing else, I know I've got to do something." She paused for a moment, then spoke again, tentatively. "Hey, do you think I'll get fired?"

It was an excellent question. According to standard protocol, she was supposed to lose her job. An RA is a role model, and failing as a role model is failing as an RA. I knew Elaine was different, though. She cared about her floor, and she wasn't failing an as RA. She was failing as herself.

"I honestly don't know, dude. Everything says you should, but I hope they'll make an exception in your case. You never know."

"I guess we'll see. I just want to stay here. I know I can start doing a better job."

There was nothing more either of us could say, so I left Elaine, who continued to rest, and went about my business for the rest of the day. Late that evening, I received another phone call from Elaine. This one wasn't good news either.

"Hey, I just got fired! How awesome is that?"

Elaine sounded hysterical. The crazy kind of hysterical that makes you wonder whether or not the person on the other line is going to jump off of a building.

"Elaine, where are you?"

"I'm in my friend's room right now. Angelica is here, keeping me sane."

Angelica was another mutual friend of ours from freshman year. She was an RA in another building, so I could breathe safe knowing that Elaine wouldn't do anything too drastic. It upset me that she was fired, though. I understand the principle of it and I do think it was the correct decision to make at the time, but it still upset me. The entire RA staff signed a petition to reinstate Elaine, of course to no avail. On Monday, Elaine moved to Kensington Gardens, a multi-class dorm located just a few feet away from New House. Eventually, Elaine worked out a deal with Student Life that allowed her to resign instead of being fired. Word was starting to spread on the floor about what happened. It was my job to let everyone know that Elaine resigned as an RA at New House for personal reasons, and that a replacement would soon arrive. But everyone knew. Every RA, every New House resident, everyone who knew Elaine was told the story by someone. I felt bad for her. People make mistakes, and hers was publicized because of the position she was in.

I helped Elaine move into the other dorm. She was somber, but she maintained her positive outlook, something I had never seen Elaine do before. Her optimism in this situation showed me she was already starting to change her approach to life.

"This really sucks, man. But it's what happens, I guess. I'm going to start meeting with Ryan, the housefellow for Kensington Gardens."

I knew Ryan. He was a nice guy, and someone Elaine would get along with well. The girls and guys on the floor were upset about it, but they also told me that since Elaine was rarely on the floor anyway, they didn't really feel like she was gone. And though her presence was missed, she came back to visit quite often. You can take the person out of New House 5, but you can't take New House 5 out of the person.

Elaine's situation did two things for me: it gave me another perspective on the importance of my position as an RA, and it essentially put the entire floor in my hands until a replacement was hired. The attention given to Elaine's situation made me see that as an RA, I was a mini-celebrity. Students pay close attention to their RA's personal and social activities at Ashford because the RA is such a big part of the residential experience. I didn't immediately change anything I did, but I did start thinking more about being a role model.

I also volunteered to remain the RA for the whole floor, knowing this would never happen. Especially in a freshman dorm, it's important for the girls on the floor to have a female RA to talk to. But until we found one, I was the go-to guy. So during the few weeks when New House 5 had only one RA, I made an extra effort to spend every second I wasn't sleeping or in class being on the floor. I kept my door open and I walked around, stopping in random rooms and talking to people I didn't know well. I became even closer to everyone on the floor. I became friends with some of the girls I never had a chance to talk to and learned more about the personal lives and aspirations of the guys on my side.

Eventually, we did hire a replacement, Laura. She was a senior and a sorority girl who had a lot going on in her extracurricular life, much like Elaine. She did a great job integrating herself into the community, but for the most part, much of the floor viewed New House 5 as "Andy's Floor," with Laura there to help. I give all the credit in the world to Laura for accepting this role and thriving in it.

Some people continued to call it "Andy and Elaine's Floor." This may have been a lot more accurate than you'd think, even though Elaine lived a dorm away. She was still a presence on our floor, and she was by no means finished having a large impact on New House 5.

GARY

Don't go chasing down those dark runways
Don't lose yourself
- Solo

I haven't talked much about Gary since Orientation. You may recall him as the guy who serenaded the floor with his song about killing a former crush with HIV. Gary was a great kid, funny and enthusiastic, but he had some issues as well. For Gary, the problems were identified, it was a matter of figuring out how to solve them. While he seemed carefree to the world around him, he was far from it. He had never dealt well with stress. At the beginning of the year, he blew off his work and spent most of his time doing a whole lot of nothing. He missed the comforts of his home, his friends, and his family, and the homesickness sunk in at some times more than others.

One afternoon, Gary stopped by my room to talk.

"Hey, Andy! What's up, dude?"

Gary looked as exuberant as ever. Although he'd grown up in a conservative Asian family, Gary was as far from conservative as a person can be. He survived by listening to emo music, a modern type of rock that consists of simple chords, screaming tone-deaf voices, and sad, emotional lyrics that make you want to kill yourself. I listened to a few of these bands so Gary and I had a musical connection. I knew Gary had just gone to see Dashboard Confessional, one of the most popular emo groups.

"How was the concert, man?" I asked him.

"Dude, it was awesome! I've seen them a couple times already but it's always cool. I started a mosh pit a few rows from the stage, it was sweet, man. I was going crazy. And he played all of his really old stuff. I had a blast!"

"That's great."

"Yeah, I'm going to come in and chill with you for a little bit."

"Okay, that's cool."

Gary sat down on the futon and breathed in deep. I knew he wasn't doing so hot in school. I figured now was as good a time as any to ask him about it. Sitting back when you know there's a problem is never good.

"Hey, man, how are your classes coming? It doesn't seem like you're into them at all."

"I'm not, man. I can't take this school. It's too much work, I hate all my classes. I just want to be back home and chill with my friends and not worry about all this shit, you know? I even miss my family. My little sister especially. She calls me almost every day to talk to me and she's only five years old. I like all the people here and stuff, but sometimes I can't deal with the stress."

Gary looked down at his hands. It looked like he was trying to keep a drum beat with his fingers. His hands were moving all over the place, in no apparent pattern or rhythm.

"Oh shit!" he yelled. "Not this again!"

"What's up, man? Are you okay? Are your hands okay?"

His hands were moving more rapidly now. They looked out of control. Gary kept cursing under his breath. I wasn't sure what was going on.

"I'm not doing this on purpose," he said, as he tried to sit on his hands. "This is what happens when I get really stressed out. My hands, feet, legs, arms—my whole body starts seizing. People don't believe me because they think I'm just doing it for attention, but I really can't help it. It'll go on for hours sometimes, there's nothing that can stop it."

He took his hands out from underneath his legs. They began shaking again. It was a little scary.

"I used to take medication for it. Well, for anxiety in general. I don't take it anymore. I didn't think it worked and when I turned eighteen, I told my doctor to fuck it, I didn't have to keep taking it. So I stopped. They think this whole shaking thing is psychological. It probably is, I just wish I knew how to stop it. They say not to think about it, but seriously, how can you not think about it when it's happening?"

"I see what you mean. Do you want to go to health services to get checked out, see if they can help you figure out what's going on?"

"I'll make an appointment tomorrow. I know what's wrong. I'm stressed out from school, I miss my friends and family, it's all just adding up. But I'm not going to go back on medication, there's nothing they can do about it."

"You know, man, they might still be open. Why don't you give them a call right now and see if we can head over there so they can take a look at it?"

"Okay, that's cool. This is kind of annoying."

I handed Gary the phone. He dialed the health services phone number with his shaking hands. They were still open and they did have a few minutes to see him. We headed down to the health center, which was just a short distance from our dorm. Outside, it was chilly and the fallen leaves blew around on the ground, making miniature crimson and ochre tornadoes on the sidewalk. Gary tried to hide his shaking hand from passersby. When we got there, he was admitted immediately and I waited anxiously in the front, reading a three-month-old copy of *The New Yorker*. He had been gone for about twenty minutes when he returned to the waiting room with the doctor. As we left, I heard the doctor say, "Good luck, young man. This kind of thing is never easy."

Gary was somber as we returned to the dorm. He had been given muscle relaxers for the twitching, but he was confident that it would return soon.

"This never happens once then goes away. It lasts for a few weeks, then it just disappears. It's going to be a long month. I can't wait to go back home for Thanksgiving."

I had never seen Gary this depressed, it seemed so unnatural. When we got back to the dorm, he slipped into his room and closed the door. I later found out that Gary tried dealing with his stress in a variety of ways. Marijuana, acid, anything to take his mind off the subject at hand. What Gary needed was an adjustment period, and with the rigors of school, he wasn't getting one. I knew in my mind that Gary shouldn't have been in school that first semester. A few nights later, Gary's body told him the same thing.

I'd taken Gary to health services on Tuesday evening. I didn't see him at all on Wednesday. On Thursday morning, I stopped by his room to check in. His roommate, Ben, opened the door. Ben was the kid from Nebraska who loved the Cornhuskers almost as much as he loved to play poker. I asked Ben if he'd seen Gary around.

"Nope, I haven't. I never see him around actually, it's sort of crazy. We're roommates and I might see him in the room for like ten minutes a day. The rest of the time he hangs out on the floor and with his friends. But I'll let him know you were looking for him if I do run into him today."

I didn't see Gary for the rest of the day. That night, I trekked over to Kensington Gardens to finish up some statistics homework with a friend.

While I was working through probability proofs and the central limit theorem, I received a phone call from Sam. I didn't think much of it, but when I answered the phone, I heard a frantic voice on the other end.

"ANDY! You have to come back now, it's Gary. He's having a seizure on the floor in the hallway. It's really scary. He can't control anything."

"Okay, I'm coming right now. As soon as I hang up, call campus police and tell them what you just told me. They'll send someone from EMS over."

"We already called. Just hurry, man. People are flipping out."

I don't think I've ever run as fast to get back to my dorm as I did right then. All I had to go on was Sam's phone call. I didn't know the severity of the situation, I just knew I needed to get there five minutes ago. By the time I reached the 5th floor, my lungs felt like sandpaper. When I arrived, EMS was already on the scene.

About twenty students were gathered around the guys' mini lounge, looking down at someone on the floor. An EMS volunteer was bent over, talking to the person. As I got to the crowd, the mob parted and I saw that it was Gary, still shaking. With some help from EMS, he got up and headed for the elevator.

"Andy! Hey, man, I'm okay. My body just went a little crazy there for a few minutes. They're going to take me to the hospital. Wow, that was really scary."

Ben was right behind him, carrying a book bag and Gary's ID card.

"I'm going to go with him," he said. "I've got all his stuff here."

"Are you sure?"

"Yeah, don't worry about it, I'll be fine. I'll give you a call if I need anything."

"Yeah, keep me updated."

Gary and Ben took the elevator down to the first floor, accompanied by the EMS volunteers. As I turned around, I saw the chaos that had broken loose. There was a large group of people yelling at each other. I tried to find Sam, since he had called me initially. He was engulfed in the mob, trying to calm people down. I realized that everyone was asking each other to calm down, they were just yelling it, which wasn't helping the situation. I pulled Sam aside.

"Okay, so what happened?"

"I was sitting here the whole time. Basically, we were all in the mini lounge doing calculus homework. Gary was sitting on the ground goofing off as usual. Then all of a sudden, he turned on his side and started shaking. He was laughing and yelling while it was happening. It started off very mild, and we told him to stop screwing around. Then he started yelling more, he started shaking more. Before we knew what to do, he was in a complete seizure. Laura called campus police right away. We just watched him for a few seconds, no one knew what to do, and people started crying. It was scary, man. Then after a minute, it stopped. He just lay still on his side, breathing hard and moaning."

"It wasn't spurred on by anything?"

"Not that I could see. One minute he was laughing, the next he was rolling around on the floor. Nobody knew what to do. I think everyone's a little shaken up right now."

That was quite an understatement. There were still people in the mini lounge, yelling between deep breaths.

"Thanks a lot, Sam. What I need you to do right now is help me calm people down. Let's get everybody who was around into the main lounge and make a quick announcement."

Sam and I gathered the startled and dazed people and herded them into the lounge. I stood up on one of the coffee tables. The murmurs and muffled tears continued. I cleared my throat.

"Okay, everyone, here's the deal. You all just saw Gary get taken to the hospital. He's going to be fine, obviously. He walked out on his own power, and Ben is with him. Ben is going to call and give me updates, and I'll let whoever is up know what's going on. We all just need to settle down now. It was a scary incident, but Gary is going to be okay."

The noise died down. A few conversations continued, but eventually the crowd dispersed and people got back to their homework. I was about to leave, too, when Sam stopped me.

"Andy, I didn't see Justine at this meeting. It would probably be good to check on her. She was sitting right next to him and she was pretty shaken up."

Sam's genuine concern for others always humbled me. I thanked him and made my way to Justine's room. Justine was a friendly Asian girl who kept to herself for the most part. She wasn't introverted, but she was never a vocal person and she wasn't close with the "core" group of the floor that had become synonymous with New House 5. I actually hadn't talked to her much, all I knew about her was her major (math) and her best friend (Michelle). Michelle was another sweet Asian girl on the floor. Justine and Michelle were like twins, inseparable and always fun to be around. I knocked on Justine's door. Michelle opened it to let me in.

Justine was sitting on her bed, wiping the tears from her eyes with a tissue. She saw me come in and tried to cover her face. Michelle hopped onto the bed next to her and held Justine's head to her shoulder.

"Hey, Andy," Justine whispered.

"Hey, Justine. How are you doing?"

"Oh, I'm okay. I just felt really bad for Gary. And really scared. I know what it feels like to lose control of your body. There's nothing you can do when that happens. You just hope it ends soon."

She cried harder and Michelle held her tighter. In most cases, I would have stayed as long as I could just to be a comforting listener. But sometimes, you have to know when you're not needed. I didn't have a great relationship with Justine, and this wasn't a situation where I was going to form one. She was upset, but she was going to be alright. What Justine needed was some time with the person who knew her the best, who knew how to comfort her. Michelle was there beside her, smiling, telling her amusing stories and referring to inside jokes. They were in their own world, where they belonged, and I had no place in that room. I told Justine to let me know if she needed anything and left. Justine and I always got along well after that, but she never became one of my close friends. And that was okay, because she had Michelle, and in that situation, Michelle was all she needed.

A lot of people stayed up into the wee hours of the morning. Ben called me twice with updates. The first time was to say that Gary was out of the waiting room and being seen by a doctor. The second, to tell me that Gary was being discharged. When they finally arrived back at the dorm via a campus police escort, it was 4 a.m. Gary thanked everyone who was still up (about a dozen people) for being concerned, and he hugged a few friends who had been crying when he left. Everyone was content to see him back and breathing, and slowly they disappeared into their rooms. Before I went to bed, I talked to Gary for a few minutes.

The diagnosis had been psychological, and they recommended that he see counseling services on campus. This frustrated me a little. The man had just lost total control of his body. I had a hard time believing it wasn't something physical, even if it was ignited by a psychological or emotional reaction. But the hospital just gave him more drugs to relax his muscles and sent him home. At this point, Gary was seriously considering taking a leave of absence, and I couldn't blame him. I told him to make an appointment with his advisor the next day to talk about it.

"Thanks so much for your help, Andy. This whole thing has just been a mess. I feel bad I brought you into it."

"Don't worry about it, man. I was glad to help. And one more thing before I hit the sack: you might want to talk to Justine tonight before you go to sleep. I think she'd be happy to see you."

ฬ๏ๅ

The following day, Gary met with his advisor, met with Tamira, and talked to his parents. Everyone agreed that the best thing for him to do was go back home for the rest of the semester. Gary came into my room, looking a little down, to let me know their decision. As much as he needed to be around his friends and family for at least the rest of the semester, it was clear that he was going to miss New House 5.

"Don't worry about it, man," I told him. "You're not leaving forever. You're coming back, right?"

"Yeah, definitely. The plan is, I'm going to just head back home and chill out for a while. Let myself recuperate and de-stress. Then I'll come back next semester. Housing even agreed to keep my spot open in the dorm, so I can live here again." He laughed. "Ben's happy to have a single for a while."

"Hey, make sure you give me a call once in a while and let me know how you're doing. We're going to miss your antics, buddy."

I hugged Gary, and it felt strange. I had only known Gary for a couple months and I'd be seeing him again in a couple more. But it felt like I was losing a part of me, like any loss to New House 5 was a blow to my soul. Others felt the same way. Even those who would not miss Gary's obnoxiousness were sad to see him leave. New House 5 was losing a member, and even though it wasn't permanent, it still stung.

Before Gary left, he wrote a goodbye letter on the dry-erase board in the lounge, addressed to everyone. It read:

> Dear New House 5,
> I'm really going to miss you guys. I had a great time getting to know all of you and hanging out. I wouldn't feel bad about leaving except I loved this floor. We were like brothers and

sisters, and we still will be. Thanks for putting up with me and letting me be myself. And thanks for always looking out for me. It's awesome to know that when I come back, I'll be living in a place where everyone has each other's back. I'll see you all in January.

With that, Gary left for the year. And as promised, he returned as good as new for the second semester, refreshed and ready to go.

CLOSE PROXIMITY

You hesitate to put your heart out on the line
- Daylight Savings Time

Let's talk about a lighter subject: floor-cest. A by-product of the dormitory setting that outsiders rarely hear about. The term refers to an intimate relationship (ranging anywhere from one night to the entire year) between two people who live on the same floor. Now, with twenty-eight guys and twenty-eight girls on one floor, you'd figure it might happen once or twice. The people closest to you geographically generally become the closest to you emotionally. But I could never have prepared myself for all the relationships that went on and all the gossip that surrounded them.

With a floor that was so close, people were bound to talk, bound to start rumors. The first night of Orientation, one of the girls hooked up with one of the basketball players. I only knew this because the next morning, the entire floor was talking about it. Did you hear so-and-so hooked up with so-and-so? There were reactions from all ends of the spectrum. "Oh my God, it's only been one day. People are such sluts." "Good for them. At least someone's getting some action." Or my personal favorite from the guys: "Which girl was it again?"

Counting the one-night stands, the accidental drunken hook-ups, and the "experiments" that I heard about, there were at least a dozen intra-floor relationships last year. It makes for some very awkward situations. It's rough having to walk to the bathroom after you wake up and see the guy or girl you made out with the night before sitting in the lounge. There's usually an ashamed "What's up?" then a quick departure by both parties. But you can't hide from someone who lives four doors down.

Eventually, people got over the mistakes. It was the long-term relationships that were a much bigger problem. The long-term relationships, the extensive crushes, and the unavoidable love triangles. They caused an unbelievable amount of tension. Everyone was forced to choose one side or the other, or be hated by both. Pick your poison. People talked about floor relationships constantly, and there was always plenty to talk about.

One morning in the middle of the first semester, I was walking to class half-asleep when I ran into Derek at the elevator. As we descended to the first floor, he issued me a challenge, which was incredibly strange, especially at 8:20 in the morning.

"I'll give you three guesses where Devon and Shannon are right now."

Devon was a great guy. A pledge at one of the fraternities, an active member on the floor, and a very opinionated, philosophical person. He was medium-sized, with dark hair, a muscular build, and a laugh that moved his entire body. Devon liked to drink, so we'd had run-ins before. Not that he was technically breaking any rules, but he was excellent at asking me what he could and could not get away with. He made it very clear that he didn't like to get drunk but he loved alcohol, and he preferred just to have one or two drinks a night. I explained to him that no, there would be no one searching his room, yes, I would bust him if he had a beer in the lounge, and that as long as I didn't see anything, he was fine. I said if he was stupid enough to let his RA see him with alcohol in the dorm he deserved to get in trouble, and he agreed. Shannon was a sweet, good-looking girl with brown hair who always stressed about class and never got enough sleep. She had also just come out of a messy break-up. Long-distance relationships rarely work in college and there's a certain two-week period in October when just about everybody breaks it off with their significant others from back home.

"I have no freaking idea, Derek. Where are they?"

"Let me tell you an interesting story. We talked, the three of us, until 5 a.m. Then, instead of going to sleep, Devon drove us to Food for Fuel for breakfast."

Devon lived in Georgia but his dad resided in Pittsburgh, so he had a car on campus. Even I was jealous of that. And Food for Fuel is Pittsburgh's form of Denny's. It's open twenty-four hours, which is good, because you'd never even think about eating there unless nothing else was open.

"After we had breakfast, I came back here to sleep. Devon and Shannon decided to go on a road trip to Philadelphia."

"What?" I asked incredulously. "Philly is five hours away. Today is Thursday. Why?"

Derek laughed. "I have no clue. Shannon was really upset about her boyfriend last night. They broke up about two weeks ago, but I think it's really beginning to hit her now. She never sees him anyway so it didn't really feel like they were broken up. Then last night, it did. We just talked to her for a long time. When I got out of the car this morning, Devon said, 'You know what? I have an aunt that lives in Philadelphia. You want to go visit her?' I said no because I've got an exam today but Shannon would have agreed to anything that took her mind off her ex. They're probably about a couple hours outside the city right now."

Students always say "I want to just run away," but rarely do they actually do it. Still a little stunned, I gave Devon a call on his cell phone. After a few rings, a hesitant voice picked up on the other line.

"Andy?" Devon said uneasily. "How are you doing, man?"

"Devon, I hear you're in Philadelphia right now."

"Um, incorrect. We're actually about an hour outside of Philadelphia."

He said it with such conviction. I laughed into the receiver.

"Oh good." Devon sounded relieved. "I thought you might be upset that we just picked up and left with no warning. And well, for no good reason either, I suppose."

"It's all good, man. It doesn't matter to me what you do. I just wanted to call and check in, make sure you two are okay."

"Oh yeah, we're fine. We made a couple pit stops, grabbed some food. I think we're going to drive around Philadelphia for a little while and stay with my aunt. We'll be back sometime this weekend. Shannon is really enjoying herself. I think this trip will be good for both of us. Here, let me put her on the phone."

After a few seconds of static, Shannon's calm voice came through the line.

"Hey, Andy. How are you, hon?"

"Not too bad. How's the drive?"

"Oh, it's great! We're having a blast. It's awesome, to just kind of pick up and leave spontaneously. I never do anything spontaneous anymore, it feels good. And neither one of us has anything due or any exams coming up. It was the perfect time to do it."

"Sounds good. Just be safe and give me a call if you need anything. We'll see you two sometime this weekend."

They returned to campus Saturday night. On the floor, their story had quickly become a legend. As soon as they stepped off the elevator, Devon and Shannon were bombarded with questions and high fives. Some people just wanted to congratulate them for doing something so spur of the moment. "Thanks," said Rob, "for doing what no one else had the balls to do." Others wanted to know what they did, where they stayed, how it went. After the novelty of their return had worn off, Devon and Shannon retreated to Devon's room. No one saw either one of them the rest of the night.

The next few days made it very clear to everyone on the floor that more had developed on the trip than Devon and Shannon first let on to. Shannon began spending every night in Devon's room. For the next week, I never saw one of them without the other a few feet away. While they didn't advertise it, the two were dating, and everyone knew it. Finally, they stopped trying hide what had happened in Philadelphia. I walked by the study room one day in the early afternoon. Devon sat inside, dressed in a bathrobe and slippers. He was listening to Nine Inch Nails on his walkman, sipping a cappuccino, staring out the huge study room windows into the brilliantly colored forest across the street. I stopped in to say hello.

"Hey, Andy, how are you doing?" he asked me calmly. "By the way, um, I thought I'd let you know, officially, that Shannon and I are together. Everyone seemed to be assuming it, so I'm just confirming the details."

"I appreciate that. Yeah, we did all kind of assume, which we shouldn't have done."

"Well, we weren't exactly discrete about it. Our trip made us both realize how much we had in common and how much we could help each other. I'm just very passionate about her. More so than I have been about any other girl, I think. She makes me happy."

For Devon, this meant something. Devon was a very philosophical guy. He decided to come to Ashford to pursue a degree in philosophy instead of trying to make it as an actor in southern California. Both were very real possibilities, but I think he was happy with the choice he'd made. He loved his fraternity, he loved the floor, and he loved to think. I often found him in the study lounge, listening to hard rock and staring into space. I can only imagine what he must have been thinking about. He looked so calm, so serene. But Devon seemed never to be fully content. He was happy, yes, and got excited about certain things, but there was something missing, something that made Devon incomplete. He would later tell me that his goal was to truly change the world philosophically. To do this, he thought he needed to be unhappy. He was torn between doing what he wanted to do and doing what he needed to do. But with Shannon, right then, there was no question. She made him happy, and that was all he cared about.

"I'll leave you to your music and meditating. Take care, man."

"You too."

Devon and Shannon's relationship lasted well into the second semester. It accomplished two things on the floor. One, it brought people together who were never friends before. Devon tended to hang out with people like Rob and Chad when he was on the floor, Shannon with her roommate Julie, and Hillary. A new bond between Devon and Shannon created more new bonds, like a domino effect. On the flip side, it also divided people at times. And the people it divided had nothing to do with Devon or Shannon. The lounges would occasionally be filled with people arguing about whether the relationship was good for Shannon, whether it was good for Devon. Were they being intimate, should they be? Was Shannon just using Devon as a rebound, was Devon using Shannon as a trophy? And of course, was it appropriate for two people on the floor to be so close? What happens when they break up? That last question would be answered much later, but until then, Devon and Shannon gave the floor something to gossip and disagree about. Everyone knew about it, and everyone had an opinion. I couldn't help thinking that it reminded me all too much of high school. But it couldn't be stopped. Devon and Shannon were the first two people to show the floor that a serious relationship among common friends can create new connections and new divisions.

Other long-term relationships sprung up as well. And as was the case with Devon and Shannon, the floor jumped all over the new situations and talked about them continuously. Any intra-floor hooking up was considered "sketchy." In every floor-cest relationship, the rest of the floor found a reason why it didn't make sense, why it shouldn't be happening, why it was immoral. Chad and Melissa began dating towards the end of the semester. Chad, the offensive, conceited, handsome Italian who said some of the stupidest things New House 5 ever heard, and Melissa, the hard-working, over-achieving girl who was commonly seen as a slut, simply because of rumors that circulated around her. According to the floor, Chad was horrible boyfriend material; he was a mama's boy who was after sex and nothing else. And Melissa was a manipulative, controlling, power-hungry snob who only appeared sweet on the surface. Opinions varied from person to person, but you couldn't walk down the hall without hearing one. And the people doing the talking were not always outsiders. Most of the time they were close friends of Chad and Melissa. Everyone had an opinion, and very few of them were grounded in fact or common sense.

Then there was the case of Avery and Bri. Avery, of course, was the opinionated Army guy who had a sarcastic comment for everything and knew how to get his way. Bri was a very quiet, savvy blond girl who worked out every day and stayed in her room for the most part. Many people on the floor knew Bri's boyfriend, Zach, who often came to visit. They'd both gone to the same high school just outside of Pittsburgh and now were at the same college. We all liked Zach, and when Bri began hanging out with Avery, the floor threw their collective arms up in disgust. I don't know if anything even happened between the two of them, but if they were seen watching a movie together, maybe a little too close to each other on the couch, furious commentary broke out in the mini lounge.

Of course, there were the random one-night hook-ups that gave the floor plenty to gossip about too. These happened on a weekly basis, so there was never a dull conversation. At the center of most discussions was Alicia, who once told Luke, after he'd received a box of flavored condoms as a gag gift, "The strawberry ones taste amazing." Alicia had a self-confidence issue and while she had a bunch of guys at her fingertips, I wondered how many times she actually slept with the guys she brought back. I got the feeling she wore the slut label just so she had something to hold onto, so she could be identified with something. She was one of the sweetest girls I've ever met, and I genuinely felt sorry for her sometimes. She refused to talk about it, however, and lived with the rumors constantly swirling around her. She often came back from the fraternities hammered, a guy on her arm. Sometimes we'd seen the guy before, sometimes not. She manipulated them, batted her eyelashes, and used all of her femininity to get what she wanted.

And as you would expect on any floor, there was one guy who seemed to attract a lot of attention from the girls. On New House 5, it was Eric. Tall, good-looking, athletic, and outgoing, Eric was the kind of guys college girls love. His red hair symbolized his flaming Irish temper, which could be seen from time to time when he was playing sports (lacrosse and hockey) or just making a point that frustrated him. Lacking common sense at times—he once tried to shave with nothing but a razor blade while sitting at his computer—his small misgivings gave a few of the girls something to giggle about, while they swooned about other parts of him. Val, in particular, had a minor infatuation with Eric during the first semester. She made fun of him more than anyone, but always with a smile on her face. Eric marched to his own beat, and I think this was one of his attractive features. He did what he wanted to do and disregarded everything else. If he did date someone on the floor, it could have caused a disastrous rift in the community, tearing apart girls who liked him along with their close friends. But luckily Eric, who wouldn't have worried in the slightest about making members of the floor hate each other, decided the first semester wasn't a good time for him to have a girlfriend.

The most talked about floor-cest relationship following Devon and Shannon was the strange interaction between Elyse and Luke. Both were good friends with almost everyone on the floor, particularly the core New House 5 group. Elyse wasn't shy about voicing her concern about various issues on the floor, while Luke couldn't care less about what was happening socially on the floor. Opposites attracts, I suppose. While it was mainly the core group of girls who did the gossiping, the guys got their fair share in as well. And even the people who were not as "informed" as the others managed to stop by and become part of a conversation if they happened to run across one.

What actually went on between Elyse and Luke, I will never know. They did a good job of confining their actions to non-public areas. But of course people knew about it, because Luke and Elyse talked about it among their close friends. And Luke and Elyse's close friends talked about it to their close friends. You can figure it out from there. To the best of my knowledge, Elyse and Luke never dated. They were a potential couple that fell through, maybe because Elyse was getting too close too fast, maybe because Luke just wasn't that into it. For whatever the reason, it was an issue, and it got its share of airtime on the New House 5 gossip hotlines.

So it goes in a close community. When everyone knows everyone else, it's easy to be intrusive and it's easy to judge other people's lives. You come to college thinking the drama will be held to a minimum, but gossip is inevitable. Each person who talked was at one point talked about. And each successive scenario was blown even more out of proportion. The relationships can be a good thing. Sometimes two people on a floor really click and everyone is happy. Of course, with the floor-cest comes the rumors and the grudges. I thought that they'd get it all out of their systems early in the school year, but I was wrong. The Elyse and Luke situation climaxed in late October. But they weren't the last couple to cause ripples on New House 5.

UPS AND DOWNS

The broken glass is scattered everywhere
But the pieces are so small
That you can't feel them 'til you fall
- The Navigator

October tested the breaking point of New House 5 and threatened to send it into a downward spiral, to destroy everything that had been created up to that point. Every small problem grew bigger, grew more difficult to hide. On Halloween, those problems reached their pinnacle, and we all learned just how much New House 5 could take.

The Halloween season started off wonderfully on the floor. Tamira announced that there would be a decorating contest between the floors. The scariest floor, as determined by a select group of judges (namely Tamira and two other housefellows), would win a pizza party. And more importantly, the unofficial title of "Best Floor in New House." Pride was on the line, and everyone knew it. A group of underprivileged children were coming on Halloween to trick-or-treat in the dorm, so we had to make our floor frightening and inviting at the same time. I wasn't sure how the floor would respond to this. Sure, the idea was great and the stakes were high, but I assumed a lot of the students would view Halloween decorating as childish and stupid. With the homework piling up and exams looming, many of them would not want to dedicate the time. But I underestimated the devotion and enthusiasm of New House 5, something I never did again. And I underestimated the rivalry that was growing between the 5th floor and the 3rd floor.

The 3rd floor issued a challenge to the rest of New House: "We're the best floor, try us." Some people claimed the rivalry started before the decorating contest, but Halloween is what really set it off. They viewed us as a bunch of introverted, cliquish, snobby humanities students. We viewed them as a bunch of uninspired, drunk, stupid engineers. The 5th floor personality tended to take after me: involved, enthusiastic, proud, goofy. The 3rd floor tended to take after their north side RA, Rohan: laidback, fun to be around, random. The 3rd floor had even named themselves "Thorn Side," an anagram of "North Side." The 5th floor was just New House 5. The connotations with that phrase on campus were already positive. But the 3rd floor decided that they were going to win the decorating contest. When we caught wind of this, school and relationships took a backseat to the competition.

About a week before Halloween, the race began. A few of the girls spent an evening cutting out decorations from construction paper. It started slow: Kristen created a giant Frankenstein that was placed right next to the elevator, and Julie, Hillary, and Shannon brightened the study room and lounges with homemade pumpkins and bats. Then Rob and Luke noticed a few decorations going up on the 3rd floor, like a clever sign that said "Welcome to Thorn Side" in fake blood. As the day approached, more little things went up on our floor, then on theirs. We strung fake cobwebs throughout the lounges and hallways. They placed clothes, stuffed to look like dead bodies, underneath sofas and chairs. For our every action, they had a reaction. It was almost scary.

But even though pride was on the line, the truth is that no one would have participated if it wasn't also fun. There were group trips to CVS, Target, and thrift shops. Costume ideas changed daily, and picking one out became a floor event. Luke, with the help of a few girls on the floor, made a Homestar Runner costume. Elyse planned on being a wench. Devon dressed up as his big brother at the fraternity. Aaron (who was Jewish) chose to go as Jesus (and did an excellent job of it). Rob told me he had the best costume idea ever, but I'd have to wait until Halloween to find out what it was.

The night before Halloween was chaotic. The floor was buzzing with anticipation and last-minute preparations. We couldn't do anything too drastic until the night before because of fire codes. So at 9 p.m., there was a mad flurry of decorating. We covered all the lights with black construction paper, making the hallways dark. Kristen collected bed sheets from people and hung them from the ceiling, creating a maze for the trick-or-treaters to walk through. Orange and black streamers were hung from the ceiling in random places. Loud shrieks and evil cackles played on a radio in the background. Homemade cardboard tombstones lined the area just outside the elevator, their epitaphs personalized and goofy: "Here lies Aaron Weinberg, he slipped on an iceberg," or "Rosalyn Morales fell on her ass." A moving hand that responded to noise was placed right outside the entrance to the maze. And for the finishing touch, Alicia purchased an eight-foot inflatable spider. We put it in the lounge, beneath the cobwebs and surrounded by darkness. The large purple spider had a light bulb inside it, which glowed brightly in the dark, and the lounge became the spider's lair, the maze became the cave leading to it. The last decorator went to bed at 4 a.m. The 5th floor was ready for action.

A quick walk around New House the following day revealed the contest to be a two-horse race. And it was going to be tight. The 3rd floor was good. Really good. Whereas we had focused all our energy on the girls' side of the floor, they had decorated both wings. They lined every wall, ceiling, and carpet with black trash bags. Walking down the hall felt like walking through the basement of a run-down haunted house. Fake dead people littered the floors, random objects dangled from the ceiling, caution tape marked off "danger" areas. The effort was there, the creativity was there. It was a coin flip at this point.

I normally don't encourage skipping class, but I didn't say anything when a few people cut out early to help with last-minute preparations before the kids arrived at 3 p.m. Kristen dressed up in a vampire costume. Her job was to greet the children when they got off the elevator and take them through the sheet maze. Aaron sat in a chair, placed strategically in the middle of the maze. He wore a fake pumpkin on his head, and at first glance, looked like a large scarecrow. With good timing, Aaron planned on scaring the daylights out of every kid that walked by. Everyone else hung out in their rooms, waiting with candy for the trick-or-treaters. I waited in the main lobby for the kids. When they finally arrived, only a few minutes late, I called Kristen to let her know. The children were in awe. In awe of New House and of college students. I forget sometimes how big we seem to little kids. I forget sometimes how big we're supposed to be. I think we all do. But these kids, with their wide eyes and dropped jaws, were a pretty good reminder. They were dressed in their own costumes: Pittsburgh Steelers players, Freddy Krueger, ballerinas, butterflies. Hesitant and excited at the same time, I led a group of fifteen kids up the elevator.

"We're going to the 5th floor," I told them. "It's the top floor of the building, and I hear some crazy stuff lives up there. I'd be careful if I were you."

They weren't sure whether to believe me or not. Some of them covered their faces, hiding looks of utter fear. Others laughed nervously, trying to convince themselves I was joking. But amid the fear and wonder, each of them wore a grin. Scared or not, they were determined to have a good time. And we were determined to make that a reality.

When the elevator door opened, they stepped into the darkness. Faint lights glowed in unseen places. A detached hand crawled in front of them. A girl screamed. She jumped back and burrowed her face in a peer's shirt sleeve. Sinister laughing and merciless screams reverberated through the halls. A female vampire appeared from the dark entrance to a beckoning lair. "Welcome," she whispered, "to the 5th floor. Come with me."

The haunted maze was a huge success. Aaron jumped out at kids as they walked by, and just as he planned, he elicited quite a few screams. About six groups of kids toured the floor. Between groups, Aaron came out of the maze, sweating and breathing hard, and grinning ear to ear. "I'm dying in this pumpkin, man. But I think I've made about seven kids cry so far."

There was screaming, there was crying, there were a few kids who flat-out refused to go into the maze. "I heard a kid got lost in there last year," I whispered to an eight-year-old vampire. "Someone told me he's still trapped inside." The little boy looked at me, eyes the size of dinner plates. He opened his mouth to ask something, then realized he'd rather not know the answer.

Despite their fright, the children really enjoyed themselves, even the ones who were scared to tears. At the end, all of them got candy and Aaron even revealed himself in the light to prevent any nightmares the children might have. I walked around the 3rd floor to check on their progress. Several of the residents were dressed in all black and jumped out at random places. A quick run through the rest of the dorm showed mostly last-minute decorations, done with little thought or planning. I was silently proud of both the 3rd and 5th floors for taking the contest seriously. I should have been happy merely with the effort, but I got caught up in the competition as well. After all the kids had cleared out, I made my way to the New House lobby. Tamira was there, talking to Jimmy. They were surrounded by representatives from the 5th and 3rd floors, many of them still decked out in their costumes. The room was buzzing. Aaron was bragging about his crying kid total, Shannon and Julie were discussing which parties to go to. Tamira cleared her throat and the room went silent.

"I want to thank all of you for participating in this year's decoration contest. I knew that New House would really get into this. I know my house is the best on campus. This is the first year New House has even been open, and I think we've already created a new tradition."

Tamira went on for a few more minutes. She was long-winded, and there was no way around a drawn-out explanation. We were told about the criteria, about how proud she was of New House. Finally, it looked like she was wrapping up.

"It was a very difficult decision to make, but we do have a winner." Tamira paused for a dramatic effect. "Our very close runner-up is the 5th floor, with their sheet maze and spider's den. And the winner of a pizza party is the 3rd floor. Congratulations to both of you."

Cheers erupted from the 3rd floor contingency before Tamira even finished her sentence. I was much more upset than I thought I would be, maybe just because we'd invested so much time and effort into decorating. I felt worse for my floor than for myself, but it was still a sick feeling. I congratulated Rohan and headed up the stairs without making eye contact with anyone. When I got to the floor, everyone who had helped was there waiting for me. A few were starting to clean up a little. I looked at them and shook my head.

"I'm really sorry, guys. It's bullshit. But I'm still going to buy you all pizza. You totally deserve it."

After I said that, I looked around at the people standing in front of me. I noticed that no one looked sad. In fact, they all had goofy grins on their faces. After ten seconds of dead silence, Luke started laughing and the rest of the floor followed suit.

"Andy, dude, it's okay. I mean, yeah, it was bullshit and we look better, but we already know we're the best floor in New House." He said it in a sarcastic, matter-of-fact tone. "Honestly, I don't think anyone was really worried about winning. We had a ton of fun just getting together and decorating. We wanted to make it awesome for the kids who came through, and they loved it."

"Yeah, man," Ben chimed in. "Who cares about the contest? You think we're going to let some random judging ruin our Halloween? I want to go through the scary maze!"

With that, Ben ran through the sheets, hands flailing in the air, yelling at the top of his lungs. The chatter picked up again. People started to clean up some of the easily removable decorations while they jubilantly talked about their plans for the evening. Some were already preparing their costumes in the lounge. Others discussed which fraternities were going to have the best parties.

I learned something about the 5th floor right then. I learned how mature they were. More mature as a group than I was individually at the time. The purpose of a contest is simply to encourage everyone to participate. Sure, there's some pride involved, but if you worry too much about what everyone else thinks, you're going to be miserable. New House 5 didn't care. They did what they wanted to do, they had a blast doing it, and the title was only a minor detail. For the 5th floor, the decorating contest was a chance to come together for a different reason than usual, for something other than study groups and pick-up basketball. And they genuinely enjoyed that. It's always important to get enjoyment out of what you do, to do things for yourself and not worry about what others think.

On Halloween, I learned that a group of people can think the same way as a rational human. On Halloween, I learned that sometimes a group of people can be more rational than a single person ever could.

ço∂

After the children left, the festivities really began on the 5th floor. We took down a few of the decorations but left most of them up. We could clean up the next day, and it would be cool to show off to visitors that night. At around 7 p.m., I got to see Rob's secret costume. I walked into the lounge and erupted with laughter. Standing between the couches was Rob, wearing my green RA t-shirt from Orientation, my navy New York Yankees hat, a pair of cheap glasses, and my guitar. Rob's costume was me. To this day, I have no clue how he managed to get all this stuff out of my room without my noticing, but he did, and he had the undisputed best costume of the evening.

Elyse took pictures of the two of us standing side by side. Rob wasn't the only person who received compliments for his costume, though. Tom wore a French maid outfit, one of the slutty, tight-fitting ones that girl wear to pick up guys on Halloween. Chad dressed as a traditional girl, complete with a skirt and lipstick. Julie went as Marilyn Monroe. Roger, who lived in Lancaster,

Pennsylvania, was the perfect Amish man. And Rob changed his costume to an Asian cook, since at parties, people might not understand his original costume.

At 11 p.m., all the preparation and talking had been done; it was time for the parties. I didn't dress up as anything since I was on duty. I'd been warned that Halloween duty is never fun, which makes sense. For many fraternities, Halloween is the biggest party of the year, and in the past, it's been the busiest night for the emergency room. The core group headed out together to check out all the parties. The Asians went to a friend's house. And even the quiet residents left their rooms to check out the Halloween festivities on campus. When I walked around the floor at midnight, I could hear the air conditioner sputtering. It had not been this quiet on the 5th floor since the first day I moved in. That was scary in itself. Every person who lived on the 5th floor was either sleeping or out. I sat in my room and watched college football, waiting for the real "fun" to begin.

At about 2 a.m., people started coming back to New House. And trust me, fun is not the word I would use to describe the next few hours.

I was already tired at 2 a.m., but since no one had returned yet, I figured it was going to be a long night. People came back sporadically, in pairs and trios, most of them drunk. The first person I saw was Lindsey, sitting on a couch in the mini lounge, with her face buried in her hands. I bent over to ask if she was okay. Lindsey looked up at me. She wasn't crying, but she was clearly upset. "So let me tell you what's been happening."

Lindsey was Rosalyn's roommate. She was a smart (and some would say snobby) math major who sort of did her own thing. She wasn't part of the core New House 5 group, but she hung out with a lot of people on the floor individually. Lindsey was a tall, blonde-haired girl, dressed for Halloween in an Indiana Jones outfit. And despite the fact that she kept mainly to herself, she had managed to put herself smack dab in the middle of the Elyse and Luke chaos.

Two weeks before Halloween, Elyse and Luke stopped hanging out. It was abrupt and unexpected, and initiated by Luke. As far as I could tell, Luke was concerned with how close they were getting, and wanted to keep anything further from happening. He had a girlfriend back in Maryland and wanted to avoid temptation. Elyse was confused and hurt. Soon after, Luke and Lindsey, two seemingly incompatible people, became as close as any two people on the floor. I would walk by Luke's room on occasion and see the two of them sitting next to each other, watching a movie on his computer. Lindsey had told me once before, "I spend more time in Luke's room than my own." Of course this upset Elyse, and Elyse let the world know about it. In a variety of ways.

Let me introduce you to the wonderful world of weblogs. The bane of my existence and the eventual downfall of civilized humanity. Actually, "blogs," as they are called, have the potential to be a great tool for a college student, but all of my experience with them has been negative. There are many internet sites that host blogs. You sign up for free and you're given a website address. The purpose of a blog is to serve as an online journal. A log of your everyday activities and feelings, on the web. A web log. A blog. Get it?

I discovered blogs my freshman year. I even have one that I never use. For some people, keeping a journal in electronic form is quick, convenient, and fun. Plus your friends can check out what you're doing and thinking without ever having to talk to you. At college, so many people have blogs that it becomes a daily ritual for people to check their friends' journals. Most sites let you leave comments on a particular journal entry, so you can let the person know how you feel about what they've just said. Sounds messy, huh? Well as I said, these can be great tools for keeping in touch, but the problem arises when people begin using blogs to vent their anger and their grudges. Most services give the user the option to make an entry private (only the user can see it) or public (anyone with internet access can see it). You could say that the problem with blogs is that occasionally, an entry that should be private is made public.

I've said before that people put poetry and song lyrics in their instant messenger profiles. They can also include links to websites, and a lot of times, people will insert a link to their blog. In these cases, a person's blog can be found by any number of people. So if you write something about someone who you don't know reads your blog, it can cause problems. Issues tend to arise, as I said, when someone uses their blog to vent. Letting the whole world see your irrational thoughts and angry outbursts is not always the best idea. But it happens, and you wouldn't believe the tension it causes. If people took blogs for what they are—online journals that shouldn't be taken too seriously or out of context—there would be no problems. But you try asking a college student to think rationally.

Back to Elyse and Lindsey. Elyse had a blog, a link to it in her profile, and a tendency to use it to vent. When Luke and Lindsey started hanging out, Elyse blogged about it. She was upset that Luke had "chosen" Lindsey instead of her. She wasn't upset at Lindsey, just the situation. It was sketchy, and that's all there was to it in Elyse's mind. Meanwhile, Lindsey was in her own world. She did her own thing and had no idea what was being said behind her back. Until one day when she stumbled upon Elyse's blog. While Elyse didn't use any actual names, Lindsey easily figured out the girl Elyse was referring to. Lindsey explained to me what I already knew. Then she gave me her perspective.

"I honestly never thought about me and Luke as a couple. He has a girlfriend, I have a close ex-boyfriend at home. We're just two friends who hang out a lot. Then I read that Elyse pretty much hates me and the whole floor thinks we're going to start dating. It's just so stupid."

I found it hard to believe that Lindsey never considered the idea of her and Luke together. The way they handled themselves, the amount of time they spent with each other. For example, one night the whole floor was watching a movie in the lounge. Luke and Lindsey curled up next to each other, giggling and holding hands. Elyse was outraged. "Friends don't do that shit." I had to agree with her.

But Lindsey went on. "Even though I never really considered us a couple, maybe Luke sort of did. I asked him about what Elyse said in her blog and he talked about how they kind of ended their friendship on bad terms. Luke never denied that he considered dating me, but he did say not to worry about anything. Then tonight I went over to his fraternity to hang out. He got really drunk. Like, totally plastered. And he tried to kiss me. I pushed him away, but he tried again. Then I yelled at him. He pulled back quickly and started moaning to himself, something about 'I shouldn't have done that.' I was freaked out, so I came back here."

She sighed and massaged her forehead. "I just don't want everyone on this floor to hate me for something I have no control over. I just want a good guy friend who I can talk to and hang out with. I don't want it to be a problem, but now, that's inevitable."

"It appears so," I said. "I think you need to talk to him about it. If he has a girlfriend and you're both looking at your relationship differently, it sounds like things need to get straightened out. Forget what the floor thinks, do it for yourself."

"I'll talk to him tomorrow. I think I'm going to bed now. I've had enough for the day."

Lindsey walked drearily back to her room. I felt bad for her. She was just trying to mind her own business, but by association, she had been pulled into the drama that she was trying to stay away from. It occurred to me then that maybe the closeness of the floor as a whole deterred the closeness of individuals, especially people who may have felt uncomfortable around the core group of New House 5. That frustrated me. I wanted New House 5 to be a community, not an all-inclusive soap opera. But they come hand in hand sometimes. It made me think that in some cases, it's not good for everyone to be super-involved in the community. In some cases, it's the last thing a person would want. Lindsey was one of those people.

I walked the floor again and found a few more people coming back in. Rob, who was a little tipsy but not too gone, sat on the couch in the girls' lounge looking bored.

"I'm waiting to hear from Elyse and Audrey. Elyse doesn't drink, but Audrey was in bad shape, I guess. We'll see."

"Hmm, keep me updated," I told him. "I'll be around the floor."

They continued to trickle in as it grew later. By 3 a.m., I had seen just about everyone I was worried about. Luke, who was as plastered as Lindsey claimed he was, stumbled off the elevator and nearly knocked me over. Hillary, Shannon, and Julie came back, a little drunk and very giggly. Kim and Meghan, both of whom did not drink, pulled Kristen back to her room. Many of the guys, like Aaron and Ben, returned tired and went right to bed. Avery came back from his fraternity looking more pissed off than anything. I asked him if he was okay, and he said he would explain it to me in the morning. Finally, Elyse came back with Audrey. She smiled at me and mouthed, "She'll be okay," then helped Audrey back to their room. Thinking my night was just about over, I went back to my room. Halloween had been eventful. My talk with Lindsey, random discussions in the hallway with Luke and Kim. I was about to turn off the lights and give in to my drooping eyelids when Rob came running in.

"Audrey is in her room screaming. She locked the door, and we don't know how to get in." His speech was slurred, not because of alcohol but because of worry. I had never seen Rob so upset in my short time knowing him. I followed him down the hall to Audrey's room. Outside, Elyse and Hillary were talking quietly. Kim and Val were standing beside them, looks of apprehension on their faces. At first there was silence. Then a loud, eerie moan came from inside the room. It was definitely Audrey's voice.

"Ahhh. No, don't let them. I can't help it."

The color drained from Elyse's face. She turned around and looked relieved to see me standing next to her.

"I took her in to pass out and then went to the bathroom," she stuttered. "When I came back, the door had closed. My key is in the room, we have no way to get in. I'm really worried about her, Andy. I have no clue what's going on. She's been really strange lately. And she had a lot to drink. I don't want anything to happen to her."

"Look, guys," I said, "I know you probably don't want to, but we have to call campus police."

As soon as it came out of my mouth, Elyse picked up her phone and dialed. We waited silently for the policeman to get there. Audrey screamed again, sending a shiver up our spines. Hillary yelled, hoping her voice would penetrate the door and wake Audrey up. We pounded, we pried, but nothing. After what seemed like an hour, the policeman arrived. We explained the situation to him. He knocked on the door before getting his master key, but to our surprise, Audrey opened it first. The police officer spoke sternly.

"I heard you were screaming in there. Is everything okay?"

Audrey was very dreary but immediately fell back into a defensive mode. "Yeah, yeah, I'm fine. Don't worry about me, I'm okay."

We stood patiently as the two talked. When the policeman was convinced Audrey was fine, he let Elyse into the room, thanked us, and left for another call. For a moment, no one spoke. Rob broke the silence.

"Audrey, do you know what just happened?"

"Yeah, I was sleeping. What was he talking about? Something about screaming?"

Hillary and Rob looked at each other.

"Why don't we go chill in my bedroom for a bit?" he said. "We can talk about it there."

So off went Elyse, Hillary, Audrey, Val, Kim, and Rob to talk in Rob's room. As they left, Rob pulled me aside and assured me they'd keep an eye on Audrey. I trusted Rob, and he was more concerned about Audrey at that moment than I probably would have guessed. I shut my door and collapsed into bed. I looked at my clock. 4:23 a.m. As tired as I was, it took a long time to get to sleep. Every time the wind blew outside, I listened hard to make sure it wasn't Audrey screaming across the hall.

❧❧

The next morning, I received some explanations. The night was hectic enough for me at face value, but when I found out some of the underlying reasons for what had happened, I realized how bad the night really was. The first person to offer some information was Rob. In the early afternoon, he stopped by my room to talk.

"Hey, Rob, how did the rest of the night go?"

He smiled and laughed. "Let's put it this way. At one point I was lying on my floor saying to myself, 'Please make this night end!'"

"When we went back to my room, we talked to Audrey for a little while about what happened. At first she didn't believe us, but then she admitted that maybe she could have been talking in her sleep. Then we tried to figure out why she was doing it. She wouldn't say why. It's something really, like, psychological. Something with her family maybe, she wouldn't tell us. But that was scary, you heard it yourself."

"How long were you guys up?"

"Hillary and Audrey ended up sleeping on my bed. We talked until about 6 a.m., then Elyse, Kim, and Val left. I was on my floor, trying to fall asleep without a blanket. My roommate walked in at 8 a.m. and was so confused. I was like, 'Don't ask, dude.' I didn't fall asleep until 9 a.m., so I got about three hours of sleep. Hillary, Audrey, and I just talked about random shit for a while. I wish Audrey would tell us what's up. She's been acting very strange and reclusive lately."

"If I were you, I would probably talk to her about it today or something."

"Oh yeah, I'm going to. But she's still not going to tell me anything. I mean, if she didn't tell me anything when she was drunk, she won't tell me anything today." He laughed uneasily.

"I'm sure your help last night was appreciated," I assured him. "It's pretty awesome having you on the floor for stuff like that, when people are hesitant to get me."

"Yeah, I just wanted to help her out. I like Audrey a lot. I've talked to her more the last couple weeks and she's a really cool girl. I think it was awesome that everyone was there for her. I mean, we were all there for her last night one hundred percent. I just wish it hadn't happened at all, obviously."

"Yeah, I know. Well, I'll let you go do your work and get some sleep. Thanks a lot for letting me know the deal."

"No problem, man. I'll let you know how it goes."

Less than ten minutes after Rob left, Hillary stopped in to give her rendition of the story. She sat on my futon and told me some of the same details I heard from Rob. She was more uncomfortable talking about it, and spent most of the conversation speaking into one of my pillows.

"But Rob may be the awesomest guy I have ever met. He was there for Audrey totally last night. We all were, actually. I'm just nervous about talking to Audrey about it. Rob and I decided we're both going to talk to her. I don't want it to be like a confrontation, but last night was bad, and I don't want it to happen again."

Hillary buried her face in my pillow.

"You guys are doing all you can," I said.

"I know. That's what scares me."

Hillary left to do some reading and write a paper. Then, when he saw that Hillary was gone, Luke swung by for a few seconds.

"Hey, man," he said, "I just wanted to apologize for being hammered last night."

"Haha, don't worry about it, as long as you're okay."

"Um, yeah." He paused. "So I heard I did something stupid last night."

"I've heard the same thing."

"Dude, I'm so dumb. Lindsey kind of gave me a quick rundown, and we're going to talk more about it later. She told me she talked to you. God, it's just stupid stuff like this I get myself into. And I'm chill about it, but obviously not everyone involved is. I just don't want people to be mad at each other and mad at me. I guess I should go see if I can take care of this." He sighed. "The problem with getting yourself in shit is that you have to get yourself out."

"That may be the most profound thing I've ever heard you say, Luke."

"Thanks, man." He punched me jokingly on the arm. Two minutes after he left, his roommate Avery knocked on my door. I felt like my room was a revolving door, but I was glad people were willing to use it.

"Andy, how are you? I told Luke to let me know when he was done talking to you so I could stop by."

"I'm good, but you seemed pretty pissed off last night."

"I was. Very much. It turns out my fraternity lied to me and to the entire pledge class about who they were."

"What do you mean?"

"I'd rather not go into it in detail right now, but you'll find out soon enough. Basically, they blatantly lied to us about something we asked about before deciding to pledge. They told us they were something they are actually not, and it's pissed off a lot of people. I have to go talk to some of the other pledges right now. All twelve of us are thinking about de-pledging."

The pledge process for fraternities is sort of a complicated process. After you rush, if you decide to join a fraternity, you become a "pledge." Pledges complete a variety of tasks and tests for about a semester and then become "brothers." If a pledge doesn't like what's going on in his fraternity, he can "de-pledge" before completing the process and get out before it turns into a logistical nightmare.

"Wow, it's pretty serious then?" I asked.

"To us it is, yes. Simply because we were lied to and we don't feel like we can trust a fraternity that lied to us. I can't be part of a brotherhood that disrespects potential brothers. I'm going to go meet with a few of the guys now. I'll let you know more details when I can."

"Okay, good luck, man. Let me know what happens."

Halloween night had extended into the morning of November 1st, and the fallout was just beginning. Every member of New House 5 was affected, in one way or another.

$$\sim$$

Some of the issues were resolved, but many were not. After creating a game plan, Rob and Hillary did talk to Audrey about what happened. As they expected, she blew them off and denied everything they told her. It frustrated Hillary and Rob, but you can't help someone who doesn't want it. You can just be persistent and patient, and maybe eventually the person will open up. Audrey revealed very little to the them on November 1st. In fact, she kept what was bothering her to herself for most of the year. Rob ended up getting through to her towards the end of the second semester. I don't know if anything substantial came out of their conversations, but at least Audrey knew she had people to talk to. Some things remain mysteries forever.

Luke and Lindsey had a long discussion about what each of them did and did not want. They decided it would be best to not be so close for a while. They remained acquaintances at first, but by the end of the year, they rarely talked to each other. Some things just aren't meant to be. Halloween helped Luke and Lindsey understand that.

Avery and his entire pledge class ended up leaving their fraternity. They de-pledged because they were hazed, which is illegal. As Avery said, he and the others had asked about hazing before deciding to pledge. The brothers said it didn't exist, and the guys trusted them. Then, during parties, they were hazed. Avery later told me the hazing itself didn't upset him, because it was nothing he couldn't handle. It was the deceit that upset him. Avery didn't join another fraternity after that.

Big decisions are made based on little events. Big discoveries are made through minor slips of the tongue. On Halloween, I saw this firsthand. From one standpoint, Halloween reinforced the community that New House 5 had become. Everyone has each other's back, one person's pain is everyone's pain. If someone had a problem, everyone had a problem. But it also showed that some people don't want to be a part of that type of community, that some people want to be their own person and find their own group. I had to rethink what it meant to be a community and figure out if New House 5 was truly ideal, or just ideal on the surface.

And more than anything else, Halloween showed everyone on the floor that there are deeper problems and concerns than schoolwork and meetings. We all have our weaknesses, we all have our baggage, and we all forget that everyone else is in the same boat. As much as New House 5 rocked, there's no way a floor can kill demons that have been growing for years. No matter how strong a community is, it can't dissolve the weaknesses of the individuals that make it up. But it can help the individual to heal the deep-rooted wounds and confront the weaknesses. Some people accept the help, others don't.

For New House 5, Halloween showed us that some problems can be solved immediately, others never will. But Halloween also showed us that with a little effort and patience, a community can make a difference in the life of every member. New House 5 would encounter more individual concerns as the year moved forward, and we would deal with all of them, one demon at a time.

CHANGES AND DISCOVERIES

When the icicles catch fire
Make sure you've got the right attire
For the official end of all our sanity
- Perfect Sense

November brought a sweeping chill to the Northeast. It brought the first snowflakes of the season to Pittsburgh. And it brought a lot of changes to New House 5. Aside from the debacle of Halloween and the new friendships that were forming, there was a different atmosphere on the floor. After what transpired over the week of Halloween, people thought that we could get through anything as a floor. We didn't brag about being a community anymore, we knew we were more of one than anyone could imagine, and that was good enough for us.

The floor was becoming more accepting of Laura, the new girls' RA. At first, some people refused to get to know her. "She's not Elaine," some said. "I don't want to help her in any way." With all of this hostility, I don't know how Laura managed to survive, but she did. Laura worked her way into the New House 5 community slowly. At first, she kept her door closed and made little contact with the residents. One girl kept a tally on her door of how many times Laura walked by without saying hello. But gradually, she got to know some of the girls. She made friends. She talked about being a senior, being in a sorority, and what it felt like to be graduating soon. Meghan really liked her. She said to me one day, "If the girls would just give her a chance, she's a really cool person."

There were a lot of people, including Meghan, who thought Elaine was never a good RA to begin with, since she was rarely on the floor. After Elaine resigned, she began meeting with Ryan, the Kensington Gardens housefellow.

I honestly think the time she spent with him made a huge impact. Elaine was able to really understand where her fears and problems stemmed from. Even though she didn't necessarily know how to combat them, she at least knew where to begin. And for Elaine, the starting point was New House 5.

Elaine began visiting New House 5 with great frequency. In all of her trips here, I think she may have seen Laura once. It was strange how they were never in the same place at the same time, but there was a constantly looming RA somewhere, you just never knew where. I think the girls viewed Elaine as more of a friend when she spent time on the floor. They viewed Laura as more of an authority figure, someone they could look up to, but never really get close to. Elaine went shopping with Alicia, visited Luke at his fraternity, and generally seemed much more content with her life. She was getting more help than I realized, but I didn't find out about that until the second semester.

❧

Our school prides itself on diversity. Diversity of race, color, religion, and anything else you can think of. The thing is, many students don't know this when they come here. And occasionally, they'll meet a kind of person they've never had to interact with before. Like someone who's gay. Meeting your first openly homosexual man or woman is always sort of a shocking experience. Not because you're against their way of life, but because until that point, homosexuality is something just talked about in movies. The first gay person I met was at Ashford my freshman year. And the first openly gay person many of the people on my floor met was Bradley, a New House resident who lived on the 4th floor. Bradley fit every stereotype of a typical homosexual male. Outgoing, flamboyant, well-dressed, effeminate mannerisms, and an excellent dancer. Bradley never introduced himself as a homosexual, but the information got around quickly. Most openly gay men don't flaunt the fact that they're gay, they simply explain it if someone asks. This is what Bradley did.

What bothered me was how people acted different around Bradley when they found out he was gay. I can understand it, because it's a big culture shock for some people. But Bradley hung out on the floor all the time before his sexuality was common knowledge. Everyone got along with him well. Many of the guys hung around with him, occasionally joking after he left that he must be gay. But when the news surfaced, people changed their attitudes around Bradley. Some of the girls stopped hanging out with him. They found him less interesting because he was unavailable, to them at least. The guys responded in a variety of ways. Some, who simply disagreed with homosexuality without any questions, stopped talking to Bradley, stopped acknowledging his existence. When he visited the floor, they shut themselves in their rooms. A few continued to talk to Bradley, but with much more inhibition. The only people who didn't change the way they viewed Bradley when they found out he was gay were the people who had dealt with open homosexuals before, which was a surprisingly small number. What people failed (or refused) to understand was that Bradley was still a human being. Not a freak, not a novelty item, not something you call your mom about. Just a normal human who practiced a different type of lifestyle, a lifestyle many of the residents on New House 5 had never been exposed to.

Bradley made a few close friends on the 5th floor, but for a while, he stopped hanging out in our lounges. This upset me, because I knew he felt uncomfortable around people who felt uncomfortable around him. But without knowing it, Bradley brought up an issue on the 5th floor that was impossible to compromise about. Some people felt very strongly one way, some felt very strongly the other. And with Bradley being around, these opinions came to the forefront. While very few people would openly speak out against homosexuality, there were those who quietly disagreed with it. Elyse, who had joined Allies, the straight-gay alliance on campus, was vehemently for gay rights. She had known homosexuals in high school and was good friends with many gay students on our campus. I always respected Elyse for sticking up for her beliefs on such a controversial topic. It just came naturally to her.

The problems on the floor arose with the use of derogatory slurs. It's typical for high school and college students to call something "gay" if it's stupid or someone a "fag" instead of a dork or a loser. I did it in high school, and while I'm not proud of it, I understood all the people who came to college using the same terminology. For people on the floor like Elyse, the use of these comments was unacceptable. And this caused problems. One evening when a few people were relaxing in the lounge talking about their favorite actors, the problem came into full view. Avery, the very conservative Army ROTC participant, was known for his tasteless choice of wording on occasion. While everyone slipped occasionally, usually one of the girls would ask them to stop and it was cut out for the most part. Avery, on the other hand, couldn't care less what the others thought, and exercised his right to free speech whenever possible. The argument began, as you can guess, between Elyse and Avery.

"Colin Farrell, no question, I love him." It was one of the girls hanging out in the lounge. "I'm going to have his children."

"No! He's so gay!" yelled Avery. "Seriously, that man is possibly the biggest fag I've ever seen in my life."

"Um, Avery," said Elyse in a very matter-of-fact tone. "First of all, I would really like it if you didn't use those words in that context, as I think I've asked a billion times. And two, why does it matter?"

"Well, first of all, I have the right to say whatever the hell I want to, and two, it's just a comparative reference. Gay people are gay. As in, they take it in the ass."

Avery laughed at his own joke. He leaned back and flicked a soda can tab into the air. To Avery, this whole ordeal over calling something gay was a joke, and if anything, he did it more frequently just to bother Elyse. She did her best to keep her cool, but her face was turning red. The others in the group kept silent, growing more uncomfortable with each passing second. When she had gathered herself, Elyse spoke again.

"Avery, something like ten percent of the population is homosexual, but so few are open about it because of people like you. It's a different lifestyle. If you're so stubborn and closed-minded that you can't accept that, I feel sorry for you. You don't even have to accept it, but you do have to respect them and not make them out to be some sort of evil, unnatural being."

"Yes, I am stubborn and closed-minded actually!" Avery was yelling now. He was calm, but he was yelling, and he was going to make sure he got his point across. "And I'll say whatever the fuck I want to say. You're not even gay, Elyse. You have no right to tell me what I can and can't say about an issue you have no business talking about!"

By this time, the screaming had attracted other students to the lounge area to listen to the exchange. Elyse and Avery were both upset. They each had their strong beliefs and they refused to budge from them. It was a battle that couldn't be won. Elyse stood up from her seat. She opened her mouth, but before anything came out, she smiled sarcastically, pumped her fist in the air as if she was about to say something profound, but thought better of it and walked away from the lounge. Avery sat in semi-shock, then began laughing.

"Holy shit, I cannot believe she got upset about that. HAHAHA!"

Avery looked around the room of spectators and was clearly surprised. The room was silent, aside from his own laughter. To Avery, our decision to not laugh with him was a sign that we supported Elyse. In reality, we didn't know who to support, and we definitely weren't going to voice our opinion right then. Avery took this personally and left the room.

"Whatever, you guys. I can't believe you're just going to sit back. None of you agree with her. You just don't feel like arguing, and I do."

All due respect to Avery, who was one of the nicest guys on the floor— he helped people with homework, advised people on workout techniques, and hung out in the lounges all the time—but he was very opinionated and occasionally an asshole, which sometimes sent an uneasy ripple through the 5th floor. As much as I've talked about all the people who added to the community atmosphere of New House 5, there were also a handful that made coming together as one entity difficult at times. People like Avery didn't try to cause problems, but their personalities sometimes created them anyway. It seems impossible for one person to tear apart an entire floor, but situations like this made me wonder.

This was the last public argument about homosexuality I ever witnessed on the 5th floor. As much as it shocked and startled everyone, it also made people realize this was an issue they couldn't just avoid. Generally, people began to get used to the idea of homosexuals. While not everyone agreed with the lifestyle, almost everyone got to the point where they at least respected it. No more comments were made in the open, and Bradley began coming back to the floor. It turns out that most people just needed some time to adjust to the idea of a good friend being gay. As Bradley explained, "Just think of me sitting here talking to you instead of hitting on you."

I always asked myself whether or not it was even a big deal. Recently, a lot of people have made an issue out of homosexuality in modern society, both for and against it. I've always looked at it as something that exists, just like there are people of different races and different religions. Maybe I adopted that ideology after coming to school here, where there is so much diversity that you have no choice but to adapt. Homosexuality should be a non-issue. There shouldn't be people disrespecting gays, there shouldn't be people who act differently around gays, there shouldn't be people who run up and down the halls espousing gay rights. And after the initial shock wore off, all of these things went away. People like Avery quieted down. Elyse and some of the other Allies didn't find it necessary to talk about bigotry on the floor anymore. And a majority of the floor learned to accept homosexuality as something they would be around. It was no longer a big deal, and that's how it should have been.

꩜

Not all the discoveries that took place on New House 5 were controversial. It was around this same time that the floor got to know Jeremy better. Jeremy, the 6'6" basketball player, was one of the most memorable characters I've ever met. He was a half-Italian, half-Asian guy who looked goofy enough to be in a cartoon and crazy enough to belong in college. Jeremy could often be found sitting in the lounge watching television, eating food from Taco Bell, which he was known to compulsively buy. A lot of students on the floor were intimidated by Jeremy. He was big, he was good-looking, he was an athlete. Not your typical Ashford student. But even though the floor was intimidated by Jeremy, he refused to be intimidated by the floor. Jeremy wanted to be part of the community just like anyone else. He started to go out to eat with a few people on the floor, and he was always out watching TV in the evening, which is when we learned some of the interesting things about Jeremy.

If you polled college students around the country, almost everyone would love to be on MTV's *The Real World*. One of the first ever reality shows, the MTV staple asks college-aged kids to send in videos of themselves as applications. From their thousands of submissions, they choose a handful each year to be on the show. A lot of people apply, few get called back. Jeremy got called back. And it made sense. He seemed like the kind of guy who could pull off a role on television. He had the looks, he had the quirkiness, he had the personality. And for two weeks, Jeremy was hounded every day with questions about *The Real World*.

All Jeremy did was send in a video of himself, just like every other applicant. MTV liked him more than the others, and called him back to fill out a long questionnaire. This is when the floor started getting interested. Only a hundred or so of the thousands complete this survey, and Jeremy was one of the lucky few. We'd ask him everyday how the application was coming, when he would find out, how he'd managed it. Jeremy filled out the application and sent it in. His trek ended there. But it didn't matter. Jeremy had solidified himself in the floor's collective mind as a charismatic guy who was likeable and fun to be around. Jeremy was now an initiated member of New House 5. And as luck would have it, Jeremy was a little more fortunate with his next crazy idea.

I found Jeremy in the lounge one day, lying down on a couch, buried in a book. I looked closer and read the spine; it was a *Harry Potter* book. The turn-of-the-century children's book craze had branched out from adolescents to high school students, college kids, and even adults. When Jeremy saw me walking by, he closed the book and sat up.

"What's up, Jeremy? A little *Harry Potter* action?" I asked him.

"You know it, man. Do you read them, too?"

"Definitely." I saw that he was about halfway through the book. "That one is pretty good, though it looks like you haven't gotten to the really crazy stuff yet."

"Dude, don't tell me! I love the surprise. Hey, man, I have this great idea."

"What's that?"

"Well, I have a plot for a children's book I want to write."

"Really?" I was intrigued. I knew Jeremy was a writing major.

"It's in the *Harry Potter* style. It's nothing like *Harry Potter* plot-wise, but it's a series, a children's fantasy kind of thing. I got the idea when I was reading *Harry Potter* one day. I said, 'You know what I want to read a book about?' And when I realized no such book existed, I thought I'd write it myself."

"That's awesome, man. Are you actually going to write it?"

Jeremy grinned from ear to ear. "I already have. I've been spending my weekends writing this book instead of going out. It's developing really well. I'm going to send it to a publisher when it's finished."

Amazing. I had met some ambitious and talented people at school, but this one took the cake. Here was a guy, a freshmen, who just decided one day to write a book. And was writing it. Seriously. I guess that's how non-professional authors usually write, but it just boggled my mind. The news of Jeremy's book got around quickly. People asked him about it, what the plot was, when it would be finished. He never revealed any information. It was always, "I can't tell you the title or the plot, you can read it when it's finished," or "Just wait. It's almost done." After weeks of badgering, most of the floor gave up. Then one day, Jeremy came out of his room into the lounge, beaming. He was carrying a thick packet of paper. There were about ten of us in the lounge. We all looked up at him.

"Ladies and gentlemen, you are looking at a published author. This is my copy of the book contract. Signed, sealed, and delivered."

Pride illuminated Jeremy's body. We were in awe. Each of us took a turn flipping through the contract, feeling it, smelling it, confirming it was real. It seems so ridiculous now, how big a deal we made about it. But at the time, it was huge. Someone we were close to, someone in the community, was publishing a book, a real book. The contract signed Jeremy on for a six-book series, just like he told us. The money wasn't great—Jeremy was due to receive a small percentage of sales—but that didn't matter. What mattered was that the publisher thought highly enough of Jeremy's work to put it in print. In a sense, Jeremy's pride was New House 5's pride. When one person failed, we all failed with them; but when one succeeded, we all shared in the joy. Jeremy's book wouldn't come out until the following academic year, but if you asked anyone on New House 5 to tell you their favorite author, most of them would have said Jeremy Spinelli.

⊱⊰

The discoveries being made on New House 5 were rarely as profound or publicized as Jeremy's book. A lot of little things were being noted. The floor discovered (or more accurately, Meghan and Kristen discovered) that Rosalyn had a tendency to bite people. Playfully, but it was still biting. Val had a habit of dreaming very strange things. In one instance, she had a dream involving everyone on the floor. Apparently we were chasing her across campus yelling "Fraud!" because she was practicing magic without a license. I don't ask questions when I hear stories like that. Aaron, who had extremely long hair, wasn't just a lazy, scruffy guy. He was growing it to cut and donate to charity. So when he returned one weekend with his head shaved bald, it came as quite a shock to the floor. Ben, who looked about as athletic as a bowling ball, turned out to have an excellent three-point shot in basketball. He became the secret weapon when the guys played pick-up games at the gym. Kim made good on her statement that she liked to dance by participating in our school's biannual Symposium. We all turned out to support her, and made a point to yell her name as loud as we could when she came on stage. Sam was gaining a reputation as an eternal pessimist but an excellent artist. The list goes on. Each member of New House 5 was showing their true selves to the people they trusted the most at college. We learned some good things, we learned some bad, but we were always accepting.

In many cases, friends were finding out about each other's pasts, acquaintances were learning about each other's hobbies, and conversations switched from boys and parties to philosophy and religion. The times for superficial friendships were over. The friendships on New House 5 were turning into real friendships, the kind people keep for the rest of their lives. We weren't even through the first semester and already some of the quieter students felt comfortable sharing their life stories with people they couldn't tell apart twelve weeks ago. Change is inevitable, it's the oldest cliché in the book. Sometimes it's good, sometimes it's bad. But it always opens your eyes. And on New House 5, the changes being made opened our eyes to the fact that while none of us were perfect, we all had something to contribute to the community, we all had something to contribute to each other. Little contributions add up. You can't make a sandcastle without all the tiny grains of sand. Each conversation, each learning experience, each unspoken understanding was a grain of sand. Welcome to the castle we like to call New House 5. Bring a little, take a little, learn a lot. I hope you enjoy your stay.

FEELS LIKE HOME

Don't feel sorry for the lonely guy
He does it to himself
- Solo

As I dedicated more time to being on the floor, I began drifting away from the friends I'd made during my freshmen year. I remember my freshman year fondly, but I was definitely the stereotypical lost, confused college kid. I tried to get good grades, I didn't get involved in much on campus, and I never really left my dorm except to eat and go to class. And of course I became infatuated with a girl who, looking back, was wrong for me in every sense of the word. I've never been big on dating someone just for the sake of dating. I'm content biding my time until the right person comes along. But during my freshman year, I was too eager to find the right person, and I jumped at the first girl I met. The first girl who I thought could be the right one. I go for the sweet, smart, cute, independent, understanding girl who has high self-confidence, self-respect, and likes to watch sports. Like just about every other straight guy in America. So good luck to me. But life is about being patient, it always has been. Sometimes you have to remind yourself over and over again. Sometimes you learn the hard way.

During my freshman year, I made a few really good friends. We hung out a lot in the dorms, liked the same kind of music, and talked about whatever was on television at the moment. I enjoyed these times immensely, and I enjoyed helping out my friends when they were in need. Sometimes it was a family problem, sometimes it was a relationship issue, sometimes it was a mental breakdown. But for all the pleasure I got out of being with them, I could never help thinking that our friendships were sort of superficial. I didn't have much in common with any of them. While we had similar interests, it seemed like we were worlds apart on how we viewed ourselves and how we viewed our environment. Maybe some of it was due to their upbringing in primarily upper class, upper-tier families, while I was raised in a rural, blue-collar area. One of my friends told me fifteen percent of his graduating class went to an Ivy League school. I laughed and replied, "Fifteen percent of my graduating class went to college."

And maybe some of it was due to my own hesitance. I was intimidated by them sometimes, by their money, by their status, by their futures. It was the most ridiculous fear ever, but it existed, and it kept me from being myself around them. I still keep in touch with a few of them, particularly Neha and Josh. Neha is one of the most mature people I know, an Indian girl from Philadelphia who always kept me in check. I still thank her for that. She shared my love of baseball, and that alone will ensure that Neha and I remain friends to some extent for the rest of our lives. Josh is a thoughtful, whimsical guy from San Jose. Tall, thin, and compulsively clad in a knit beanie which, along with his goatee, makes him look like a rock star, Josh is your typical Californian. Josh and I talked about girls. He was the first guy I ever felt comfortable talking to about relationships. We're juniors now, and we still try to see each other a few times a semester, which can be difficult given our schedules and workloads.

But back to last year. I spent so much time on the floor and with my residents that I often forgot I even had friends from freshmen year. I felt awful when one of them would call me and ask if I wanted to go out to eat. I would have to decline because I was playing basketball with my floor or doing homework. Finally, a few of us were able to consolidate our schedules, and beginning in November, we started going out to breakfast each Saturday morning.

The trips were always fun. It was usually three or four of us, sitting in Pamela's, home of the best breakfast in Pittsburgh. Just being in the restaurant eased my mind. The smell of thick, buttery pancakes, the sound of crisp bacon sizzling on the fryers, the aroma of fresh coffee and rich hot chocolate. It relaxed my senses and lightened my mood. And our conversations were always interesting. We'd update each other on how our lives were going. Neha had a new love interest, Josh talked about his internship with a computer game magazine, Anne praised her new sorority. And of course, since they all lived on the SHS floor the previous year, they wanted to know how my floor was doing. I always told them it was going well, but I don't think I could have explained in words just how well. I talked about the different activities and programs we did, about the comfort level of everyone on the floor, about the amenities of living in a brand new dorm. But I found that trying to put into words what New House 5 had become was impossible. It wasn't something you could explain, only something you could experience.

Someone who didn't know anything about New House 5, who didn't know anyone on the floor, could tell that it wasn't just any residential living quarters. Neha stopped by to visit me once, and she walked around the floor to check it out. When she came back to my room, the look on her face told me she understood why I couldn't fully describe it.

"This is crazy, Andy. Everyone has their door open. Everyone said hi to me because they assumed I was someone's guest. One of them said, 'If you're one person's friend on this floor, you're everybody's friend.' There were kids walking in and out of rooms, opening up closed doors without knocking. Two girls just came up the elevator with a pan of cookies. Is this normal?"

It was normal. It was just another day. On the floor, we didn't think twice about it anymore. To us, some things that Neha found amazing were as natural as going to class in the morning.

My freshman year friends and I continued our breakfast outings, but as the weeks wore on, we ran out of things to talk about. At times, the conversation and smiles seemed forced. Everyone was happy to be there, but no one felt at home. I'm sure everyone else had their own reasons, I knew mine. The only time I felt at home was on New House 5. When I was in class, at a meeting, eating food, I could never stop thinking about getting back to the dorm. Even if I was just sitting at my computer, talking to Rob and Kim on my futon, chilling with Meghan and Kristen in the mini lounge, watching TV with Sam and Aaron, it felt like home. For the first time in my life, the word "home" meant New House, Room 515, not Rochester, New York.

We started planning the breakfast meetings more sporadically. We started losing close touch with each other again. I know I regretted it to some extent. I cared a lot for the friends I made during my freshman year, and I wanted to keep them as long as I could. While I still talk to them, I know we aren't as close as we were before and I know we'll never be that close again. But as sad as that made me, I knew that we weren't the most compatible people in the world. Maybe our friendships were forced. I looked around New House 5.

How many of these friendships were forced? How many were just because of proximity, because people need other people to hang onto?

You know what? It wasn't very many. To this day, I still don't know how it happened. It was partly luck that such a compatible and open-minded group of people were put on the same floor. It was partly fate that all of them had similar academic interests in the sciences and humanities. It was partly the work of Elaine, Laura, and I, bringing them together through encouraged interaction and activities. But it was mainly the desire of every member of New House 5 to be open with each other, to learn from each other, and to support each other. It was everyone being comfortable talking to someone else about a problem they might be having. It was the Friday night conversations with Meghan, the rainy day comforting of Rosalyn. It was the concern of Rob, the opinions of Avery and Elyse, the motherliness of Val. If you took one person off of New House 5, you'd change the entire dynamic of the floor. Sometimes, the stars line up, and all you can do is smile.

ᕤᗄᕩ

One thing being an RA did was give me more ideas for songs. As I said before, I had written about half a dozen prior to the start of the school year. My various conversations and new friendships opened my mind to new ideas. I started to write songs, and I wrote a lot. Most of the time, lyrics would start in the margin of a notebook while I was in economics class. Sometimes, I'd be at a staff meeting and a verse would pop into my head. All of my songs are built on one or two distinguishing lyrics. I always write the words first. I start with lyrics that are "quote-worthy." College students love quoting song lyrics in their instant messenger profiles, on postcards, or when an appropriate situation comes up in a conversation. So I tried to make my lyrics thoughtful, unique, clever. My six songs quickly multiplied into ten, fifteen, twenty. Each song was different, based on a different story, a different theme. And I had a reason for writing each one.

The music came after the words. I would try to think of a tune I wanted, then spend some time strumming chords on my guitar, figuring out a chord progression that matched the tune I was looking for. Since I'm not a great guitarist, this usually took some time. But eventually, I figured out the right chords. I recorded my songs on my laptop, using scratchy free software I downloaded from the internet. I would set my laptop on top of textbooks so the built-in microphone would be an equal distance from my mouth and guitar. I tried everything I could to make the recordings sound better. But with free software, sometimes that just isn't possible.

Regardless of the quality, people listened to them. And they liked them. My floor asked me to write more, asked me to write specific songs about specific people. I still don't know if they actually enjoyed the songs or if the novelty value of me singing was enough, but it was pretty cool to have fans, even if there were only fifty-six of them. Though most of the songs I wrote last year related to the floor in some way, I never told anyone how, and I never intend to.

Rob and Kim often asked me how I benefited from being an RA. I always responded that I simply loved to help people, and being given an opportunity to help fifty-six freshmen was like a dream come true for me. It was the truth, but it wasn't exactly what they were looking for. They wanted to know what tangible, physical gains I received from being an RA. When I started sharing my songs with the floor, I figured out what it was. I had fifty-six close friends, people who knew me, who respected me, and who wanted to help me as much I helped them. When I sent my songs out to people who asked for them, the feedback I got was incredible. Kim, who was a creative writing major, gave me insight into the use of words. Hillary, who had an incredible voice, gave me free voice lessons to develop my vocal chords, which were, to say the least, untrained. Meghan judged my songs like she would judge any other: by how much she was able to connect with it. Eric, who is one of the best guitarists I've ever met, gave me tips on the chord structure of my songs. And Sam, an amateur songwriter himself, let me know if I was being too cliché or outdated. When it came to my music, I was no longer an RA, I was just another person on the 5th floor, another person that everyone tried to help in any way they could. I asked Rob and Kim how they benefited from living on the 5th floor. I told them, "Whatever you answer to that question is my answer to yours."

And of course, New House 5 would not have been New House 5 without the myriad of practical jokes the guys played on me. It got to the point where every Saturday morning, I hesitated before I opened my door, because I wasn't sure if I'd be alive a few seconds later. After Aaron's prank phone call on the bus, it was an unspoken challenge to see who could pull the best practical joke on me. The first weekend of the year, I opened up my door, groggy and half-asleep. When I looked out, I thought I was in some sort of crazy dream. I saw pure white in front of me instead of the dull yellow wall. I blinked. Twice. I reached out my hand to touch what was in front of me. My hand ripped through it. Paper towel. I broke through the layer of toweling, much to the amusement of Elyse and Luke who were sitting in the mini lounge. A few of the guys had sealed my doorway with layers of paper towel at around four o'clock in the morning. It didn't end there.

The culprits were always the same people. Devon, Luke, Rob, Aaron, Eric. Always the same five guys, always a different practical joke. One Saturday I walked out of my room in the morning to find a hundred large toy ants, whose stretchable legs had been wrapped around others in a variety of sexual positions. Once, I opened my door and a pulley system sent a large cylindrical pillow directly at my face. I dodged most of it, but I still was sent flying back into my room. Another time, I returned to my room to find it had been filled with potted plants taken from each floor of the building. Farther back were Rob and Luke, hidden in the forest they had created. And of course, they performed the classic college practical joke: removing my entire door with screwdrivers when I left for the bathroom.

I hate to call practical jokes community-building events, but in a way, they really were. The entire floor usually came together to participate in them. Two in particular stick out in my memory.

Each year, our school hosts several "sleeping bag weekends." On these weekends, prospective students come to the school and spend the night in a host's room. The "baggers," as we call them, attend classes the next day and get a feel for what it's like to live in a dorm. A dozen people on the 5th floor volunteered to host baggers for the first sleeping bag weekend, which was in early November. The floor was excited to show potential students how to enjoy themselves in the dorms. Rob stopped by my room before they arrived.

"Andy, we want to do something special for the baggers when they get here. Do you have any suggestions?"

"Not really. But if you think of something, as long as it doesn't involve alcohol or breaking anything in New House, go for it. Just run it by me first."

Rob was trying to suppress a grin. It kind of scared me. He scratched his chin and nodded his head.

"Okay, that sounds good. I'll let you know if we come up with anything clever."

Rob walked away silently. I wondered what he had planned. I didn't have to wait long to find out.

When the baggers did arrive, we had a gathering in the lounge area. The high school seniors and juniors were overwhelmed by the attention they were getting and the chaos of the 5th floor. I introduced myself to all of them. They seemed like nice kids, eager to learn about the school and see what college life was all about. One of them asked me if I had a course catalog. I told him I did and ran to my room to grab it. When I turned around to go back, they were on me. Luke, Eric, Rob, and Derek attacked me from all sides. Luke produced a roll of US Postal Service tape from his pocket. While the other three held me down (which they did an excellent job of, despite my kicking and yelling) Luke wrapped the tape around me, fastening me to my chair. After a minute or so, he had taped me well enough that Derek, Rob, and Eric could let go of me and I couldn't move. I tried wiggling my hands. Nothing. I tried moving my legs. Nothing. All the while, a crowd had gathered outside my room, watching and laughing as I struggled. I tried to rock back and forth. Bad idea. I tipped over, and probably would have hurt myself had Luke not caught me and placed me gently on the ground. While I squirmed on the floor, yelling at Eric to untie me, Rob cleared his throat.

"Ladies and gentlemen, we wanted to do something special for all of you sleeping baggers this weekend. So we decided to start a tradition. Welcome to the First Annual Sign Your RA Day!"

The people present clapped and cheered sporadically. Rob pulled two permanent markers out of his pocket. He found a spot on my arm and signed his name, nice and large. Sign your RA day. He really meant it. After Rob had finished, he passed the marker to someone else. Eventually I was signed by over fifty people, baggers included. I had signatures on my arms, legs, thighs, feet, forehead, and stomach. People took pictures of me from all angles, and everyone but me had the most enjoyable time in the world. When the floor had finally gotten its fill, the crowd slid away. Rob and Luke untied me and ran off to their rooms.

I have to say that I wasn't happy with them. I wasn't genuinely pissed off, but I didn't have a great time either. The permanent marker took a few days and about a dozen showers to fully erase from my body. But as much as it sucked for me then, I laugh at it now as hard as anyone else. The pictures are hilarious, and the floor still remembers the event like it happened yesterday. The First Annual Sign Your RA Day, as it officially became called, showed the baggers that, for all the academics and social drama that college is associated with, there's more to it that just schoolwork, parties, and philosophical discussions. And as ridiculously simple as this sounds, sometimes it's easy to forget. More than anything, college is about enjoying yourself. You can enjoy yourself in a ton of ways, but sometimes, good old immature fun can work wonders for a stressed out college student.

The second big prank the 5th floor pulled on me called for the active participation of every resident of New House 5. All for the purpose of publicly humiliating me. I first noticed something strange going on when I walked by Sam's room one evening. There were four people just inside the door, whispering and giggling to themselves. Their backs were turned to me. I walked by and asked what was up. They jumped a mile. The three people standing outside (Aaron, Rob, and Kristen) scattered and Sam quickly slammed the door shut. I was confused. Sam didn't drink, so I knew he wasn't boozing in his room. It was a strange assortment of characters. I knocked on the door.

"Sam, what's up, man? That was crazy."

"Don't worry about it, Andy. It's nothing. We'll let you know in a few days."

I left it at that. Over the next week, I realized that whatever was going on in Sam's room had something to do with me. Whenever I walked by, the omnipresent group of people quickly scattered and Sam made sure to close his door. People would walk by me after exiting Sam's room and cover their mouths in laughter. Rosalyn popped her head into my room one day and shook her head.

"Wow, do they have a surprise for you," she said.

It was a Saturday night, around 3 a.m. I had gone to bed about an hour earlier, after talking to Hillary for a while about her own songwriting. When she left, she told me I probably shouldn't fall into too deep a sleep. My phone rang. At night, when I plug my phone in to charge, the volume setting changes to extra loud. If I'm ever sleeping and my phone goes off, I don't miss it. I looked at the screen. "Incoming call—Rob." Oh man, what the hell was this? Could be someone drunk that needs to go to the hospital, could be something even more serious. I answered and, in the most awake voice I could muster, said, "What's up, Rob?"

"Andy, we need you to come outside. It's really important."

I found my glasses, fumbling as I slipped them on. I grabbed my phone and flip-flops. Wearing nothing but boxers and my glasses, armed with only my cell phone, I opened the door. I may have still been half-asleep, but what I saw certainly woke me up.

First, to the left, was about half the floor, smiling, cameras ready. And right in front of my room, taped to the wall, was a life-sized replica of a person. I rubbed my eyes. Rob spoke.

"She couldn't knock, but she needed to get in."

The people behind Rob began laughing. I took a step closer to the model. It was a replica of a girl, about 5'5", wearing a tie-dye t-shirt and gym shorts. She was made out of plastic bottles. Coke, Pepsi, juice—every type of plastic bottle imaginable went into the construction of this figurine. Her head was a giant milk carton. Her face was drawn with cheap markers. A large round hole had been cut out for her mouth. I couldn't help laughing at that. Pinned to her chest (which was quite generous) was a note. It read:

> Dear Andy,
>   My name is Milky. The 5th Floor made me for you out of plastic bottles. It's what they've been doing in Sam's room for the last week. They spent a lot of time and duct tape on me. Everyone contributed something: design, ideas, plastic bottles. I want to sleep with you tonight, and maybe we can have some fun. My mouth isn't shaped like this for no reason.
>
>   Love,
>   Milky

Stunned, I looked at the large group gathered around me. They were still laughing and taking pictures, watching my every move. I scratched my head.

"I don't know what to say, guys. Thanks?"

With that, the hallway erupted in laughter. Rob patted me on the back and told me to go easy on her. I took Milky into my room, propped her up against my wardrobe, and went back to sleep. In the morning, I thought it may have just been a dream, but when I looked over to my wardrobe, there was Milky, perky as ever.

The floor always gave me a hard time about not having a girlfriend. I explained to them that I wouldn't have time for a girlfriend, what with the time I spent being an RA, so they decided to make me one. It was amusing.

And while it was a prank, it was touching as well. I examined Milky the next day. They had spent a lot of time on her. She could stand up by herself, and proportionally, she did look like a real person. Kristen later told me it was the floor's way of saying, "We made you a girlfriend, she's all you're allowed to have." While Kristen was joking, it was nice to feel needed. I told her not to worry, nothing would come between me and the 5th floor, and I meant that with every inch of my body.

The adventures of Milky didn't end there. After the novelty had worn off, she sat in the corner of my room and deteriorated. Sam and Aaron took her out of my room one day when I wasn't paying attention. The next morning, I opened up my door and found a piece of Milky's leg in front of my room. It was outlined in chalk, with a place card marked "#2" on it. As I walked to the bathroom, I saw more pieces of Milky, each marked with a different number. I searched the entire floor and found thirteen pieces of "evidence." Aaron and Sam even went as far as to make a fake police report, saying that I sexually assaulted and then dismantled Milky. A copy of that report was sent via e-mail to the entire floor, and signs were posted all over New House. The ingenuity never ended. Milky had finally died, but not without one final hurrah.

Milky and her death were fantastic pranks, but they were not the last. One time, Rob and Luke moved my dresser, with all of my clothes, into Elyse's room while I was in the shower. I had to walk around the floor in my towel for half an hour. Each time they played a prank, they left a note that said something along the lines of "Ruben was here." "Ruben" became the code name for a practical joke. Every time something bad happened, it was Ruben's fault. Ruben struck many more times before the year was over, and each time, it was with something new. I may not have loved all the practical jokes, but New House 5 certainly kept them interesting.

Practical jokes, while they were nearly all at my expense, really did bring our floor closer together. I say this about a lot of stuff, but it's never just one thing. A combination of small things created a friendly, loving atmosphere. It wasn't just the practical jokes, it wasn't just the study sessions, it wasn't just the movie nights, it wasn't just the comfort we had with each other. It was all of these things and more combined, creating an atmosphere that we thrived in. The lunch trips with my freshmen year colleagues were important for a reason I never would have imagined at the time: they showed me how much I needed this floor, how much I loved it, how much it helped me grow. The practical jokes showed me how much the floor needed me, how much I was a part of what went on. On New House 5, no one was left behind. Not even me.

POETRY IN MOTION

All of those I-Love-You's
Were accompanied by tears
- Spirit of the Midnight Moonlight

By late November, I was developing very close friendships with a handful of people. In particular, I was becoming close with Rob, Meghan, and Kate. Rob and I talked everyday about everything from baseball to economics. But my relationships with both Meghan and Kate were very different.

Meghan and I were close as friends. We talked about our childhoods, our families, and our life philosophies. Or more appropriately, she talked, and I listened. I didn't mind this at all. In fact, I liked it. I've always enjoyed listening to what other people have to say more than I like telling them what I have to say. It worked out well. I disagreed with Meghan on many issues, but we had an understanding that allowed us to call each other out and be civil at the same time.

When my conversations with Meghan didn't focus on world issues, they always came back to the same thing: Rick, Meghan's ex-boyfriend from high school. Rick had been her best friend for most of high school, and he was the only person she felt comfortable talking to in any situation. When they broke up her senior year, she had nowhere to turn, and she fell into a state of minor depression. Meghan frequently spoke of Rick's bad characteristics, like his poor people skills and drab personality. She talked about how in college he changed for the worse, letting his hair grow long and starting to smoke. But she tried to speak highly of him as well. Either way, it was clear from the tone of her voice and the distance in her eyes when she talked about Rick that she missed him. She hadn't seen him since they'd graduated from high school.

There was one particular time when I talked with Meghan about Rick while we were walking on campus.

"Now that soccer is over, I have more time to think about Rick. It's not that I miss him so much as I wish I could talk to him. For a few minutes."

"Why don't you? Can't you just call him up?"

She laughed uneasily. "It's not that easy. We both have too much pride, too much to lose if the other doesn't respond. He goes to Altech University. I went down there for a soccer game, and I saw him in the crowd. I was nervous the whole game. Afterwards, I went to talk to him, and it was the coldest, most awkward conversation I've ever had. It lasted for two minutes, then it was over. Now I might never see him again. I just want to sit down and really talk with him for a few minutes."

"That sucks," I said consolingly.

"Yeah, but who knows. Everything happens for a reason, I truly believe that. It will all work out."

That was something she said a lot. I was never sure whether she believed it or not. Sometimes I think she was just trying to sound optimistic, because she wanted to believe it. Personally, I do think everything works out in the end. But who's to tell when the end is? Who's to tell what "working out" means?

"I just want to know what I did wrong," she went on. "I guess I never told you this, but when we broke up, it was Rick's doing. He said he needed space, that he didn't want attachments when he went to college and stuff. I accepted that. But through friends, I heard that he just couldn't stand me anymore. Something about my mannerisms, my attitude, I don't even know. I wish I could find out. I wish I could have my best friend back."

We walked the rest of the way in silence. Meghan was probably thinking about it too much, but you can't always control your thoughts. She needed to get some things cleared up in her head. Later, she would get her chance to talk to Rick, but it didn't work out how she planned.

⚘

With Kate, our conversations were less frequent and more tense. And more often than not they reverted back to Kate's family. She was an only child, and her upbringing in an upscale part of New Jersey differed greatly from my upbringing as the oldest of three children in rural New York. Kate often talked about how overprotective and irrational her parents were, but I got the impression that she respected how much they cared about her. Few only children I've known have really understood how spoiled and babied only children tend to be. Kate was well-aware, and talked about it in stride.

Initially, I liked her parents from the stories I heard, but as Kate talked about them more and more, I sensed a trend. I noticed that every time she talked about them, her mood changed. If she was happy one second, she would be gloomy and introverted the next. Sometimes one of the girls would make a joke like, "I won't talk to you for a week if you fail this test," and Kate would jump in, embarrassed. "Please don't say that. My mom used to say that." The stories Kate told about her parents were sometimes amusing, sometimes angry, but never positive. I heard about their strict rules, their high expectations in academics, their strong tempers, their use of Kate as a bargaining tool. Kate told me that when her parents fought, one would threaten to leave the house for a while and yell, "Kate is coming with me!" The other stood across the room and yelled back, "No, she's staying here. She wants to be with me!" All while she was standing in the middle of the room, upset and unsure what to do. The stories were never fun to hear, because they were always accompanied by a sad expression on Kate's face.

I felt uneasy about Kate's parents as her stories turned more and more sour. I started telling Kate how cool her parents were after every story she told. I picked out something they did that I found amusing or clever and exclaimed, "You have the coolest parents ever." Whenever I said something like that, I could see Kate holding back a cringe. I could see her eyes trembling as if to say, "Are you serious?" I kept doing it, waiting for Kate to snap and prove me wrong. I realize now how manipulative and cruel that was. I was trying to trick Kate into telling me something she clearly was trying to hide, and it racked her emotions every time. But I wanted to know the story behind her family, I wanted to know what she was covering up. I was in no position to be snooping for this information, and I did some stupid things to get at it. But through all of this, I just wanted to find out why Kate was so upset every time she talked about her parents. I wanted to know if I could do anything to help. Finally, one day, I discovered what I'd been looking for.

Kate was talking to me about her parents' strict dating policies. It was a cool Wednesday evening, and I had the window in my room open. The gentle breeze was refreshing after a week of harsh November wind. Kate was sitting on my futon, hugging a pillow and staring straight ahead. The rest of the floor was quiet. The sound of scribbling pens and shuffling papers were the only noises. I had just finished telling Kate how clever her father's technique of screening her male friends was—he made sure to privately invite them over when Kate wasn't there, just to get to know them better. She rolled her eyes and punched the pillow she was holding.

"My parents are *not* as cool as you think they are. Just trust me, and stop."

"Why?"

"Do you really want to know?"

"Yes, Kate, I do really want to know. I would actually love to know, because I'm very curious."

She stared at me blankly for a few seconds. Then she shrugged her shoulders, stood up, and headed for the door saying, "I'll be right back," as she left.

She would be right back, and when she returned, I learned everything about Kate's past that I ever wanted to know. And some things I probably never should have known.

ॐ

"Here's proof that my parents aren't as cool as you always say they are."

She handed me several pieces of paper doubled over each other. While I sat in my chair unfolding them, she settled down on my futon and tucked her legs neatly underneath herself. She stared straight ahead with an empty look in her eyes, waiting for me to react. She wouldn't have to wait long.

On the papers were poems. Written by Kate. Not frilly poems with clever rhyme schemes, but slick literary pieces that jabbed you in the gut. For many reasons. The first poem was called "Learning the Hard Way." It described how her parents physically abused her all through high school. Her mother would hit her, pull her hair, push her down stairs. Her father would throw her into walls, leaving bruises all over her body. And every time, they would deny doing it, always tell her that they loved her. I cringe now thinking how I felt when I read that first poem.

I looked over at Kate. She turned her head to make eye contact with me. I said nothing. I looked back down at the paper and read the next one. This one was even worse. In it, Kate recounted cutting herself with a pair of scissors. She talked of the blood, of watching it flow from her body. She did it to escape her parents. To get back at them, to make them sorry for what they did to her. It was gruesome. And it brought me to the edge of tears.

"Kate—"

"You can't tell anyone. I mean, I know you wouldn't, but it's important. I can't believe I showed you those. Only one other person knows about that. Oh my God, this is crazy, I don't even know you and I'm trusting you with something I won't even admit to myself sometimes. I need those back."

She snatched the papers from my hand. Smoothing them out, she stared at them for a few seconds before looking back over at me. I wasn't sure exactly what to say, but I knew exactly what not to say.

"Does this still happen?" I asked.

"Which?"

I decided to talk about her parents abusing her first.

"The first poem, about your parents," I said.

"It hasn't in a long time, not since junior year of high school."

"And nobody else knew about it?"

"Only Jared. That's why I always spent so much time at his house. It was my safe place. I could go there and talk to him about it. Or sometimes, I would just sit down on the couch and turn on the TV. He would know not to say anything."

"I'm going to be honest with you, Kate. This part doesn't surprise me. The way you act around other people, the way you talk about your parents and about violence, how did no one else pick up on this in high school?"

"I wore long-sleeved shirts and pants so no one could tell. My classmates used to think my favorite clothes were turtlenecks. I wore them because they covered up the bruise marks on my neck. If somebody ever asked about a bruise, I'd say I fell or something. I had the spiel down."

Still sitting up, Kate curled up into a ball and bit her knee. She looked so unsure of herself, so vulnerable to the world. I could tell she was very uncomfortable talking about this, but I could also tell she was relieved to be able to talk to someone about it. She was proud of how she concealed her bruises and scars, but she wasn't proud of having them.

"Andy," she was whispering now. "How could you tell? I always thought I hid it so well."

"Little things. The way you always speak poorly of your parents. You're never happy when you talk about them. Your mood changes sometimes when they're brought up. It's almost as if you're scared of them or scared of telling people about them."

"I always felt like it was my fault," she said. "Like I was the bad kid, I deserved it. That's why I never told anybody. My parents just cared. Maybe too much, but they wanted me to be strong, to be able to take it. They wanted me to know there would be consequences when I screwed up. That's the only time they'd do it. When I did poorly on a test, when I started to gain weight. Everything has a consequence. I learned that at a young age."

It boggled my mind how someone could just take physical abuse from their parents like that. Not even once or twice, but almost daily, as she later explained to me. I just couldn't imagine how someone could believe that it was alright. But I figured now wasn't a good time to ask. I wanted to hear Kate talk about it as much as she comfortably could.

"I guess in some sense, I wonder if it ever really happened," she continued. "I mean, I have the bruises and the scars, I have the memories. But sometimes, I don't know. I used to ask my parents about it. Ask them why they did it. When I did, they would look at each other and laugh. 'What are you talking about?' they'd say. 'You get everything you ever want, you are spoiled rotten. We would never touch our little angel.' It was only two years ago, but sometimes, I still wonder if they were telling the truth, if I dreamed it all up. Some nights, I'll wake up screaming, sweating, caught in a nightmare where I'm being dragged down the stairs or hit with a shovel. And then I wake up and it's all gone. Maybe it was all like that. Maybe I'm just hallucinating."

She talked about what happened to her, but she never actually associated those things with her parents. Kate could not bring herself to accuse her parents of abusing her; the abuse and her parents were separate entities. She refused to admit that the two were connected. Maybe I would have, too.

"It doesn't sound to me like you're hallucinating at all," I said quietly.

"I know, but I try to justify it, somehow. My parents haven't touched me in a while. I guess they thought I was finally strong enough. That I finally understood. But the memories are always there. Whenever I cried, I got yelled at, I got punished. They told me never to cry, especially in public. It showed weakness and vulnerability. They wanted me to be strong and self-sufficient. I never cry now. I don't think I can anymore, I don't know how to. See, they were just looking out for me. Maybe they knew what they were doing after all."

Kate told her story with no emotion at all. She stared at the wall and hugged my pillow tightly. When she finished, I let the silence ring through the room. When I thought she was done talking about her parents, I asked her about the other poem.

"So what about the second poem? About hurting yourself. How long has it been since you've done that?"

I was scared. I was scared that her answer would be a bandage on her wrist or a wound on her leg. She looked at me helplessly.

"It's been a long time. Longer ago than the other one. I guess it was my junior year of high school too, the last time it happened. I sort of stopped after my parents stopped. Jared got me into it. That's how I started. Jared did it, too. He did it before me. I used to get so scared. When I was a freshman, he did it to himself right in front of me. I threw up once. I asked him to stop. I cried, I yelled, I threatened to tell his parents. But he knew better. He knew I would never tell anyone. Finally, one day, I told him I was going to do it to myself to show him how it felt. To show him what it was like to watch the person you cared more about than anyone else in the world hurt themselves. He told me not to. He said he would kill me if I did. I took a pair of scissors and... and after that, it became a habit."

I cringed. Self-mutilation is something I have never understood and never will. I don't understand what the purpose of cutting yourself is, I don't understand what it accomplishes. Kate had her own theory.

"A lot of my friends were masochistic. I had plenty of experience with it. Allan, one of our good mutual friends, almost killed himself once. He had to go to the hospital. He somehow talked the doctor into believing he fell off his bike. I remember thinking in my head, 'You idiots! He has a problem! He needs to be in a psych ward somewhere.' But then I realized maybe I did, too. We all did it. We all took care of each other if something went wrong. I would go to the store to buy bandages for Jared, and he would call my mom to tell her I was staying at his house for dinner while I frantically tried to stop the bleeding. I had to wear long-sleeved shirts at school to cover the scars. Sometimes, I wasn't sure where the scars from me ended and the scars from... well, other sources began.

"People who... who do this to themselves don't want to die." She refused to use the word "cut." "At least most of them, anyway. I never did. I just wanted to escape. When you're feeling lost, helpless, and dead, it can do wonders. I was beginning to lose my ability to feel emotion in high school.

When I c— When I did *it*, I felt pain, a burning sensation. It was an emotion, it made me feel alive. Watching the blood pour from my skin, it was like watching something living flowing from my body. It woke me up. I got good at it. I could make myself bleed and two hours later, the scars would be too small to see."

I was speechless. I didn't know how to respond. Kate talked about cutting herself like it was a release, like a drug. I will never understand how someone can get a high from hurting themselves, and I never want to know. What concerned me then was the way Kate talked about it now. I knew the thought was in the back of her mind, to revert to masochism, to see if the same sensation would still exist.

"Kate, you said you haven't done this in a few years? Seriously?"

"No, I really haven't. I got scared. I'm not going to lie, when I stopped, I had a withdrawal period. I never got tired of it, the desire never went away. The thing about it is you do gain a tolerance, and you have to do more each time to get the same sensation. A bigger gash, a hotter instrument. That's how Allan almost died. That's what scared me, what made me stop. I didn't want to get to the point where I needed to practically kill myself to get through the day. I haven't done it since junior year of high school, and I don't intend to ever do it again. Jared stopped soon after I did, but I wouldn't be surprised if he's doing it now. He always needed it more than I did.

"Amy does it, too. She still does, at college. I don't think I've ever told you about Amy. She's probably my best female friend from high school. We were the quiet girls. We hung out together because, well, no one else really wanted to hang out with either one of us. She goes to a small school in Detroit. She's the worst. She's into hardcore drugs and cuts—damn, I hate saying that word—probably two or three times a day. One of these days she's going to kill herself. She fully expects to, eventually. By accident, of course. But it doesn't bother her."

Kate said this with a straight face, almost matter-of-factly.

"I talk to her on the phone three or four times a week. Sometimes we'll talk for hours about nothing. Occasionally I'll have to yell at her to put a knife down. She tells me when she's about to do it to herself. It's pretty scary. When the best friend you have left plans on eventually killing herself. I've been trying to convince her to go see counseling, but she refuses. It's a pride thing, and I can understand it. I guess that's been worrying me, too. I guess a lot of stuff has. And now my past has come up again."

I wondered why she had never mentioned Amy before. I started thinking there was a whole lot about Kate that I didn't know. That no one knew. That no one would ever know.

"Have you ever considered doing it again?" I asked hesitantly. I tried to seem confident and relaxed when I said it, but I know it sounded shaky and uncertain.

She squinted, and the reflecting light gave her face the impression of a distorted mask.

"No, I never have. I'll never do that again." She said it definitively.

I knew she was lying. I could tell even at that moment she was thinking about it, wondering if the pair of scissors sitting in her desk drawer could make her feel alive, even for a few seconds. There was no point arguing with her, though. All I could do was watch. And hope I was wrong. Kate's overall mood had dipped considerably in the last few weeks. She had always been quiet, but it was a happy kind of quiet. She had been hanging out more on the floor and making new friends. But recently, Kate had appeared more solemn, more lost in thought. She had been spending more time in her room, reading poetry, listening to music, and thinking.

"These last couple weeks have been sort of stressful," she said. "For no reason, either. I'm not sure why."

"Is it classes or anything?"

"Nope, I actually think it's the opposite. The novelty of classes has died off. I haven't had a ton of work recently, so I haven't been busy. I've just had time to think. That's never good for me. I always over-think."

"I'm the same way. Sometimes it's good, sometimes it's bad. Over-thinking can definitely take over your mind and body for a while."

Kate shot me a confused look. "When I over-think, it's always bad. I think about this stuff. My parents, my past. I wish I could change my past, everything about it. But then I think about it more and if I was given the chance, I don't know if I would take it. I haven't been sleeping much lately, I've just been going over scenarios and situations in my head. Second-guessing myself, thinking about life. And mostly, I've been thinking about my family and about Jared. I don't know why."

"Have you ever considered going to counseling yourself, just to check it out, see what they can do?" I asked.

Kate laughed hard this time, like what I said was genuinely funny. When she realized I was serious, she turned her head.

"Andy, that's never going to happen. First of all, my parents would kill me. Second of all, I am *not* going to some shrink. I don't have any mental problems that I can't handle myself. Third, I have a serious trust issue. Even if I went to one, I would never tell the person anything. I can't even believe I'm telling you. I don't even talk to Amy about it, I just talk to her about her problems."

"If you're trying to convince Amy to go to counseling, why aren't you considering it?"

"Don't pull that reverse bullshit on me." She was angry.

"I'm not, Kate. If nothing else, it seems like it would strengthen your argument with her if you were going yourself, if you want to think about it mechanically like that. You can tell yourself you're going for her sake."

"Andy, I think I know myself better than you do. I think I know if a psychologist would even have a chance at helping me. And trust me, they would not."

I believed her. I genuinely believed that she was right, that she would not be open enough with a doctor to resolve anything. But that didn't mean I was going to give up on it. I would drop the subject for the night, but I planned on bringing it up again. I thought I might as well try, because no one else seemed to have helped Kate throughout her life.

There was a knock on my door and we both jumped. It was Aaron, who needed to ask me a few questions about course registration. Registration, the day when all the students sign up for spring classes, was quickly approaching and the entire floor was worried about their selection time, the availability of classes, and fulfilling requirements. Just like that, our conversation ended. It was probably for the better. Kate left the room quietly. She mumbled something about calculus homework and waved goodbye. When Aaron sat down on my futon, he pulled two folded pieces of paper from underneath him.

"Are these important, Andy?"

"They are actually, let me have them. Thanks a lot, man."

I tucked them away for another time.

ço∞

Over the next couple weeks, I kept a close eye on Kate. She had come out of her shell a little, hanging out more on the floor again, appearing fairly chipper. I could never tell if it was an act to get me and other concerned friends off her case, or if maybe our talk had allowed her to get some things off her chest.

I regret two things about our conversation. One, I wish I had pushed counseling on her more. Even if it didn't help, I really would have liked to see her try it out. We have free counseling services on campus that are totally anonymous. In the back of my mind I knew it probably wouldn't do anything, but even farther back, I knew there was nothing to lose.

Luckily for me, Kate started going to counseling services anyway. And it was because of Elaine. Kate told Elaine about her inability to sleep. When Elaine delved deeper, she found out about Kate's parental problems, though not the self-mutilation. Elaine made Kate go to counseling, threatening to tell someone higher up in the administrative food chain if she didn't. Kate begrudgingly went, getting in two sessions before the end of the semester. Kate came to my room after each session to complain about the pointlessness and embarrassment of the sessions, but I can honestly say, even after just two meetings, Kate's psychologist seemed to be making progress. She was getting Kate to say some things she didn't want to, to admit to things that happened. I was glad it seemed to be helping, even if Kate refused to admit it. And I was glad Elaine stepped up to declare an ultimatum when I was hesitant.

The second thing I regret was not telling Tamira right away, or at least someone in Student Life, the department of our school that handles student issues. Elaine and I agreed to not tell anyone unless it got any worse, for the simple reason that we'd promised Kate. She had begun telling us a lot, telling us things she would not tell anyone else. And it was based on her trust in us, based on promises we made. But looking back now, it was stupid. As it turned out, we eventually did let higher people know, for reasons you will learn later. But had we let someone know earlier, we could have gotten Kate more help. Even if I had just told Tamira that someone on my floor was having these kind of issues without giving a name, she could have kept an eye on any incoming information. Maybe there were other cases I didn't know about that fit into a puzzle. Regardless, I didn't tell anyone, and the rest of the semester, Elaine and I kept a close watch on Kate, with no backup but each other.

Kate stayed close to Elaine and me despite our constant disagreements and unsolicited advice. Many evenings, she came into my room and lay on my futon for half an hour, letting me know how she felt and what was going through her mind. She called Elaine (or Elaine called her) almost daily, just to talk and keep in contact. I'm glad Kate was receptive to us. It made it easier to help her, easier to make suggestions. And though it sounds like a lot of time, this only went on for two weeks. After that, the semester was over. Elaine, Kate, and I were about as close as three people could be by the end of the fall term. And none of us felt comfortable around each other. There was a sense of tension, a sense of awkwardness, and sense of despair. I just tried to hold on tight, to keep myself and the situation under control. The secrets Kate revealed to me on that night in late November were the first of many. What unfolded that night impacted the entire floor in ways I could only imagine.

WINDING DOWN

So hold me close now
As the sun sets on today
I am here now, don't you worry
Baby, everything's okay
- Daylight Savings Time

With all of the drama and personal issues that were coming to the forefront, academics got lost in the mix. It was easy to forget that the primary reason for being at school is, well, school. New House 5 was certainly forgetting. The workload picked up speed and gave everyone a swift kick in the rear during late November. Thanksgiving was coming up, which meant people were happy to be going home and scared to death that final exams were just around the corner. For a few weeks, New House 5 the community took a backseat to New House 5 the freshmen college dorm, which was probably a good thing for all of us.

It wasn't hard to tell which classes were giving people the most trouble. Some introductory classes were purposely not too difficult, because all freshmen had to take them. What they did require, however, was effort. Writing a paper isn't hard, but making yourself do it can be. So one night before a World History paper was due, I walked into the lounge to see people typing away at their glowing laptops.

"What's going on? There's like fifteen of you out here. It's 2 a.m., go to bed."

Shannon laughed. "Oh Andy, we have a history paper due tomorrow. Guess how far all of us are on it?"

Hillary broke out into a nervous, forced laugh. "Andy, I haven't even thought about it yet. I have two papers to write by tomorrow. I think I'm probably just going to jump in front of a bus and not do either one of them."

Everyone in the room looked up and pondered this idea, going over its merits in their heads.

Chad looked blankly at a stack of papers. He was clueless. "What is this paper supposed to be on?"

"The last two books we read, *Things Fall Apart* and the book about the slave guy," Meghan answered.

"Huh? Did we read those?"

"We were supposed to."

"I'm pretty sure I never bought them because I didn't have any money."

I shook my head. "Chad, what are you doing? This isn't a joke, man. You have to pass World History or you're not going to graduate."

"Wait, what's World History?"

He was only half-joking and I wasn't laughing. Chad grew up in a very wealthy family. His mother was an ambitious woman who worked in the government after immigrating from Italy. Chad went home every weekend to help his mom, and in exchange, she paid for every penny of his tuition. He took college about as seriously as he took relationships.

"Instead of writing this paper, I think I should go find a hot sorority girl, have sex with her, and tell her to write the paper for me as a thank you." Chad awaited compliments for his clever idea, but received only silent stares. There was no point giving all of them a lecture on getting work done ahead of time, I had tried that several times throughout the semester. Normally, they agreed and said, "What a great idea," but it rarely worked in practice. It takes a long all-nighter and a really bad grade to make you realize that writing a paper four hours before it's due doesn't work all the time. I left them to their work. The next day, I saw Hillary walking to class. She looked like a zombie, only less attractive. Her hair was all over the place, she was walking crooked, and papers were falling out of her backpack.

"Do you need those, Hillary?"

"Probably not, and even if I did, I don't care. I got twenty minutes of sleep last night, Andy. I'm not in the mood to chase down papers."

So went the two weeks leading up to Thanksgiving. Economics exams, seminar papers, psychology experiments, physics quizzes. It's no secret that the academic workload here is a little more rigorous than your average school.

Students feel like they're slackers if they aren't taking at least five classes and haven't declared at least two majors. Even though the personal problems are always present, schoolwork is without the question the number one stressor at Ashford. Everything is very technical, very precise, and very difficult. You sink or swim. And regardless of how you're doing, you always complain, because if you didn't you'd go crazy.

It's true that once in a while there will be a student who is simply a genius. Someone who breezes through the homework, thinks the exams are a joke, and scoffs at a 4.0. But there aren't many of those. Even students who do well work their asses off, and for that reason, I have a lot of respect for the students here. But I also feel sorry for them sometimes. Most students who come to Ashford were at the top of their class, big fish in a little pond. Then they get to college and everyone falls into the same category. So of course, there will be some who do well, and some who do not. There are students who have never gotten below an A- before who end up with a 2.2 for their first semester GPA. Not because they're stupid or they don't work, but because with a thousand bright students, there still has to be a lot of B's and C's and D's. There is absolutely nothing wrong with getting a C, but try convincing some of the students at Ashford that. I try to explain that a C is average, and being average here is still pretty damn good. No one ever buys that, though. They just mope and complain about it. That's when people start to over-study or burn out. You have to learn how to relax. Do your best, because it's all you can do.

A lot of the time, students don't get upset about their grades, they get upset about what their parents will think. For many of the students at this school, Ashford was not their first choice. Usually it was an Ivy League, Cornell or Harvard or something like that, but for whatever reasons, they didn't get in, so they fell back on one of the other top-tier schools. Students come here already feeling "stupid" because they couldn't get into an Ivy League, and the grades they get make them even more miserable. I've heard that at some Ivy's, over fifty percent of students graduate on Dean's List. I don't know if that's true, but if it is, come on, that's just dumb. Dean's List means something here, it's not easy to attain. But the parents don't always realize that. There's constant pressure coming from parents to do well in school, to get a good job, to marry well. I asked Meghan once why she wanted to be a doctor. She couldn't come up with a concrete answer. "I guess my parents always pushed it on me, and I don't not want to be a doctor. Who knows." A lot of people fell into that category.

In the age of cell phones and e-mail, some students receive messages from Mom or Dad everyday. "Have you done your homework? How did your last test go? Why did you only get a C?" And forget academics, some people turn off their cell phones when they go out simply to avoid an awkward confrontation with Mom when they're at a fraternity. I get so upset at parents sometimes for making their children miserable at college. Sure, they want the best for their child, and it's not all parents, but it's still frustrating. Let your children make up their own minds, let them do what they want to do. Kristen wanted to major in psychology originally, but was told not to by her mother. "She says I can't get a job with a psychology degree, but I really like it. So instead I'm taking these awful pre-med classes. Bleh." Forget making gobs of money, forget the prestige of wearing "Yale" on your sweatshirt. Your freshmen GPA will not matter in ten years. What will matter is what you learned about yourself in college. Very little of what happens in the classroom will affect your job. Your interactions with people, the connections you find, the social decisions you make—*those* will matter. College students, forget what your parents want you to do for a few minutes. Figure out what you want to do. And do it. Even if it doesn't pay the most money, even if it isn't what Grandpa did. Because if you're not happy, it's not worth it. I saw so many students make themselves miserable over classes they didn't want to be in. What a crappy way to go through college. If you're going to struggle, it should at least be over something that interests you, not something that interests your parents.

That's not to say you should just give up, because college is hard. Some people wanted to throw in the towel, and that's never the answer. The answer is to rethink what you want to be doing. It's deciding what kind of future you want and moving towards that. Because if you're moving towards a future that doesn't make you smile, you're going to struggle the entire way. Eventually, some students figured this out. They said, "Screw it, I'm not going to make myself miserable over something I don't want to be doing." But others never figure it out. There are doctors and lawyers walking the streets today who daydream about being a teacher. They could have, but they didn't. And that's sad. Rosalyn always threatened to transfer when she did poorly on an exam. "Ros," I would tell her, "transferring isn't the answer. But reevaluating what you're doing here is a start." She took that advice to heart.

She picked up a Spanish minor, because she truly enjoyed speaking the language and learning about the culture. She stopped trying to overload classes. She considered joining a sorority to enhance her social life. Solid, concrete steps. I admire people who can do it.

There is such a fine line between doing what you want to do, doing what you need to do, and doing what you're told to do. Just because a class is hard doesn't necessarily mean you should drop it. Just because you get a C in biology doesn't mean you're not cut out to be a doctor. So when I saw these things happening to my residents, I made an effort to figure out what each problem was. For some people, they were simply not used to a rigorous course load and extensive amounts of homework. They were still adjusting. For some people, they were simply not smart enough to get A's at Ashford. Some of their weaknesses may have been covered up by grade inflation in high school, and these people had to cope with the fact that they would never be 4.0 students. It's a hard thing to accept, but the sooner you do, the better off you'll be. Some people were indeed making themselves miserable to please their parents. As inappropriate as I think that is, there are a lot of people who think it's disrespectful to not take into account what your parents want. So while some sided with me, others went right on doing as they were told.

And of course, there were always the people who had their grades and goals under control and just occasionally got stressed out. It happens to all of us. Regardless of which type you were, when Thanksgiving finally arrived, it was like a Godsend.

❧

The short holiday refreshed all of us. We came back ready to buckle down and finish the semester strong, both academically and socially. The collective mood on the floor during the time between Thanksgiving and winter break was jovial, excited, and relaxed. "Turkey Day" had given us all a breather. It gave us a chance to be away from each other for a little while and a chance to realize that living on New House 5 definitely beat living at home. Whenever I go home, I'm happy to be by myself for the first day. After that, I get creeped out that there aren't always people walking by my room, and I'm ready to go back.

We also found time to do some minor floor decorating. There were the traditional streamers and cardboard cutouts of Santa Claus and gifts. We purchased a small, potted evergreen tree and, so as not to offend anyone, we called it the "Finals Tree." It wasn't until we got the Finals Tree and decorated it with everything from cut-out menorahs to playing cards that I realized how religiously diverse New House 5 really was. There were ten practicing Jews, several Catholics, one girl who was Hindu, and of course every denomination of Christianity I had ever heard of. Diversity comes in all shapes and sizes, and the Finals Tree pointed out just one more way New House 5 showed that. Race, religion, creed, sexuality, location, ethnicity. When you live in a place like this, you learn so much about other people, sometimes without even trying. What a cool place to live.

And of course, we had a Secret Santa gift exchange. I decided not to organize it and instead handed off the reigns to Rosalyn and Kristen. They e-mailed the floor to see who wanted to participate and laid some simple ground rules. They decided on a ten-dollar maximum gift price and set a date for an exchange party: the last Friday before finals. Over the next week, there was much discussion about what to give certain people. When the party came around, the entire floor showed up just to see what people would get. When I walked into the lounge, it was buzzing with excitement. People who weren't participating stood in the background, whispering to each other. The thirty or so people who did participate sat anxiously around a pile of neatly wrapped gifts in the center of the lounge. Rosalyn thanked everyone, and we began opening the gifts, one at a time. The next half hour was one of the most amusing experiences I had on New House 5.

The crowd responded louder to each progressive present. Since everyone knew everyone else so well, it was easy to think of a great gag gift for each person (or at least ask around to figure one out). Eric, who we constantly teased for being extremely pale, received a jar of tanning cream, along with a pair of boxers. Luke received a box of flavored condoms and a cigar, which he was instructed to "use wisely." When it was all said and done, I had laughed so much that my stomach was pulsating with pain.

When all the presents had been opened, Kristen stepped to the center to make an announcement.

"Before we all leave, since this is the last time we'll all be together before winter break, there's something we'd like to do." She pulled a large package from behind one of the couches. Taking care not to rip it, she brought it to me. "Andy, this is from New House 5 to thank you for being the awesomest RA in the world. We love you."

I opened the package amidst claps and whistles. Inside was a penguin-themed bed comforter. It was common knowledge that penguins were my favorite animal; I had various penguin paraphernalia in my room, and my instant messenger name contained the word "penguin" as well. Any and all things penguin were now associated with me, and I was totally cool with that. I let out a burst of laughter, and the rest of the room followed suit.

"Thanks, guys," I said. "I don't know what to say. You all have been awesome this semester. You've made my job incredibly fun. Seriously. It makes things easy for me when I plan stuff and you all come. And it makes things easy for me that you all are willing to talk to me."

"Oh, come on, Andy," Julie chimed in. "The only reason we feel comfortable coming to talk to you is because you're the nicest guy we've ever met."

"And you've also always got your door open, and you're always in your room," added Elyse.

"That's because I have no social life," I laughed. New House 5 laughed in agreement and the crowd broke, ending the fun and sending everyone back to bury their heads in notebooks and review sheets. I stood for a few minutes, stunned. Honestly. I guess I always knew my effort and enthusiasm made a difference on the floor, but hearing it directly from them gave me a sensation I had never felt before. It's one thing to be genuinely appreciated and respected by a single person. It's an entirely different thing to be genuinely appreciated and respected by fifty-six of your peers. Knowing that I had something to do with making New House 5, and hearing it from them, it gave me chills. I stood holding my comforter, hoping I'd never lose that feeling. It sounds crazy that the moment I felt the most content and humbled came during a Secret Santa exchange, but last year, it did. For that first semester, for my determination to make New House 5 a community, for my willingness to go the extra mile to let the floor know I was there for them above all else, I was proud of myself. And I didn't know it then, but when the second semester rolled around, I would have a chance to be proud of my floor.

When the feeling finally wore off and I realized I should probably go study for my exams as well, Rob came up to me with another wrapped package.

"This is from me, Luke, Eric, and Micah. 'Cause you know, you don't have a girlfriend because you're always here for us, but we don't think that should stop you from having a good time."

I opened up the oblong package. It was a DVD: Tour Bus Hotties, distributed by Playboy. They got me porn. I just shook my head and smiled.

"Thanks a lot, I appreciate the gesture. Let me know if you ever want to borrow it."

Rob smiled and patted me on the back.

"Okay, man," he said. "Thanks for everything. This floor wouldn't be the same without you."

"Thanks to you too, Rob. I can honestly say the same thing about you."

"You know what? I think we could say the same thing about anyone on this floor."

❧

Finals week progressed and New House 5 started to empty. As each person left, they stopped by my room to say goodbye and wish me a great holiday. Jeremy left after the first day, since most of his classes had a paper in lieu of a final exam. Ben headed back to Nebraska before the first week ended, and Sam was on his way to Michigan by Saturday. On Monday, the second to last day of finals, the floor really emptied out. Kim caught her flight to Houston and found out on her way to the airport that she'd be sharing a plane with Desta. Rob headed off to Boston, Meghan was on her way to Texas, and Luke was bumming a ride back to Maryland. On Tuesday morning, everyone except the RAs had to be out of the dorm. Elyse and Val left early in the morning. Aaron was leaving to drive back to Philadelphia as I walked into the bathroom to brush my teeth. I took a last lap around the floor at 1 p.m. It was completely empty. It hadn't been this way since the middle of August, and it felt strange.

I didn't leave until later that evening. After I walked the floor, I sat in my room and thought for a while. About the semester that just ended, about the semester that was quickly approaching. Yes, New House 5 had truly become the New House 5 I dreamed about. Not everyone was friends and not everyone agreed, but it wasn't supposed to be a utopia. It was supposed to be a community, a brotherhood. And it had certainly become one. Of course bad things come with that. Talking behind people's backs, nasty confrontations, heated disagreements, heartbreaks. But for every bad thing I could think of, I came up with a dozen good ones as well. The late night conversations about nothing, the pranks, the museum trips, the inside jokes, the help given when others were in need. New House 5 was something special, and I felt fortunate to be a part of it.

The next semester would bring a lot of changes to New House 5, which was only natural. But it also brought a lot of new problems that I never could have foreseen, and it tested the mettle of the entire floor. Things started to fall apart in the second semester, and we tried as hard as we could to keep the community we worked so hard to build together. The second semester tested all of us. It tested our courage, our strength, and all of our previous beliefs. I learned a lot about myself during the spring semester. But I learned a lot more about our floor. I learned what it truly meant to be a part of New House 5, and I couldn't put it into words if you gave me forever.

SPRING SEMESTER 2004

BACK HOME

Going back home didn't feel like going back home. It felt like a job, like a chore, like something I didn't have any choice in. When I first arrived in Rochester in late December, I was genuinely happy to be there. After a crazy first semester, I was looking forward to being in my bedroom, relaxing, doing absolutely nothing. I spent the first week doing what every college kid does during winter break: going out with high school friends, visiting old stomping grounds, and raiding the refrigerator. It felt good.

I never had any "best friends" in high school, but there were a handful of people I went to concerts and played video games with. We had known each other for ten years, so it wasn't a matter of if we were going to hang out, just a matter of when. I guess it was strange that given how long we'd known each other, we weren't very close, but I did enjoy not having to worry about anything when I was around them. I could just be myself and that was cool. I think that's what friendship is, and it's something we all take for granted.

I never thought I'd go back to visit my high school, and during my freshman year of college, I made a point not to. It's not that I disliked my high school. I had a decently good time there. I just felt bitter towards it. I wasn't one of the most popular kids, I wasn't the biggest nerd, but I just didn't fit well in my high school. I'd always felt like I was forcing myself to enjoy it, so when I graduated, I decided that would be the end. My sophomore year cooled me off a bit, though, and I decided it would be okay to go back and say hi to a few of my favorite teachers. So my buddy Tim and

I hopped into his maroon Honda Accord on the Tuesday before Christmas and made the ten-minute drive to Hilton Central High School.

Driving there was nostalgic in itself. I remembered making the same trip every day for four years of my life. But walking around the school, seeing the same structures but different people, it was a strange experience. It made me feel even less at home. High school was supposed to be about making friends, having no worries, and enjoying yourself. I hadn't been able to do that, for a variety of reasons. But I was able to do it at college. That's where I belonged. I respected my high school for preparing me to go off into the real world, but it didn't hold a special place in my heart. I was happy when we left. When we got in the car and began to drive away, I told Tim, "I have a feeling I'm never coming back here. Ever again."

Christmas came and went, and all I could think about was getting back to Ashford. By the beginning of January, I was sick of sitting in my room alone, sick of not being around people. I missed being able to walk out of my room at any hour of the day and find someone sitting in the lounge, sipping coffee and fooling around on a laptop. So when it came time to leave, I was ecstatic. I needed to be back by Friday evening. I loaded up my car Thursday night, and at 6 a.m. on Friday morning, I started my car to make the five-hour trip to Pittsburgh. I was ready to go back home.

It was snowing when I pulled into the parking lot at school. Not the wet, disgusting snow, but the light, fluffy kind you see in movies. The kind of snow that makes you love living in a place where winter means snowball fights and sledding, no matter how old you are. Looking around, I felt more at home then I ever had in my life. I took a deep breath, feeling the frigid air and soft snowflakes tickle the inside of my mouth and fill my lungs. It was like breathing in newness, cleansing myself of everything I didn't want to be. Here at school, I was free to be myself. And I was part of New House 5.

I stood for a few minutes, silently looking at the quiet campus. It was covered in snow. One lone person walked to the library, bundled up, head down, trudging against the wind. I wish I'd had a camera. The scene looked like a postcard. Beautiful, pristine. The snow made it look like a playground, a place where all your dreams could come true, if you let them. The perfect college campus. I saved that image in my head. I'll never lose it.

I returned early for an RA training refresher. Our staff spent most of Saturday afternoon and part of Sunday talking about what had been accomplished last fall and what our goals for spring were. It was interesting to see our entire staff together again after we had all weathered a semester as RAs. After hearing their stories, I realized that we had all had similar experiences. Maybe everything didn't go as well for them as it had on New House 5, and maybe different situations were popping up on other floors, but we all had the same general feeling: being an RA was an incredible experience. But it ate up more time and effort than any of us anticipated. For some people, like myself, this was okay. I spent most of each day being an RA. But others on the staff had a difficult time balancing being an RA with other activities. I rarely saw most of the staff since they were always so busy. Laura, for instance, was in a sorority and applying to medical schools. Jack was a member of the marching band, an editor for the school paper, and took a rigorous computer science course load. I admired how they were able to do everything and stay sane at the same time.

After a session about setting goals for the next semester, Sara stopped me before I went up the elevator.

"Hey, Andy, how did your interview go?"

I had told Sara before we left that I had an interview with a minor league baseball team for a summer internship. I thought it would be a fun and interesting way to utilize my economics experience, so I gave it a shot. The interview had gone very well, and I appreciated Sara asking.

"It went really well, I think. I have to wait another couple weeks to hear from them, but I don't think I could have done any better. How's your job search going?"

She rolled her eyes and sighed. "About as well as it's been going the last two months. I think I've sent out over two hundred résumés, and I've gotten one lousy phone interview. I'm going to be unemployed after I graduate."

It boggled my mind that Sara was having a problem finding a job. She was a business major, coming from one of the most prestigious undergraduate business programs in the country. She wasn't picky about where the job was, and she had all the credentials to be a top employee: school involvement, excellent grades, well-rounded.

"You're just overqualified for every job available," I told her. "If worse comes to worst, you can always stay in my room next year."

"Thanks. Be careful about saying that, though. I might take you up on it. I'm leaning towards becoming a prostitute. I have good people skills, I think I'd be good at it." She laughed.

"Let me know how the money is, I might join you. But seriously, I'm sure you'll find a job. I guess you have to pick it up now that we're in the second semester, but if you're persistent, you'll be fine."

"I keep telling myself that, but it's still frustrating. I don't even know where I'm going to be living next year!" She shook her head. "Well, I have to go call my boyfriend. He said something about going out tonight. I'll see you tomorrow."

"Yep. Later, Sara."

As I walked up the stairs to the 5th floor, I realized how close I was to being in Sara's position. I was a sophomore, and in two years, it would be my turn to start thinking about the real world. Most college students have been in school their entire lives. They have no clue what it means to not have classes everyday. It was a scary thought, finding a real job somewhere I've never been before. I tried not to think about it, but I couldn't help it. It all related back to the floor. To being an RA, to learning about other people. It costs a lot of money to go here, and I'm sure the education isn't that much better than at a top public school. But it's worth every penny to me because of the people I get to meet. I learn about so many different kinds of people here that I never would have known existed if I stayed in Rochester. International students, rich snobs, New House 5—they all gave me different insights into the world around me. I can't think of anything better to prepare me for the real world than seeing what the real world has to offer.

Spring RA training finally ended. When I returned to my room Sunday afternoon, residents were starting to come back. One by one, another bundled up student would carry new boxes of clothes and food to his room and holler "I'm back!" at me. The 5th floor was becoming New House 5 again. I hoped the long break hadn't made people forget what it meant to be a part of New House 5. I had a feeling nothing could have made them forget.

Sunday night flew by. It was like a reunion. Everyone was happy to be back, happy to see their friends after a one-month hiatus. There were hugs and handshakes, gossip to catch up on, lives to be updated, and stories to be told. On Sunday night, New House 5 felt more like home than ever before. Without the distraction of classes or exams, we stayed up late into the night, talking about absolutely nothing.

I informed everyone (much to their chagrin) that they had not reached the 3.5 required to get me to dye my hair pink. But they came close with a 3.3 and I was very impressed with them for getting even that high. They said I lucked out this time and I acted relieved, but in reality, I don't think I would have minded losing the bet. The pink hair would have been worth their 3.5.

Gary was back, and everyone was glad to see him. The time at home had been good for him. He got his act together, figured out how to control his stress—how, I still don't know—and he hadn't changed a bit. He was still the same old Gary, obnoxious and offensive as usual. He had written a couple new songs in his spare time and offered to play them for us. We all politely declined, but thanked him anyway.

I checked in on Kate as well. I'd talked to her a couple times over the break on the phone, just chatting for a few minutes each time. She always seemed to be in a good mood, but I had learned never to trust what it "seemed like" with Kate. I stepped into her room while she was still unpacking.

"How was your break, dude?" I asked her nonchalantly.

"Eh, it was alright. Nothing too exciting. I guess I had a good time, but I'm glad to be back. There's just a lot of stuff I'd rather not deal with at home."

I could tell she was lying to me about having a good time. About everything being alright. She was too obviously trying to make it sound like things were fine.

"What kind of stuff?" I asked.

"I don't know. Just… stuff."

I left the conversation at that. It would only be a matter of time before I badgered her to find out what was wrong. Because something clearly was wrong, and I had my ideas about what it might be.

Meghan stopped by my room just before I went to bed. "Andy," she said. "Oh, you're going to bed. Well this isn't really important, but sometime soon, I'll have to tell you a story. I had a run in with Rick over break. I was going to call you and tell you about it, but I was, um, unable to for… reasons. Anyway, it was really awkward, and you're the only person here I talk to about Rick at all. I sound like I think about him all the time, which is really lame, but yeah. Goodnight!"

She ran off before I could say anything, so I decided to let her go. Meghan did eventually tell me about her run in with Rick but it wasn't until a few weeks later. And it wasn't until I had to talk to her about it.

ৡৡৡ

Winter break had come and gone. It was a different experience for everyone. Some people had a great time at home with their high school friends, others were miserable. Regardless, I think everyone was happy to be back, in some way or another. New House 5 wasn't always the easiest place to live, with the lack of privacy and constant activity. But to most of us, it did feel like home.

I looked around for distinct changes in people. I wanted to see if the break had really affected anyone, if it had changed who people were. From what I could tell, there weren't any major differences. And while I was probably right, what I didn't see right away were the smaller changes people were making. Everyone was evolving in some way; forward, backward, sideways, it didn't matter. Everyone was making little adjustments that would eventually turn into much bigger realignments. New House 5 was locked and loaded for the second semester. None of us knew exactly what it would bring, but there was a strong sense of optimism on the floor. That sense of optimism didn't last long. Things became very different very soon, and I don't think any of us saw it coming.

DEMONS

No one can hear her
No one ever has
- Unnamed Girl

Every time there's a blizzard, it reminds me of the movie *The Shining* with Jack Nicholson. I love the snow, but there's something about blizzards, about snow so thick you can't see in front of your face, that creeps me out. The first blizzard of the year took place on the second weekend we were back at school. We spent all of Saturday outside, making snowmen and snowballs. I still remember how much fun we all had. Kim and Meghan, both of whom lived in Texas, weren't used to snow. They had both seen it before, but never had the chance to just wake up in the morning and see the ground blanketed in white. Ski trips are one thing, but you can't beat a pick-up snowball fight. Kim was bundled up in her new winter jacket. Watching her come inside made me burst out laughing.

"Shut up, man. It's warm, and that's all I care about," she growled at me.

"You look like an Eskimo. You can't even put your arms down because your coat is so puffy. Do you even have a head in there?"

"I'm making a face at you under my scarf right now, take my word for it."

"I guess I'll have to."

Right after Kim left to shower, Rob came up the elevator, wearing jeans and a t-shirt.

"Someone needs to tell these people it's not that cold out," he announced. "This is like April in Boston."

"It's like July in upstate New York," I countered.

Behind Rob, Elyse and Aaron got off the elevator. Distracted by my weather conversation, I didn't see the giant snowball being heaved at my face until it made impact. If you've ever had a giant ball of ice smack you in the face, you know how I felt. They laughed and walked away to warm up.

"I'm glad nothing's changed," I said as I wiped most of the snow off my glasses. Ben walked by and smirked. "I can't believe you fell for it, man. Why do you think Rob would talk to you as soon as he got off the elevator? Should have been an immediate tip-off."

"Hey, Ben, why don't you go back to Nebraska or something?"

"It's too cold there." He patted me on the back and walked to his room.

When he was about halfway there, he turned around. "Andy, I'm thinking about applying to be an RA next year. Do you think you could write me a letter of recommendation?"

"Of course, dude. Just get me the info I need."

"Cool, thanks a lot, man. I'll make sure to put in a good word for you during the interview. I was thinking about it over winter break. I think it would be a fun thing to do, you seem to enjoy it, and it looks like it has a lot of benefits. I figure there's no harm in applying."

"Yeah, definitely, man. Might as well give it a shot."

Roger walked off the elevator just as Ben and I were finishing our conversation. Roger, who was from just a few hours away, was used to the cold as well. He was wearing only a sweater and a knit hat.

"You're cool like us, no need for the crazy winter gear," said Ben.

"Well, I've got my nice round body to keep me warm." Roger put his hands around his belly and did his best Santa Claus impression. As he pulled off his glasses to wipe away the condensation, he brought up the idea of being an RA as well.

"I talked to you about it a little before break, but I'm definitely going to apply," he said. "I'm not sure if I'll interview well because I'm sort of shy and soft-spoken in that atmosphere, but I'll give it a try."

"You really should. If nothing else, you'll get some experience interviewing. It's not always about being the loudest, just being the most thoughtful."

Roger smiled at the idea. He was a very soft-spoken guy, but he was also very thoughtful. I liked the prospect of Roger being an RA, but I agreed that the interview process might weed him out. It disappointed me that a guy like him might not get an opportunity just because he didn't speak up as much as someone else.

Actually, until Ben and Roger brought it up, I had totally forgotten about RA applications. They were due in two weeks and a bunch of people on the floor had expressed interest in applying. It made me feel good, that they'd had a positive enough experience on the floor to want a floor of their own. Kim, Desta, Claire, Roger, Ben, and Chad all planned on applying, and I was more than happy to write a reference for all of them. The application process wasn't for another two weeks, though, so I had time to think about it.

 споку

The snow came down hard for the remainder of the evening. Most people stayed in and watched movies or chatted. I was sitting in my room watching *Field of Dreams* on my laptop when Kate knocked on my door. She looked worried. Even as she came in, she was shaking. She closed the door cautiously and sat down on my futon, breathing harshly. She stared straight ahead. The air turned cold. Goose bumps ran up my spine. A zombie had just walked into my room. After several minutes of silence, I decided to speak.

"Are you okay, Kate?"

"I'm fine." She spoke in staccato, continuing to stare straight ahead. Her breathing grew slower now. She was wearing a pale blue turtleneck I had never seen her wear before. She looked different in it. Somehow, not as lively, not as real.

I hadn't talked to Kate at all about her break or what transpired last semester. We had both been busy with other things. From what I heard around the floor, she had an excellent time back home. I knew that probably wasn't true. But maybe being back was making her even more miserable. She moved her head, looking down at the floor. She leaned forward, placed her chin in her cupped hands, and stared emotionlessly.

"How was your break?" I needed to say something, anything to end the silence.

"It was fine. My friends and I had a good time. My parents and I had a ton of fights, and I got kicked out of the house twice. I didn't care, though. I didn't want to be there anyway."

"Fights about what?"

"Oh, stupid stuff. Me not calling when I was coming home late, having friends over without telling them, the usual. They're good at frustrating me.

But it was fine. I just got in my car and drove away when they yelled. I didn't even respond to them."

"Hmm. How are your friends doing?"

"They're all good. It was a lot of fun seeing them actually. It was weird. So many of them changed. I guess I figured that we'd all leave for college then come back and it would all be the same. But they changed. I changed. They said I seemed colder, more distant. Maybe they're right."

Kate's blank stare hadn't left her face, but she was talking more freely now. She untwisted her body and sat in a more comfortable position on the futon. She sighed deeply before going on.

"I talked to Jared over break. It was really strange. He was even more different than when I talked to him on the phone. He was genuinely mean to me this time. He swore at me, told me how horrible of a person I was for everything I did to him back in high school. I didn't know what to say."

I didn't know what to say either. Where to begin. "What kinds of things did he say?"

"He regretted all the time he spent with me. He regretted doing everything he did for me. I wanted to shove it right back in his face. I wanted to remind him who saved him from near-death. I wanted to remind him that he was the reason I started doing… bad things. I wanted to remind him of everything he ever did to me. But I didn't. I just stood there and took it. I ran home and cried in my bedroom. I was trying to be quiet but my parents heard me. They yelled at me, so I left. I drove around for an hour, crying. I felt like there was nothing in the world for me."

She sat silently. We could hear the blowing wind, threatening to break through the window. For a moment, I thought it would. Kate turned her head and made eye contact with me. She looked lost. Genuinely lost. Her eyes, her demeanor, her expression. Silently, she begged the question, "What do I do?" The look on her face turned to one of shame. She opened her mouth, then closed it abruptly, as if her conscience sat on her shoulder, whispering what to reveal and what to keep quiet. Her eyes moved back and forth. She fought with the demons in her head. When one side came out victorious, she spoke.

"I did something bad, Andy."

She rolled up the sleeves of her turtleneck. Her arms were marked with cuts. Some deep, scabbed over, almost healed. Some were fresh, still red and wet. It looked like she had fallen on a bed of razor blades. She might as well have. Her eyes stared into mine. They looked for answers, but I only responded with shock.

"How did you do those?"

"There are ways. Scissors, knives, curling iron, ball point pens. If someone wants to do it, they will find a way."

"When did you start again?"

"After I drove that night. I got back home early in the morning. I felt dead. Emotionally, physically, mentally dead. I took a knife from my kitchen drawer and sat on my bed. I held it for an hour, thinking about what to do. Talking to Jared brought back memories of doing it. I remembered what it felt like. I wanted to feel it again. I did it. Deep. I did it across my arm, not lengthwise, so I wouldn't kill myself. I watched the blood pour out of my skin, bright and flowing. I felt alive. For a few minutes, I felt alive.

"Afterwards, I couldn't believe what I had done. I cleaned up quickly. I made sure not to leave any signs. It was high school all over again. I knew exactly what to do. They next day I wore a long-sleeved shirt. And the next night, I did it again. I did it every night after that, sometimes a lot, sometimes a little. And each time, I felt horrible afterwards. But it was worth it for the few minutes when I sat in my room each night and watched my body come alive. I don't know how to explain it. It kept me going."

"It looks like you've continued to do it here."

"It's addicting. But I know I can't keep doing it. If you haven't figured it out, I have serious trust issues. I would never tell anyone I trust them, but I'm telling you about what I'm doing now, and I wouldn't tell anyone else. You can take that for what it's worth. I need to stop, but I don't know how to."

"Well, first thing's first: are you still going to see counseling?"

"Every Thursday morning. I did at the end of last semester too. I thought you would have figured that out, since I'm so miserable every Thursday. It's not helping. I tell Elaine it's not helping. But I don't know what would help."

"Listen, Kate, I need to tell someone about this."

"You can't." It wasn't a plea, it was a demand. I wouldn't tell anyone, and she expected that.

"But Kate, I'm going to be honest, I have no clue what to do. Withholding information like this, if anyone ever found out, could get me fired. And for good reason. Maybe if we told Tamira, we could figure something out…"

"YOU ARE NOT TELLING TAMIRA!" She laughed nervously. "This is between you and me. I want you to help me. That's why I'm asking you!"

She was putting me in an awkward position. I knew I needed to tell someone, anyone, but I didn't want to alienate Kate. At least she was coming to me, and I could figure out what to do in the meantime. Looking back, it may have been the biggest mistake I have ever made, because it endangered someone's life. But at the time, I did what I thought I had to do.

"Okay, let's clear that up then. I will not tell anyone, I promise. But you need to make some promises to me. If someone found out I knew this and I didn't tell anyone, I would get fired."

"I really would kill myself if you got fired because of me."

"I'm just having a difficult time balancing being a friend with being an RA here. It's very irresponsible of me to not tell anyone about this, even if you don't want me to. I feel sort of sick knowing I'm going to keep this to myself. You're putting me in a tough position, I really want to tell someone."

"But you're not going to," she said gravely.

"So what about counseling? Why don't you think it's helping? Listen, if we can't figure out some solid steps here, I am going to tell someone. I'll call Tamira right now if I have to."

She knew I was serious. "Okay. I'll be totally honest. I think counseling isn't helping—well, I know counseling isn't helping—because I'm not really telling the counselor anything. She's been prying and trying to figure stuff out and I've already told her more than I'd like, but I don't want to tell her any more. It's her job. I don't want someone to help me if it's their job. It makes me feel like another statistic."

"You need to keep going and you need to start opening up. You need to tell her the truth. You need to help her help you. You forget that it's her job because she went through years of training in it, Kate. This is ridiculous. If you don't start telling her things she can work with next time you go, I really am going to tell Tamira."

Kate was silent. She knew I was serious about telling someone if I felt I needed to, just like she was serious about not talking to me again because of it.

"I wish I hadn't told you any of this," she said under her breath.

"I'm trying to help you, Kate, and if that means doing something you don't want me to do, then so be it."

"You don't want to help me. You want to do this and be a fucking hero and make it look like you're the world's greatest human being. Well, congratulations, you're helping a fucked up little college girl. I hope it makes you feel good about yourself. I hope when you jerk off at night you think about how much good you're doing in the world!"

The word enraged is not strong enough to describe what Kate's tone was at that moment. She was quiet and controlled, but the words flowing from her mouth were the angriest things I had ever heard her say. Her face was bright red. She caught me off guard with the outburst, and I was silent as her face drained back to its normal color.

"Does anyone else know about this?" I asked her.

"Elaine does. I told her about it a few days ago. She said the same thing you're saying. She's worse than you, though. I'm like her project. She has her own self-esteem issues. Once she's given up on me or I'm cured or whatever, she'll move on to something else. It makes her feel good about herself."

"Even if you don't want to admit it, you're still telling both of us. That means something."

"It doesn't mean I trust either one of you, if that's what you're implying. I never have, even if I told you that. All it means is that I need to tell someone, and I recognize that."

"You just implied that you trusted me."

"Don't read into what I say."

"If I don't feel comfortable going to sleep tonight, knowing that you might not be alive tomorrow, I'm calling Tamira, so you better convince me right now that I have nothing to worry about."

"You have nothing to worry about," she tried to assure me. "Oh my God, this is so stressful. Andy, my coming to you is my cry for help. I wouldn't tell someone if I thought it wasn't a problem, I'm telling you because I know it is a problem. I want help, Andy. I want help. But I'm not going to kill myself, I know my limits. You have to believe that I know what I need."

She was practically in tears. Her hands were clenched in fists, held in front of her chest. She kept the pose for a moment, then fell back onto the futon.

"Okay," I said quietly. "You need to go to bed. You need to bring me everything in your room that you could possibly hurt yourself with. Not because you couldn't find something else, but because of principle. I'll talk to Elaine."

"Don't talk to Elaine. I can't stand people talking about me. Please don't."

I ignored the request. "And you're going to open up to the counselor. We'll see where everything stands in a couple weeks. But remember, if I am at all concerned, I will not hesitate to call someone. Understand?"

She nodded obediently. For the first time, she was submitting to my demands. Kate left the room and returned a minute later, her hands full of scissors and plastic knives. She placed them on my desk. Without a word, she left my room. I didn't see her again until the following morning. When I got up at 8 a.m., the first thing I did was check her away message. "Today is a good day."

It certainly was. I let out a deep breath.

I did talk to Elaine. She had the same concerns I did, but neither one of us had any extra information to give the other. Kate was careful about not telling either of us more than she had told the other. She clearly had experience in this, and it was frustrating. We discussed what action to take next. Both of us wanted to tell someone, anyone higher up. But in the end, we decided to keep it to ourselves and try to fix the problem without any outside intervention. Not telling anyone else was not only stupid, it could have meant someone's life. As I said before, even telling Tamira that a girl on my floor was cutting herself, without using a name, could have been helpful, but I was too stubborn and confused to see the importance of that information. So Elaine and I talked about it frequently, but the information never went beyond the two of us.

We kept a close eye on Kate for the next few weeks. And we did see a marked improvement. Both of us were confident we had made the right decision. Now we didn't need to force anyone else into a situation that was clearly solving itself. Kate came to my room almost every night, even if just for a few minutes. Sometimes we'd talk about her psychologist or her parents, but most of the time we just talked about our days and classes. It was small talk, but it made both of us feel comfortable. Kate knew I was there if she needed anything, which was a big step for her. It was genuine trust, even though she would never admit it. And I was able to see her progression each day, see her growing happier, stronger, more content. She knew I appreciated her coming to see me, so she stopped by sometimes without saying a word.

She sat on my futon and turned on my TV, watching for a few minutes before walking out.

Kate talked to Elaine more often than she talked to me, online, on the phone, and in person. She stopped by Elaine's dorm frequently, and whenever I saw Kate on the phone, it was with Elaine. Kate constantly complained about Elaine, about her biases, her fakeness, and her flaws. But she kept talking to her anyway. One evening, I walked by Kate sitting in her room, her phone at her ear. She looked up at me and rolled her eyes. "Elaine?" I mouthed. She nodded and made a talking motion with her hand.

Twenty minutes later, I walked by when she was off the phone.

"I'm going to kill her!" Kate yelled. "She is so annoying! She talks forever about herself and her stupid problems. I cannot take it!"

Ten minutes after that, I saw Kate getting in the elevator, bundled up in her coat and gloves.

"Where are you going?"

"Um, I'm going to Kensington."

"To see Elaine?"

She didn't answer. As the door closed, I smiled to myself and thought how nice it was for both of them to have a good friend, even if neither one admitted it.

Kate was definitely getting better. She told me that she was telling her counselor more and more about herself. At times, it seemed like the counseling was helping her figure out the roots of her problems and in turn, how to start fixing them. But as soon as I mentioned it in a positive light, she would quickly turn the conversation and bad-mouth her counselor in every way she could think. I noticed she was wearing short-sleeved shirts again. The scars were gone. She generally seemed to be enjoying college more. She remained close with the friends she had made on the floor during first semester, particularly Meghan, Kristen, and Elyse. I saw them hanging out in the mini lounge one day and sat down to chat for a few minutes.

"Andy," Elyse said, "We're trying to figure out what kind of guy Kate needs."

"I don't care what kind of guy she dates. It's none of my business," Meghan said, staring down into a novel. Meanwhile, Kate was just shaking her head and reading a biology textbook.

"We're thinking the tall, dark, mysterious type," said Kristen, looking thoughtfully at Kate.

"Which means we need to find her a guy *not* from Ashford." Elyse snickered at her own joke. Kate tried to muffle a laugh.

"Oh, come on, Kate. We'll find you a nice boy here somewhere," said Kristen confidently.

"It's not that I want a boyfriend. I was just saying I wish I knew more guys here," said Kate, correcting the other girls. "You three can twist anything."

"Only because we love you, Kate," said Elyse. "But I have a newspaper meeting to get to, so we'll have to put this off to another day. Later, girls."

Kristen and Meghan got up as well. "We have some meeting for the concert committee, I don't even know. I think we're late. Oh well." They walked away unconcerned. Kate's face was still buried in her textbook.

"Are embryos that interesting?" I asked her.

"Actually, it's mitochondria, and yeah, they are." She looked up at me with a smirk.

"Why are they giving you a hard time about finding a guy?"

"Who knows? I can't stand it."

"I think you enjoy the fact that you're cool enough with each other that they can give you a hard time."

"Oh, you think so?"

"Definitely."

She shrugged her shoulders and went back to her mitochondria. Things were getting better. My only fear was that Kate's problem could be triggered again. And I knew in the back of my mind that if something did happen, it would be worse than what I'd seen in my bedroom. I shuddered to think what that might mean. But it didn't matter. I had to tell myself it wouldn't happen again. Besides, Kate was smart enough to not go too far. I mean, she had gotten help once, so she would get it again. Wouldn't she?

SWEEPING CHANGES

Too bad we all believe that
To keep up we have to rush
- Give Up

February taught me that change is truly a continuous thing at college. When I thought I had everyone figured out from my interactions with them first semester, they all surprised me. Nothing was good or bad, just different. At least in my eyes.

One of the most drastic changes I saw was in Meghan. I remained very close to her, talking to her almost every day. And our conversation was still dominated by Rick, indirectly or directly. During winter break, Meghan had a run-in with Rick. She told me about it the first week we were back at school. We were walking to class, shivering in the wind, as she recalled her encounter.

"I went to a friend's house because she was having a party. I didn't ask if he was going to be there because she knows not to invite me if he's coming. But when I got there, I saw him across the room and my heart started beating through my chest. I was so mad at my friend. She just looked at me and said, 'You didn't ask.' How frustrating is that? She knew exactly what I was thinking.

"I tried avoiding him all night. I didn't want to leave because he had seen me, and I didn't want to come off as a baby. I knew he'd been talking about me behind my back. Stupid stuff. Saying that I was possessive, that I was a bitch. My friend told me he bragged to her about hitting on other girls and drinking and smoking when he was still dating me. Stupid high school stuff. I thought I'd finally gotten away from that."

"So did you run into him?"

"Yeah, he came up to me actually. He said hi, and we were civil. We talked for a few minutes. Then he started bitching me out. For no reason at all. In the middle of a party, the entire place went quiet listening to him yell at me. I was so scared, I wanted to just shrink away. I didn't know what to do. I was whispering to him to stop it, I was almost crying. He wouldn't. He just kept yelling, calling me a bitch and a slut and every awful thing he could think."

"How long did that go on for?"

"I don't even know. A few minutes? I don't even want to think about it. Then I did something really stupid. I drank. A lot. I had like eight shots in about ten minutes. Do you know how much that is for someone who doesn't drink?"

This stopped me dead in my tracks. Meghan didn't drink. She was one of the people that looked down on anyone who had ever had a sip of alcohol in their life. She saw how shocked I was.

"Don't be condescending," she said snobbishly.

"I'm just surprised. You know I'm not against drinking. But you are. That's why I'm surprised."

She whined defensively, "I know. It was bad. I'll never do it again. I still don't know why people drink, it really is dumb. My friend Linda had to drive me home. She was making fun of me the whole time because I always used to give her a hard time about her drinking. I don't know, I just needed something to take my mind off what happened."

With that comment, Meghan sped ahead of me and slipped inside Bergin Hall to her next class. I blew off Meghan's mistake as just that: a mistake. But as the semester wore on, I realized it wasn't a mistake. It was a growing trend. Though she tried to hide it from me, she started drinking every weekend with the rest of the floor. I would see her in the hallway at 1 a.m. on a Friday night, still tipsy. Once, she hopped behind her door before I called her name.

"Shouldn't you be sleeping?" she asked me.

"Shouldn't you?" I replied.

"Maybe. Goodnight." She closed the door uneasily.

The first couple times I didn't think much of it. I made a mental note but never called her out on it. I should have. Meghan was not the kind of person who drank, and she clearly wasn't doing it to have fun. She was using the weekends as her only form of stress relief, to take her mind off bigger things.

Drinking isn't always bad, but in Meghan's case, it wasn't the answer. One night, Rob came to my room laughing at 2 a.m.

"When you see Meghan tonight, ask her how the fraternity party was."

"What happened?"

"Let's just say, she had a little fun on the dance floor."

Meghan walked by as Rob was telling me this. She yelled at him and took a weak, off-target swing as he ran the other way.

"How was the party, Megs?"

"Um, I think I did something not good."

"Like what?"

"Like make out with a guy on the dance floor."

"What happened?"

"I don't know. We were talking, then we were dancing. I had a couple drinks, I think. Then he started kissing me. And I kissed him back. Then I was like, 'This isn't good,' and I told Kristen we needed to leave. Everyone on the floor was standing to the side laughing at me." She shook her head. "I don't know why I'm telling you this. I'm going to bed."

"Come by tomorrow morning when you get up, if you remember."

"I'm not that bad, I'll remember." She said it arrogantly. The next morning, she did stop by. She looked ashamed and unsure.

"You wanted to see me?" she said uneasily.

"Yeah, dude, what's up with the recent drinking binge?"

"I thought you were cool about drinking?"

"I am, but I get the feeling you're doing it for the wrong reasons."

"What's a good reason to drink?"

"I suppose there's no good reason, but there are acceptable reasons. Like to have fun, be social, blow off steam. I get the feeling with you, it's to forget everything, which is never good. Because it's dangerous, you don't know how far you'll go. You never drank during the first semester. As a matter of fact, you hated it. Every time someone came back drunk, you'd thumb your nose at them and talk about how irresponsible it was. Now that irresponsible person is you."

Meghan couldn't think of a good response to this. She decided to stop standing in the doorway and found a place on my futon. After a moment of thought, she slouched over and started talking.

"I don't know what I'm supposed to be doing. Who's to say what's right and wrong? I mean, I'm not. And it was stupid of me to judge people for drinking just like it's stupid of me to drink now, but I don't know what else to do. It does take my mind off of things for a while."

"What are you trying to take your mind off?"

"Rick. You know that, don't ask stupid questions. I knew things would never be the same, but I think I hoped they would be. In the back of my mind I hoped. Rick is a huge part of my life, he will never go away. He's why I listen to REM, why I love reading Steinbeck, why I became a debater. The only thing he didn't affect was my soccer, and even when I play soccer, I think about how he used to come to my games. It seems so childish, I know it is, but I just can't get used to the change. I lie awake at night and think about it sometimes. And then I can't sleep, or I think too much. I wonder how much of it was my fault."

"I think you put too much pressure and blame on yourself. I know it's hard to just stop thinking about that stuff, but the drinking isn't going to do anything. It'll make you feel worse, and sometimes it'll make you do stuff you regret, like last night. What if something more had happened?"

She knew what I was implying. "Andy, come on, it's me. I'm not going to do anything more with a guy."

"Well three weeks ago, I wouldn't have thought you would be drinking every weekend. And I wouldn't have thought you, the girl who calls herself asexual, would be making out with a frat guy you didn't know in public."

She contemplated this and nodded.

"I know," she agreed. "I'm just not sure what to do."

"I think at this point we can't sugarcoat it anymore. Rick is not going to be close to you, at least not for a while. But you don't need to cut him off. You should remember him, not resent him. It starts with meeting new people, forming new relationships and stuff."

"I don't know how."

"Neither do I. If I did, I'd tell you. But I think you'll figure it out once you stop hiding what's bothering you and start trying to make it go away."

Meghan's silence was her way of agreeing with me. She had too much pride to admit to her mistakes, but she knew they had been made. Our conversation ended there. Meghan left my room and after that, we never talked about alcohol again. Of course we talked about Rick still, but it happened less and less. Meghan did stop drinking for the most part, but she also opened her eyes to other viewpoints. She stopped looking down on certain people, she stopped writing off everyone who did something she disagreed with. She continued to casually drink with friends once in a while. And because of all this, the close friends she had at college became closer. I think that really helped her. She found that she could have an understanding with someone besides just Rick. Alcohol wasn't the answer for Meghan, but in this case, it helped her figure out the problem.

ာ၈

I stayed in close contact with Elaine throughout the second semester, for a couple of reasons. One, we checked in with each other about Kate, and two, Elaine was going through her own tough times. The end of the first semester was rough for Elaine, and the beginning of the second wasn't looking much brighter. After she was fired, she went into a state of depression. She was constantly second-guessing herself, wanting to transfer, hating everyone around her. One afternoon back in November, I'd gotten a phone call from Jimmy, my CA. Jimmy and Elaine were very close, and it was probably Jimmy who helped Elaine, more than anyone else, get through her difficult times. He was with Elaine when he called me.

"Andy, I'm in Elaine's room right now. Why don't you come join us?"

"Um, I'm sort of busy right now." In reality, I just didn't feel like making the trip over to Kensington Gardens at that moment.

"Actually, Andy, you should really come visit us over here at Elaine's."

His tone was forceful. I knew something was up and I told him I'd be right over. Five minutes later, I arrived breathless outside of her room. Her door was open so I walked right in. Elaine was sitting on her bed, a goofy smile on her face. She was clutching a large stuffed elephant and waved at me as I entered. Jimmy was standing a few feet away. He was clearly frustrated and worried. His face was red. It was the only time I have ever seen Jimmy's face red. He's one of the most patient and understanding people I have ever met. Seeing him like that scared me.

"Andy, Elaine and I were just talking. I'm glad you came." He spoke tentatively and motioned with his hand for me to come closer. I moved to stand beside him.

"What's up, Elaine?" I asked.

"Nothing, Andyman. I just suck at life and I can't do anything right. And I want to leave Pittsburgh and never come back again. I hate it here, I hate the weather, I hate the people."

"You've got a lot of friends here, Elaine, let's be serious."

Jimmy nudged me. I looked at him and his eyes darted to the side, instructing me to be more observant. I snuck a peek behind his back and saw that he was clutching something in his hand. Something small and white, maybe plastic. I quickly looked away so Elaine wouldn't be suspicious, but I had a feeling she knew anyway.

"Nope, I don't think so. Everyone here I know thinks less of me now. I don't feel like going to a school that doesn't appreciate me."

While she spoke, I took another look behind Jimmy's back and realized what he was holding. It was a small plastic bottle, labeled Advil. Elaine was threatening to take the whole thing, I knew without asking. I don't know if she actually ever would. In fact, I'm pretty sure she wouldn't. But she had threatened Jimmy with it, and you can't take a matter like that lightly.

Jimmy seemed satisfied that I had seen the Advil. When Elaine stood up to open her refrigerator, he motioned for me to leave the room again.

"Well, Elaine, I'll let you guys talk. I don't want to interrupt anything. I'll see you later."

Elaine was well-aware that Jimmy had purposely called me over so I would know what was going on. I'd made the trip to his room in New House (which merely required walking down a single flight of stairs) many times to ask how Elaine was doing. And each time, Jimmy would tell me I didn't need to worry. It frustrated me that he didn't tell me more, but it was a confidentiality issue, and I respected Jimmy for showing a lot of maturity.

I didn't talk to Elaine much after that until our problem with Kate started. When the second semester rolled around, I asked Elaine about it one day. We were sitting in the on-campus coffeehouse, talking about ourselves instead of Kate for once. Elaine was talking my ear off, as usual, about her bad day, her untrusting friends, and her extracurriculars.

"Hey," I said, "I know I never brought this up before, but what ever happened last semester with the, um, the time I came over to your room? When Jimmy was there." I would have felt awkward mentioning the pills before she did, but I didn't have to wait long.

"You mean the Advil thing?"

"Um, yeah."

"I guess I never told you about that in detail. So yeah, Jimmy took away my Advil because he thought I was going to overdose." She said it casually, shaking her head as if she couldn't believe anyone would think that. "Like I'm going to kill myself."

"I'm sure he was just worried, dude. I'm sure he didn't take it away for no reason."

"Well, I jokingly threatened I would do it, but I wasn't really going to."

Elaine was talking about the subject nonchalantly, and I didn't feel like making the conversation more serious than it was. I was just glad she was talking about it at all.

"So what happened after that?"

"He made a deal with me. He said he'd give me back my Advil if I started going to counseling. I didn't really need my Advil. I just wanted it back on principle, 'cause it's mine, you know? So I argued with him for a while and finally I gave in. I told him I'd start going to counseling but he couldn't tell anybody, I didn't want it getting out."

It suddenly became clear to me why Jimmy never said anything more about Elaine than, "She's fine."

"How did that go?" I asked curiously.

"I'm actually still going. But I think I'm going to stop. I really hate it sometimes. The counselors over there are dumb. They have no freaking clue what's going on. I'm like, 'You've got the degree, help me.'"

"So why are you still going?"

"I don't even know. I guess I thought it was helping initially, but then it turned out it wasn't. They don't really tell me anything of substance."

I knew that for each time Elaine wanted to quit, there was likely another time when she didn't know how she ever survived without counseling. She was still going, which made me think it was really helping her. If she didn't want to go, Elaine is the kind of person who would have just stopped going.

"I've been talking to Ryan a lot, too," she said. "I'm going to apply to be an RA again next year."

"Do you think that's a good idea?"

"I wasn't sure at first, but I talked about it with Ryan. I think I've really figured out some of the things that were bothering me earlier in the year. And I learned my lesson. I think I deserve another chance."

Whether or not she deserved another chance, I don't know. But she certainly had improved since she was fired. After the initial shock, when she threatened to down a bottle of painkillers and transfer, she settled down. She got involved in more school activities and focused on getting her own life back in order. And of course, she helped me out on the floor, especially with Kate. But the real turnaround seemed to start when she began talking to people like Ryan and her counselor. For Elaine, maybe all she needed was an authority figure. Someone who wouldn't sugarcoat anything or take her occasional bullshit, someone who would be firm and realistic with her.

"That's cool," I told her. "Good luck with that. I think you were a great RA, seriously. You helped make our floor what it is today. And it's unfortunate what happened. If they do give you a second chance, I think that says a lot about what they think of you."

"I'm a little nervous about it, but there's not much I can do right now."

"Yeah. Okay, I have to go to class. I have an exam in economic analysis."

"Oh, fun. Good luck, Andyman."

I walked away from the table knowing that Elaine still had a lot of personal issues to work out. What her counselor decided was at the root of her problems, I don't know, but at least Elaine was admitting the problems were there. The closed-mindedness and wavering self-confidence were still there, but not as much as before. As Elaine was discovering more about herself, she was closing down the defense mechanisms in her mind and coming to terms with her conscience. Maybe losing her job was the best thing that could have happened to her.

The changes were not limited to Kate, Meghan, and Elaine, though. It seemed like everyone was doing something different in the new semester. Eric, whose opinions often came back to haunt him, was one of the guys who had made fun of fraternities during the first semester. Now he was thinking about joining one. Micah was still that random kid who walked around in his boxers, the kid who no one took too seriously. They had both made a few friends at one particular fraternity. Eric knew a few of the hockey players, and Micah knew a couple of the guys on the club baseball team. And despite what they said, both of them struck me as fraternity-type guys in many ways. They liked to party, liked girls, and liked to be cool. Whatever cool means. But they also had attributes that didn't coincide with the "frat guy" stereotype at all. They were both very smart. Eric studied harder than Micah did, but both of them strove to get good grades. It was their number one priority. And both of them were really nice guys. They could both be jerks sometimes, but for the most part, I could count on Eric and Micah to take care of business. And I knew I could count on Eric to protect the floor. Once during the first semester, Roger had knocked on my door at around 3 a.m. It was a Saturday night, and I was just falling asleep. I came to the door, groggy and irritable.

"What do you want?"

"Sorry to wake you up, Andy, but there's some random dude in our lounge trying to pick a fight. He's really wasted."

I threw on my glasses and grabbed my keycard. When I entered the lounge, about ten people were standing in a circle around two guys. One of them was a large, shirtless male wearing a sombrero. I could smell the alcohol on his breath, even from several feet away. The other one was Eric. Eric, who was completely sober, also had his shirt off, probably because he was about to sleep. The two of them were having a heated exchange when I came in.

"Dude, I'm not going to try to pick a fight with a whole floor," said the sombrero man.

Eric laughed. "Clearly that's exactly what you're doing. Just fucking leave and there won't be any problems."

"I can be here if I want to, man."

"But we don't want you here." He was frustrated. His face was a furious red, and I could tell he was about to explode. "You're annoying and disturbing everyone. So just get the fuck out before I do something I regret." The way Eric said it was out of some Western movie. For a moment, I admired Eric's fearlessness and tenacity. Then I realized I didn't want any blood on the carpet. I intervened, my heart pounding, rehearsing what to say to the guy.

"Is there a problem man? I'm Andy, I'm the RA." I extended my hand to the guy in the sombrero. He immediately backed off.

"No, dude, there's no problem. I'm leaving, I'm leaving. We're cool."

Apparently the thought of an authority figure scared him off. As the guy walked away, Eric was still fuming. I looked at him but didn't say anything. He spoke first.

"That guy was a fucking douche bag."

"Is everything cool now?"

"Yeah, everything's cool. He just came in here wasted, saying he was going to kick everyone's ass. I have no idea what his problem was."

"Well, thanks for protecting the floor. I just don't want anyone getting hurt."

"Oh, I know, man. It's cool. I'm just not going to let some random guy come up here and mess with us. Who the fuck did he think he was?"

After that, I respected Eric a great deal, even if his temper got the best of him sometimes.

Micah, on the other hand, was just one of those guys you tell your parents stories about. He was known for making drunk phone calls and stupid, non-politically correct comments. Both he and Eric ended up joining the fraternity they had been considering. I still couldn't get over the fact that they were going to be in a fraternity. I stopped them one evening before they headed over to their pledge night celebration.

"Hey, guys, I see you decided to pledge."

"Yeah, we thought about it for a while," said Eric. "I mean, I had a tough time making a decision. I'm not exactly a frat guy, but it has a lot of benefits. I'll be able to be around my good friends here a lot more now. Plus, next year I can live in the house and have a car on campus, which I wouldn't be able to do any other way. And there's the benefit of being an alumni. The big reason for me was having those kinds of connections when I need to find a job."

"Yeah, same with me," said Micah. He was wearing a lime green suit. I tried to suppress a laugh. "I mean, I like drinking, and I like girls, and they're both at a fraternity, but they're also both at a lot of places. But I like the guys over there, and I like the idea of being part of a brotherhood. It'll be fun." Micah shrugged his shoulders.

As they walked away, I thought about the other guys who had pledged during fall semester on the floor. Devon and Luke weren't the typical frat guys either. It came naturally to think of them as frat guys now, because for most of the time I had known them, they belonged to a fraternity. But both Devon and Luke were caring, thoughtful, smart, selfless individuals. Even Gary decided to join a fraternity when he got back. It took me until my fourth semester at college to overcome my bias about frat guys. And it was overcome by taking the time to get to know some of them. If nothing else, I knew the guys on my floor would help to break down those stereotypes that existed.

≫∞≪

Everywhere I looked, I saw more changes taking place. I ran into Aaron at the University Center one day and sat down with him to eat. I used to see

Aaron several times each day during the first semester, but since the start of the spring term, I rarely saw him around the dorm. Aaron was munching on a slice of cheese pizza, and I opened up the mustard dipping sauce for my pretzel while I took my seat. The biggest change in Aaron was his physical appearance. He had come to school with flowing hair, almost a foot long. He didn't look scruffy, just unrefined. But when it got long enough, he donated all of his hair to charity.

"That's the whole reason I grew it out," he said. "Otherwise I couldn't stand the long hair." When he did get rid of it, he shaved his head bald. That was several weeks ago, and now his hair had grown back to a normal length. Clean-shaven, well-groomed, and bursting with a new sense of enthusiasm, this Aaron was a lot different than the Aaron I'd met during Orientation.

"Hey, man, I haven't seen you around at all lately," I said to him.

"Yeah, I've been doing a lot of stuff. See, I figure I've gotten to know a lot of people on the floor and I've made a lot of good friends. So this semester, I've been trying to get off the floor and do more stuff around campus. Meet other people in different groups."

"What kinds of groups have you been getting involved in?'

"Crew, for one. That's taken up a lot of my time. With workouts, practice, and meetings, I'm all over the place."

"How did I not know you were on crew?"

"Well, you wouldn't know unless I told you. I get up for it at 5 a.m. each morning when no one else is around. And I go to bed really early since I have to get up. That's why I'm not on the floor as much anymore. But I still try to hang out sometimes."

"Yeah, that makes sense."

"Ben and Gregory are doing it with me, so we all go together and it's not so bad. Plus I'm helping out with the chemistry student advisory council. Let's see... Oh yeah, and I've been doing a lot more stuff with Hillel. I'm being a good Jew this semester."

"That's crazy, man. I didn't realize you were doing so much stuff."

"Yeah, I sort of kept it to myself. I'm not big on telling the whole world what I'm up to. If you ask I'll tell you, but I won't be the guy telling everyone I see what's going on in my life."

"I'm the same way, man. I respect that."

As Aaron chewed on his crust, I thought about his evolution throughout the year. He started off as a slightly nerdy and immature kid who had no clue what to expect at college. But instead of hiding in his room, he treated Ashford like a coloring book. He scribbled all over the place, learned what worked and what didn't. All in order to find his niche in the community. He was no longer the guy who came to every floor event. He was now the guy planning some of those events, setting up soccer teams for tournaments, organizing group trips to baseball games. I was proud of him, sitting there watching him eat. It felt so weird. I was like a father watching my son grow up, except Aaron was only a year younger than me. But that's how I felt sometimes, like a proud parent. And once in a while, I was appreciated like a parent, too. Those were the moments that made it all worthwhile.

ৡৢ∂৶

Back at the dorm, poker continued to be all the rage. Its popularity never changed, but the seriousness with which they played did. There were still small money games on the floor almost every night. And when I say small money, I mean small. Most of the time, we played with a dollar, so each person got twenty chips worth a nickel each. Even I played with them once in a while. But when the "better" players started getting tired of making just a couple dollars each game, they turned to a different platform: the internet.

The domino effect was in full swing on New House 5 when it came to internet poker. Avery, MinYoung, and Ben were the first to join. All of them were smart, cautious players. And all of them made money. Not a few dollars, but a lot of money. Avery and Ben pulled in almost one hundred dollars on some days. MinYoung had made over a thousand bucks in a month. And of course, their success attracted the attention of the other poker players on the floor. When I walked into the lounge one afternoon, Ben and Taylor were huddled around a laptop on the couch.

"You playing some poker, Ben?"

"You know it, man. I'm doing good today. Just won a tournament for fifty bucks."

I shook my head and looked at Taylor. "This kid is nuts."

Taylor stared intently at the computer screen. "I know. I think I'm going to start playing online soon. I'm a business major at Ashford. I should be able to make a little money on this. Ben is showing me the basics."

Getting into online poker is a simple process. You deposit a certain amount of money into an account using a credit card. Then, depending on which website you use, you just download the software and open up the program. It's a three-dimensional interactive "poker table" on your computer screen, with all sorts of controls and buttons. One wrong click of the mouse and you could be a thousand dollars in the hole. It was a scary thought.

"Just be careful," I said. "I would never play poker on the internet. Too dangerous. It wouldn't feel like real money to me, and I don't like that."

Still focused on his game, Ben grinned ear to ear. "It's a little tense sometimes, but you get used to it. YES!" Ben had just made a big gain, and that seemed to be the final straw for Taylor.

He jumped up excitedly. "Okay, I'm going to sign up. Let's make some money." He rubbed his hands together and walked away. This was an epidemic I couldn't control at all, but I knew that eventually it was going to put someone in a very bad position.

A handful of guys signed up to play online and fared horribly. Chad lost fifty dollars in a matter of ten minutes, and Aaron accidentally called a twenty-dollar raise with a pair of threes. These and a few other similar mistakes seemed to curtail the online poker interest. The buzz died down, and soon enough, it was back to just Ben, Avery, and MinYoung, all of whom knew what they were doing. At least, I thought it was just down to them. Then Ben stopped by my room with a concerned look on his face and sat down on my futon. He picked up a plastic football and threw it up and down in the air. As he tossed it to himself, he said, "So you know how Taylor started playing poker online a couple weeks ago?"

"Yeah, how's he doing?"

"Not too well. In fact, he's down several hundred dollars."

"Several hundred?" I couldn't believe it. I had walked by when Taylor was playing poker online before. I asked him how it was going and he always said, "Alright. I'm down a little today but I'm okay overall," or something like that.

"Yeah. I'm not sure how he lost the first couple hundred, but after that, he started playing recklessly to make up his losses. We didn't know about it until a few days ago. MinYoung and I just changed his password so he can't play. Have you noticed he's never out on the floor at all? He doesn't play for real anymore either. He just sits in his room and plays online poker because he needs to make up his losses. I don't even think he does work anymore."

"Oh geeze. What is he thinking?"

"I have no idea. But I'm pretty sure he just signed up for a different website now that we changed his password on the one he normally uses. I don't know what to do. He won't listen to us. When we knock on the door, if he knows it's us, he'll just ignore us. Or he'll take his laptop somewhere else on campus and play where we can't find him. He's becoming an addict."

Ben tossed the football into my crate of sporting equipment. "I just wanted to let you know, because we may tell him to come talk to you if nothing else works. I don't want him to be, like, ten grand in the hole, you know? Although at this rate, he might be. I'm up a few hundred overall, but I'm going to stop playing. For a while at least. Because what happened to Taylor scares me. I don't want to end up like that."

"That's probably a good call, man. Thanks for letting me know."

Later that day, Taylor stopped by. Apparently nothing else Ben or MinYoung could do worked. Taylor walked into my room looking upset and dejected. He wasn't wearing his normal navy blue cap, and his curly blonde hair hung messily off his head. Without his hat on, Taylor looked naked, vulnerable. It reminded me of the first time I'd talked to him, during the first semester. Ironically, it was poker that had integrated him into the floor to begin with, and it was poker that was alienating him from the floor now.

"Hey, Taylor, what's going on, man?"

"Oh, you know what's going on." He laughed. "Andy, I feel like an idiot, but I've definitely got a gambling problem."

"How much have you lost?"

"About six hundred. It's money I had, I didn't borrow it. But now it's gone, and I'm practically broke."

"Are you going to stop?"

"I want to, but I don't feel like I can. You know, each time I sit down at my computer, I think, 'If I take one big hand, it'll be good.' Then I lose more." He sighed and scratched his head with both hands.

"You just have to stop, man. Cut your losses now and learn from it. All you're going to do is lose more."

"I guess I have no other choice. Aw man, I didn't think it would go this far. I was just trying to make a few bucks."

"I think we forget sometimes that poker is a game, it's supposed to be fun. When we start thinking about it in a business-like fashion, it gets dangerous, 'cause when it comes down to it, it's still just a game of chance."

"It really is." He sighed. "Okay, I'm going to stop. I'm really going to. Ben and MinYoung kept telling me to, but they didn't give me a reason. Avery talked to me about it earlier too. He said it's not worth it to lose this much. And you're right, I've just got to cut my losses."

I nodded. "It seems like you're getting cut off from everything. Classes, friends, your social life. You can't let it take over like this."

"Shit, I know. Okay, I have to go. Thanks. This is going to be rough."

He left abruptly. I didn't see him again for the next few days. I worried that he crumbled and gave in to playing again, but when I did see him, he was all smiles. It turned out he took a break from everything. He didn't use his laptop and just hung out with his friends in another dorm, doing homework and watching television. It refreshed him. Taylor was a new man, and I could tell. It had cost him six hundred dollars, but Taylor realized that he needed to stop before things got any worse. We'd all told him to stop, but he had to figure it out for himself. He was just lucky it only took him six hundred dollars to learn instead of six thousand.

My residents weren't the only ones changing. Things were different for me too, particularly with my friendships on the floor. I was becoming a lot closer to Kim, for one thing. She was one of the most active people on the floor during the first semester, aiding in all the practical jokes and becoming close friends with a lot of my residents. Kim was able to connect with a lot of people. She went to parties, but didn't drink. She was generous and easygoing. Because of her personality, I got along with her very well. I never talked to her too much during the first semester because, well, she didn't really need me. Like Rob, she was almost an assistant RA. But during the second term, we found a lot more common interests. She introduced me to a lot of music I had never heard of, and Rob and I reinvigorated her interest in Houston sports. She became one of the guys to a certain extent. From that point on, I looked at Kim like one of my close friends who I never had to worry about upsetting or offending. It was a good feeling. Kim was also applying to become an RA, which gave us a lot to talk about. I explained to her what I thought an RA should do; she told me why she wanted to do it. In the coming weeks, I would talk to Kim a lot more about the RA process, and I would learn a lot more about her.

On the opposite end of the spectrum, I found myself drifting away from Sam. While we had never been really close during the first semester, we had talked several times about Sam's life and perspectives. He was an eternal pessimist, and he was perfectly content that way. "I'll never be happy, no matter what I get or do. Miserable is my way of life," he once told me. We drifted apart for two reasons. One, Sam was more comfortable talking to girls about his problems. All his friends back home in Michigan had been girls, and he talked a lot to Elyse and Elaine at school. It was nothing personal against me, just a preference he had. I respected that. Two, I just became frustrated with his constant moping and cynicism. Sam was a Dean's List caliber student, a good-looking guy, and had a great sense of humor. But after the talks we had, I could tell he just didn't want to be happy. He claimed to make efforts, but from what I could see, Sam was happy feeling sorry for himself.

"Sometimes I feel like the whole world is out to get me," he told me one day when we were walking across campus. "I know it sounds stupid, and I know it's not true, but it just feels that way sometimes. Whatever, I don't even care. I'll always be depressed."

To me, Sam was a great kid. But he was one of those people that still didn't get it, someone who was still learning about his place in the world. He had reasons to be frustrated, like his inability to decide on a career path. But he didn't see that a lot of other people had the same issues. Sam didn't have the deep-rooted problems I saw in people like Kate. He just had a negative attitude that he was working to overcome. Sam and I still talked, but we didn't become good friends until much later in the semester when he began to change his attitude. We had similar personalities, just different ideas of how the world around us worked.

New House 5 grew and changed constantly. There were no pauses, nothing was static. And as much as I hated to see the changes, sometimes it was good. For all of us. Because change is part of life, and that's something I'm still learning, slowly but surely. Most of the changes were for the better, but even the ones that weren't taught us a lot about ourselves and about each other. The changes taking place were a product of New House 5 maturing as a group, and as individuals. I still don't like change, but New House 5 would have been a pretty boring place without it.

CONFLICT

I try to compromise
But that just makes me realize
That nothing in this world ever changes
It's only your perspective that does
- Another Day

Sometimes I remember New House 5 a little too idealistically. Then I remember the month of March. In March, New House 5 began to fall apart. It started small, then escalated. I watched in horror as unspoken fears led to messy confrontations, as developing rumors led to lengthy grudges. Over the next few weeks, we all uncovered the beast created by New House 5 and tried our best to tame it.

March came in like a lion. On the first Friday of the month, a bunch of the residents decided to hang out on the floor. Most Friday nights were quiet. Some people went to party, others went to see movies, others just slept early. But on this night, everyone chose to stay in. It was pretty cool to see everyone hanging out with each other when there were a lot of other options. A popular spot on nights like these was my room. I sat at my desk playing stupid computer games, chatting with the people who came and went. Rosalyn, Chad, Meghan, Elyse, and Kristen were in my room, sitting on the floor or the futon and talking about random stuff. Those times when we sat around and talked about nothing are some of my fondest memories of New House 5. There aren't a lot of people I feel comfortable talking to about nothing.

Rosalyn and Meghan were in a manic mood that evening. They sat on the futon, throwing pillows and yelling obscene things at each other. Elyse and I laughed all the while. Chad looked around confused, trying to figure out what was going on.

"Meghan, you're such a slut," yelled Rosalyn.

"Oh yeah, because I've hooked up with *so* many guys this year."

Meghan was comfortable saying this because everyone in the room knew it wasn't true. Under different circumstances, she might have ripped Rosalyn's head off, but this time, she just played along.

"At least I'm not the one who dates a black guy for, well, you know," Meghan sneered.

Rosalyn jumped up from her spot with a look of shock on her face.

"You bitch!" she screamed jokingly. She threw a pillow at Meghan's face. With her quick reflexes, Meghan deflected the pillow away and it hit Chad, who was sitting on the ground.

"Hey, hey, hey, now!" he said. "Let's chill out. And then have sex with me."

He laughed for a few seconds before he realized no one was going to join him. Elyse and I were having a side conversation about what her nickname should be.

"I'm really liking 'Reindeer' since your last name is Randolph. Elyse the Reindeer Randolph."

"People call me Randy, which is kind of cool, but I don't know about Reindeer."

Chad jumped into the conversation, mainly because he had nothing better to do. "I think it should be Reindeer. Watch."

Chad picked up the pillow that had just hit him. Lifting it over his head, assumingly to imitate antlers, he made a swift, poking motion with his head. In the process, he happened to hit Rosalyn square in the face.

"Oww! Chad, I'm going to kill you."

Amused and a little scared, Chad jumped up and bolted out of the room. Rosalyn, being in a frenzied mood, followed him. Meghan rolled her eyes.

"Oh Ros, stop flirting. Where are they going?" She jumped up and chased Rosalyn out of the room.

Elyse scratched her chin. "This could be interesting. Let's go check it out."

We followed their loud yells and ended up by the elevators. Meghan was standing to the side, laughing hysterically. Just outside the elevator, Rosalyn was wrestling Chad. Well, trying to. She had a firm grip on his leg and was writhing on the floor. Chad was standing up, laughing just as hard as Meghan. Then Rosalyn managed to remove one of Chad's shoes. She got up and ran the opposite way with it, and Chad took off after her. She came back around to the elevator with Chad nowhere in sight. She was still laughing and short of breath.

"Watch this." Rosalyn pressed the down button on the elevator. When it opened, she put the shoe inside it and pressed the button for the first floor before getting out. Chad was now coming around the corner and saw his shoe trapped inside the elevator. He arrived a second too late.

"You bitch! You fucking bitch! What if someone steals my shoe?" Everyone quieted down. We weren't sure if he was serious or not.

"It's on the first floor, Chad," Rosalyn said tentatively.

Chad scampered down the stairs to retrieve his shoe. Rosalyn looked offended. "Was he really upset?" We all shook our heads, not knowing the answer. We waited patiently for him to return. After a few minutes, the elevator opened up, revealing Chad, very red in the face, holding his shoe. He stepped out and came face to face with Rosalyn. She looked up at him. He was breathing hard, but we still thought he was joking around. We were mistaken.

"WHAT THE FUCK ARE YOU DOING? YOU DO NOT FUCK WITH MY SHIT! DO YOU UNDERSTAND ME? I DON'T FUCKING CARE IF IT'S JUST A SHOE, I WILL BEAT THE FUCK OUT OF YOU IF YOU EVER DO THIS AGAIN! DO YOU FUCKING UNDERSTAND ME?"

We all stood in shock. Chad raised his fist, as if he were about to punch Rosalyn across the face. Luckily, Melissa had arrived in time to grab his arm and lead him away, still fuming. I don't want to think about what would have happened if she hadn't gotten there. If Chad really hit Ros, we all may have gone crazy on him.

For a second, no one knew what to do. We had never seen Chad like that before. Rosalyn was standing in the same spot, panting, the smile wiped from her face. Tears were forming in her eyes. She walked slowly back to my room. We all followed her.

Rosalyn sat down, frowning and sniffling. We all sat down as well. No one said anything. Meghan was the first to break the silence.

"Are you okay, Rosalyn?"

"I'm fine. Let's talk about something. Anything." She said it calmly. It was our cue to forget what had just happened for the time being, but no one took the hint. We did start talking about something, but that something was Chad.

"That was totally inappropriate," said Elyse.

"Yeah, I'll talk to him about it later," I said.

"Don't talk to him about it," Rosalyn said. "There's no point. It's not going to stop him. I'm not going to feel comfortable around him anymore. People don't just fucking explode like that."

"Rosalyn, I'm sure he didn't mean it. It was a one-time thing." Meghan had a point: we had never seen him do anything like that before.

"How can you say that?" Rosalyn started getting upset. "You have no clue, no right to say that. We've known him for less than a year. What if it happens all the time but we've just never pissed him off before? He did that over a shoe. He almost hit me over a fucking shoe."

"Rosalyn, I'm not condoning what he did," Meghan said defensively. "I'm just saying there are different ways to look at it."

"Yeah," Elyse chimed in, "I think if you talk to him tomorrow when things have cooled off, it'll be okay."

"I think we're taking this a little too far. It was scary, but it's over now, and it won't happen again." My comment pushed Rosalyn over the edge.

"Taking it too far? You've never had to live with someone like that! I HAVE! None of you understand any of this, and I don't expect you to!" Within seconds, Rosalyn was bawling. She sprinted from my room. Meghan and Kristen looked at each other. They were Rosalyn's two best friends. Kristen stood up to follow her.

"I forgot about that," I said quietly.

"I think we all did. She can't compare everyone to her dad, though," said Meghan.

Elyse looked concerned. "Will she be okay?"

"Yeah, she just needs to be by herself tonight. I wouldn't talk to her until tomorrow."

Chad walked in the room. We all looked up at him, unsure of what to expect. He was smiling now. "Did she really just run out crying? She needs to chill out. I wasn't really going to hit her. Fucking A, man, we were just fooling around. She took my shoe."

"Yeah, man," I said, "but I'm not going to lie, that was pretty scary. We really thought you were going to hit her."

"Whatever, dude. I'll apologize to her, but this is ridiculous." Chad threw his hands up in disgust and walked away.

"If he had hit her, I would have killed him myself," Meghan said grimly. We all nodded in agreement.

"I think we should all go to bed," I said. "It's getting late."

"I agree, Andy. It's bedtime for Elyse." With that, she left for her room.

Meghan followed her out, but before she left, she turned around and said, "I would talk to her tomorrow morning. Don't worry about what you said, though. She was ready to blow up anyway."

I still felt horrible. I hadn't even thought about what triggered the extreme emotion in Rosalyn. I figured it was just the stress of nearly being punched by an angry guy. But it went deeper than that. The next morning, I knocked on Rosalyn's door. She opened up and said hi shyly. She let me in and closed the door. Her hair was a mess and her face looked tired. It was clear she hadn't gotten much sleep the previous night.

"What's up?"

"Hey, Ros, I just wanted to apologize for what I said last night."

"It's okay. It's not your fault. I shouldn't have flipped out." She spoke in a monotone voice, reciting an answer she had devised in her head.

"No, dude. We can't possibly understand what it's like for you to be in that situation. You had every right to be upset about it, even if we didn't understand why."

"No one could possibly understand. I will never feel comfortable around Chad again. Ever. It was like watching my Dad, and it scared the fuck out of me. That's how he was. He would be fine one minute, fooling around and being cool. Then something small would happen and he'd just flip out. He'd hit, he'd throw shit… Oh my God, Andy, I can't even explain it. When Chad was standing over me, I saw my dad. I saw him hitting me and throwing me against the wall."

The tears were forming in her eyes again. She tried to wipe them away.

"God, I always cry when I'm around you. It's okay, Andy, really. I was just upset when everyone said not to worry about it, that he didn't mean it. They never mean it. But it still happens, and that's unacceptable."

"Yeah. I can promise that I'll be more sensitive about it."

She laughed. "Thanks. And Chad apologized, too, for what it's worth. It did nothing for me, but I'm sure you told him to. My dad apologized every time, too. Every single time."

That was the end of our conversation. Putting yourself in the other person's shoes isn't always easy, nor is it always fun. None of us could really understand what Rosalyn felt. We could only imagine, and be happy we weren't in the same position. Rosalyn and Chad still talked once in a while, but Rosalyn always tensed up whenever Chad was around. She couldn't be herself around him. That made me angry.

ৡৢৢৣ

The stronger personalities on the floor were bound to clash at some point—clearly it had already started—but the problem really came to a head when the residents of New House 5 started thinking about where they would live the next year. Since New House was a freshman-only dorm, none of them could stay in their current rooms. That meant they would all be splitting up to different parts of campus. Just the thought of that, though it was still several months away, scared everyone. To try keeping a large group of the floor together, a few of the girls looked into Special Interest Housing. SIH was an opportunity for a group of eight people to live together in a dorm on campus in exchange for doing a community service project. Since many of the girls liked volunteering anyway, they thought it would be a great idea to apply for SIH and stay together.

The problem arose when the girls realized that only eight people could be a part of it, and twice that many wanted to be involved. Meghan and Rosalyn initially had the idea. They filled out the forms and applications, submitted them, and attended the mandatory meeting. They came back on a Tuesday afternoon from the meeting, looking flustered. Rosalyn asked me to follow them into the study room. When we sat down, they both wore looks of concern.

"So here's the problem," Meghan explained. "Only eight people can be in Special Interest Housing. Fifteen girls on the floor want to do it. I don't want to hurt people's feelings, especially since we might not even get the housing because a lot of groups are applying. But they need a definite list of names by next week, and we wouldn't know if we got it for another month. How do we figure out who gets to be in it and who doesn't?"

Rosalyn expressed her concern as well. "Like, should we do an interview? That would just feel so awkward, and everyone would get upset. But then again, no matter how we do it, people will be upset. If we do an interview, it will be me and Meghan interviewing people, and everyone will think that we're trying to take over. If we pick randomly, people will complain that we didn't choose based on who would contribute most to a community project or to helping out around the dorm. There's no good way to do it. We're all friends, and some people are going to get hurt. We don't want that."

I folded my hands on the table and sighed. "It sounds like there's no way around it. If you guys really want to do this, you have to suck it up and figure out how to choose. You are the two who took the initiative to do this, so it's your call."

"But we were just the first people to print out the application," said Meghan. "All the girls talked about it. Alicia even started filling out the forms, but then she found out we were too and decided to let us take care of that part." She sighed. "I wish we'd let Alicia fill them out. Then we wouldn't have to be making this decision."

"Well, what's wrong with a random drawing?"

"We want people in the house who have good ideas about what to do for our community project," said Meghan. "We want to make sure the girls in it aren't just in it to be with their friends and mooch off us. We want to make sure they'll contribute in a lot of ways."

"If that's what you want, then it sounds like you have to do some sort of interview process. That seems kind of weird and it might upset some people, but these are the problems that come with something like this. People are going to get left out."

"Yeah, we were leaning towards that," said Rosalyn. "Would you help us do interviews?"

"Sure. But like I said, the girls are going to have to respect that you are both taking the initiative and going to meetings and stuff. It's your decision, and if they say you didn't give them a chance to help, you can say they didn't offer. Which I'm assuming is true. It's not a fun thing."

"Well, I'm going to go tell everyone who wanted to do it what's going to happen," said Rosalyn. "I guess we'll do interviews today, if you have time, Andy. This feels so awkward. I have a bad feeling about this."

Meghan gathered up the girls and had them all sign up for a ten-minute time slot. The interviews would take place in the study room. Rosalyn,

Meghan, and I planned on asking each girl a few simple questions: Why did they want to be part of the housing? What would they contribute to it? When the interviews started, everyone in the room was uneasy. The first person interviewed was Shannon. She was just as nervous as Rosalyn, Meghan, and myself, and I began to think maybe this interview process wasn't the best idea after all. But it was too late now. It took over two hours to go through each girl. Shannon, Julie, Kristen, Kate, Elyse, Hillary, Val, Alicia, Melissa, and a handful of other girls all wanted to stay with the group. When the interviews had ended, the three of us sat down in my room to talk about them.

"This sucks. I have no idea what to do." Rosalyn buried her face in a pillow.

"Neither do I," said Meghan. "How do we choose between our friends? Some of them we just really like and we know we would enjoy living with. But some of the other girls, like Shannon and Julie, just had really great ideas about what we could do for the volunteering and they seemed really enthusiastic about it. This is horrible."

"Well, you've got a few days to think about it," I reassured them. "Why don't both of you take a break for tonight and not worry about it. You can make the decisions tomorrow or something."

"We're going to take a break," said Meghan, "but there's no way we're not going to think about it."

"Ugh, I don't want to go out there and face the girls." Rosalyn looked disgusted. "They probably hate us right now. This whole idea was stupid. But I really want to do it. Why are things so difficult?"

When they left my room, I figured they were overreacting. While the girls may not have loved the idea of being interviewed by Meghan and Rosalyn, I figured they would understand that it was the only choice. I was wrong. Very wrong. A few hours later, Rosalyn came into my room and slammed the door behind her.

"Andy, I can't take this. I don't want to do this Special Interest Housing anymore. Seriously. We shouldn't have done interviews. I didn't want to, it was Meghan. She wanted to be all mechanical about it and stuff. We hurt so many people's feelings just by interviewing them. Meghan can deal with people being mad at her, but I can't. I really don't want to do this anymore."

"Whoa, whoa, whoa. What happened?"

"Every single girl we 'interviewed' has said something to me in the last two hours. Kate said she didn't agree with Meghan and I making the decisions, Julie said she didn't think it was appropriate to do an interview of friends, Hillary thinks the whole process is being blown out of proportion, Elyse thinks it's going to rip people apart. It's too much hassle. It's not worth it. It's going to cause so many problems. We have to live with these people for another two months, but at this rate, we won't be able to."

"Okay, maybe interviewing wasn't the best idea. But based on what you guys wanted to do with the housing, it was the only option."

"I would have been happy picking straws or something." She opened the door and peeked outside before she left. "I don't know what will end up happening," she said nervously. "I'm sure Meghan will talk to you about it later, though. It's going to be a long night."

The clash came later that evening, between two people I wouldn't have expected. At around midnight, I heard loud yelling coming from the girls' side, so I walked over to see what was going on. When I turned the corner, I froze. Standing in the hallway, less than a foot away from each other, were Alicia and Meghan. They weren't screaming, but their voices were loud enough to hear across the hall. Alicia appeared angrier. Meghan was trying to keep her composure, responding to each remark by Alicia strongly but with a calm tone. Apparently it had been going on for some time because a crowd had already formed around them. When Alicia saw me approaching, she backed down. Meghan turned around and, seeing me there, stepped away as well. The crowd dissipated. Alicia returned to her room. Meghan was left standing in the middle of the hallway, stunned. I tapped her on the shoulder.

"Are you okay?"

She stared at me blankly. "I'm going to sit in your room."

I followed her in. "What happened?"

"Alicia can't deal with rejection, that's what happened." She spoke coldly, bitterly. "She confronted me and said I had no right to be interviewing people. I told her that since Rosalyn and I did all the work for it, we were going to decide who got picked. She said she would have done it if someone asked her. I told her no one asked us. Then she just blew up. She started yelling at me. She called me every name in the book. She said I was ruthless, mechanical, uncaring, and arrogant. She said I was going on a power trip and trying to be manipulative.

"I just stood there and took it. I can't yell at people. I don't know how to. I was scared. I defended myself by trying to be rational with her, but it wasn't working. I can't take being yelled at, Andy. I just can't take it." She looked up at me timidly. "Andy, I don't want to lose friends because of this, but I really want to do it. Not just to be with my friends, but to do the whole community and service thing. Is it worth it, though?"

"That's your call, dude. I can't make that decision for you."

She looked away, disappointed. "I'm going to apologize to her tomorrow. And I'm sure she will to me too. She was just being irrational because she can't handle the idea of being rejected by her friends. I remember her crying for hours one night when some guy at a fraternity rejected her. She's used to getting everything she wants, so she becomes really defensive when that's in danger. But I guess I am being power hungry about it. I want this done a certain way and I'm going to do whatever it takes to achieve that, even if it means hurting some feelings. We're all too scared about offending other people sometimes. You just have to fucking deal with it."

Meghan was contradicting herself. First she didn't want to lose friends and she couldn't stand being yelled at. Then she decided losing friends was part of the process. It was hard to tell which version was the real Meghan, and which was the Meghan she wanted herself to be. I think she was afraid to have strong feelings for people, especially after what happened with Rick. Maybe she was trying to make herself not worry about her emotions. Who knows. But telling yourself how to feel never works.

Once Meghan had finished venting, she picked herself up. "This is going to suck. I'm not even sure if we're going to go through with the application process. And I know Alicia and I are never going to be the same again. This is so stupid."

The girls ended up deciding to not submit the names and their quest for Special Interest Housing died. I think it relieved everyone, and though it took some time, most of the girls got over it. They understood that Rosalyn and Meghan had to make a decision, and they respected the two girls for realizing their mistake. Rosalyn and Meghan learned that it wasn't worth having to choose between friends, that it wasn't worth tearing apart the floor. I never said it to them, but I agreed. Even if everyone ended up in different dorms the next year, it's only a short walk to get from one end of campus to the other anyway.

As for Alicia and Meghan, they both realized their irrationalities and mistakes. They apologized, but it was purely political. They were never close again, simply because they were too similar. And it was all because of an idea that didn't even happen.

The whole episode made me realize that when people are comfortable being around each other, they tend to be comfortable telling each other how they really feel. Even if how they really feel isn't always rational or intelligent. Even if how they really feel could dissolve friendships. I watched in disgust as these things happened, and there was nothing I could do but hope everything would work out in the end.

Another problem was brewing on New House 5, one I didn't see coming until it smacked me right in the face. With as much actual floor-cest as there was, I forgot that there were probably also a lot of potential relationships that never panned out. Rob and Kim hung out a lot. During the second semester, I saw them together every day. Eating, studying, talking. As I said before, they were similar, so their friendship made sense. They were both selfless, caring individuals with a unique sense of humor. They were both easygoing people who everyone on the floor got along with. And they were both single. Occasionally they'd come up in floor gossip circles, but no more than any other two people who were good friends. However, as the semester progressed, it definitely seemed to me like there was more there. I made a note to keep an eye on that. I didn't know if Rob liked Kim or not, but it definitely looked that way to a discerning eye. Either way, this wasn't the actual problem. The problem came later on, when the Rob and Kim issue became a triangle. Like I said, I never saw it coming, because initially it just seemed like a simple college crush to me. But in reality, it was the beginning of one more conflict that would end up having a big impact on New House 5.

All these minor conflicts added up to a community that was heading downhill. Many of the bonds and ties that were created during the first few months turned out to be weaker than we all thought. The fights, the arguments, the grudges, they all led to tension on the floor. The community I had watched form was tearing itself apart. It was frustrating to see it happening, and it was frustrating that there was nothing I could do about it.

But it's part of the process. Not everyone will be close. Some personalities will clash, some conflicts will occur. New House 5 was definitely heading in the wrong direction, but the strong sense of community was still there. Yes, the community itself was crumbling on its foundations, and it would only get worse before it got better. I just hoped it would get better eventually.

A NEW FRIEND

The waiting makes her dizzy
While her life it keeps her busy
- November

     Resident Assistant selection for the next year took place in March. It was a stressful time for everyone involved, myself included. A handful of my residents were applying to be RAs, and I was hoping that at least a few of them would get a position. It made me feel good that whatever I had done made them think being an RA was cool, and if they were accepted, there would be a certain sense of pride in knowing a few of my residents turned into RAs themselves. I had already decided to return as an RA for the next year but I wasn't too worried about that. I was much more anxious for the residents on my floor, and they were much more anxious than I was.

     Four of the boys ended up applying. Roger, Chad, Ben, and Tim. They were all good guys, really nice and really smart, but I had a tough time envisioning any of them as an RA. Tim was Roger's roommate. A tall Asian guy, Tim didn't start hanging out on the floor at all until the second semester. I wondered how a guy who didn't even spend time on his floor as a freshman would find time as a sophomore. Roger seemed a little too quiet and submissive, not the take-action kind of guy most RAs are. Chad was too offensive to ever become an RA, and he was applying more for the single room and freshman girls than anything else. I secretly hoped his interviews went horribly. Ben was the one guy who I could see becoming an RA. He was sort of laidback, but he knew what was going on and he wasn't afraid to assert himself. In the end, though, my opinion wasn't what mattered. It was up to the Student Life office to make that decision.

Three of the girls ended up applying as well. Desta, a little Indian girl who many people found annoying but I found refreshing, was excited about working with freshmen. She definitely had the enthusiasm, but I worried about her sometimes since she tended to walk around with her head in the clouds. Claire was a nice girl who I didn't see much of because she had a lot of things to do on campus. I always thought of her as sort of an oddball. She rode her scooter around the dorm, made very strange jokes, and was only close to a couple people on the floor. But maybe that was a good thing. Of all seven people who applied from my floor, the one who I wanted to become an RA the most was Kim.

In my mind, Kim had everything it took to be an RA. She connected with people, from the partiers to the nerds to the daydreamers. She wasn't afraid to take action or make a tough decision. She was enthusiastic, involved, friendly, and more than anything else, she was genuinely excited about helping people. There was nothing fake about Kim, and that's why I thought she would be an ideal RA. The one thing I thought would hurt Kim in her interviews was her demeanor. Kim was a very soft-spoken girl, and in a thirty-minute interview, that could be misconstrued as shyness and timidity. She needed to make sure she presented herself as a strong individual, and everything else would follow.

I talked to Kim infrequently during the first semester because, as I said before, she didn't really need me as an RA. But during the second semester, we found a lot of common ground and I started talking to her more as a friend. She was a creative writing major and took an immediate interest in my songwriting. I sent her a few of my songs and that served as a catalyst for many of our conversations. She gave me critical feedback and helped me a lot in developing my lyrics. In exchange, Rob and I made sure she didn't leave school without a newfound respect for baseball. I felt comfortable around Kim because she rarely got upset and she had a sense of calm and confidence about her. But as RA interviews and selection approached, our conversations turned more serious. She was interested in what she needed to do during the interviews, as well as what it took to be an RA. The night before her interview, she stopped by my room to relax. It was mid-February and snow was falling lightly outside, taking a break after a week of harsh blizzard conditions.

"Wow, I'm really nervous about this," she said as she walked into my room.

"Don't worry about it, dude," I told her. "You'll be fine. Just remember to be yourself, that's all they want to see. If you go in there trying to show them you're the perfect RA, it won't go well. Just be confident and you'll be fine."

"Yeah, I know. I'm sure it will go okay, it's just nerve-wracking. I really want to be on this floor next year since Laura is graduating. I think it would be such a cool place to be an RA."

"It is a really cool place to be an RA. And I don't want to give you false hope or anything, but I think you've got a good shot at getting on this floor."

She frowned at me. She stuck her hand in her pocket and pulled out a keychain. Fingering through the different pieces dangling from it, she separated a chain holding three wooden beads and held it in her hand. Kim made a fist and knocked on the beads lightly.

"Don't say stuff like that. You're going to jinx me."

"What's up with the beads?"

She laughed. "Well, I don't believe in jinxes, but I definitely do believe in karma. I think there's balance in the world. So whenever I say something, or a friend says something, like 'I think so-and-so good will happen,' I knock on wood as a sign of respect to the universe. You know, letting the universe know I'm not trying to undermine it. One of my good friends gave these beads to me as a gift so I'd always have some wood around to knock on."

"You're such a weird kid."

"Haha, I know, but what can you do? You have any new songs for me?"

"Nope, not yet. I'm in the process of writing one, but I need to record it still. Sam told me about some good free recording software, so I need to check that out."

"Cool. You have to send it to me as soon as it's done."

"I know. I have to send you the song, Meghan the lyrics, and Hillary the music." I rolled my eyes. "But you guys help me out, so it's all good."

"We try. A little in return for everything you do for us."

"Yeah, yeah. Well, I'm going to go wish everyone else who has an interview tomorrow good luck. Good luck to you too. You'll be fine, just be yourself and remember to breathe."

She smiled. "Yeah, breathing, that would be good. Thanks, Andy. I'll let you know how it goes."

I talked to the rest of the guys and girls who applied for a few minutes each. All of them were nervous, just like I'd been before my interview. The

RA selection process is rigorous and competitive, and it always leaves people feeling bad about themselves. This year was even worse because a lot of RAs were coming back, like me. There were probably two hundred people trying to get about sixty positions. Not a good ratio. And everyone knew it. I assured everyone they would be fine as long as they kept their composure. It's tough to figure out if someone would be a good RA in a thirty-minute interview, but that's how RAs are picked at Ashford. And they usually do a pretty good job of it. The application questions and letters of recommendation are nice, but when it comes to being an RA, it's all about that interview.

During class the next day, I thought constantly about the potential RAs on my floor. I shouldn't have been nervous about it, but I was. As soon as I got back to the dorm early in the afternoon, I looked all over to find the people who had interviewed. The first person I saw was Ben. He was sitting in the lounge watching *Full House* reruns.

"How did it go, man?"

"Okay, I think. I interviewed with Tamira, so it was cool because she knew me. I tried to be myself like you said. I cracked a couple jokes, got a couple good points in there. We'll see what happens. I'm actually not too worried about it now that the interview is over. I've done all I can. They'll make their decision."

Ben was looking at it the right way. It's tough to not worry afterwards, but he was right. He had done everything he could. I talked to the other guys as they got back. Everyone said the same thing: the interview went okay, and none of them knew what the interviewers thought of them. Kim was the last person I saw. I ran into her getting off the elevator early in the evening.

"So?"

"I don't know, Andy. I really have no idea. I'm usually good at telling if I had a good interview or not, but I have no clue. Which is kind of scary. I guess we'll find out."

The next two weeks were not fun for the applicants. All they could do was wait. I tried my best to put in a good word for those who I thought would make good RAs when I was in the Student Life office picking up my mail, but it was all for nothing. I knew the housefellows would make their decisions and that was the final word. The CA for each house also had some input, but each housefellow was very meticulous about picking their staff. I made a point to send Tamira an e-mail to recommend Kim for the soon-to-be-vacant 5th floor position and Ben for a first-year area. In Kim's case, I did want to work with her, but I also knew that she had all the qualities to be a great first-year RA. I just hoped her interview had convinced Tamira of that.

If it seems like I'm picking out Kim and Ben as favorites, it's simply because I knew them the best. There were a lot of residents who I did consider my close friends and in turn, I knew them much better than some of my other residents. Rob, Aaron, Kim, Meghan, Rosalyn, Ben—all of them were people I connected with on some level, so I did everything I could to help them out.

March 1st was judgment day. Everyone who applied was to pick up a letter from the Student Life Office after 1 p.m. Their letter would either say "Congratulations, you're invited to become an RA at..." or "We're sorry, there were a lot of qualified candidates, bullshit, bullshit, you're not hired." Watching people open their envelopes was intense. That piece of paper would alter the college life of every individual who received one. The morning of March 1st, I left a note on each applicant's door. I told them to talk to me as soon as they could. I couldn't sit through class. I couldn't focus on anything. I rushed back to my dorm at 12:30 p.m., skipping my last class of the day. I sat and waited for people to come back with looks of joy or devastation.

Again, Ben was the first person I saw. He walked into my room. He looked at me sternly, then shook his head, smiling. "No go, man. I'm an alternate, whatever that means."

"I'm sorry, dude. Being an alternate is something, though. Occasionally people don't accept their position, so keep an eye on it. But I'm sorry, there were just so many people applying."

"Yeah, I know. It's not the worst thing in the world. I would have liked to do it, but now maybe I can get a house with Derek or something. We were talking about it, just in case this RA thing didn't work out. I'm going to go play some poker to ease my suffering."

He walked away, and I knew his "suffering" wouldn't be much. I was proud of how Ben handled it, with grace and rationality. I hoped everyone else would handle it the same, regardless of whether or not they got a position.

A few minutes later, I saw Roger and Tim walk towards their room together, both with solemn looks on their face. I didn't even want to ask. I didn't have to. When they saw me approaching them, Tim threw his hands in the air in disgust.

"Nope," sighed Tim. "Neither one of us got it. Nobody is. We just saw Chad, and he didn't get a spot either. He didn't seem too pissed off, though. This is no good, Andy. No good."

Roger had a slightly more positive outlook. "I was kind of expecting this. My interview didn't go great and, well, I'm not the most outgoing guy in the world. But whatever. It's not a big deal."

I was surprised that none of the guys who applied got a position. I was sad for them and disappointed that there wouldn't be any males from New House 5 running their own floor next year. But I could definitely see that none of them had a distinct RA personality. I turned around and headed for the girls' side. As soon as I turned the corner, I ran into Desta. Her face was glowing.

"Andy! I'm going to be an RA next year! In Palmer House! I'm so excited! I'm going to be just like you, only a girl. I have to call my mom."

"Congratulations, dude," I told her. "Palmer House is cool, you'll have a ton of fun over there."

"That's what everyone tells me. Okay, I'll come talk to you about it later. Thanks again for the help."

"No problem, Desta. Congratulations again."

I was somewhat surprised that Desta got a position, but I was happy for her. She was a little ditzy, a little irresponsible, and a little offbeat, but you couldn't fault her enthusiasm. She wanted to do it, and the one thing interviewers look for is desire. I was confident in her ability to become a great RA with her newfound responsibility. I walked around the floor for another half an hour, waiting for the rest of the girls to return. The floor was silent. It was so strange walking around during the afternoon when everyone was at class and on campus. Suddenly there came another loud "Andy!" from behind me. I turned around and saw Claire standing there with a huge grin on her face.

"Andy, I got an RA spot. At New House! How cool is that?"

"Congrats, Claire. Great job. So we'll get to work together next year."

"Yup. I'm not sure if I'm going to be on the 5th floor yet, but I hope so."

"Yeah, I don't know either. You look like you're in a hurry, so I'll let you go. I just wanted to see how everyone did. Go celebrate!"

I tried to get away from Claire as quickly as I could; I needed to think. If Claire had gotten a spot in New House, it was probably for the vacancy on the SHS floor. So where did that leave Kim? I was worried now. I wondered where Kim was. I hoped I was wrong. I paced around for another hour or so before going back to my room. She probably had class. I would just have to wait for her come to me. And she did, later that evening. When Kim stepped into my doorway, her expression told me all I needed to know. It wasn't angry or even sad. It was a look of resignation, of exhaustion. Kim wasn't going to be an RA.

"So how'd it go?" I asked the question I already knew the answer to.

"I didn't get it. I'm an alternate, whatever that means. Can I come chill in here for a while?"

"Yeah, definitely."

She collapsed onto the futon and rested her head on a pillow. She let out a deep sigh and closed her eyes.

"I got my hopes up way too high," she whispered. "I told you how I believe in balance in the world, right? Well, I had a bad feeling about this the whole day. I took an exam last week that I thought I bombed. I got it back today and I ended up getting an A. For some reason, it gave me the worst feeling in the world. I was sitting in biology half an hour ago and Derek kept talking to me about picking up my letter. I didn't even want to. I knew it wasn't going to be good news."

"I'm not going to feed you the cliché bullshit," I said. "You know I think you should have gotten a spot, you know I made all the recommendations I could. I don't get it. But I guess it's not our place to try to understand."

"I know there were a ton of qualified people and in the back of my mind, I knew I didn't have a great shot. I was a little hesitant in my interview, I didn't get to know a lot of the housefellows. But I guess the entire last month, everyone on the floor has been talking about me as the next RA of the floor. It hasn't been 'if,' it's been 'when.' And I started to buy into it."

"I have to say I'm partly at fault for that, too," I admitted. "I know I told you that I expected you to get this job a lot of times. I got your hopes up."

"But it wasn't just you, it was literally the entire floor. Everyone expected it. I would go as far as to say that most of them wanted it. So I started expecting it, too. This is what happens when you don't respect the universe." She smiled lightly and closed her eyes again.

"I'm going to do the paperwork and stuff to become an alternate," she said. "Just because I don't want to be dumb about it. But this is going to hurt for a while. I was planning on being an RA. Even without saying anything out loud, I was expecting to be living on the 5th floor for another year. And now, all of that is gone."

At times like these, the best consoling you can do is listening. Nothing I could have said would have made Kim feel any better. But for her, just speaking her mind, telling someone how she felt, eased her pain.

"It seems like whenever something bad like this happens to me, I remember all the bad things that have ever happened to me. I wish I could stop that. I go through a diary in my mind. I see everything that's occurred throughout my life. I don't want to sound like I'm whining, but it's not fun."

"What kinds of things do you remember?"

She opened her eyes to look at me. Then she smirked. "I haven't told many people this. Just Rob since I got to school, actually. He's been my best friend here. But I feel like none of my friends can really know who I am or where I am mentally without knowing what I've been through." She sat up straight, leaned forward, and redid the ponytail in her hair. "So do you want to hear the story of my senior year of high school?"

I leaned back in my chair and put my hands behind my head. "Sure, why not?"

She had a huge grin on her face. It was one of those grins that said, "This should be interesting." She breathed in deep and began to talk.

"During high school, I dated this guy named George. I know, who's named George anymore? He was just a nice, normal Asian boy from Houston. He was the first boyfriend I ever had, so I sort of dove in headfirst. He became my entire life. I look back on our relationship sometimes and I wonder what I was thinking. He had good intentions, and I still talk to him on the phone and stuff, but he had some issues. I'll tell you more about George later, but all you really need to know is that he meant everything to me during my senior year. And he had crazy things going on in his head.

"The whole problem started in early January. And it started over a stupid note he wrote to his friend in class. I still can't believe that's what caused the problem."

She paused, lost in thought.

"Sometimes, I have to laugh at it," she said. "It sounds so stupid, but here's what happened. George had a run in with a Hispanic guy when he was out getting his hair cut. We have a large Hispanic population in Houston, obviously. He was furious at school the next day so he wrote a note to his friend that said something very derogatory about Hispanics. He was just ranting, but I don't support him at all in what he wrote. It was absolutely horrible."

"What did he say?"

She paused. "I can't say. Not right now anyway." To this day, I still don't know what George's note actually said.

"So anyway," she continued, "the note was intercepted before it reached its destination. And it was intercepted by a Hispanic guy who then passed it on to all of his friends. We had Hispanic gangs at our high school, and they started threatening George. Through phone calls, e-mail, in person. The gangs spray-painted 'Kill George' all over our high school. They even found out where he lived and killed his dog."

She paused for a moment. Kim had been going full force with her story. She took a few breaths and continued.

"And while he was being threatened, I was sort of in the middle of it. I was his girlfriend, the person he could trust and talk to, and one of the only people who was on his side. At school, most of his so-called friends stopped associating with him. They didn't want to get killed just for knowing the guy. It was on the news a few times, and it got to the point where George had to be escorted to every class. They must have quadrupled the security in our school for a couple weeks. Every single person knew it was for George. And even while George was being threatened, he was being blamed at the same time. He was valedictorian at our high school, but they didn't let him give the valedictorian's speech at graduation because of what happened."

"Andy," she continued, "I don't think I can explain how scared I was for myself and for George. I really went to school everyday for a couple months not knowing if I would come home alive. Have you ever been in a situation where you honestly think someone close to you will die before it's over? I can't even explain it. I have so many vivid memories about it. I need to write them down someday, write down everything that happened. It was such a big part of my life. But right now, it's too close behind me to think about too much.

"I remember sitting at the table one night, eating dinner with my parents. They sort of knew what was going on, but I never told them the full extent of it. They wouldn't have let me go to school if they knew, and I certainly wouldn't have been allowed to see George. Through all of this, I did stay by his side, and I'm proud of that. But anyway, I remember sitting at the table eating broccoli. And I thought to myself, 'I need to wear tennis shoes tomorrow. That way if there's a fight, I can run faster.' Who thinks that? I left for school every day hoping more than anything that George and I would be able to walk home at three o'clock. And I was never really sure.

"I was never sure how it would go down. They had guns, they had knives, they had numbers. But nothing ever did happen. I can't say there was one moment when everything ended, though. For George, he didn't feel safe until June, when we graduated. I started feeling safer in April, I guess, when things started to die off and I could sleep easier at night. I broke up with him in the beginning of the summer. Not because of this—well, not directly. He had become crazy, even more so than in the beginning. He was possessive, paranoid, confused, careless. My breaking up with him isn't important; what's important is how much the… incident, I guess, changed his life. And mine. It gives life new meaning."

She paused again. With a story like this, there are so many little details, so much that happens that never gets revealed. But I understood the concept, and that's all Kim wanted me to understand.

"Even after all we went through, I felt sad when I knew things could never be the same between us. I cried when I was driving home from his house after we broke up. He still does some stupid and inconsiderate stuff, and I would never think about being with him again at this point, but we will always share a bond because of what happened. So yeah, that was my senior year in a nutshell. Pretty crazy. I guess everyone has their story, though."

"I'd be willing to say that yours is a little more intense than most people's. Wow, dude, the whole thing sounds so surreal. I can't imagine anything like that. I feel like I've had such a benign life to this point."

"It changed how I look at things in a lot of ways," she said coolly. "For one, I don't take anything for granted. Anything. Not when something as simple as an angry rant to a friend can mean you're running for your life. And I've learned to respect the universe. It's why I do the 'knock on wood' thing. Everything happens for a reason. It was definitely a learning experience."

"I guess when you put it all in perspective," I said, "nothing is ever too bad after going through that."

"No, it's not. And even though sometimes things don't work out how I hope, my mind goes back to last year, and I'm quickly reminded that things can always be worse."

"They certainly can," I said.

Kim and I talked for another hour about random and pointless things. After hearing about her senior year, almost everything seemed random and pointless. I had a new respect for Kim, as a human, as a friend, as someone who was not afraid to stand up for what she believed in. This was one of those conversations that created a bond. I spent a lot of time talking to Kim during the rest of the semester about everything, from George to our concerns about the floor. But part of me still couldn't believe Kim's story. I mean, I believed it was true, but I couldn't believe it happened. Especially to someone like Kim, someone who seemed so innocent, so passive, so inexperienced. But innocence isn't always something that's given away; it can be taken away just as easily. In Kim's case, it was taken by brute force. But her pride and her principles remained intact, and I think they'll remain intact for many years to come. Knock on wood, of course.

When word leaked that Kim hadn't gotten an RA position, there was a collective uproar from the floor. Everyone wanted to know what kind of phony and corrupt system was being run. In the middle of the scuffle was Claire, and I felt terrible for her. While she wasn't the most popular girl on the floor, nor the closest person to me, I couldn't help thinking that she must be wondering, "Why don't they think I can do it?" It wasn't that anyone thought she couldn't, they all just thought Kim was more ideal. People congratulated Claire, and publicly no one showed any kind of animosity towards her. But in private conversations, people would whisper things like, "She can't connect to people at all," or "I would kill myself if she were my RA." The hostility died down only after Kim stepped forward and asked everyone to stop. Claire seemed almost apologetic that she got the position instead of Kim. After they talked, however, the situation was smoothed out. There were no hard feelings between the two of them and the floor got off Claire's case. Claire is my co-RA this year, and while some of the concerns the floor brought up last year have been valid, she's doing an incredible job. All you can ask for in an RA is someone who puts in the effort. And she certainly puts in the effort.

Rob felt so strongly about Tamira's decision to not hire Kim that he scheduled a meeting with her to talk about it. Rob told me after their meeting that, as he expected, Tamira basically said a whole lot of nothing and defended her selection. But Rob was happy he did it. "At least she knows what I think now. And she knows how we all feel. I just wanted to make sure that she understood what was going on. That we all thought Kim would be the best person to complement you as an RA for the SHS cluster next year. Nothing will change, but maybe it'll make Tamira think a little differently about things next time."

Tamira was just as happy with the meeting as Rob was. "It was a little inappropriate for him to question my judgment," she said, "but I think it says a lot that he wasn't afraid to talk to me about it. I'm glad he did. At least I know what the general sentiment is now."

And then there was me. How did I feel about the selection? I had no doubt in my mind that Claire would be a fine RA, but I would be lying if I didn't say I was disappointed in how things turned out. But maybe that's okay. Kim bounced back. She got involved in some other things on campus that being an RA would have prevented her from doing. And a week after she received her rejection letter, she confidently told me she planned on applying the next year. As for Claire, I began talking to her more about being an RA and about the SHS cluster. She was enthusiastic about it, and she thought about things differently than I did, which allowed us to combine ideas and come up with better ones. She was your typical nerdy physics major, but she thought outside of the box, and maybe that's what Tamira was looking for.

On a side note, Elaine ended up getting a second chance. She was offered an RA position in Palmer House, the same dorm Desta would be working in, and I was happy for her. She had reformed and I knew she could help a lot of people. Some of my floor was confused and concerned. Meghan said to me one day, "I feel bad that Elaine got a spot just because of her connections when someone like Kim could have been an RA instead." She had a point, but Elaine had come a long way. And I believed in her as much as she now believed in herself.

So what did I learn? I learned that things don't always go how we want them to, even things we think we have control over. I don't question Tamira's decision anymore. I do wonder sometimes how things would be different, but it worked out alright after all. And as much as I think Kim deserves to be an RA, deserves to be allowed to help other people out, I think she will eventually get that chance. Would I change things if I had the chance to? Would I replace Claire with Kim? Maybe. But maybe that's why I'm not making the decisions. What I did gain out of the entire mess was a new friend. As selfish as that sounds, maybe Kim and I wouldn't have been as close if she had been chosen. You can question people who make decisions, but you also have to keep in mind that there's a reason they're in the position to make these decisions. Maybe more than anything else, I learned that even when I'm confused as hell, it's always good to show a little respect to the universe.

DOWNFALL

The sun is going down for another lonely night
It's me against myself in the Friday evening fight
The first thing I always ask when I wake up and scream
Did that really happen or was it just a dream?
- Insomniac

While the RA situation wasn't fun, it didn't affect the floor community a great deal. We all consoled Kim as a group and individually, and we congratulated Desta and Claire. We went out with the guys, who just wanted to blow off some steam. But New House 5 wasn't in the best shape. On the surface, things were going as well as ever. I was still getting compliments daily about how great the floor was doing, how we were setting an example for Ashford. But time was beginning to take its toll on New House 5. Living with fifty-six of your closest friends is never easy, and in late March, on top of the already growing conflicts, new problems arose. Stress was causing people to speak and act irrationally. The downfall of New House 5 was in full swing. A lot of good was still happening, but man, it sure seemed like the bad was taking over.

At this point in time, there was no big, looming problem that was on everyone's mind. That would come later. In mid-March, it was a lot of little things that added up. And for the first time, they started to directly involve me. I was sitting in my room one night chatting with Rob, Val, and Luke about our futures. What a scary thought. Everyone talks about what they want to do when they graduate, but no one knows for sure. Conversations about careers and graduate school are always a little strange. But it's fun to imagine the possibilities. Rob and I were in a similar position. We both wanted to figure out some way to make a career in sports. We threw around internship ideas and talked about different connections we had. These connections were usually something along the line of, "I think I know a guy who used to have season tickets for the Red Sox." Wishful thinking, as I said. Luke wasn't sure what he wanted to do after school. "I don't know, guys," he said. "If you think of something I would be good at, let me know. Could I get a job being a slacker?" Val was even more clueless. But of all four of us in the room, she had the best outlook. "I don't worry about it, really," she shrugged. "I mean, my major is ridiculous, I have no clue what I'm going to do with it. I'll just wait until I find something interesting and go from there." Val was an Ethics, History and Public Policy major, and Val liked to say, "It's a whole of words to describes a whole lot of nothing." We sat in my room eating tortilla chips and salsa, talking lightly about the real world. Then Elyse knocked on my door.

"Come on in and join the party," I said.

"Ha, party. Thanks, guys. I'll chill here for a little while, so I don't kill myself."

"What's up, Elyse?" asked Val.

"Oh, the usual," she responded. "Biology and English are eating my soul. Like everything else at this school. I'm so frustrated right now. This work is insane. I'm so stressed, I want to just go home and do nothing for a few days. But I can't do nothing, or I'll fall so far behind that I'll have to drop out of school."

"Aw, Elyse, come on. Is it that bad?" I asked.

"Oh, yes, Andy, it is." She spoke angrily. Apparently, it was that bad. "I just want to do well this semester. I didn't do poorly last semester but I know I could have done better. So I'm making a conscious effort to study more and remain focused. But honestly, that's just burning me out and making me sad. So I'm taking a break right now."

"Elyse," I said, "how much time are you giving yourself to have fun this semester? It seems like I haven't seen the bright and cheery Elyse as much the last few weeks."

"Honestly, like none. I've been so swamped with work, it's ridiculous."

"Tell me about it," Val chimed in as she tipped the bag of Tostitos upside down, hoping there were a few more left at the bottom.

"Elyse," I sighed, "you have to take some time out for yourself. Like actually schedule it in if you have to. You're going to get burnt out before finals, and that'll just kill your grades even more."

"Argh, I know," she said. "I know, I know, I know. But I can't. Trust me, I would if I thought I could afford it. But tonight for instance: paper due tomorrow, problem set due tomorrow. The next night? Same thing. Sooo frustrating. I've been trying to do some fun things, like watch movies and eat with people and stuff, but I want to stay on the ball with my academics. This school is eating my soul, Andy, really."

Val let out a laugh. Rob agreed with me. "Elyse, he's right. You're not looking real good right now."

"The deal is, grades are important obviously, but how important?" I asked. "It all depends on how you look at them. Your freshman GPA is not going to matter in ten years. It might not even matter in one year. If grades mean a lot to you, then that's great, but there are other things that are important too."

"I know that, Andy," she said in a flustered tone. She was half-laughing, probably to keep herself from breaking down. "I know all of these things you guys are saying. But right now, I have my priorities. I need to figure out what I'm going to do with my life. And for me, getting good grades so I can get a good job is at the top of the list right now."

"Elyse," I said, "do you know Sara, the RA on the 4th floor?"

"Um, sort of. I've seen her around before."

"She's a senior business major. She has a ridiculous GPA. 3.95 or something like that. So here's Sara, an attractive girl with a high GPA, a great résumé, excellent people skills, graduating from one of the top business schools in the country. She's been looking for a job since October. She's sent hundreds of applications and résumés around the world. You know how many phone calls she's gotten back? A handful. How many interviews? Two. How many job offers? None. And she's graduating soon. It baffles my mind, but I'm telling you this to show you that your GPA doesn't mean everything. In Sara's case, she's just been unlucky. It's a little fate, a little skill, a little who you know, but it's mostly ambition. And you can't be ambitious if you're burnt out."

Elyse sighed deeply. She rested her forehead on the back of her hand. She closed her eyes and let out a nervous laugh. "Andy, that's not what I wanted to hear. That doesn't make me feel better at all. Grades are the only thing I have, the only thing I've consistently been good at. I'm sort of a failure at life. This just depresses me even more and makes me want to never talk to anyone again."

It was Luke's turn to open his mouth. "Elyse, you're not a fucking waste of life. I don't mean to sound harsh, but you just need to chill out and relax. You really do need a day of just having some fun. It'll clear your mind so you can focus again. Listen to what you're saying, you're being a fatalist. There are people who go here and lead great lives. A lot of them. What you're saying is ridiculous. You're only a waste of life if you make yourself one."

"Look, guys, I know you're trying to help, but it's not working. I don't want to hear any of it right now. Let's change the subject."

Elyse was fuming. I figured anything we said would just give her another outlet to vent, so I kept my mouth shut. But Val broke the silence.

"Elyse, I should adopt you, that way I can legally beat you and yell at you for being dumb. This is ridiculous."

"Awesome, Val. You can adopt me and be waste of life, too."

"What?" asked Val with a puzzled look.

Elyse was going off. She was thinking of anything and everything to rant about. "Nothing, nothing, nothing. Whole 'nother issue. I just think anyone who adopts is a waste of life."

"Why do you think that?" I immediately inquired. She had my attention now.

"Well, not everybody," she said. "People who have at least one child then adopt are fine. But I can't stand people who adopt without having their own children unless they physically can't. They're being a waste of life. We're meant to reproduce, to extend the species. What's the point? You're being sort of selfish if you adopt." She shook her head. "This is stupid. I'm going to start saying things I'll regret. I'll see you guys later."

With that, Elyse whisked away to her room. I was stunned. Elyse was the only person in the room who didn't know (or maybe didn't remember) that I was adopted. I didn't know what to say. Rob and Luke looked at each other. They both got up, patting me on the back as they left. Val rolled her eyes and walked into the hall to see if Elyse was in sight. Seeing no one, she turned back around to face me.

"Andy, I apologize for what just happened. And I'm sure Elyse will, too. She didn't know. Obviously. I'm going to go talk to her."

Elyse's comments didn't exactly bother me. I disagreed with her, but everyone is entitled to their own opinion. And I honestly think if Elyse was given a chance to think about what she said, in a rational mindset, she would have rescinded her argument. But she was upset, so she went off. And in doing so, she could have severely offended one of her good friends: me. She hadn't, luckily, but her words had disturbed me. I had never before heard anyone say anything negative about parents who adopt. I spent the rest of the night trying to read an economics textbook, with very little success.

I didn't sleep well that night. I just kept thinking about what Elyse had said. Even if she didn't really mean it, how many people shared her viewpoint? I hoped not many. I can't express how thankful I am for my adoptive parents. I don't know where I'd be without them, and I don't like to think about it.

The next morning, I woke up to find a long e-mail from Elyse in my inbox. It was essentially an apology. For everything. For the adoption comment, for being pessimistic and belligerent, for creating a tense and uncomfortable atmosphere in my room. I'd expected Elyse to send an e-mail, but it was still greatly appreciated. I knew Elyse was genuinely sorry, and I knew she felt awful after finding out that I was adopted myself. I never held it against her, and I've never brought it up since. There's no need. I sent her a response letting her know that she was allowed to vent and be stressed, but also to take into consideration the advice we all gave her the previous night. I hate to say it, but sometimes screwing up like Elyse did can open your eyes to what you're doing wrong. I don't know if it opened Elyse's eyes, but I do know that I never again saw her as frustrated as I saw her that night.

Elyse was forgiven and there were no hard feelings on anyone's part. But this is just one example of many minor explosions that took place on New House 5, just one of many scuffles and disagreements that were slowly tearing apart the bonds that had formed so easily during the first semester. I didn't hear about most of them, but they happened, and it was obvious when they did. And they caused a downward spiral. When one bad thing happens, it usually turns into a lot of bad things.

New House 5 was deteriorating, but that didn't mean it was turning into nothing. It just meant the utopian New House 5 was giving way to the more realistic New House 5. Through all of the arguments and grudges, there were a few things that remained constant throughout. Maybe that's why the defining moment in the downfall of New House 5, the moment when everyone realized that we couldn't just cover up the problems, was when Shannon and Devon broke up.

Shannon and Devon never appeared to be the most compatible people in the world. Shannon was the sweet, caring college femme who turned heads and watched *My Little Pony*. Devon was the philosophical frat guy who listened to Nine Inch Nails and A Perfect Circle. But they made it work somehow, and it was a sort of inspiration to all of us. They were telling us, "Screw what the world thinks. You can do whatever you want to, especially when you live on New House 5." It made everyone happy. They seemed to be getting along great. Everyone knew the routine: Shannon would take her work into Devon's room each night and sit there, talking and reading until the early hours of the morning. On weekends, Shannon and Devon could always be found at Devon's fraternity, dancing and having a good time. Nothing was wrong, everything was perfect. Then one Saturday night in late March, Rob came to my room just after midnight. He was sweating, his breathing was shallow. He looked upset and confused.

"Andy," he said hesitantly, "I just want to warn you, tonight might be a rough one for the floor. Devon broke up with Shannon."

Looking back now, it's hard to believe that I was so concerned with a boyfriend/girlfriend conflict. But as soon as Rob said this, I wanted to know exactly what happened. This wasn't just any relationship problem. This was Devon and Shannon.

"What happened?"

"Okay, first of all, it was the most random thing ever. Like seriously, no one saw it coming. We were all at Devon's fraternity, chilling and stuff. A few people were dancing, a couple of us were just hanging out off to the side having a drink. There were probably a dozen people from the floor over there. The entire night Devon seemed a little off. Like, he was keeping to himself and being sort of a hermit. Which was strange, because he invited us all over there a couple days ago. Finally Shannon grabbed him and brought him out onto the dance floor. They started dancing and everything was fine. Then after they had been dancing for a few minutes, Devon seemed to turn away from Shannon angrily. That's when it happened.

"He just turned back around and yelled something at her. The music was loud so no one knew exactly what he said. Then he took her off to the side and talked to her for a few minutes. She started crying, but everyone was too far away to figure out what was going on. When they finished talking, Devon went upstairs to one of his brother's rooms and Shannon came over to us. We were all sort of huddled up in a group waiting to hear what happened. She said he broke up with her and that she wanted to leave. Man, Andy, it wasn't that she was crying harder than I've ever seen before, but the tears were, I don't know, real. She was upset."

"Did anyone figure out why he broke up with her?" I asked.

"Um, not really. She told us he said it had nothing to do with her. She said Devon told her he was happy with her and cared about her. But he was almost too happy. He needed to be by himself. It was about him, or at least that's what he told Shannon. I don't understand it. All I know is this isn't some drunk thing Devon said. It's for real, and tomorrow morning, it'll still be real." Rob shook his head in disbelief. "This is crazy, man. I'm going to go see where everyone is. It's going to be a rough night."

Rob left my room to search for the rest of the group. In the meantime, I sat at my desk with my door open, listening for the sound of anyone else who might come and give their perspective. I was rarely present when stuff like this happened, so I depended on the testimony and opinions of other people. I felt fortunate that they were willing to tell me. Otherwise, I would have been clueless about half the stuff that went on last year. An hour passed. I didn't hear any screaming or shouting. In fact, I didn't hear anything. Just before I started to get worried that it was too quiet, Hillary stopped by my room. She looked sad. Not depressed, just sad. She sat down on my futon and sighed deeply.

"So I'm sure you've heard about tonight's catastrophe," she said. Hillary was one of Shannon's best friends on the floor. And earlier in the year, Hillary had nearly dated Devon herself. Instead of tearing Hillary and Shannon apart, though, their connection with Devon brought them closer. Hillary didn't want Devon, but she wanted Shannon to be happy. And right now, Shannon wasn't happy.

"Yeah, Rob told me. How's she doing?"

"Better, better. At first she was just a wreck. Sobbing, talking nonsensically about her inability to maintain a relationship and how ugly she was. But we've calmed her down a little. The girls are all still in her room talking to her. Elyse, Julie, Alicia, and Kristen are all over there with her. I think we're all going to bed soon. It's getting late."

I looked at the clock. 3:28 a.m.

"So did we figure out why this happened?" I asked.

"Sort of," she said hesitantly, "but I hope I'm wrong. Here's the thing with Devon. I know this from talking to him earlier in the year since, you know, I almost dated him. But that's beside the point. See, he has his whole philosophical mindset and these crazy ideals. He really thinks he's going to change the world, Andy. Change it through new ways of thought and all that… shit. And he really thinks he has to be unhappy and hate the world to do that. As stupid as it sounds, I think he broke up with her because he thought he was too happy."

"I can't think of a stupider reason to break up with someone."

"Neither can I, Andy. Neither can I. But I can sort of understand it, in a weird, twisted way. He thinks he needs to step back for a while and do some more living. As much as I'm upset with him right now, I know he cares about her."

She sighed.

"Well, I just wanted to make sure you knew we were all okay," she said. "Like I was saying, we're probably going to bed soon. It's been a rough night for all of us."

"Thanks for telling me. And even though Shannon will probably say it a billion times, thanks for helping her out. You girls are awesome."

She laughed. "Yeah, we've all got each other's back." As Hillary left my room, I was reminded of the Halloween incident with Audrey. Hillary had been one of the girls who took control, just like this time. Hillary wasn't someone you'd expect to rely on in that situation. She was sort of a slacker, she hated homework, and she did nothing but complain about being at school. But when it came down to it, Hillary made an impact when it really mattered. She thought rationally. New House 5 gave her an opportunity to shine during times when most people wilt. The same can be said for Elyse. Elyse had her moments on the 5th floor, moments she'd probably rather forget, but when it mattered, she rose to the occasion. Everyone contributed in a different way.

The next morning, it was clear that everyone had heard about the previous night's events. But no one was talking about it. I spoke to Hillary briefly about it. She told me Shannon was doing well and that the girls were still taking care of her, keeping her company and lending a shoulder whenever Shannon needed to cry. I also ran into Shannon's roommate, Julie. Julie was so upset at Devon that it was difficult to talk to her. Everything out of her mouth was "He's just a stupid bastard," or something like that. But she also told me that Shannon was doing a lot better. I let Julie go, since she was on her way to get something from J.T.'s, a popular on-campus food joint. "Shannon just needs some greasy food right now," Julie said as the elevator doors closed. I laughed as I thought how lucky Shannon was to have the friends she had on New House 5.

It wasn't until a few days later that I actually talked to Shannon or Devon. I decided to let their close friends help them out first. The Tuesday after the incident, I stopped by Shannon's room to see how she was doing. She was sitting on her bed, typing away at her laptop. Alicia was sitting next to her, giving her a massage. "Hey, guys," I said as I knocked gently on the door.

"Andy!" yelled Shannon. She set her laptop down and jumped off the bed. "I haven't seen you in forever." I stepped into the room and she gave me a hug.

"How are you doing, bud?" I asked as I sat down on the floor.

"Much, much better," she said. "My girls are awesome, they've been keeping me sane. And I'm not talking to any boys right now except you, Aaron, Rob, and Ben. I just don't get it, Andy. He broke up with me because he was happy. HAPPY! Argh. I just need some time to myself, and I'll be fine."

I was glad that she felt comfortable enough to talk about it. She had gotten over the initial sadness and now she just sounded bitter. But that was to be expected. She was definitely recovering well, and that was good to see.

"Alicia and the girls are going to take me out to dinner this weekend," Shannon continued. "Just the gals. We'll probably hit up a few parties afterwards. I hope Devon and I can work this out, though. At least so we can stay friends. I guess time will tell."

Shannon definitely had the right attitude about it. She was depending on her friends in a time of need, which is what friends are for. And she was being rational. It was going to be hard to avoid Devon when he lived a hundred feet away. The answer wasn't avoidance, it was compromise. Shannon recognized that, but accomplishing it was a much more difficult task.

Talking to Devon about the break-up was a very different experience. I wouldn't call it more difficult, but it was certainly less direct. I saw Devon sitting in his usual spot in the study room one afternoon, listening to music and drinking coffee like he always did. I stopped in to say hi. As I opened the door, I found it ironic that this was the same place where Devon first told me he was dating Shannon. When I entered the tiny study room, Devon took off his headphones.

"Hey, Andy, how are you? Take a seat."

"Thanks, Devon. I'm doing pretty well. But I'm interested to know how you're doing."

He looked up at the ceiling and tilted his head. He laughed a little. Devon knew exactly what I was talking about, even though I hadn't mentioned Shannon's name. I knew Devon didn't like the idea of me "checking up" on him, but since he viewed me as more of a friend than RA, I figured he'd talk.

"I'm doing alright," he said, nodding. "Things have been a little rough recently. I've been asking myself some questions, going over various situations." Devon talked like a thoughtful professor, and it was strangely soothing to listen to him speak. "But I stand by my decision. Not to say I don't think about it. And it's been worsened by the fact that a lot of people have been talking on the floor and, well, in my opinion, not giving me a fair chance. But I knew that was going to happen. This is something I thought about for a long time, and eventually I made the decision I thought I needed to make. But yeah, I'm doing okay."

When Devon finished talking, there was finality in his voice that said the conversation, at least for the time being, was over. And I was fine with that. He needed his space, and I was more than willing to give it to him. I liked Devon, and while I wasn't sure why he did what he did, I didn't question him. He said he was doing okay, and I believed him.

When the girls came together to support Shannon, it created a lot of tension on the floor. Devon was alienated from the girls' side. In turn, people like Chad, who hung out with Devon a lot, were alienated as well. It was unfortunate for everyone. Devon and Shannon did talk and try to work out a compromise. How successful it was, I don't know. But I do know a lot of the girls got upset at Devon for maintaining close contact with Shannon. For the next few weeks, Devon and Shannon went out to lunch and hung out occasionally. Some of the girls saw this and thought Devon was being manipulative: he was enjoying all the benefits of a girlfriend without the label or the responsibilities. Hillary and Alicia specifically tried to deter Shannon from staying so close to Devon. And that's when things started getting messy. Through his conversations with Shannon, Devon implied that Alicia and Hillary were trying to control Shannon's life. He accused Hillary of being jealous that he hadn't dated her in the beginning of the year. Then Hillary retaliated by saying Devon wasn't good enough for her or for Shannon. Every time Devon was in the same room as one of Shannon's friends, the tension gave everyone present an uncomfortable feeling in the pit of their stomachs.

Devon and Shannon, who had once been the epitome of how close New House 5 was, were now an example of how far New House 5 had fallen. The love affair was ending. How much was left, no one knew for sure.

ڡ

Individual people were falling apart as well. When I say falling apart, I don't mean literally, I mean mentally. It was easy to have a breakdown at Ashford, and a lot of people did. Most of the time, it was related to academic stress. Hillary and Val were perfect examples. They were both very chill, very upbeat girls. Socially, they were all over the place: on campus, at the fraternities, in the dorm. But when it came to school, the stress settled in, and during the second semester it took over both of their lives.

A lot of people made goals to study harder during the second semester after a subpar first term. Val and Hillary were no different. Both of them had the same major in the history department. The problem was, both of them also wanted to double major in something else. Hillary, who had been speaking German since early in high school, wanted to pick up a German double. Val, who had begun writing for the school newspaper, was looking for a double in technical writing. It still makes me angry that students at our school feel like they have to double major or they're being slackers. Having too much work will cause you to be a slacker, because it's easy to lose motivation when you know you've got eight hours of work ahead of you on any given night. Students in the school of humanities particularly take a lot of flak from computer scientists and engineers for having lighter workloads. But that's not always the case. Hillary and Val were living proof of that.

Neither of them had a difficult time with the actual work itself. Both had mainly writing and reading to do. But when the work piles up, it can be overwhelming. Hillary dropped by my room one Monday evening, almost in tears. "Andy," she said, "there's a Red Wings game on tonight. They're playing Colorado. I've been wanting to watch for like two months, but I can't. I have three papers to write and seven hundred pages to read by Wednesday. Why does this school suck? Why is it slowly but surely making certain I leave depressed and crazy?"

No sooner had Hillary finished her spiel than Val walked in as well. "Hillary, are you venting about having too much fucking work?"

Hillary sniffled. "Yes."

Val laughed maniacally. "Good," she said. "So am I." She sat down on my futon next to Hillary. Noticing the bag of Doritos on my desk, Hillary asked if she could partake. I told her to go ahead. There were a few seconds of silence while the two girls chomped away on week-old Doritos.

"What kind of work do you have, Val?" I asked.

"Oh, the usual bullshit. Article for the newspaper, paper for my history class, have to read a book by tomorrow. I won't be sleeping tonight. I don't fear not having a job when I leave school, I fear not having a soul." Both girls laughed.

While I sat there watching them eat voraciously, I felt sorry for both of them. I never was too stressed about school, maybe because of my time management skills, or maybe just because of my ability to work really fast. And if I was stressed, it never lasted for more than a couple days. But with Val and Hillary, it was literally every day. The work piled up for both of them. They tried to chip away at it, but even if you know you're capable of writing a paper in an hour, it becomes a lot more daunting when you know there are two more right after it. It's not doing the work that's the problem; it's starting it, finishing it, and staying focused. But it's easy to lose focus when there are a million things to focus on instead of just one.

They looked bad, too. Val and Hillary were both deceptively attractive girls. They both had pretty faces and pleasant personalities, but the lack of sleep had taken its toll. Their eyes sagged, their faces were colorless, their demeanors were boring, snappy, and anxious. I watched before my eyes how school could turn beautiful people into zombies. As Val finished off the last of the Doritos, she said, "I'm thinking two hours of sleep tonight sounds reasonable."

Hillary cackled. "Oh Val, if I get one, I'll be thrilled."

They threw away the empty Doritos bag and looked at each other. "I guess it's time to get back to work," Hillary said. "And by work, I mean staring at my computer screen and crying. Maybe if I didn't procrastinate this wouldn't happen. But it probably still would."

They left the room. I didn't say anything. What could I say? I had already told both of them everything I knew about time management, stress relief, academic development, and all that good stuff. I had recommended that they take some seminars relating to their problems. They went, but they found them very unhelpful. Hillary and Val were extreme cases, but almost everyone at Ashford falls into the same boat to some extent. School is stressful, we all care about grades, and sometimes, the pressure takes people out of their element.

As the semester wore on, both Val and Hillary did do a better job of getting work done and spreading things out. This meant less partying on the weekends to set aside Saturdays for assignments, but with a little sacrifice and effort, it worked out. That's not to say that there weren't still stressful nights where two hours of sleep seemed like a gift, but there were fewer of them. Everyone had nights like that, and it was on those nights that I realized life on New House 5 was dragging. For a lot of reasons. There were the conflicts and bad blood between people, there were the academics that kept people from being upbeat and excited, and there was the fact that everyone was seeing the foundations that built New House 5 fade away. There weren't as many late-night conversations, there was more gossip and less acceptance, people were seeing the bad in their friends when they were tired of just seeing the good.

I have to say that things still weren't nearly as bad as they could have been. I once talked to another RA on campus about her experience, and she told me about how one overweight girl, Teri, became the butt of everyone's jokes on the floor. They ridiculed the girl endlessly, and no one could stop them. Early in the second semester, the girl's roommate, Janet, told her RA that Teri had been missing for three days. Janet said Teri had returned from Winter Break, then after a week or so, she just sort of disappeared. After some phone calls, they located Teri at her home in eastern Pennsylvania. She was taking a leave of absence, but she hadn't told anyone.

All of her stuff was still in the dorm, so Teri's mother asked Janet to pack up a few things and ship them home before they drove down and got the rest. When Janet opened her roommate's wardrobe, she gasped. Sitting in the back of the wardrobe, lined up on the floor, were glass containers filled with a gross, yellowish substance. And as soon as she opened the wardrobe, a horrible stench filled the room. She almost threw up. And then she realized what was in the containers. Vomit. Since coming to school, Teri had become bulimic. Some bulimics, as my friend told me, keep their vomit in jars so they can measure how much weight they've "lost." It turns out that Teri usually emptied these every week but because she left, they just sat and rotted in her wardrobe. She had started about midway through the first semester. And while she likely had similar problems dealing with her weight in high school, her floor community at college didn't help. It could always be worse, I thought.

Yes, New House 5 was in decline, but I kept my morale high and continued making efforts to help everyone out. At that point, all I could do was try to stop the bleeding temporarily until things got better. I couldn't single-handedly turn New House 5 back into what it was during the first semester, but I could at least show the floor that I was trying. Maybe they would follow suit. I kept telling myself to keep my head up, that it would get better soon. I hated the yelling, the moping, the evil looks people who were once great friends shot at each other. I knew it would be okay if we all just kept moving forward. But my morale was dropping, and somehow I knew it was going to get worse before it got better.

LOOKING AHEAD

I'm by your side
I am far away
Here tomorrow
I'll be gone today
- Fade into the Night

Amidst all the trouble brewing on New House 5, it was easy to overlook the fact that we only had two months left at school. In a few short weeks, I would be a junior, and the rest of New House 5 would become sophomores. It was crazy to think about us all getting older. It was even crazier to think about every person on the floor going their own separate way. New House 5 would be inhabited by fifty-six new people next year. It was a scary thought.

Room Draw got everyone thinking about next year. Room Draw is the process of selecting your dorm and room for the next school year. It's a lottery system, and it drives people insane. Anyone who wants to live on campus submits a small housing reservation fee. Once you submit it, you get a random number between 1 and 1200, or however many students there are in your class. The lottery goes by seniority—juniors, sophomores, and finally freshmen—and then by Room Draw number, lowest first, highest last. By the time freshmen choose, there isn't a whole lot left. Usually the top fifty freshmen get their first choice, but after that, it's all up in the air. Sometimes, people in the 1000's are stuck living in a crappy dorm with incoming freshman, or somewhere farther off campus. It's a stressful process that takes place at the end of March and reminds everyone that the school year is coming to a close.

Of course with Room Draw comes roommate selection. This is where things can get sticky. Triples are hard to come by, singles are even harder. So almost everyone has to have a roommate, and only one. How do you choose? How do you try to get all of your friends into one dormitory? How do you tell your current roommate you can't stand her hygiene and need to room with someone else? How do you tell your best friend that you're going to live in the fraternity house and he needs to find someone else to live with? In the end, there are always some people who feel left out, shafted, or pissed. But it's part of the process.

On New House 5, the whole Room Draw fiasco began back when the girls decided to not apply for Special Interest Housing and it became clear who was and was not going to be an RA. Then people started making plans in their heads. Some things were a given, like the fact that Shannon and Julie were definitely going to room together. One of the advantages of the Room Draw process is that if you have a roommate with a great number, you can discard your 1215. Shannon's number was in the mid 400's, Julie's was in the high 600's. With Shannon's number, they would have no problem getting a double in Kensington Gardens. They were great friends, there were no hard feelings, and everyone was happy for them. Perfect. The same went for Sam and Aaron. They planned on getting a double in Kensington Gardens or Hamilton House, the other dormitory adjacent to New House. Aaron had a number in the 200's, they would be fine. But not all the situations were so simple.

The girls particularly found it difficult to figure out who was going to be where. A few of the girls, like Rosalyn, Audrey, and Elyse, had extremely high Room Draw numbers. They were confident they could all get triples, so they planned an elaborate scheme that would make everyone happy. With the guys, the process definitely left people feeling gypped, but it was much smoother. And even though some people were left out, everyone managed to find a roommate. Every plan caused a chain reaction, but everything seemed to be working out. We all hoped there would be no glitches the day of Room Draw so everyone could get the room and roommate they wanted.

A few people, as is always the case, were left out of the ordeal. Kate, whose roommate planned to live with Lindsey, was stuck with a mediocre Room Draw number and no one to room with. "This really sucks," she told me. "I'll just put myself in a random room and housing will assign me some random roommate. But I guess that's the same as this year. It's my own fault for not getting to know more people. I think I could room with any of the girls on this floor, but they all have friends they are closer to. I don't feel like getting involved in their whole master plan and making it more difficult. I'm fine taking my chances on a new roommate." Kate was definitely much more social now than she was at the beginning of the year, but she still wasn't comfortable enough with any of the girls to ask them to be her roommate. I'm sure it was frustrating for her, but she didn't show it. She didn't show much emotion at all actually, not since we'd talked a few weeks earlier.

The day of Room Draw came and no one knew for sure how everything was going to work out. The entire floor was riding on the master plans of Elyse, Audrey, Rob, and everyone else with a high Room Draw number. If one thing went wrong, a lot of things could follow. Living with someone for a year is no small thing. We all held our breaths and hoped it would turn out okay.

It was a stressful day for everyone involved, but in the end, everyone got something. A few people were unhappy with their new dorms, but everybody ended up with the roommates they wanted, which was the important thing. Room Draw came and went without a big problem. One bump in the road, met and passed. But it definitely got everyone thinking about next year. People were already sad about leaving the floor, others were excited about getting away from the drama. As Rosalyn told me, "I love the people on this floor. They're my best friends here—hell, they're some of my best friends in the world. But living with them is not smart. It's going to make me hate them. I'm glad next year we can just visit and we don't have to live with each other. It'll keep some friendships intact."

෪෨

I said before that Kate had been showing very little emotion about anything since the night she talked to me. She was still going to counseling and Elaine and I were still checking up on her, but neither of us were really worried about Kate. We thought she was getting things under control. For all we could tell, Kate was really turning over a new leaf. We were wrong.

It was the first warm day we'd had all year. One of those late March days when you walk outside, see the sun shining, and take deep breath of spring. It always fills me with utter joy. When the sun went down, clouds entered the skies. It started to sprinkle, but it was still warm out. I was walking back from picking up my mail at the University Center when the rain hit. I got to the dorm just before it started to come down hard. I went up to my room and pulled out a book. Before I started reading, I noticed that Kate had sent me an instant message while I was away. I pulled up the message.

"Today sucks," it said.

I frowned. I typed back to her, "Today was beautiful out. How can you say today sucked?"

She responded, "I don't know, Andy. I don't know. It did."

Then, abruptly, she signed off. I decided to go over to her room to check up on her. When I got there, she was running around her room frantically.

"Kate," I said. "What are you doing?"

She stopped dead in her tracks and looked at me curiously. "I'm cleaning. This is what I do when I don't know what else to do." She sounded nervous and upset. She went back to her manic cleaning. She picked up a pair of jeans from the floor and placed them back on the floor, a few feet away from where they'd started. "You can stay here, just don't get in the way," she said nervously. Her face was bright red. Her hair was up in a ponytail and she was wearing her winter jacket.

Wait a second. She was wearing her winter jacket? We hadn't had weather this nice in months. And she had clearly been indoors for quite sometime anyway. Who wears a jacket indoors?

"Kate," I said hesitantly. "Why do you still have your jacket on? It's kind of warm in here."

She looked at me coldly. Without saying a word, she pushed me from the room and closed the door. I went back to my room to think about what just happened. And to decide if I needed to do something.

When I got back to my room, I sat silently in my chair for a few minutes, going over things in my head. I had a feeling the jacket was to cover up her arms. I toyed with idea of calling campus police, but in the end I decided to just call Elaine and go from there. Before I had a chance to do anything, Kate was at my door. She had an eerily empty look on her face and something in her hand. I looked closer. It was a curling iron. Still smoking. Kate handed it to me.

"Careful, it's hot. You need to take that. I'll be back."

As I set the curling iron down in a safe spot, I noticed why it was smoking. On the end of the iron were pieces of flesh, covered in fresh blood. I got up to find Kate, but she found me first. My cell phone rang. I answered it and heard Kate's meek voice on the other end. "I'm in my room in the corner. Come in, and close the door behind you."

When I entered Kate's room, I didn't see her at first. I didn't know which corner she meant. Then after a few seconds of looking, I found her curled up in a ball, sitting in the small space between her wardrobe and her refrigerator. I knelt down in front of her. There was only room for one person in her spot. She sat upright, holding her knees close to her body, shaking uncontrollably and crying.

"Hey, bud, can you come out here so I can sit next to you?" I asked quietly. She shook her head. I asked again. "Please? Just come out here. I'll sit next to you and we can talk."

She crawled out from her spot and leaned against her wardrobe. I moved to sit beside her, and she buried her head in my shoulder and cried harder. I put my arm around her and pulled her close. We stayed like that for several minutes. I didn't say anything. Finally, she pulled away from me and removed her jacket. Her arms were a mess. It was clear where she had used the curling iron, and it looked like she had used a lot of other things, too. The bleeding had stopped. She had covered most of the cuts with bandages.

"They're fine now," she said. "I'm used to taking care of this stuff. I used Neosporin and everything."

"I'd feel a lot better if we let EMS check it out," I said.

"No," she said firmly. "We're not calling EMS, I don't want to make a scene. My arms are fine, it's nothing new to me. I called Elaine, and she said she'd be here in a little while."

"Why did you do this? I thought you were doing better."

"I was doing better. A lot better. The counseling was still stupid, but I think I was getting something out of it. Andy, I only called you and Elaine because I know I needed help. I didn't know who else to call."

"Do you trust me?"

"I called you, didn't I?"

I left it at that. It was the best answer I was going to get.

"Everything was fine," she said. "Then today, Amy called me. She hurt herself pretty bad last night. She had to go to the hospital. Andy, I can't tell you what it feels like to wonder every day if your best friend is still alive. I yelled at her. I told her she could have killed herself. She said she knew. She wasn't trying to, but she knew. I told her she was being selfish. She didn't listen. She told me she didn't care, nothing mattered. I hung up. I didn't know what to do. So I did what I always did in high school. It's the only thing I knew how to do. I knew I was going to regret it afterwards, but I couldn't stop myself. I can't control it, Andy. It's a problem, I know. But I don't know how to stop it."

"Kate, I don't care what you say, we're taking you somewhere tonight."

"Haha, no, you're not," she said stubbornly. "Andy, I only told you because I know you don't do what you're supposed to do in every situation. You do whatever you think needs to be done. And trust me, I'm okay right now. I have a counseling appointment tomorrow. I'll tell her about it. Listen, I'm not going to kill myself. I'm not that dumb. But I do need to figure this out. And that's why I called. Not because I want to go see an emergency shrink in the middle of the night."

"You say you won't kill yourself, but how do you know you won't go too far once? Or that in the heat of the moment, you'll say, 'Fuck it, I'm going all the way'? Kate, we need to do something, we need to tell someone."

"No, you have to trust me. I know myself better than you or anyone else does, I'll make the decisions. I just want you to help me. And you can't tell anyone. Not Tamira, not anybody."

If nothing else, Kate was livelier now. She rubbed some more cream on her cuts and re-covered them with bandages. For someone who had just mutilated her arm, Kate seemed very thoughtful and spry. As Kate covered the last cut, we heard a knock on the door. It made both of us jump.

"Hey, it's Elaine. Are you in there, Kate?"

I stood up to open the door. When Elaine came in, she gasped. "Kate," she yelled. "What the hell did you do?"

"I'm okay, Elaine, seriously." Kate was an entirely different person from ten minutes ago. The girl who had been running around frantically, crying in the corner was now the Kate we saw everyday, sarcastic and stubborn as ever. I wondered what changed her mood so quickly. Maybe it was just me being there to comfort her. Maybe something just clicked off in her mind. I had no clue.

"Andy," Kate said. "Do you mind if I talk to Elaine in private?"

"Not at all. Listen, Kate, I'll be in my room. I'm going to come check on you later, but…"

"No," she interrupted me. "I'll be fine. As soon as I'm done talking to Elaine, I'm going to bed. I'm tired. I'll talk to you tomorrow."

I dropped the subject and left.

Ten minutes earlier, I'd known for a fact that as soon as I left the room, I was going to call campus police. Kate was in a state of shock. But now I was hesitant. She seemed okay. Was it something she could just snap into and out of like that? Was she really fine now? Did she mean what she said, that she'd never go too far? Even if it was the truth, she was still cutting herself, and that was a huge problem by itself. In the end, I didn't call campus police, although I should have. I was too hesitant, too unsure of myself. I decided to wait until Elaine had finished talking to her. I knew Elaine would stop by my room when they were done, so I waited patiently.

Elaine came to my room about half an hour later. She looked as confused as I was.

"What do we do, Elaine?" I asked. I knew Elaine would have some sort of opinion.

She sat down on my futon and told me her thoughts. "Here's the deal," she said. "I'm not going to do anything tonight, although I threatened it."

"So did I."

"But I don't think that's necessary. She seems to be doing fine. As usual, she told me to promise not to tell Tamira. But I'm going to. Someone else needs to know because honestly, I'm kind of struggling with what to do here and I'm kind of scared. I have a meeting with Ryan tomorrow, I'm going to tell him too. Then when I'm finished, I'll tell Tamira."

"That sounds like a plan. I was toying with whether or not to call anyone tonight as well. It's a tough decision. Part of me wants to not make a big deal out of a small one, since making a call would definitely turn it into a big deal, but I can't get over the fact that one minute she was crazy, the next she was fine. It's just too weird." I shook my head. "And I keep saying 'small deal.' This isn't a small deal. This is huge deal. It's kind of sad that I'm referring to it as a small deal just because I don't think anyone is going to die."

"Yeah, it's so weird, dude. How does she calm down that quickly? I don't get it. But I don't think we need to call tonight. She went to bed when I left. I saw her turn the lights out. Someone else needs to know, though, in case something happens again. I just don't know what to do with her anymore. Nothing seems to be helping."

"Yeah, and it seems like it can only get worse if we let it stew. I'm going to talk to Tamira tomorrow or the next day if I can, too. We don't have a choice."

Elaine left my room, but neither one of us felt satisfied. In the back of our heads, we both knew we should have taken Kate to counseling or health services that very second, but neither of us wanted to betray Kate's trust. We were too scared to do something wrong that we didn't step back and do what the best thing for Kate was. There are not many things I would take back about last year, but if I had the chance, I would have called someone that night.

I had a tough time falling asleep. I'm sure Elaine did, too. It's ironic that of the three of us, Kate probably got the best night's rest.

The next day, I saw Kate on campus going to class. She looked like her normal, moody, sarcastic self, and it lifted my spirits. Elaine got a chance to talk to Tamira before I did. When I stopped by in the late afternoon, Tamira knew exactly what I was there to talk about.

"Andy, what's going on?" she asked me as I took a seat in her office.

"Well, you know what's going on. I just wanted to stop by and see if I could offer any more information."

"Well, I had a nice talk with Elaine today. I'm glad you both are coming to tell me this now, but I'm going to ask you the same thing I asked Elaine. Why didn't you tell me earlier?"

"Honestly, Tamira, I don't know. I mean, I know my reasons, but I don't know why I thought they were good ones. I was unsure of the situation, but I thought Elaine and I could handle it by ourselves. I didn't want to betray Kate's trust. Her biggest thing through all of this was that she only told us what was going on because she trusted we wouldn't tell anyone about it. And I felt like it was a bigger risk to tell someone and have her find out than to not let anyone know what was going on. Up until this point, I didn't think anything was life-threatening. I don't even think this is, but it's gotten to the point where I needed to tell someone higher up."

"Andy, I don't think it's life-threatening either, but you have to trust us to help you, just like Kate trusted you to help her. I have a lot of information about different people and other situations that you don't know. Maybe a little more information can help me a lot. You have to let me know when this kind of thing happens so we can work on it together."

I knew she was right, but it frustrated me to be scolded by Tamira. I knew I had made a few poor decisions regarding Kate, but I was admitting my mistakes by telling Tamira now. Better late than never.

Tamira and I talked for a few more minutes. I told her I would keep her updated and Tamira assured me she would keep our confidentiality. But she also said she was going to make a point to check in on Kate in discreet ways. I had my doubts about Tamira's "discreet ways," but I decided not to make a big deal about it. As much as I disagreed with Tamira on many things, she had made a lot of good decisions so far, and I wasn't about to second-guess her. I also knew that withholding serious information from Tamira, like the fact that one of my resident's was cutting herself, was sufficient grounds to fire me as an RA. So I decided to swallow my pride, learn from my mistake, and try to do better the next time.

I thought Kate's situation was getting better, but as we found out, it was only getting worse. And I didn't know why. That was the most frustrating thing. I wanted to help Kate more than anything, but I didn't know how. And I didn't want to try something that might worsen the situation. So as usual, Elaine and I just kept a close eye on her. But now we had another person to help us out.

Over the next week, things seemed to get back to normal. Kate was her usual self. She hung out on the floor and was cheery with her peers. I talked to her almost every day, though not about what happened. I did talk to her about Amy, though. Kate knew Amy would be okay in the long run, but she worried about her when bad things happened.

"Amy knows I need her," Kate told me. "For that reason alone, she won't let anything happen to herself. It works like that both ways."

That was all Kate told me relating to her problem, but it made me feel a lot better.

෴

I was able to put Kate's issues aside for at least one weekend in April, and that was the weekend of Spring Carnival. I wish I could explain to you everything Spring Carnival is, but I may need a whole different book for that. Still, I'll try my best.

For some people, Carnival is simply a four-day weekend where you're drunk for ninety-six straight hours. Carnival starts on Wednesday night, and I've seen kids passed out on the sidewalk by Thursday afternoon. Each year, it goes from one Wednesday night to the following Sunday. And it involves everything you might expect from a Carnival, plus a whole lot more.

For starters, the school clears out the very large parking lot behind the Kensington Gardens dormitory to make what's called "The Midway." On the Midway, the school hires a company to come set up carnival rides and games. Also, all the fraternities, sororities, and any student organization who wants to builds a booth. "Booth," as it is referred to, is one of two main events during Carnival, and it's intense. Every year there's a different theme, and the goal is to build the best booth relating to that theme. The student and Greek organizations each spend thousands of dollars to vie for the coveted trophies. They are graded on creativity, design, environmentalism, aesthetics, and of course, the game. Each booth must have a carnival game, hence the name "Booth," hence Carnival. Children and college students alike play the games. It's a chance to be a kid again for four days in the middle of a grueling academic year.

A lot of residents on New House 5 got involved in Booth in some way. Elyse helped out with the Allies booth. It turned out that she ended up carrying the bulk of the load, so a bunch of people from the floor went out to the parking lot on Tuesday night to help her finish it up. Eric and Micah helped their fraternity build a booth, though they were eventually disqualified for not having a game. Still, I was happy to see many of my residents get involved in Carnival in some way.

While Booth is a relatively normal thing, the other main event that takes place during Carnival is not. Officially, it's called Sweepstakes. Endearingly, it is referred to on our campus as "Buggy." Explaining Buggy will be tough, but again I'll try my best.

Essentially, it's a race. At the starting line, there are four people, dressed in colorful outfits provided by their organization. Fraternities, student organizations, anyone who has the resources to compete does so. At the sound of a whistle, each "pusher" as we call them, begins to push a "buggy," a five foot long contraption that looks like an airplane without wings. Inside the buggy is a person. A real, short, person. It's amusing because girls under five feet tall are treated like princesses at Ashford. Fraternities start training for Buggy in September. For an event that takes place in April. That should give you an idea how intense it is. It's the biggest competition on our campus.

The rules are endless, the competition is fierce, the equipment is incredible. Tons of people turn out each morning to watch the races. It's one of the most unique things about our school, and it's always a trip to watch for the first time. Each buggy is painted differently, each team buys t-shirts specifically for race day, and everyone has a great time.

A few people on the floor got involved with Buggy. Meghan, Rosalyn, and Bri, all of whom were excellent athletes, were recruited by Gary and Luke's fraternity to push for their women's team, and Grace, who was about five feet tall, was recruited to be a driver. Melissa decided to push for another fraternity's women's team. Being involved in Buggy is not at all glamorous, though. You have to get up at 6 a.m. on weekends to practice, be very secretive, and be very competitive. Despite the ridiculous hours, everyone who participated on the floor had a great time. A bunch of us got up early on race day to go out and watch the pushers and drivers from our floor. Meghan and Bri's women's team placed in the top three, so we all had something to cheer about at the end of the day.

Carnival is simply the biggest event of the year at Ashford. In addition to Booth and Buggy, all the fraternities have parties, and various events happen all over campus to complement the four-day weekend. Alumni come back to hang out and have fun. It's a time for everybody to get involved and have a great time. If you can't enjoy yourself during Carnival, I don't know when you can. Drinkers and nondrinkers, partiers and non-partiers, competitors and non-competitors—there's something for everyone. That's what I love about it.

New House 5 enjoyed the Carnival experience, but it was also a reminder to everyone that the end was near. When Sunday came and we all got back to work, we realized that there was only a month left in the school year. Only a month. It was scary, and everything that was happening pointed to the fact that New House 5 wasn't going to be around for much longer. At least not the New House 5 we all knew and loved.

But you can't worry about that. You can reflect on it, you can be nostalgic about it, but you can't worry about it. All good things come to an end. When the end approaches, that just means it's time to get the most out of it while you still can.

જ્જ

It was around this time that I also noticed Meghan acting a little differently. She had recovered from her early semester troubles. She no longer looked down on people who drank, and she seemed more open. There were still those who called her a hypocrite, but for the most part, Meghan got along with everyone on the floor. Her mind seemed to be cleared. She didn't have Rick looming over her head all the time. I think she finally realized Rick and her just weren't meant to be. When she accepted this, she was able to move on and be more relaxed.

This meant she became more active on the floor. And it also meant she could consider the idea of having another boyfriend. She'd had a quasi-boyfriend during the summer, but he was just some guy to take Rick's place, a "rebound," as they like to say. Meghan wasn't the kind of girl who would date anybody just for the sake of dating, so it was a surprise when, instead of shrugging off the idea of having a boyfriend, she opened up to it. And for Meghan, this meant she had a lot of opportunities. She was a very attractive girl, and whether or not she wanted to admit it, she knew it.

I wasn't the first person to notice when Meghan started hanging out with one of the guys from Luke's fraternity. She met him when she pushed their buggy. I couldn't imagine Meghan ever dating a frat guy, but then again, stereotypes are made to be broken.

At first it was just a joke. The guy obviously liked her. A lot. He was tall, muscular, white, and scruffy-looking, with dark hair and a mature face. His name was Alex. He was a junior engineering major from Ohio. I never got a chance to really talk to the kid, but I said hi to him when he was sitting in Meghan's room chilling. He came into my room and watched the end of a baseball game once when a bunch of people were hanging out, Meghan included. But he seemed sort of quiet, reserved, shy. He had a sense of confidence and maturity about him, though, and I think Meghan liked that. We teased her in the beginning, then we realized that maybe the interest wasn't a one-way thing. Maybe Meghan liked him as well. Some people kept making the jokes. I stopped.

Meghan claims they were never actually dating. Initially I didn't believe her, but I would later learn something that changed my mind. Either way, after a couple weeks there were subtle signs that told everyone that, in some sense, Meghan and Alex were together. He put his arm around her during movies, they hugged when they left each other for the night, they went out to eat almost every weekend. It was nice actually, to see Meghan happy with someone.

As it turned out, Alex was graduating early so Meghan didn't plan on pursuing anything long-term with him. Hell, she refused to admit they were together for the remainder of the semester. But I could tell there was a new bounce in Meghan's step. She had gotten over her past, however simple or complicated it might have been, and moved on. That's what people do at college. They learn from the past and push towards the future.

But Meghan's relationship (or non-relationship, however you want to refer to it) wasn't all blue skies. There was a backstory and a subplot, as there usually is. But I wouldn't learn about that until a few weeks later.

⇛⇚

It was time for everyone to start looking ahead towards the summer and the next year. For me, I didn't have much to worry about. I knew I was going to be an RA again next year for the SHS cluster on New House 5. And I knew that over the summer I was going to have my dream job: an internship with the Rochester Red Wings, a minor league baseball team in my home city. I had gotten the internship through a couple phone calls and a good interview, and I was pumped about doing it.

But not everyone was in my boat. In fact, most people were clueless. Rob was searching desperately for some sort of sports-related job. He thought he had a summer job helping out a statistician who worked for Fox Sports, but that fell through.

"This sucks," he said. "It would have been perfect for me. The guy said I would have to be up until like 3 a.m. every night figuring out baseball stats. I do that anyway."

It turned out that the guy gave the job to someone else, so Rob was left still searching for something to do with himself.

Most people were content finding any kind of paying job over the summer. No one can fault you for not having an internship right after your first year of college. And to be honest, most companies won't hire freshmen. So it was back to the bakeries, the restaurants, the grocery stores, and the family businesses.

Meghan had a job lined up at a local eatery. "I'm the hostess at a seat-yourself restaurant," she liked to say. Aaron was one of the lucky few. He found a job at a chemical company in Philadelphia, which matched up with his intended field of study. Kim was planning on working for her parents, helping them out with the newspaper they ran in the Houston area. And of course there were some people, like Chad, who were fully content not having any kind of real job. I was jealous of those people, because it's hard to really enjoy the summer when you're worried about internships and jobs.

We were nearing the homestretch. The end of the year was approaching, and that was a bittersweet thought for New House 5. For one thing, it would be good for all of us to explore more of Ashford the next year, get away from the drama and the bad blood that had formed. And on a broader scale, it meant we were all getting older, maturing, moving one step closer to the real world. But on the flipside, it saddened all of us to think about leaving New House 5, to think that New House 5 would never again exist as it existed right then, as it existed in our heads. It wasn't something to mope about, but it was definitely on everyone's mind.

It was only April, there was still a month left. But even so, people were already asking if they could visit me next year, asking if I would miss them. I could only laugh. Miss them? Miss isn't a strong enough word. But I hoped to keep in contact with most of them. I think I've done a pretty good job of that this year. Even with everything that happened during the second semester, New House 5 was still a community, and it was still great to be a part of it.

I was walking on campus with Elyse one day when she said to me, "Andy, it's going to be so weird next year coming back to visit you and seeing different people in all the rooms. I don't know if I'll be able to handle it. It'll be like we're replaced."

"Elyse," I said sternly. "There are not fifty-six people in the entire world who could replace you guys. Next year will be different, yes, but this year was something special. I can't even say why, but maybe I'll be able to put it into words someday. In the meantime, let's enjoy the time we have left."

The year wasn't over yet. Not by a long shot. And the last month of school would turn out to be the longest month of the year.

GROWING TENSIONS

I'm on my way back
I might slip between the cracks
If you want to find me
It'll cost you one apology plus tax
- Stratosphere

Late April was supposed to be a time for relaxation. Not the case on New House 5. Late April is when things really got sticky on the floor. And it all started around Rob and Kim, the two people who had been the glue for New House 5 the entire year. Irony has a way of kicking you in the ass like that sometimes.

I said earlier that it seemed like there was something going on between Rob and Kim. Secretly, I kind of hoped there was. They were both great people, and they seemed to complement each other very well. It's one of those situations you look at and smile about. Regardless of whether or not anything had or would happen between them, the feelings were there on Rob's side, and they were obvious. I never got a chance to talk to him about Kim, but it wasn't something he tried to hide. It was a non-issue for the most part, however. Everyone did their own thing and there were no problems. At least not until Kristen and Rob began to hang out.

I guess Kristen and Rob started becoming close sometime during the month of April. I'm not sure why, it could have been for a multitude of reasons. But it doesn't really matter. The point is, they hung out. A lot. And slowly but surely, the rumors starts to circulate. In this case, it was clear that Kristen had very strong feelings for Rob. Rob, on the other hand, didn't seem sure of what he thought. He knew he still liked Kim, but he wasn't getting a strong response from her. Meanwhile Kristen was responding avidly. He was torn. From what I gathered by talking to him, he didn't want any kind of commitment. He just wanted to do a little exploring and figure out what he needed. And with Kristen, he had that opportunity. He took it.

As much as they tried to keep it under the radar, everyone on the floor knew: in some capacity, Rob and Kristen were together. They flirted wherever they were. In class, in Kristen's room, in the lounges. And of course, people began to talk. We all assumed they were making out when they closed Kristen's door, and we all assumed they knew our suspicions. But it wasn't until Rob decided he needed to talk to someone about it that anyone knew anything for sure. As usual, he turned to Elyse and Kim, the two people he felt the most comfortable around.

Elyse wasn't shy about telling Rob how sketchy she thought the situation was. Rob and Kristen were friends, they lived on the same floor, and they acted like love-struck middle-schoolers in public. But Rob didn't care. Neither did Kristen. And for all the talking that went on, I really respected the fact that they didn't care what other people thought. A few people were upset that they were so obnoxious in public areas, such as the lounges, which I can sort of understand. But the bottom line is, they did what they wanted to do and didn't let anyone else deter them. Some people viewed this is a good thing, other viewed it as bad. But it was clear that both Rob and Kristen were, at least for the time being, happy with the situation.

The first time I noticed anything was one afternoon when I was walking around the floor. Rob and Kristen were sitting in her room chatting, as they often did. I stopped and talked with them for a few minutes, but I didn't make anything of it. At the time, Kristen was sitting on her bed holding a book. Rob sat Indian-style on the floor playing with a plush soccer ball that Meghan had left lying around. I told them I had to go to class and ran off to the elevator. But just as the elevator door opened, I remembered that I had to remind Rob that we had an intramural softball game that night. I rushed back to the room to let him know. When I got there, I was at a loss for words.

Kristen was still on the bed, but Rob had joined her. And they weren't just sitting there. Rob sat in one corner, his legs hanging over the side of the bed. Kristen was curled up next to him, lying on her side, her head resting in his lap. Rob had his right arm wrapped around her shoulder, and his left hand was interlocked with one of Kristen's. They didn't see me. Both of them were giggling softly, talking in very quiet voices. To avoid an awkward situation, I decided to leave them alone. I could tell Rob about the softball game when I got back from class. But it was obvious from that scene that Rob and Kristen were more than just friends.

Other people began to catch on as Rob and Kristen started caring less and less about other people seeing them. They began flirting in the lounge areas and leaving the door open when they were lying on Kristen's bed. They kept most physical contact with each other private and away from public view, but we all made the assumptions, and neither one of them denied anything. That's when the situation got sticky. Because people began to talk. And when people talk, bad things happen.

The fact that they were so public about their relationship, whatever their relationship actually was, made them an easy target. This is why Rob went to Elyse in the first place. He didn't like the fact that everyone was talking about them. Rob had never been one to bad-mouth other people or gossip about things he didn't know about, so he didn't appreciate it when it was done to him, especially by his close friends. Rob was being pulled in two directions: on the one hand, he wanted to have his fun and do a little exploring. On the other, he didn't want to lose the respect of his friends.

It got to the point where he asked Elyse, "What should I do?" And even though I have no clue what advice Elyse gave him, or if Rob took it, it showed that he had a large concern with how his friends were reacting. It wasn't that public opinion was going to change his mind; Rob wasn't the kind of guy who would let that affect him. But he didn't like the thought of losing friends or creating enemies over something he wasn't sure about. It definitely made the situation a little tougher.

It seemed like each person involved had some sort of individual problem with the entire situation. First there was Rob. He was confused, to say the least. He didn't want to make a commitment to Kristen, but he also didn't want to be "that guy who hooks up with his friends," as he told me.

Once when Rob, Elyse, Melissa, and Meghan were talking in the lounge, the subject of hooking up with friends came up. "It's totally inappropriate," said Melissa. "It's not what friends do."

Meghan agreed. "I totally concur. I mean, if they don't intend on making something more of it."

And as this dialogue was taking place, Elyse began to crack up. As Meghan would later tell me, at first she was confused. She had no clue why Elyse found her comment so funny. Then she saw Rob's face turn bright red and realized what she had said. She turned to Melissa, both of whom now realized that they were, inadvertently, making fun of Rob in front of his face. The ridicule and judgment upset Rob to the point that he never felt comfortable on the floor when he was in his relationship with Kristen. To Rob, the whole ordeal was one giant headache.

It wasn't any easier for Kristen, although she made things difficult for herself sometimes. Kristen was upset that Elyse and Val seemed to like talking about her behind her back. I'll be the first to support Kristen on this; Elyse and Val were incredibly immature about how they handled the topic initially. They joked and gossiped with no regard for Kristen's feelings (though at times, everyone did that sort of thing). However, Kristen's problem was how she dealt with the gossip surrounding her. She could have done two things that would have made it go away. One, she could have totally ignored the gossip. It's tough to do, but sometimes, it's necessary. Or two, she could have talked to Val and Elyse to let them know how she felt about what they were saying.

But Kristen would have none of it. Instead of talking to Elyse and Val or just ignoring them altogether, Kristen let the problem fester. She complained about it indirectly to her friends, who then let it slip to Elyse and Val. Before long, Kristen was talking about Elyse and Val just as often as they were talking about her. Still Kristen refused to talk *to* either one of them, and they gave her the same silent treatment in return. It got to the point where the grudges were so bad that Kristen refused to even acknowledge their existence. And of course, this just gave Elyse and Val one more thing to talk about.

I've said it a few times already, but I really felt like I was witnessing a high school soap opera. Val and Elyse got themselves involved by angering Kristen. Kim was involved due to the simple fact that Rob had a crush on her; Kristen hated her for that reason alone. Meghan and Rosalyn, Kristen's two best friends, also became part of the chaos. They defended Kristen, her relationship, and her right to privacy against gossip. So as Rosalyn and Meghan fought on behalf of their friend, they also became alienated from Elyse and Val. It all started off slowly and grew with time. A downward spiral, a domino effect.

The whole thing stemmed from the uncertainty of both Rob and Kristen. Rob thought it was kind of cool that Kristen liked him so much, and he didn't mind the physicality. But he also didn't like the hostile atmosphere around him. Kristen was sure about wanting Rob, but she wasn't sure about anything else. Rob relied heavily on advice from his friends, Kristen refused to accept any. And all of these strange factors added up to one giant mess. Everyone took a side, and for the last two weeks of April, there was a lot of hostility and tension on the floor.

"Rob," I said one day when he was sitting in my room, hiding from the rest of the floor. "I don't even know what to say about all of this. I just feel sort of bad for you."

"You know what, man," he said. "I don't know what to say about all of this either. And as bad as you might feel, I guarantee you I feel worse. I feel like I'm responsible for pulling friends apart, and I hate that feeling."

As I said, this sort of stuff happens. But it disturbed me because it was such a bad way to end the year. The situation only worsened as April progressed. For a while, we were distracted by a number of other things, but at the end of the month, the problem of Rob and Kristen would still be alive and kicking.

ᔐᕍ

Late April also brought a few trips to the emergency room. I wish I had saved my hospital visitor stickers throughout the year, because I would have had a nice collection by the end of the semester. The first incident happened on a Thursday night, and it was incredibly unexpected. I was sitting in my dorm watching a hockey game on TV when Meghan stumbled into my room, gasping for air. She sat down next to me on the futon, breathing in and out, wheezing each time.

"Are you okay, Megs?" I asked worriedly.

"I… think… I'm… having… an…. asthma… attack."

"I'd probably agree with that. I'm going to call EMS."

She shook her head violently. "I'll be fine… It's happened before… I just need to calm down." She took a few more deep breaths. Meghan the soccer player was the last person I would have expected to have an asthma attack.

"What were you doing?" I asked.

"Just sitting… I've never admitted that I have asthma… I was never diagnosed…"

I decided to get Audrey, who also had asthma and would know what to do better than I would. I grabbed her from her room and brought her to Meghan's side. Audrey sat down next to Meghan and started talking to her like a mother. Her presence calmed me down almost as much as it calmed Meghan.

"Hey, Meghan, having an attack?" she asked soothingly. "It's okay. I just need you to stay calm and keep the deep breaths coming."

Meghan had only gotten worse since she'd come to my room.

"Should we call EMS, Audrey?" I asked.

Again, Meghan shook her head. Audrey looked at her and sighed. "I'm going to go get my nebulizer. It's a machine that lets you breathe in asthma medication. If that doesn't help, we're taking you to the hospital. Understand?"

Meghan nodded begrudgingly. Audrey hurried off, leaving Meghan and I sitting in the room alone. She laughed between wheezes. "So how's it going, Andy?"

"Not bad. How's Alex doing?" I asked.

"Shut up," she said half-sarcastically, half-seriously.

Before I could respond, Audrey returned with a crazy-looking contraption. She spent a few minutes putting it together before giving Meghan a pipe-shaped tube. "I'm going to turn on the nebulizer and we'll hear it start to hum. Then you have to breathe in and out through the tube. It'll make you feel a lot better."

As Audrey turned on the machine, I noticed a crowd starting to form around my room. Kristen, Rosalyn, Sam, and Rob were all looking in. As she breathed in through the machine, Meghan laughed at the fact that she had become a novelty item.

After ten minutes, Audrey pulled the tube away from Meghan's mouth. "Feel better?" Audrey asked. Before Meghan could respond, she started coughing even harder than before. Audrey turned around to look at me. "Call EMS."

If we hadn't already created a scene, EMS certainly did. They brought in two medics and three policemen, and crammed all of them into my dorm room. At first they just asked Meghan questions, then decided that she needed an oxygen mask with medicine. They had been in my room for about fifteen minutes before deciding that Meghan needed to go to the hospital. The policeman, followed by Meghan, made his way through the crowd outside my room.

"Audrey," I said. "Let everyone know that she's going to be alright. It's just an asthma attack. I'm going to go to the hospital with her."

The ride on the ambulance was uneventful, and the waiting room at the hospital was just as boring. Meghan was discharged at around 2 a.m., several hours after she had gotten there. She was fine, but tired. After a few doctors' appointments, Meghan finally ended up with an asthma diagnosis. All the doctors were shocked that no one had figured it out before.

Meghan was fine, but I couldn't believe how much was happening on the floor right before the year ended. I told myself that with only two weeks left, I was going to try to avoid the hospital for the rest of the year. That lasted two days.

On Saturday nights, I'm used to being woken up at random hours. Most of the time it's to help a drunk resident, and occasionally it's got something to do with a practical joke. But the Saturday after Meghan's incident, I was woken up by Kristen, who looked both sober and worried.

"Andy," she said. "Rosalyn isn't feeling too well. We think she got food poisoning from J.T.'s. She's been throwing up and dry heaving for the last two hours. We weren't sure what to do, so we decided to get you."

Ah, J.T.'s. Your typical on campus eatery complete with disgustingly greasy and fried foods. I absolutely love the place, but it's definitely not somewhere you can eat more than a few times a week without dying.

I threw on my glasses and sandals and walked over to Rosalyn's room. Rosalyn sat on the floor with her head over a garbage can. She looked awful. Dehydrated, tired, and angry. Hillary and Meghan sat next to her, rubbing her back and holding a bottle of water. Rosalyn looked up when I came in.

"Hey, Andy, what's up?" she said with as much energy as she could muster. "J.T.'s is the devil."

She paused to throw up into the garbage can. I had to turn away.

"We called campus police earlier," said Hillary. "They told us to call if it got any worse. She's been like this for a few hours. I think she needs to go to the hospital."

"How are you feeling, Ros?" I asked her.

"Haha, um, I've felt better. I'm never eating there again."

"I don't think I am either," said Hillary. "Maybe you getting sick will make all of us stop going there."

"I'll still eat there," I said, "but right now, we're going to get you to the hospital. You've probably lost a lot of fluids. I'm sure they'll cram a couple bags of IV solution into you."

"Oh Andy, you're going to make me sick again talking like that," Rosalyn groaned.

"I'm just messing with you, dude."

I called campus police. They had an EMS volunteer over in five minutes. They asked Rosalyn the standard questions and eventually decided that she really did need to make a trip to the hospital. Rosalyn was loaded into the back of the ambulance while a policeman escorted Hillary and me to the emergency room waiting area. When I checked in with the receptionist, she gave me a confused look. She was young girl, probably just out of college. "You look familiar," she said to me.

I smiled back. "Yeah, I probably do."

Hillary and I waited for a few hours while Rosalyn was treated. They gave her some antibiotics and an IV. Rosalyn was released at 4 a.m., and we took her home to get some much needed rest. We had all suspected it was food poisoning, and the medical examinations confirmed that. As it turned out, there was an epidemic that happened that night. At least half a dozen students who had eaten at J.T.'s suffered severe stomach illnesses. Some were diagnosed with food poisoning, others with salmonella, others with just a bad bug. But it all came from J.T.'s, and many people swore off the restaurant for the remainder of their college careers.

Though neither of these incidents was life-threatening or detrimental to the floor, things like this continued to drain all of us. With only days left in the semester, we all just wanted to ride a wave of calm out to summer. But the random hospital trips, the growing tensions between the girls, and studying for final exams kept everyone from being relaxed. Yes, school was almost over, but it wasn't letting us leave without a few more smacks across the face. We were exhausted, frustrated, and ready for the year to be over. It's not the way I wanted to see the year end, not on such a sour note. There was still time, though, and I hoped for a miracle.

As if life wasn't stressful enough without worrying about Kate everyday, I did anyway. She had already proven to me once that what looked like recovery was just a cover-up. At least now Tamira knew, and I hoped that alone might keep Kate in check. But I was never sure. I do have to admit that Kate seemed to be doing a lot better during the last couple weeks of school.

And when I say a lot better, it wasn't the same as what I thought during the middle of the semester. She didn't look like she was forcing herself to be social, she looked like she really wanted to be. I wasn't sure why until the last day of April.

April 30th fell on a Friday. It was supposed to be a calm night. The weather outside was warm (though a little damp) and a lot of people were staying in to get a jump start on finals studying. So I was a little surprised when Rosalyn stopped by my room, cell phone in hand, looking ready to go out.

"Where are you going, Rosalyn?"

"Um, nowhere right now. Kate and I were supposed to go to see a movie like half an hour ago but I can't find her anywhere. I saw her literally like forty-five minutes ago and she said she'd come get me when she was ready. Her roommate has no clue where she is, and she's not picking up her phone. I thought I'd check here since she hangs out in your room a lot. Have you seen her?"

"Nope. But if I do, I'll let you know."

"Grrr. I wish she'd let me know if she can't make it, then I wouldn't have to wait around for her. Alright, thanks, Andy. Have a good Friday!"

Rosalyn wasn't too concerned. Kate was known to disappear from time to time, maybe for a couple hours. But no one else on the floor knew what she tended to do to herself during that spare time. I got a little worried. I tried to forget about it and do a little more reading, but quantitative economic analysis isn't the most exciting subject and my mind quickly reverted back to Kate. What the hell was she doing? I decided to drop by her room myself and see if I could figure out where she might have gone.

When I got to Kate's room, Allison was just about to leave. "Hey, Andy. I have no clue where Kate is. You can chill in here and wait for her if you want to. I was going to leave it propped open anyway because I'm not sure if she has her key or not. I'm going out to eat with my friend from Pitt."

"Okay, thanks, Allison. I'll see you later. Have a good time!"

As she closed the door behind her, I looked around for anything that might clue me in to the whereabouts of Kate. I felt sort of like a stalker, but I was just trying to look out for her. Her jacket was gone, so she was probably outside somewhere. Her cell phone was sitting on her desk, which would explain why Rosalyn couldn't get a hold of her. It just didn't seem like Kate to be inconsiderate to Rosalyn. If nothing else, she always let people know if she was going to be late or miss something. So maybe she had a valid excuse. Maybe she just forgot her cell phone because she was in a hurry. As soon as I'd convinced myself that I was overreacting, Kate came plowing into the room.

Her face was beet red. She had obviously been running, or doing some sort of physical activity. She was breathing hard. She looked angry and distraught. She was wearing her light winter jacket over a plain white t-shirt and gym shorts.

"What the fuck are you doing in my room?" she yelled.

"I was trying to figure out where you were. Allison told me I could stay in here for a few minutes. Rosalyn is looking for you."

She stared at me and squeezed her lips together, as if to say, "I really want to punch you right now." She walked by me in a huff, grabbed her cell phone, and headed for the door. When she turned around, I noticed the back of her shorts and legs were covered with a thick layer of mud.

"Hey, are you alright?"

"I'm fine. I'm leaving now, so I don't know what you're going to do in here."

"Where are you going?"

"For a walk."

"Can I come with you?"

"What you do is your own prerogative."

"I'm not going to force my company on you. Would you like me to come?"

"Do I look like I'm in the state of mind to make any kind of decision right now?"

I took that as an invitation to join her. I followed her to the elevator without grabbing my jacket. I was still wearing my flip flops and a t-shirt. She was silent as we took the elevator downstairs and as we walked out the door. When we left New House, she turned around and said, "You're going to be cold, I hope you know."

"That's fine," I said. "Where exactly are we going?"

"I don't know. Just for a walk." She still spoke in an angry, pointed tone. Her face was still bright red, and she walked at a quick pace. We turned towards the back of New House, cutting through the Kensington Gardens parking lot. As we got to the pavement, the skies opened up and it started to sprinkle. I laughed out loud. Kate shot me a confused look. I just smiled back. The rain had a way of showing up at the most opportune times.

"Okay, Kate," I said. "We're walking now. Can you tell me what's up?"

"It's stupid, it's nothing, you'll laugh. I just need to get away." She picked up a stone and threw it as hard as she could against a sign denoting a reserved parking spot. The loud clang it made rang in my ears for several minutes afterwards.

"Kate, I won't laugh at you," I told her. "You're obviously very upset, I'm just curious about what."

She stopped dead in her tracks. I almost lost my footing stopping with her. We were now standing right underneath a light post. She looked up into the light. I did as well. It was a cool sensation. Watching the water particles flutter to the ground, illuminated by the light. I felt like everything was happening in slow motion, like everything around me was focused on the light. The misty rain fell on my face as I stared skyward. It felt good.

"This is kind of cool, Kate."

"Everyone's been talking about how this guy Alex likes Meghan." The subject surprised me, but I didn't say anything. She continued. "She knows him because I introduced them. I thought they could be friends. But not this. I met him earlier this semester. I went over to the fraternity all the time to hang out with him. That's why I was feeling a lot better during the middle part of the semester. Because I was with him.

"We never did anything, we barely even held hands, but I felt at home with him. I didn't tell him a single thing about myself, but I felt like he really understood me. Then when the other girls started hanging out at the frat, I introduced them all to him. You know, to be a good friend. And then Meghan and him started hitting it off. And now, well, now you see what's happened. He totally ditched me.

"It's not even like I'm ugly, Andy. I know I'm not. But he doesn't even talk to me anymore. He refuses to acknowledge that I exist. The last time I… had a problem… it was more than just Amy. It was the first time I saw Meghan and Alex together. They were just sort of cuddling, but it made me sick to think about. Then Amy pushed me over the edge. I called her to talk about Meghan and Alex, and we ended up talking about her."

She paused and looked down at the ground. She stuck her hand out into the night and closed it, hoping she could change the fate of a few raindrops before they hit the ground.

"Then tonight," she went on, "I saw them again. At the elevator. It was when I was going to get Rosalyn. I know Meghan, and I like her a lot. She doesn't act like a girly girl in public. But there they were, in front of the elevator. They thought no one was around. And they kissed. It was a long, real kiss. And that's what people who are together do. It was too much for me. I had to get away from it. So I ran. I ran as hard and as fast as I could. I don't even know where I was, but I ran up a hill and slid down it when I lost traction. That's the only reason I came back." She looked at the mud on her backside.

"It's stupid, Andy. I know it is. But I believed that maybe this guy, even though he knew nothing about me or my past, could be the one guy to help me get out of my rut, to help me overcome everything I've been through. It was fate. I met him by accident, when I dropped some papers at the library. We talked for a couple hours, just sitting there in the library. It was right out of a movie. I don't do that stuff, Andy. I don't. I've been alive for nineteen years, a ton of guys have talked to me, hit on me, asked me out. But Alex was different. I don't even know how. I told myself, 'Andy and Elaine are right, I can get through this.' Then, it all falls apart. Like always."

She appeared to become dizzy all of a sudden. She sat on the cold ground and covered her face. I sat down next to her, still looking up at the light. Kate started to cry.

"I put all my hope into these little things. I think that if they work out, maybe it will restore my faith altogether. But they never do."

"I know this sounds kind of crazy, Kate," I said soothingly, "but have you ever considered talking to him? Just maybe about what went wrong? Maybe he thinks you're upset at him or something."

"I couldn't," she said. "I wouldn't know how to. This whole thing must sound so ridiculous. I'm out here crying, having a breakdown because of a guy. Oh man, if someone had told me this would happen a year ago, I may have just killed myself right then. I can't do anything right."

"Kate, listen. We're going to go back inside. You're going to clean up, you're going to apologize to Rosalyn for making her miss the movie, and then you're going to set up a game plan for talking to Alex. Even if it's awkward, even it's just for a few minutes. That way, you can know the deal for sure."

"First of all," she said, "don't tell me what I'm going to do." I smiled. Even in a breakdown, she didn't lose her desire to control her life. At least the aspects she could control. "Second, I don't know how to talk to someone about this kind of stuff. I'm the one who makes fun of everybody who does. I'm the girl you can look at but never touch."

"I'll give you time to think about it," I responded. "But I think when you do, you'll realize that talking to him would make a world of difference. You can't control what other people feel, but you can at least explain how you feel. Maybe that's enough."

She looked up at me and wiped her face. I couldn't tell the tears from the rain. I'm sure she preferred it that way. Without saying a word, Kate got to her feet. She was already walking back towards the dorm before I could pull myself up. We walked back together without saying a word. As we parted ways when we exited the elevator, she whispered one thing to me.

"Thank you."

It was all I needed to hear.

I don't know if Kate ended up cutting herself that night, I don't know if she had already done it before I found her. But I was pretty sure she didn't, and I kept our conversation to myself. I didn't even tell Elaine about it. This was a truly private matter, and it was something that Kate knew she had to deal with in a mature way. I knew that eventually she was going to talk to Alex. I just hoped she would muster enough courage to do it before the semester ended. Maybe killing one demon would have a domino effect. Or maybe I was still thinking a little too optimistically.

⚭

While Kate was having her problems, things continued to fall apart on the floor over Rob and Kristen. Kristen still refused to talk to Elyse, Hillary, and Val because of their gossip. She still refused to talk to Kim, just because, well, you can't be friends with the competition. But now Kristen's friends began to get more involved. Meghan and Rosalyn didn't want to sit back and see Kristen get her feelings hurt. So they stood up for her, in a variety of ways.

For one, they stopped hanging out with Val and Elyse. When people went out, Meghan and Rosalyn went with Kristen, while Val and Elyse went in the other direction. And of course, there were heated exchanges over blogs. Excuse me while I smack my head against the wall. Yes, some people, Elyse and Meghan especially, took out their frustration by expressing their feelings on the internet for the entire world to see. Elyse made it clear that she thought Kristen was being an over-reactive little baby. Rosalyn voiced her opinion that what Kristen did was no one else's business. Everyone on the floor was forced to take sides. You supported Kristen, you supported Elyse, or everyone hated you.

And to make matters worse, the people on the same side started getting upset with each other. One evening when Kristen, Rosalyn, Meghan, and I were walking towards Pitt to get some food, Rosalyn and Meghan started talking about the situation. Kristen was upset by it. "I don't like how you guys always talk about it. You're worse than Elyse and Val. Why can't you let me do what I want to do? I just want to be happy."

"Oh, Kristen," Meghan said. "We want you to be happy, too. But we wouldn't be good friends if we didn't tell you what we really thought. And Rosalyn and I both really think that you're getting in too deep. We just want to make sure you don't get hurt when Rob isn't even sure what he wants."

"Well, it just sounds to me like you guys are trying to rain on my parade," sneered Kristen. "You know what? I don't feel like eating. I'm going back."

Kristen turned one hundred eighty degrees and scampered back to the dorm. She was mad, but she was also sad and upset. Meghan and Rosalyn were trying to help her, but in Kristen's mind, they were just adding to her misery.

On the other side, Elyse and Val continually told Rob that the whole ordeal was stupid.

"It's not worth it, Rob," Elyse told him. "You said yourself you don't want to date her. Okay, so you get to hook up, but it's not worth all of this."

Rob disagreed. He wasn't going to let his friends control his life, he just wanted their support.

The tension was pulling everyone apart. There never used to be any animosity on New House 5. You were either friends or acquaintances with everyone. Not the case anymore. Everyone had some kind of grudge against everyone else. Even the people who weren't directly involved got pulled in somehow. Aaron and Chad served as a refuge for Rob when he wanted to get away from it all. Kristen started spending time with Melissa when she felt like she was losing her other friends. New House 5 was officially in shambles. And I didn't know what to do.

Kim stopped by that Friday night after I had gotten back from walking with Kate. She let me know the newest developments in the Rob and Kristen soap opera, and she wanted to know how I was doing through all of the New House 5 agony.

"Honestly, K, I'm really, really sad. I don't want everything to leave like this. I don't want everyone to go away for the summer with a bad taste in their mouth. Because as great as this floor was—is—has been—everyone is going to remember the last thing. I don't want this to be the last thing. I want everyone to remember how great of a place this was, how much fun it was to live on New House 5, what it meant to be part of a true community. And I don't think everyone is going to remember it like that. It really saddens me."

"Andy," she said. "I honestly don't think that will happen. First of all, this won't last all summer. We'll all get back next semester and realize how stupid this was. The good outweighs the bad, even if the bad is fresh in our minds. And second, the semester isn't actually over yet. Maybe everything will get resolved."

She was right. There was still time left. And during that time, one more big thing did happen on New House 5. One thing that brought everything full circle, one thing that affected every person who lived on New House 5. It was like everything that could have possibly gone wrong did. All on one night. The universe decided to test how strong New House 5 really was. And with finals coming up, we weren't prepared for the surprise exam.

COMING FULL CIRCLE

When the jokers started crying
And the hummingbirds stopped flying
I smiled while I was sighing
It's tumbling into sweet perfection
- Stepping Stone

The floor community had been deteriorating since the middle of the second semester. The Rob and Kristen saga had been going on for three weeks. Kate ran into the Kensington parking lot crying on Thursday night. And on Sunday, everything came together.

Early in the evening, at around 7 p.m., Meghan made the trek over to the fraternity quad to hang out with Alex. It was her custom every Sunday evening. She sat at his computer, looking up song lyrics and checking e-mail, while he sat on his bed doing last-minute homework and complaining about being an engineering major. On this particular night, Meghan planned on throwing a kink into the routine. She had noticed Kate checking them out sometimes. Meghan suspected that Kate and Alex had something going on before she met him, but Alex assured her that Kate was just a friend, nothing more. Meghan was beginning to think that Kate didn't share those same sentiments. She just wanted to clear things up, that was all. But that could cause a problem. Alex didn't have a bad temper, but he tended to get upset about little things.

"This is going to suck," she whispered to herself as she walked across the fraternity quadrangle. That day was warm and breezy, but the night air was cool against Meghan's skin. She put her arms across her chest as she walked into the fraternity house.

She arrived at Alex's door and knocked softly.

"Yeah, it's open," Alex yelled from inside.

Meghan pushed the door and slowly walked in.

"What's up, Megs? Why did you knock? I don't think you've done that since you started coming over here."

"I thought I'd be polite today," she said capriciously. She sat down at his desk.

Alex was sprawled out on his bed as usual, his nose buried in a textbook labeled *Fluid Mechanics*.

"This test is going to fucking blow," he groaned as he rolled over on his back. His new position on the bed allowed him to reach out and grab Meghan's t-shirt. Meghan moved forward in the chair, just out of his reach, as she usually did. But this time, instead of ignoring him, she jumped at the chance to bring up Kate.

"You always try to grab me, but it never works. Why don't you try it with Kate or something?"

Alex sat up immediately. "What's that supposed to mean?"

"Nothing," she said. "Just seems like she wouldn't mind it if you grabbed her."

"How many fucking times have I told you? She's a friend. She introduced me to you, in case you forgot."

"Don't cuss at me, and don't raise your voice to me. I'm just asking a question. I want to make sure I'm not being taken for a ride."

"Listen to me, Meghan." He was calm now. "I'm not going to say I love you or any of that shit. You know I'm not into that, and I know you aren't. But you have to trust me when I say I have no feelings for Kate at all. I hung out with her, I even flirted with her, but that stopped when I met you. She's nothing, she's an empty shell of a person with no emotion." He sighed. "Would it make you feel better if I talked to her about it, to clear things up?"

"What you do is up to you. I don't need you to prove anything to me. I just wanted to hear it from you because I know she's been checking us out and I know she still has strong feelings for you. And you know it too."

"Listen, I'll talk to her tonight. To clear shit up for all of us. So she knows that I'm committed to you right now, even if this isn't going to go past next year."

"You don't need to do that, Alex, seriously."

"I know I don't, but I'm going to."

Alex and Meghan spent the next hour in silence. In the back of her mind, Meghan was glad Alex was going to talk to Kate. Maybe it would stop her from always watching them. It did creep Meghan out. Did it make her a bad person, that she wanted to get Kate out of her life? She liked Kate, a lot. In Meghan's mind, Kate was an intriguing and mysterious girl, someone who she wished she could get to know better. But not right now. Right now, she was the enemy. Right now, Meghan couldn't stand Kate. Maybe that would all change someday.

ഗ✤ഗ

Kate sat in her room, staring at her computer screen. She was watching her star screensaver, the one where the small white specs look like they're flying at your face. She was thinking about exactly what to say to Alex. Yes, she was finally going to do it. Forget the fears, the inhibitions, the shyness. It was time to take a stand.

"Andy was right," she thought. "I need to suck it up and talk to Alex about how I feel. I need to ask him what went wrong, find out if it's something I did. Maybe I can learn from it. Breathe, Kate. Breathe."

She sat silently for an hour, staring at those stars. She imagined herself flying through space, lost and alone, free from the distractions and problems that had plagued her life. Then she leaned forward in her chair and began to type out exactly what she wanted to say to Alex. "We need to talk…"

"You need to do this," she told herself. "Come on, Kate. Everything that's happened is your own fault. You need to make things happen. You need to take a stand."

For the next two hours she typed and retyped, reading it over in her head, memorizing each word, each pause, each emotion. It wasn't exactly how she felt but, well, Kate wasn't the best at conveying exactly how she felt to those around her.

At 9 p.m., Kate rose from her chair. She slipped on a clean pair of jeans, a white hooded sweatshirt, and a pair of Nikes that were falling apart. She looked at herself in the mirror. "Okay, Kate, it's time. You've been through a lot. It never goes away, but this? You can control this. You can start controlling your life. Baby steps, Kate. This is simple."

She took a deep breath and glanced out the window. It looked chilly. She thumbed through her closet and pulled out her light jacket. It was five years old. The once vibrant blue color had turned pale. She brought it to her face and breathed in deeply. It reminded her of those days in high school when she walked in wearing a jacket during a warm front. "I just get chills sometimes," she'd told her friends.

Outside, the air felt crisp, but Kate was warm beneath her layers as she walked across the street to Alex's fraternity. She kept talking under her breath, reminding herself how simple her task was. "You're just asking him how he feels, Kate. All you want to know is what you did wrong, why these things never work out. God, why are you getting so worked up about a guy?"

She walked and mumbled, her head angled down at the ground as she went over the speech she'd planned. It had to be perfect. Then maybe she could convince him that she was really the girl he'd been looking for. She knew he was the guy that could make her problems go away. He was the only guy.

Kate was so caught up in her silent rehearsal that she didn't see Meghan walk right by her. The two passed without a word, just two dark figures, looming in the night. Every dark figure is someone important, someone with a story, someone with a mission. Sometimes the stories collide, sometimes the missions conflict. Kate knew her mission. She was seeking the truth, no matter how much it hurt.

When she arrived at the fraternity house, Luke let her in.

"Kate! Haven't see you here in a while."

"Yeah, I know. Is Alex around?"

Luke snickered. "Yeah, he's upstairs in his room. Meghan was just here, she left about two minutes ago. You've got to get your piece too, huh?"

"Something like that. Thanks, Luke."

Kate ascended the staircase and stopped outside Alex's door. "If you don't knock now, you'll just turn around and walk away. Knock on the door, Kate. Do it. Just fucking do it!"

Kate knocked. Alex yelled from inside the room. "Come in!"

❧◦❧

Rob sat in his room at 8 p.m., pondering his next move. He knew he had to do something. He couldn't put up with the ridicule from his friends anymore, not over something he didn't even care that much about. But man, he just couldn't bring himself to tell Kristen he really wasn't ready for a relationship. He had tried to tell her before, sure, but it was always kind of in passing. He knew Kristen blew it off. Tonight he needed to make it absolutely clear. The fling had been fun. Kissing, cuddling, touching. He wasn't used to any of it, and it felt good. But that time was over. He knew he couldn't live like this anymore. He was losing his friends, he was losing respect, he was losing his mind.

But Kristen had been so nice to him. So sweet and sincere. He knew she liked him. A lot. Had he taken advantage of that? Maybe a little. But not on purpose. They were just two college students, learning about love and all that good stuff. Now the learning experience was over. It was time to move on.

Rob met up with Kristen at 8:30 p.m. They were supposed to walk to Squirrel Hill to get ice cream and see a movie. "God, what the hell am I doing?" he asked himself. When they met at the elevator, Kristen knew something was off. Rob wasn't ready to drop the bomb just yet, but Kristen could tell there was something on his mind.

"Is something wrong?" she asked with a concerned tone.

"No, no. I'm just tired. What movie are we going to see again?"

"You wanted to see *Miracle*, right?"

"Oh yeah. Cool. Alright, let's go then."

They walked silently for ten minutes. Kristen enjoyed just being with Rob, looking to her side and seeing him there. She always tried to hold his hand in public, but he pulled away from her every time. She could deal with that for now. It would change with time.

"I don't care if he's not really committed to me yet," she thought. "There's no else in his life right now, so until there is, he's mine. Well, there's Kim, but she doesn't even like him. I don't know why he likes her anyway. She's too innocent."

Kristen had been thinking a lot about things recently. Maybe it wasn't the most orthodox relationship ever, but it worked for her, and it seemed to be working for Rob. With everything running through her mind, she didn't realize Rob hadn't said a thing. Not until they were halfway to the theater.

"Rob, what's wrong? Something's not right here, I'm not an idiot."

Rob stopped dead in his tracks. It was time. Here in the chilly April air, with random strangers walking by, it was time. Now or never.

"Kristen, we have to stop this."

"What?"

"You know what I mean. All of this. The sneaking around, the sort-of-dating, the hooking up. All of it. It needs to stop. Listen, I care a lot about you. Seriously, I know that sounds corny, but I do. But I don't want to date you, and I'm tired of not being sure what's going on. I don't have feelings for other people, but I can't do this. I don't want a relationship with you. It's not fair to either one of us. So… yeah."

Kristen was stunned. She'd expected this before. Maybe two weeks ago. But now things seemed to be getting better. Rob was hanging out with her more in public. He stopped worrying about whether or not her roommate came back when they were spending time in her room. So what was all this? It took her by surprise, and she couldn't contain herself. The tears came, and they came hard and fast.

"What are you talking about? I don't get, it Rob. I don't get anything. I don't get you. Things were going so well. How can you say you don't have feelings for me? With everything we do? What, am I just your self-esteem builder because you know I want you? What the fuck is this?"

"Kristen, come on. It's not that. I was unsure when I got into this, and I'm still unsure. But I know for a fact that I don't want to be with you and that's not going to change. So let's stop now before anything else goes wrong or anyone else gets hurt."

"Fuck this!" she screamed into the night. "You just listen to your stupid gossiping friends. They don't know anything about us or about what goes on. I don't care how much you tell them. You're so worried about what everyone thinks, about your fucking reputation. Who cares? Do what you feel. You're too scared to do what you want to if you can't justify it. Elyse and Val are controlling your life because you're letting them."

"What are you talking about? Elyse and Val try to help me because they're my friends. They tell me what they think, but I do what I want to do. If I listened to them, you'd have been gone a long time ago. I never let other people affect what I do. I'm doing what I need to do now."

"Well thanks for taking my feelings into consideration."

"What the hell? I am! I just said I don't want to draw this out anymore. I screwed up, what do you want?"

Kristen threw her hat at Rob in disgust. She turned around and walked in the opposite direction. The tears still streaming down her cheeks felt cold in the wind, but she didn't care. She didn't know what to do or think. She didn't even know where she was going. Just not here.

Rob called out to her as she walked away. "Kristen, come on. We can still go to the movie. I just needed to tell you that so we didn't keep on like this. Where are you going?"

It was useless. She was out of earshot by the time he finished yelling. He stood still in the night for a few seconds after she was out of sight.

"Well, that went well," he said out loud.

He laughed to himself and started walking back towards the dorm. Maybe she'd be calm by the time he got back. He wanted to make sure things were unambiguous, but he also wanted to make sure Kristen understood he had good intentions. He didn't dislike Kristen, she was one of his good friends. But that's as far as it went. Why was that so difficult to understand?

Kate entered Alex's room. Something felt very wrong. If she could have, she would have turned around and walked out that very moment. It wasn't right. The time, the place, the situation. She had a bad feeling about this. But it was too late now. Alex would know something was up. So she swallowed and stepped forward.

He was too stunned to talk. Alex opened his mouth but nothing came out. He hadn't seen her in two months. Things had ended on a bad note, and he knew it. What did she want? He didn't have to wonder long.

"Alex, I know this probably seems really strange, but I needed to come talk to you. It's serious, and it's been bugging me for a while. So just let me say everything I want to say, and then we can go from there. Is that cool?"

He nodded and leaned back against the wall. Kate closed the door before settling beside Alex on his bed. She sat cross-legged, her back straight. For the few seconds before she began, she looked like the queen of the world. She felt like it, too. She knew exactly what she was going to say, exactly what she'd come for.

Then Alex touched her hand. A small gesture, probably out of nervousness. But he did it. Ever so gently, he wrapped his fingers around her hand and looked into her eyes. A rush of emotion came over Kate's body. Emotion that she hadn't felt when she was imagining what to say.

"Come on, Kate," she thought. "Hold on. Just hold on and say what you need to say."

But she couldn't do it. She lost control.

Kate started bawling on Alex's bed. Everything she'd planned on telling him became a distant memory. She sat crying for a few moments before she leaned against his shoulder and buried her face in his shirt. Between sobs, she spoke.

"What did I do? What did I do that was so bad?"

"What are you talking about?" Alex spoke in a soft, consoling voice, but his tone made it obvious to Kate that he didn't really care. It made her cry harder.

"Alex, you're the first guy I've ever met that I feel like this about. I didn't even feel this way about my boyfriend in high school. When I was with you, I felt alive, I felt free. Oh God, this sounds so fucking ridiculous. You're different, Alex. But you haven't talked to me in two months. Meghan came along, and she was your new pet. And we… we just stopped."

She paused to cry some more. Alex didn't respond. He sat next to her, like a statue. Whatever moved him to touch Kate's hand was gone now, and he just wanted her to leave. "Girls are so melodramatic," he thought. "I bet she's done this a thousand times."

"What did I do?" Kate went on. "I know I did something to make you hate me. It wasn't just Meghan. I did something. I need to know. I need to know! Do you understand this? I need to know what I did."

"Okay, okay! Chill out," Alex said shortly. He was pissed. He stood and opened the door, peeking around the corner to make sure no one heard the commotion.

"Listen, Kate," he said as he sat back down. "I'll be totally honest with you. First of all, you're blowing this thing way out of proportion. I never told you to stop hanging out with me. You stopped coming over here when I started dating Meghan."

"I figured I wasn't invited. You stopped calling and stuff."

"Just because I had Meghan didn't mean you had to stop calling either. Look, Kate, I didn't try to hurt your feelings, I'm sorry if I did. But I stopped calling once I found Meghan because we really connected. I wanted to stay friends with you but when you stopped talking to me, I figured it was because you had some sort of grudge against Meghan for taking me or whatever. And to be honest, I really didn't care, and I still don't." He wasn't trying to be mean, just direct and clear.

"But what did I do that made you want Meghan instead of me?" she begged.

"What are you talking about, Kate? You didn't do anything. Maybe I was inconsiderate, maybe I was leading you on or whatever. I never knew you felt this strongly. I thought we were just friends who liked to flirt, or whatever you want to call it. I never thought of having a real relationship with you, and I thought you felt the same way. That's why I liked hanging out with you. We were just a couple people who needed somebody else, you know?

"Then I met Meghan, and I really liked her. A lot. So it was time to stop fooling around and really be committed. Kate, come on. We were never really good friends. I mean, we never told each other anything about ourselves."

"A couple people who needed somebody else?" Kate screamed, jumping off the bed. "I am not that kind of girl, Alex! I don't mess around with guys! I don't... I don't do that shit!"

"Well, okay, I'm sorry. I didn't know. How the fuck am I supposed to know that? You're introverted, conceited, you don't trust anyone or talk to anyone about yourself. You mope around like you have the worst life ever. I liked hanging out with you sometimes, but dating you would have made me depressed."

Kate stood silently in the doorway. She was surprisingly calm, all things considered. Now that she was done yelling, she wiped the tears from her eyes. She looked confident once again. Like a girl who knew exactly what she wanted.

"I don't know how you can expect anyone to take you seriously, Kate," Alex said angrily. "I never felt like you were a real person. I don't know how to explain that, but it's what I think. You want to know what you did wrong? There's your answer, I guess."

"Thanks," she said sarcastically as she walked out and shut the door behind her.

Kate didn't know what to do or think. She had stopped crying. There was no more emotion left in her body. Nineteen years old and tired of feeling. How sad. She walked towards New House not knowing what tomorrow would bring. Not knowing if there would be a tomorrow.

Kristen arrived back at the dorm sobbing. She hoped no one would be around when she got to the floor. All she wanted to do was shut herself in her room and cry. Meghan would probably be with Alex. The girls would likely be out getting food. She just needed to make it to her room. A little time to think, that's all she needed. Kristen found that as she rode the elevator up to the 5th floor, she had never wanted anything more in her life than to step off the elevator and hear dead silence. When the elevator came to a lurching halt, she closed her eyes.

"Please be empty," she whispered.

As she stepped into the lighted foyer, she heard exactly what she hoped. Nothing. She opened her eyes and looked around. The floor was empty. She was home free.

Just as she turned to run to her room, a voice called out from behind her. "Kristen, are you crying?"

Meghan had walked up the stairs. She was in a hurry to see if Kate was still in her room. Meghan could have sworn she saw Kate walk by her on the fraternity quad, and she had to check. But Kristen was clearly upset, and that took precedence over figuring out where Kate was. At least for the moment.

"What's wrong?" Meghan asked.

Kristen, who had stopped crying for a few minutes, began tearing up again.

"Meghan, can we just go to our room? I really don't want to talk to anybody right now."

"Yeah, that's fine."

Kristen walked quickly, hoping she wouldn't run into anyone else. But as her luck would have it on this evening, she turned the corner and ran right into Rosalyn.

"Kristen, are you okay?" asked Rosalyn.

"I'm fine. I'm going to my room."

"I'm coming with you."

Kristen threw her arms up in disgust. So much for being alone. But if she had to pick two people to be around her at this moment, they would have been Rosalyn and Meghan. Things could have been worse. She could have run into Elyse.

Once inside Kristen's room, they all sat on the floor next to each other. Meghan and Rosalyn stayed silent, waiting for Kristen to say something first. They didn't have to wait long.

"Rob told me he didn't want to be with me. At all. It's over. I hope you two are happy."

Rosalyn and Meghan looked at each other. They had seen it coming, they had been preparing themselves for it, but now that it was really happening, they felt bad. Rosalyn had even imagined herself yelling at Kristen: "We told you so, but you wouldn't listen, you ignorant, naïve bitch." But now that the time had come, she felt sorry for her. Kristen really did think she was in love with Rob.

"Kristen," Meghan said tenderly. "We're not happy. Yeah, we told you to expect this. We expected it. But it doesn't mean we're happy. We just didn't want to see you get hurt like this. What did he say?"

"I don't even remember," Kristen said, wiping her eyes. "We were walking to go see a movie and he just stopped on the sidewalk and said, 'I can't do this anymore, I don't want to be with you.' Didn't leave much room for interpretation."

"We're really sorry, Kristen," Rosalyn said consolingly. "Really."

"I know, but right now, I just need some time to myself. Can you guys leave for a little while?"

Without saying a word, Rosalyn and Meghan rose to leave. As Meghan shut the door behind her, she whispered to Kristen, "Everything happens for a reason. Remember that."

Meghan and Rosalyn went in opposite directions. Meghan went to check on the whereabouts of Kate, while Rosalyn headed to the elevators to get some food. When the elevator arrived, Elyse and Hillary stepped out, in the midst of a conversation.

"She's so dense. I don't understand how anyone can be that stupid. He obviously doesn't really like her, but she still hangs onto him like a dead flap of skin. Oh my God, it's just…"

Elyse fell silent. She had only then realized that Rosalyn was standing to the side, waiting to get on the elevator, listening to every word she said. Elyse stared at her blankly, then turned to walk away.

"Hey, Elyse!" Rosalyn yelled. "Tonight Rob told Kristen he doesn't want to be with her. You got your wish, you made your point. Congratulations. I hope you're proud that your stubbornness and self-absorption, you know, ruined someone else's life. That's real special."

Elyse raised her eyebrow at Rosalyn and took a step towards her. "What are you talking about? I couldn't care less what Kristen and Rob do, it doesn't affect me. They're free to do whatever they want in their own little world."

"That's why you were talking about them just then, right? 'Cause there's nothing better to talk about. And that's why you talk to Rob about it every night, right?"

"Listen, Rosalyn, I don't see why this has anything to do with you." Elyse was half-laughing, half-yelling. "I help Rob out because he's my friend and he asks me to help him. I give him the same advice I would give anyone else. What do you want me to say? That your friend needs to get her head on straight? Okay, your friend needs to get her head on straight! It's the truth, and you know it! But you're too close to her to tell her that. That's being an awesome friend. Good job, Ros."

Those were the last words that Elyse and Rosalyn would exchange that night. Rosalyn ran forward and shoved Elyse hard into the wall. Taken aback, Elyse stood stunned, staring at Rosalyn. Hillary had the sense to step in and pull Rosalyn back.

"Take a walk," she said. "We don't need to do this. Take a walk."

Rosalyn took the open elevator down to the first floor and stormed outside, not sure exactly where she was going or how long she'd be gone.

❧

Rob had stopped by Luke's fraternity on his way back to campus. He just wanted to say hi and give Kristen a few minutes to cool down. Now as Rob was leaving the fraternity to head back to New House, he saw Kate a few feet ahead of him. He yelled out to her, but she just walked away faster. He decided to leave her be for now. Rob made his way back to New House, and he saw Rosalyn walk briskly out the door as he walked in.

"What's up, Rosalyn?"

She gave him a sinister smile and continued walking.

"I guess she's talked to Kristen," he said out loud.

Rob climbed the stairs to the 5th floor, thinking about what exactly he should do, if anything. By the time he reached the top, Rob had concluded that he needed to suck it up and apologize for springing his decision on her, but make sure she understood that this was really the end of Rob and Kristen as a couple. He walked right up to Kristen's door and knocked, not giving himself time to rethink it.

"Go away!" Kristen yelled from inside her room.

Rob knocked again.

"I said GO AWAY!"

He gave it one more try. This time, Rob heard movement in the room, and Kristen opened the door violently, expecting to see Rosalyn or Meghan standing there. When she saw Rob instead, she lost it. Again.

"WHAT THE FUCK DO YOU WANT? Haven't you humiliated me enough tonight? What, do you want me to tell you how much I was in love with you to make you feel good about yourself? Or do you want to tell me more about how I'm not the kind of girl you date? What's it going to be this time?"

"I just wanted to apologize, actually."

"Apologize? Twenty minutes after you ripped my world apart? Thanks, Rob. Apology accepted. Way to be mature. You can sleep well tonight." She shook her head. "Don't patronize me. You told me what you had to tell me, I don't need it rubbed in."

"I'm not trying to rub it in, Kristen. Honestly, I didn't realize I was springing it on you like that. I guess I didn't really think about it. It can't work, yeah, I said that, but I don't want you to feel bad about it."

Kristen laughed hysterically at this, and Rob, unsure what to do, just stood in front of her and waited. When she had finished laughing, she slammed the door in his face.

"What a night," Rob mumbled to himself as he walked back to his room.

Meghan knocked on Kate's door and received no answer, so she figured it must have been Kate she saw walk up to the fraternity. Part of her was glad that Alex was finally going to clear things up with Kate. But part of her was a little scared. What if Kate convinced him that she was actually the girl he wanted, not Meghan? It all sounded so immature in her head, but she worried about it nevertheless. She walked around the floor, looking for anyone to talk to her. She needed to take her mind off Alex and Kate. The situation would work itself out. What had she just said to Kristen? Everything happens for a reason. Yeah, that's right. And just as she thought this, she saw Rob opening his door.

"Hey, Rob, what's up?"

He was not in the mood to talk. "Aren't you going to yell at me for being a horrible person?"

"Rob, I don't really care. I mean, I do, but we all knew it was coming. I have my own things to worry about right now."

"What, like the fact that Kate was just over at the fraternity?"

"Did you see her?"

"I went to visit Luke, and she walked out right in front of me. She seemed like she was kind of in her own world."

"I wonder where she is now."

"I have no clue. I know she hangs out in the back stairwell a lot. Maybe she's there?"

Meghan ran to the back stairwell and threw the door open. It was a quiet place, seldom used and always forgotten. But Kate wasn't there right now. Meghan stood there for a few minutes, contemplating what to do next. Then, the door leading to the stairwell opened behind her. She turned around to see Kim, who was clearly in a hurry, breathing hard, wrapped in her infamous purple jacket.

"Meghan! What are you doing here?" Kim gasped.

Meghan was too busy laughing to answer. "I'm sorry, Kim. It's just that crazy purple jacket. It's so obnoxious."

"Hey! I know it's obnoxious, but I like it. I've had it forever. It's unique, and it makes me stand out."

"Yeah, it does." Meghan chuckled again, then composed herself. "I was just looking for someone. What are you doing?"

"I've been using this stairwell recently. It's nice and quiet, and no one ever remembers it. I'm actually on my way to a movie with some friends. It'll be good to get out of the dorm, I think."

"I agree. Too much stuff is going on right now."

"Really? Like what?"

"You didn't hear? Rob finally told Kristen that things weren't going to work out."

"Oh boy, I bet that was fun."

"Yeah, it wasn't pretty."

"Hey, Meghan, really quick before I go: she doesn't still hate me, right?"

Meghan clenched her teeth. "Honestly, Kim, she does. It's irrational, totally, but she does. Maybe hate is the wrong word to use, but there's definitely a grudge. I guess part of it is because you've never actually talked to her to make her think differently. I mean, that's not your job, but I think that's why."

"Is she in rough shape right now?"

"Yeah, very rough."

Meghan explained what had happened as best she could, and for several minutes, Kim became so engaged in the conversation that she completely forgot that she had a ride to catch.

"Oh, Meghan, I'm sorry, but I'm going to miss my ride!"

"It's okay, I'll see you later."

Kim flew down the stairs and ran to the side of New House where she was supposed to be picked up. She had been running late in the first place, so she hoped the carpool hadn't left. But when she arrived, there was no car. She called her friend on the phone to see what was going on.

"Hey, Kim," she heard on the other end of the line. "What happened?"

"I'm really sorry," she said breathlessly. "I got caught up in a conversation. Where are you?"

"Um, we left like five minutes ago. We waited for a long time. I mean, I guess we could come back and pick you up…"

It was clear from her friend's voice that they didn't want to turn around.

"Don't worry about it, I'll hang just out here. Sorry for the inconvenience, though!"

"No problem, I'll see you later."

Kim wasn't too concerned. Honestly, she didn't really want to see the movie anyway. Her friend from dance club had called earlier in the afternoon to offer her an extra ticket. She didn't have anything else to do, so she told her friend she'd go along. But Kim preferred hanging out in the dorm, and she was secretly happy she'd get to spend the night at New House, even with everything going on. Recently, she always seemed to have some sort of commitment on the weekend: work, dancing, dinner outings. But not tonight. She had a feeling that tonight would be a good night to be on the floor. You know, one of those feelings that something was going to happen.

She climbed up the back stairwell, but instead of stopping at the 5th floor, she went up the last set of steps, which she often did. Above the 5th floor, there was a door that led to the roof. It was always locked, but one day Kim discovered, quite by accident, that the lock was broken. With a little maneuvering of the handle, the door popped open, giving free access to the roof. It was her private hiding place. Kim went there to sit and think when she wanted to get away. Tonight seemed like a good night to enjoy the cool air and the great view for a few minutes before descending into the chaos that seemed to be building on the floor. Kim checked to make sure no one was watching, opened the door quickly, and stepped into her own world. At least, what she thought was her own world.

ৡৣ

Kate ran back to New House, confused and upset. She didn't want to think. She knew where she had to go. There was only one place on the entire campus where she could hide away by herself: the roof of New House. She knew a little trick to get there using a door in the back stairwell. Actually, she'd created that trick. She had tried for hours once to break through the lock, and finally figured it out. After that, Kate began to spend many hours on the roof, standing tall and looking out over the campus. And when she started spending time on the roof, she stopped cutting herself. The roof was her new path to freedom, and it felt good.

Needing that feeling now, she scampered up the stairs and let herself onto the roof. The air was still cold, but it felt warmer as she stepped through the door. It always did. She made her way through a maze of piping and electrical equipment to an opening that overlooked the New House backyard. From here, she could see the huge buildings that belonged to the University of Pittsburgh, lit up like Christmas, standing peacefully in the dark. On this night, the stars were out in the clear sky. She looked up at them as she paced back and forth. "What am I doing?" she asked out loud. On the roof, she could speak her mind. Because on the roof, no one could hear her.

"What's wrong with me? I can't do anything right. Is this really worth it? IS IT?" She screamed into the night. A harsh wind picked up and slapped her in the face. She took a step backwards, balancing herself on the rubber floor.

"What's that supposed to mean?" she yelled at the sky. She spread her arms and raised them to the stars. "I don't believe in any of this religious bullshit. I don't even believe in myself. I have nothing to believe in! I have no one to trust!"

She walked to the ledge and peeked over the edge. The ledge was three feet high, tall enough to keep someone from accidentally falling over. Accidentally. She looked down for a long time. Five stories. A long way down. She'd thought about it before. Sometimes when she was up there. But she was always too scared to do it.

"If I wasn't such a pussy," she told herself, "I'd have done it a long time ago."

She wanted to. She really did. She thought about it every day, at least once. Even when things started to get better, she thought about it. And now that things were getting worse, it was always on her mind. Maybe ending it is really the best answer, she thought. It was so simple. So, so simple. Maybe this was the night she'd swallow her fear and do it. Take a chance. What is death? Couldn't be worse than this thing called life. No way. Why not do it? Look at the situation. It's perfect.

"Someone is trying to tell you you're not supposed to be here," she whispered to herself.

A rush of emotion came over Kate. Standing next to the ledge, she felt like she was on some kind of high. She smiled at the sky. Yes, this was the night. She needed to do it. For herself. Nothing ever felt more right, nothing in her life. She saw the problem. All the cutting, all the hoping, all the wanting—it was to make her feel alive. But, Kate realized, she just wasn't meant to feel alive.

She climbed onto the ledge and balanced herself. She stood looking out over Pittsburgh, her hands on her hips, like an explorer staking claim to a brand new discovery. Her hair blew in the gentle wind. Her hooded sweatshirt felt warm against her stomach. It felt right. She wanted to wait just one more minute. Soak all of it in. Feel alive for the last time, then never have to worry about it again. She took a deep breath.

᭡᭡

Something didn't feel right to Kim. She liked to walk out towards the ledge of the roof and lean against it, watching the world operate from sixty feet above. But when she turned the corner, she gasped. She wasn't alone. Standing on the ledge of the roof, her back to Kim, was Kate. She looked like she was going to jump.

Oh my God, this can't be happening, Kim thought. This isn't real. Oh my God, say something. Say anything.

"KATE!"

Kim had never screamed louder in her life. She didn't think she ever would again.

Kate turned around on the ledge. She faced Kim, a blank, sinister look on her face. "You shouldn't be here, Kim. You're a sweet girl. You wouldn't want to see this."

"Oh my God, Kate. What the *fuck* are you doing?" Kim realized it was the first time she had ever used that word out loud.

"What's it look like I'm doing?" Kate asked sarcastically.

"I can't believe this! Oh please, Kate, don't do this. What's wrong?" Kim sounded scared and nervous. But she kept her cool. She knew she needed to. Beneath her clothes, she was shivering.

Kate threw her head back and laughed. The force of her motion almost took her over the edge. Kim, fifteen feet away, put her hands out as if to will Kate back onto the ledge, but she rebalanced herself.

"Everything is wrong, Kim. Everything. Don't ask me to explain. I can't. I'm sure it all sounds so petty to you, but you can't change my mind. Just don't do anything stupid and I'll talk to you for a few minutes. But if you run at me, if you try to call someone, if you leave, then… Yeah, don't do it. You can't stop the inevitable, you can only postpone it."

❧

Rosalyn was still furious at Elyse. But she felt horrible that she'd hit her. She was turning into her father. Oh God, anything but that. She wanted to apologize profusely to Elyse and yet tear her head off at the same time.

Feeling restless, she walked around the Kensington parking lot for a few minutes. After she had cooled down, she decided it was time to go back to the floor. She needed to apologize to Elyse, even if she disagreed with her. She knew she hadn't handled the situation well, and she needed to show herself she wasn't turning into her father.

As she walked back to the dorm, she looked up at the sky. The stars were out tonight. They looked beautiful. She stopped for a moment to stare at them, to pretend everything was fine. Everything would be fine. She inhaled the cool air and brought her head back down to eye level. But something caught her eye. On the roof of New House. It looked like… It looked like someone was standing on the ledge. Was this a joke? It didn't look like a joke.

Her heart started beating faster. She couldn't tell who it was. A girl, judging by the hair, but her face was turned the opposite direction, like she was talking to someone. So someone else was there too. Rosalyn looked closer. Was that Kim? Yes, it was Kim, wearing that awful purple jacket. Instinctively, Rosalyn pulled out her phone and dialed Kim's number.

ℒↄ∞ↄↄ

Kim took a few steps closer to Kate. "I'm not trying to grab you, I just can't hear when you're so far away. Kate, I don't even know what to say."

"You don't have to say anything."

Kim's cell phone rang and startled both of them. "It's Rosalyn. Can I pick it up?"

Kate shrugged her shoulders. "Sure, just don't tell her where you are."

She answered the call.

"Kim? Are you on the roof?" Rosalyn asked.

Kim had to think quickly. "Yes, I did end up canceling the movie."

Rosalyn paused. Okay, this wouldn't be easy. Something was up. No kidding, Rosalyn. Okay, focus, think. Don't be stupid.

"Do you need help?" she asked slowly.

"Rent a movie? Yeah, that would be great. I'm running a few errands right now, but as soon as I'm done, you should come join me."

"How do I get up there?"

"What do you mean how are you supposed to kill time until I get back? I don't know, Ros. Do what I would do." Kim stressed that last sentence as subtly as she could. "And invite people to watch the movie with us. The more the merrier."

Kim wasn't exactly sure if more people would be good, but she had no clue what to do. Maybe if they combined ideas, they could figure something out.

ℒↄ∞ↄↄ

Rosalyn sprinted into New House. "Do what I would do," she kept saying to herself. As she ran through the front doors, she came to a screeching halt. Kim always took the back stairwell. Maybe she could get to the roof from there. She ran for it. When Rosalyn arrived at the top of the fifth flight of stairs, she was surprised to see Meghan sitting there.

"What are you doing here, Megs?" she asked quickly.

"Just chilling. I was here talking to Kim, then she left. Then I left, but I came back here a few minutes later. It's a pretty cool place, actually. I've never really been in here before."

Rosalyn looked up, and for the first time, noticed that the stairs went one floor higher than the 5th floor. She shushed Meghan for a moment and crept to the door. It was open.

"What's going on?" Meghan asked.

"Kim is up there. There's someone standing the ledge next to her, I think the person wants to jump."

"Rosalyn, what are you talking about?"

"I'm serious. You need to believe me. I'm going to call campus police. Go round up people to come up to the roof. Maybe all of us can help. I don't know. I called Kim, she told me to bring a lot of people. Go!"

Without thinking, Meghan ran through the door to find people. Rosalyn frantically called campus police and told them she thought there was a suicidal person on the roof of New House. She didn't wait to hear their response. She opened the door slowly and stepped quietly onto the roof.

༄

Kim hung up the phone and looked back at Kate. She had a newfound confidence. "Kate, what can I do to convince you to come down from there? At least for tonight."

Kate thought about it. "If you can prove to me that there's a damn good reason to keep trying when I've been trying so hard for nineteen years."

"How can I do that?"

"If I knew, I'd tell you, trust me. This doesn't scare me, Kim. Dying, killing myself, it doesn't scare me. That's why it's come to this. It's not something I want to do, but I'm prepared for it."

"You don't have to, though."

"I can't explain it, but I do. I know I do. I've known for a long time. I've been looking for a reason to believe in myself, to believe in other people my entire life. I haven't found one."

She dropped her head. She looked sad but content. Kim opened her mouth to say something else, but she was interrupted by a voice from behind her. They both looked up. It was Rosalyn.

"Hey, guys… How's it going?" Rosalyn was clueless. She'd felt so calm and confident before she saw Kate standing on the ledge, but now, with Kate in front of her, she was close to passing out. She had seen some scary things in her life. This was the scariest yet.

"What are you doing here?" Kate yelled.

"Please don't be mad. I saw you up here when I was walking through the parking lot. Oh, Kate, are you really going to jump?"

Kate was losing her patience. She turned back around. She tried to shut Rosalyn and Kim out, she wanted to feel the moment. But she couldn't block them off. She listened.

Rosalyn and Kim were scared. They didn't know what to do. What do you say to someone about to jump? They don't teach you that in calculus. Suddenly, calculus seemed like the easiest thing in the world.

"Kate, listen to me, please," begged Kim. "I know anyone in this situation would try to talk you out of it, but you have to at least hear me out. We care about you. I don't care if it sounds stupid or if you don't believe me, but we do. That's why I'm still here, and that's why Rosalyn came. You can believe in that. You can believe in us, as your friends, as people who want to help you."

"She's right," Rosalyn chimed in. "Maybe we aren't as close to you as you'd like, but we're here to back you up. What's Andy always say? We're a community. We are. This floor, this group of friends. I sound like a fucking sap right now, but I mean it. Kate, you've never been our best friend, but we really do care about you. We all have our fights and our stupid feelings and stuff, but that's just because we're so close."

Rosalyn heard footsteps behind her. She turned around to see Meghan standing there, stunned. And Rob, and Kristen, and Elyse. Behind them were Ben, Aaron, Val, Hillary, Melissa, Luke, Sam, Chad, and Alicia.

I brought up the rear. Meghan had pounded on my door while I was writing a paper. She yelled that someone was on the roof, something about someone trying to jump. We had all come running.

In hindsight, I can't believe that many people were even on the floor on a Sunday night, when students were usually crammed into the library and computer clusters. But at the time, I was more concerned about Kate standing on the ledge, looking down, clearly ready to jump.

Meghan stepped forward. She had been listening to Kim and Rosalyn. "Kate," she said apologetically. "It's Meghan. I'm sorry. I am. Rob told me he saw you walking away from the fraternity house. I know you talked to Alex. I know you didn't hear what you wanted to. And it's partly my fault. I acted without taking your feelings into consideration. I wish I could take that back. Kate, I really like you. I wouldn't want to lose your friendship because of a stupid guy who won't even be here next year. I'm sorry."

Kate felt tears forming in her eyes. "It's not about that," she mumbled without facing us. "There's so much more to it."

"Oh, I'm sure there is," Meghan went on. "But what happened with Alex doesn't help. All the little things add up. Believe me, I know. But Kate, turn around. Look behind you. Your friends are here. There are twenty people standing behind you right now that want to help you."

I stepped forward, my legs shaking, and my voice trembling.

"Kate, this is Andy. I probably know a lot more about what went on this year than anyone else here, and I know it hasn't been easy. But you have to let us help you. Kate, before this year even started, I knew what I wanted this floor to be. I wanted it to be a place where everyone had someone to lean on. I know you don't buy into that, but you've got a home here. You have New House 5. Whether you like it or not, you are part of us, and that means we aren't going to let you take the easy way out. We're asking you to lean on us, Kate. This isn't fake friendship. You can't brush us to the side just because you think we don't really care. Because what if we do?"

"Shut up about the fucking floor," she replied. "This has nothing to do with your 'community.'"

Before I could respond, I was tapped on the shoulder. I looked behind me to see Elaine standing there. "Sam called me," she whispered. She looked up at Kate and spoke.

"Hey, it's Elaine. I'm here too. There's no point in repeating what everyone said, but we want to help you, buddy. Let us help you."

Kate turned around on the ledge. She was facing us now, all thirty of us. Claire, Desta, Allison, Tim, Roger, and Devon had all joined us, along with a handful of others. When Elaine stepped back, Sam stepped forward. "Let us help you, Kate." Then Meghan. "Let us help you, Kate." And Elyse. "Kate, let us help you, babe." Each person stepped forward, each person said the same thing, each time with a sincerity I can't describe in words.

Kim went last. "Let us help you, Kate. You said you needed something to believe in. Believe in this. Believe that we care about you. Not because we're a cult, or an honors program, or a floor. But because we share a bond that no one can touch. We believe in you, Kate. You need to believe in us."

Kate stared at us. She didn't move a muscle. A single tear ran down the side of her face, lost, lonely, confused.

Rob stepped forward one more time. "Kate, I admit I never got to know you well. And if I did it all again, I probably still wouldn't get to know you. But not because I don't like you. We just aren't compatible people. But you don't have to be best friends with someone to care about them. You just need to know that you're on their side, and they're on yours. We probably won't ever be best friends, but why would you give up that chance? If you need something to believe in, believe in chance. Some things work out, some things don't. You've got to give them a chance, though."

໑໐

Kate looked. Looked at all thirty of us, each and every one. If someone asked her who her closest friends were, who would she say? She smiled. The people standing in front of her. She might hesitate to admit it to someone, but she wouldn't hesitate in her head.

But why? These were the people she didn't like. The people who only said they cared, who only acted like friends. No one really cared. No one was really worried about anyone but themselves.

But maybe not. Maybe these people were real. Maybe they understood her more than she would have liked to admit. They had spent the last year changing her mind, slowly but surely. They were trying to do it one more time.

I want to go home, she thought.

Home. Where was home? Images flashed through her head. All the good, all the bad. Home wasn't New Jersey. She didn't feel comfortable there. Home wasn't Alex or Jared. She couldn't be herself around them. Home was New House 5. Home was just around the corner. Home, home, home.

໑໐

Kate stepped forward onto the roof. She fell to her knees, buried her head in her hands, and cried. Elaine sat down beside her and hugged her gently. Kate wrapped her arms around Elaine. We pulled her farther back from the ledge and everyone took turns consoling her.

A confused policeman walked onto the roof a few minutes later. "Took me a few minutes to find this place," he said.

"Good thing," Rosalyn whispered under her breath.

Elyse took the policeman aside to explain the situation as best she could while the crowd began to break. I stood back for a moment and let it all sink in. It was my turn to be proud of my floor. What I witnessed that night made me proud to be an RA, proud to be a member of New House 5, proud to be a human. I knew we were strong, but not this strong. New House 5 wasn't just a floor. It wasn't just a community. It was a family. And standing there in the cool air, I truly believed that.

As Kate and Elaine were getting ready to go back inside, Kate broke from Elaine to hug me. "Thank you," she said. "Thank you for being there for me. And thank you for making this place a home. Maybe a home is all I needed."

BREATHE IN, BREATHE OUT

Let me hear your stories
I promise not to tell
Share the new dreams you pulled from
That dried up wishing well
- Whispers

The aftermath of what came to be known as "The Roof Incident" wasn't really an aftermath at all. The policeman stuck around for a little while, taking down names and information. We managed to convince him that Kate had never actually climbed onto the ledge, she had just threatened it, and that saved her from a lot of unnecessary paperwork and grief. I told Tamira and she sat down with Kate the next day to talk about what had happened and make a plan for the rest of the semester. With so little time left, they decided it was best for Kate to stick it out, finish up finals, then go home to recuperate.

But Kate had a problem, we all knew it, and she was ready to admit that. She began going to a professional counselor off-campus. She opened up to her new therapist on the first day, and after a four-hour session, she came back looking more relieved than I had ever seen her. There was something about the bounce in her step and the way her dimples appeared in a split second that I had never seen before. Her eyes didn't look lonely. They looked fulfilled.

No one spoke to Kate about what happened. It was an unwritten agreement, and I think it worked out for everyone. Kate appreciated everybody being there for her more than she could have ever expressed, so she didn't try. She just hoped they understood. New House 5 had always felt like home, but she could never admit it to herself. She may never actually say it in so many words, but she needed to realize it, and that night standing on the roof, she did.

Laura asked me about what had happened the next day, but she already knew everything was fine. I give Laura a lot of credit for dealing with a floor that never really connected to her and still managing to be a role model nonetheless. A lot of the girls looked up to her even if they didn't love her, and that's the important thing.

Soon, everyone on New House 5 knew about The Roof Incident, but it never left the floor. As far as the rest of the Ashford campus could tell, nothing had happened at all. We were still New House 5, proud and strong.

Kate continued with the counseling, telling me about it every time she went. In the last two weeks at school, she made three trips, each one more successful than the last. Our conversations no longer seemed forced or awkward. We both talked freely about our problems, concerns, and triumphs. I never talked to Kate about The Roof Incident either. She never brought it up. We didn't need to talk about it. What happened on the roof would stay up there, maybe forever. But the memory would never go away. Not from my mind, not from Kate's, not from anyone's who was there that night. It impacted all of us more than I can explain. We all saw what the power of friendship can do. It can tear down walls that have been standing for years, that have been layered with emotional scars and bad memories. It's a crazy thing, friendship is.

Rob and Kristen both realized that they were making way too big a deal out of their situation. After a long conversation, they agreed that it wasn't good for either one of them. They agreed on friendly terms to end the physical relationship, and to my surprise (as well as a lot of other people's) they both seemed cool with it. Rob needed to figure out what he wanted in a relationship (or if he wanted one at all) and Kristen needed to get over her infatuation. I figured Kristen would take a little longer than Rob, but they both were making a conscious effort, and that's all that mattered. Maybe witnessing a close friend stepping onto a ledge sixty feet above the ground will make you figure out that there are more important things in life than holding grudges and pouting.

It seemed to work for us, anyway. During the next week, there were a lot of conversations between people who used to be friends but had turned into enemies. In their minds, each of them knew they needed to make up, and that happened in a variety of ways. Elyse and Meghan were walking back from class one day when out of the blue, Elyse spilled her soul to Meghan.

"I know this is really random, but I want to make sure you know. I am so, so sorry about everything that's happened in the last few weeks. I know I was wrong. I know it was all stupid to begin with. I know I didn't respect the feelings of the people around me, and I just want to say I'm sorry. To you, to everyone, for everything." It was very thoughtful, analytical, and all-encompassing. The good old Elyse.

"Thanks," Meghan said. Hearing that meant more to her than Meghan would ever admit. "It's partly my fault, too. Everyone's fault, actually. We were all just really immature about it. I'm kind of ashamed of all of us. We turned a small deal into a big deal, and it sort of tore us apart. A few months ago, I would have called you one of my closest friends here, but during the last two weeks, I wasn't even sure if I had any friends. I'm glad it's taken care of now."

Elyse laughed. "Me too, Meghan. Me too."

Reconciliation was the word of the week. Elyse and Rosalyn worked out their differences, Val made amends with both Meghan and Rosalyn, and those two apologized to Rob for giving him a hard time. On Thursday night, just four days after The Roof Incident, Rosalyn, Val, Elyse, Meghan, Rob, and Kristen all went out to eat at a Thai restaurant in Squirrel Hill. If you'd told me four days earlier that I would witness them all walking onto the elevator together, I might have punched you. Hard.

Not everything worked out like a fairy tale. Kristen decided it was time to give up on Rob, but she still held small, quiet grudges against Elyse and Kim. She had a difficult time forgiving Elyse for causing the problem in the first place, and she couldn't ever forgive Kim for being on Rob's mind the entire time she and Rob had been an item. Call it childish, but that's how things were. But Kristen still had her close friends. She and Rosalyn were like sisters now, and she had Rob and me to goof around with. And of course there was Meghan, her roommate and unspoken best friend. I say Kristen and Rosalyn were like sisters, but sometimes I thought Meghan and Kristen really might have been separated at birth. They complemented each other very well, each giving something to the other and taking a little as well.

Speaking of Meghan, she had her own problems to sort out. Lost in the shuffle was the straw that had broken the camel's back: Alex. Meghan needed to talk to him, because all of the hassle simply wasn't worth it. Before she talked things over with Alex, she decided she needed to suck up her fear and discuss it with Kate first. In the midst of finals studying, Meghan went to Kate's room. Her door was open.

"Hey, Kate," Meghan said in the cheeriest voice she could muster. "Can I talk to you for a minute?"

"Yeah, my roommate is gone for a while. What's up?"

Meghan laughed nervously. "Okay, this is kind of weird, but I wanted to talk to you about Alex. I know we don't know much about each other, but I've always sort of admired you, and I'm getting to like you a lot more as I get to know you. I don't want a misinterpretation to ruin that. I'm not going to stop seeing Alex because of you, but I do want to know what you think."

"Thanks for saying something about it," Kate said. "I've wanted to for a few days now, but I wasn't sure if it was appropriate."

"I wasn't sure either."

"I don't want you to stop seeing him, seriously. My mind was all over the place for a while. I was thinking stupid and irrational things, and I was saying even stupider and more irrational things. I don't want my own insecurities to stop you from doing what you want. You all have helped me so much to come back around and be myself again. I did have a crush on Alex—a huge one—and I still do like him a little. But he doesn't want anything to do with me as far as a relationship goes. It took me a while to accept that, but now I have and my feelings for him are fading away. I'm fine, seriously. It means a lot that you asked how I felt, though. Thanks."

"No problem, Kate. Hey, do you want to go out to eat with Kristen and me tonight? We're going to some place in Shadyside that's supposed to be amazing."

"That would be great. I'll be here studying, just swing by and grab me."

"Sounds good."

With her conscience clear, Meghan made the trek over to Alex's room. She was glad Kate took it so well. "She really is a nice girl," Meghan thought to herself. "Maybe now that we know more about each other we can stay in touch for the rest of college. That would be cool."

Her conversation with Alex was a little awkward. Meghan wasn't sure exactly how she felt about him. She did like him, and he was a nice, good-looking guy who liked her. But there was something about him that didn't sit well with her, and that thing, whatever it was, was in the forefront of her mind. Maybe it was his lack of sensitivity, maybe it was his apathy, maybe it was his "college guy" attitude. But for whatever reason, she knew after talking to Kate that she was going to tell Alex that their relationship wasn't going any further.

"Look," she told him, "you're graduating next semester. I don't know when I'll see you again. There's just no point. I like you, and I want to stay friends with you, but something doesn't feel right about this whole thing. To be honest, something didn't feel right from the start."

"I don't get girls at all," he sighed. "Whatever. That's cool. It doesn't matter to me."

"If it really doesn't matter, then I think that's a good indication that this whole thing isn't a great idea."

"Maybe. You're starting to sound like Kate, dude. She's a nut job."

Meghan held her tongue. So much had happened in the last week that Alex didn't know about. That he would never know about. She just smiled, turned around, and walked away. As she was leaving, she said one last thing to Alex.

"Watch what you say about Kate. She's an awesome girl. You wouldn't understand."

Despite the reconciliations, there was still a lingering uncertainty in everyone's mind. Who could they trust, who was really their friend? But instead of worrying about it, they all decided that each situation would work out in the end and only time could make things better. Not everything ends like a Disney movie, but in this case, it came pretty close. We had a few kinks to work out, but it was nothing we couldn't overcome. Actually, I'm not sure there's anything we couldn't have overcome.

Everything had come together, just I like I'd hoped. All the tension of the previous few weeks had gotten to everyone, but now we could all take a few deep breaths and go back to being New House 5, the floor of floors. Cocky, yes. But we walked the walk.

I'm not going to lie, I wouldn't have chosen The Roof Incident as the single thing that would bring us all back together. But it did. Everything happens for a reason. I believe that more and more as each day passes. My entire floor had witnessed an incredibly traumatic event, but I couldn't help being all smiles for the rest of the semester. New House 5, just two weeks earlier, was a floor in shambles. There had been no sense of community, no sense of family, no sense of closeness. No sense of home. At least that's what I thought. But I was wrong. The real New House 5, the New House 5 that had become my family during the 2003-2004 academic year, had only been hiding. Hiding beneath lies and deceit and anger and confusion. We had just needed to wipe those things away and leave the true spirit of New House 5 remaining. I'd been so afraid we wouldn't be able to do that, but we did. And I couldn't have been happier about it.

We had one last floor meeting before everyone left for the semester. It was the first evening of finals and I thought it would serve as a nice study break. I wanted to wrap up the year, thank everyone, and go over a few logistical things about checking out of the dorm. But what started as a study break turned into an emotional moment for all of us. After I told everyone what I needed to say about checkout, I made one final presentation of the Lucky Fin Award.

"I'm going to give Nemo to someone tonight to keep permanently. I thought a long time about this and it was a tough decision. But with help from some nominations, I've decided to give Nemo to someone who has never gotten Nemo before. Nemo has changed hands about thirty times. And this time, he's going to someone who is always around, who participates in every floor event, who is friends with almost everyone who lives here, and who epitomizes the enthusiasm and friendship that New House 5 is known for. Aaron, take care of him, buddy."

As I tossed Nemo to Aaron, the group erupted in applause. It really was symbolic. Aaron was the guy who never did anything crazy. He never saved anybody from dying, never drove someone to the hospital at 3 a.m., but he was an anchor for the strength, stability, and community of New House 5. And for that, I wish I could have thanked him with a dozen Nemos.

After the applause died down, I quieted the group for one final announcement.

"I need to say something to all of you, while I have you here in a group. Thank you. Thanks to each and every one of you for everything you've done and meant to me this year. We've been through quite a bit together. Maybe somebody can write a book about it someday.

"I never use the word 'love.' I think it's thrown around too much. But I love this floor. I love all of you. Because I've learned more from you than you can ever imagine, and I know you've all learned more from each other than I will ever know. This floor is truly something special. It's not a floor, it's a home. And that's because of everyone sitting here right now. It doesn't matter if everyone knows your name, it doesn't matter how many stories you have, it doesn't matter if you've screwed up once or twice or a hundred times. I know you all feel comfortable here, and I know you all add something to this floor. What an incredible thing. Thanks, guys. Thanks."

In the split second of silence that followed, Kate stood up, cleared her throat, and took a deep breath.

"Before you all go, I need to say something too. To all of you." There were tears in her eyes. She wiped them away but more appeared.

"If Andy had said what he just said a couple months ago, I would have said, 'Bullshit. This is the most superficial thing ever.' But the reality is, it's not. You all know what happened last week. It doesn't need to be talked about. But what you all did for me... I can't even explain it. I am alive right now because of you."

She paused for a moment. It sent goose bumps up my spine. The entire room was quiet and motionless. She wiped her eyes again before going on.

"I never wanted to be a part of this... well, I called it a cult. It was forced friendship, it was cliché, and I don't do that stuff. But everything about this place, about this floor, is true. The people, the friendships, the community, the... whatever other bullshit term Andy uses. It's all true, and I love all of it. I was messed up when this school year started. I still am. But you all have shown me that with a little help, I can make things better for myself. You have made me believe in people again. And for that, I will always be in debt to you."

She sat down. No one moved. There were a few sniffles, a few tears, and a lot of smiles. We sat silent for a full minute. No one wanted to move. It felt so right. When we all started realizing we needed to break out of our trance, someone spoke up. And you know who spoke up? The only person I could have imagined speaking up.

"So," Rob said loudly. "Who's up for some pizza?"

It wasn't funny, but we all laughed hysterically. It was so appropriate.

We did order pizza and we sat in the lounge, talking for hours, all of us, recounting our memories of the year and our hopes for the future. Studying for finals took a backseat that night. In fact, I can't think of anything that could have been more important than sitting with my closest friends, eating pizza, and talking the night away.

The next day, I hung a huge piece of poster board next to the elevator. On it, I wrote in large letters, "New House 5th Floor, 03-04." Next to it, I posted a sign asking everyone to jot down their name and a quote or a few words of wisdom. I planned on putting the poster up in my dorm room the next year. I signed it first:

> Thanks for making my job fun and easy, double thanks for making my life a living hell. Thanks for the memories and friendships (and the comforter). This has seriously been one of the most rewarding, fun, and challenging things I've done. I'll never forget you guys… no matter how hard I try. Come visit next year.

Within a few days, most of the floor had signed it with some sort of clever remark. Eric wrote something obnoxious about the Red Sox. Ben, MinYoung, and Avery made references to poker. Aaron glued a picture of himself with long hair to the poster and wrote, "They sent this kid back bald." Allison and Hillary harped on my musical career. Melissa recounted one of her favorite drunk comments. And of course, someone signed the name "Ruben."

Finals week went pretty smoothly. There didn't seem to be any more stressing than usual. I guess the events of the previous two weeks put schoolwork in perspective. It's important to study and get good grades and all that stuff, but there are a lot more meaningful things in life. College isn't just about school.

As finals week wore on, a few people trickled out here and there. I said my goodbyes to Ben and Sam, told them I'd see them soon. That's the great thing about saying goodbye when you're in college: it's only goodbye for a couple months. Before he left, Sam made sure to tell me, "Andy, you're the sister I never had." I took it as a compliment.

Finals were spread over one full week, plus the following Monday and Tuesday. By Tuesday evening, the floor was really starting to clear out. Every five minutes someone else stopped by my room to borrow the vacuum and say goodbye. It was all sort of a blur. It reminded me of how much RA training had been a blur as well. The year had come full circle. The beginnings mesh with the finishes, and it's hard to tell where anything starts or ends. Maybe nothing really ends. Maybe an end is just a way to say a new beginning. I said goodbye to some of my closest friends. Meghan, Elyse, Rosalyn, Aaron,

Roger. They were all leaving, and they'd never live on the floor again. But they'd always be part of it.

୬◦ଏ

When Wednesday morning came, there were less than ten people left on the floor. By noon, that number would be zero. Rob, Kim, and Kate were still around, and I told them to make sure they stopped by before they left. I knew I didn't have to tell any of them, though.

Rob was first to drop in, around 8 a.m.

"This is it, man," I said when he walked into my room.

"Well, it's not really 'it.' But it is goodbye for now, and it is kind of sad. I didn't think I'd be sad about leaving because, you know, we're all coming back next year. But it just feels so weird to know that I'll never be able to call this place home again."

"It's a strange feeling, man. Maybe I'll come up to Boston this summer when I'm not busy working for the Red Wings."

"You definitely should. Just give me a call."

"I will," I said. "You know, you really helped make this place what it was this year, dude. You were sort of the floor personality."

"I just fed off everyone else's enthusiasm and acceptance, honestly. I had a ton of fun. Next year definitely won't be the same." He sighed. "Well, I have to catch my flight. I'll talk to you soon."

"Definitely, man."

As I shook his hand and he turned away, I realized I had one more thing to say.

"Hey, Rob. You said it feels weird to know that you'll never be able to call this place home again. I have a feeling, to some extent, we'll always call this place home."

He smiled. "I get the same feeling."

About an hour after Rob left for his flight, Kim stopped in to say goodbye too.

"Andy, this is so weird. There is no one on the floor. I think there are like two other people left. It feels so empty."

"But not lonely," I said.

"This place never feels lonely," she responded.

"I agree. I'm going to miss you, dude."

"Oh, come on. Don't go all sentimental on me. You better call me this summer, and I know where I'm going to camp out next year when I'm stressed. Your room is my bubble of safety. This floor can get stressful sometimes, but everybody had a place to go when they needed to get away. Everyone needs some time away from their family."

"Yeah, dude, I hear you. I know I'm going to see you guys next year, but it definitely won't be the same. You know?"

"I do. New House 5 for life, remember? I put that in my profile. Along with about a dozen other people on the floor."

"I saw that. It's pretty cool. Makes me feel all warm and fuzzy inside."

"Haha, shut up."

"I'm serious. Sort of."

Kim's watch beeped. "Andy, I'm going to miss my flight! I'd say I'm going to miss you too, but I'm sure I'll talk to you a lot over the summer." She grinned. "Thank you for everything you've done this year. For being a great RA, then a great friend. The first semester, you created this warm little community for all of us. I didn't start coming out for a month or so, but when I did, it was awesome. I really needed it. I really needed to know people cared, especially coming off my experience with George. And then second semester, you became one of my best friends here. I think a lot of people feel the same way."

"I get too much credit for what happens on this floor, but thanks, dude. It means a lot to me to hear that from someone."

"You don't get too much credit. Bye, Andy. I'll talk to you soon."

Kim surprised me with a tight hug, then turned around and ran to catch her bus to the airport.

Kim had only been gone for a few minutes before Kate dropped in. She stood in my doorway for a few seconds until I noticed her and got startled.

"Scared you, didn't I?" she asked playfully.

"I thought everyone was gone."

"There are a couple of us left. Greg is still packing a few things too. But I'm leaving now, my mom came to pick me up. We've got a long road trip ahead of us, it'll give us a chance to talk about some things. I think there's a lot I've just never had the courage to talk to her about until now."

She smiled. "Andy, I don't want to keep my mom waiting, and I'm not going to recite some sappy goodbye monologue, but if I haven't said it enough, then here it is one more time: thanks. Someday I'll be able to show you what you've done for me." She hugged me quickly, then turned to leave.

Before she left, I stopped her one more time. "Hang on a second. I almost forgot." I fumbled through my desk and pulled out two folded pieces of paper. I handed them to her. "I thought you might want these back."

She opened the folded sheets and smiled. "These are two poems that are staying in my past." With that, she crumpled them up, threw them into my garbage can, and left my room.

"Have a good summer," I yelled as she walked away. I stood smiling for a moment. It was one of those smiles that never goes away.

I walked out onto the floor. All was quiet, except for Gregory moving his last few boxes. For the first time, I felt alone on New House 5. I walked the entire floor. It was scarier than Winter Break. Then, I'd known everyone was coming back. But not this time. Now, everyone would be in a different dorm, living a different life.

As Gregory waited for the elevator, I tipped my hat to him.

"You're the last man standing, buddy. When you step onto that elevator, New House 5 is empty."

"That's a lot to live up to. But it's pretty cool being the last man standing. I wouldn't have it any other way."

Gregory got onto the elevator and waved at me as it closed. When he was out of view, I stood still for a moment and took it all in. New House 5 as I knew it was no more. There would be more people next year, and I had no doubt they would make their own memories and have their own identity. But New House 5, the pioneers, were gone. I felt empty and fulfilled at the same time. And you know what? I couldn't help smiling.

I spent the next hour doing logistical RA stuff. Room checks, cleaning up, clearing out the refrigerator on the first floor. At 3 p.m., I loaded all of my belongings into my car. Before I left for the summer, I took one last walk around the floor. It was barren now. My room, the bathrooms, the lounges.

So many memories were created here. The family that was New House 5 had gone in fifty-six different directions. I stood on an empty floor, feeling the pangs of empty nest syndrome at the age of twenty.

I hoped everyone who had been a part of New House 5 enjoyed it as much as I did. I hoped they all learned as much as I did, about themselves, their friends, their futures. A community is a place to let your imagination run wild and set your dreams free. New House 5 was a place to do that. I knew I would see everyone the next year, but I knew we wouldn't all stay close. It was impossible. I knew I would stay in touch with some and others would fade away. But for that one year, for that one magical ride we all had on New House 5, no one faded away. We were one. Now, I stood alone, the last representative of New House 5. But somehow, I knew that I had just lived the best year of my life. Somehow, I felt surrounded by every good feeling that exists in the world. Somehow, I knew that feeling would never go away. Ever.

EPILOGUE

No one knew
How this would go
But it turned out alright
Say goodnight
But don't turn off the light
- Keep the Light On

It's hard to believe that everything you've just read about happened less than a year ago. It's such a concrete memory in my mind, something I think about each day in one way or another. I started writing this book in the middle of October, and now, in the middle of December, the idea has become a reality. I don't consider myself a writer, but putting my story down on paper seemed like the most natural thing in the world. I started writing. And I kept writing. And I couldn't stop.

I'm back doing the RA thing again. I'm enjoying it again, though my experience has been much different. There isn't as much drama, there isn't as much community, and there isn't that magical feeling anymore. But this year's floor is unique in its own way, and my current residents constantly remind me, through their actions and words, that New House 5 is still alive. This year, it just means something different.

One of my current residents found out I was writing this book and said to me, "We're not as interesting as last year's floor, are we?"

I laughed and said, "Well, that might be a good thing."

It feels like everything has changed this year, but then I look, and nothing really has. Yeah, I'm on a different staff (that I love just as much as last year's) with fifty-six different people on my floor. It's weird sometimes walking around the floor and not seeing Rob or Kim or Meghan hanging out in the lounge. But I've made new friends this year, learned new stories, and dealt with new issues. And as always, I learn from all of it. If nothing else, I've realized that I have a lot of learning left to do. We all do.

I say nothing really has changed because I'm still close to the people I was close to last year. A lot of my former residents keep in touch with me through instant messaging, and occasionally I go out to eat with them or see a movie. But I still see Rob, Aaron, Sam, Kim, Meghan, Rosalyn, Elyse, Kate, and Ben all the time. They come over to chat in my room, or I go to their new dorms to hang out. Somehow, we manage to balance our schedules to make time for the people who really matter.

It's funny how my floor this year has taken to some of the people from my floor last year. Rosalyn and Rob were both Orientation Counselors on my floor this year, and they come back to visit often. My current residents know all of my good friends from last year by name and face. New House 5 has turned into a continuous community, spanning two years and across the campus.

I put the poster that everyone signed up on my wall this year. It's pretty much the only thing that has changed about my room. I knew everything else around me would be changing, so I decided to keep my room exactly the same, right down to the pictures on the wall and the furniture setup. When I taped the poster to my wall and looked it over, I noticed that Rob and Kim hadn't signed yet. It turns out that both of them had wanted to wait until the last possible second, and in the end, they forgot to. On the first day of school, they both swung by my room and signed it. Rob wrote, "Better late than never. New House 5—Forever my floor." Kim simply wrote, "NH5 for Life." Three months of summer hadn't changed anything.

Claire is doing well as the new female RA. She's had some problems connecting with students, but her work ethic and effort has been incredible. Everything works out in the end, and I'm glad this was no exception. Laura, who graduated, is now working for AmeriCorps for a little while before she goes to medical school. Elaine, who you may recall received another RA position after showing Student Life how much she reformed, is really enjoying her second chance. I'm glad she got another opportunity. I do think she deserved it.

I won't go specifically into what every person is doing, but needless to say, everyone is fine. Kate, for instance, is like a new person. I talked to her a lot over the summer, and with each week I could tell she was gaining more confidence and becoming more relaxed.

Issues still come up for everyone, and I still hear about them. I love that I'm still introduced as "Andy, my RA," even a year after the fact. I love that my former residents feel like they can still talk to me about anything. And I love that I am no longer their RA, just their friend. It's been rough sometimes this year, trying to balance school, being an RA, and being a good friend. But I think I've done a decent job of it, and I think I've made the necessary changes if I thought something was getting in the way of any of those things. Still going, still smiling, still learning.

As the fifth semester of my college career winds down, it scares me to think that soon, I'll be heading out into the real world. It scares me that soon, Aaron and Rosalyn will be more than a short walk from my room. That my best friends will be in Pittsburgh when I very likely won't be. The real world has always been scary, and thinking about going into it makes me even more nervous. But I have no doubt that I can handle it, and I know a lot of that has to do with my experiences at college. Being an RA opened my eyes to so many different things. Problems, ambitions, ideas, philosophies. Not that it affects what I do, but it affects what I think, and it affects how I view the world. It affects how I take on the world. Not with hesitance or arrogance. With cautiousness and confidence. It's a subtle difference, but it's an important one.

This story is skewed, no doubt, because I wrote it just months after I experienced it. Who knows how the story will change as the years pass, who knows what I'll think when I go back and read this ten years later. Time will change my perspective of what happened last year, but it will never take away what I learned and accomplished. The events won't change, but how they affect me will. My emotions still run high when I think about last year, as I'm sure they will for some time. Now that I've gotten a chance to catch my breath and really reflect on what happened, it all seems surreal, like a movie, like a dream. But maybe that's all life is. A dream. Make of it what you choose to. Prolong it and enjoy it. And never waste a second of it. Because one wasted second could mean the difference between saving someone and letting someone fall. Between saving yourself and losing yourself.

I struggled over the decision to publish the book. I decided to fictionalize some events and create characters who were compilations of real people so my friends would be protected. Still, what kind of person sells out his friends like that? What kind of person publicly reveals secrets that others shared with him? When it comes down to it, everything in this book is part of the past. We can't change the past. But we can learn from it. My hope is that you, the reader, can learn from our mistakes, just as we're learning from them now.

And through all of this, I have to remember that I got to have this experience because I was an RA. For those of you in college right now, or who plan on attending soon, I encourage you to live on campus, experience dorm life, and if you feel up to it, become a resident assistant yourself. It truly is a unique experience. And that chance to make a difference, well, it's not often handed to you on a dining hall platter. College is about evolution, and when I came into college as a scrawny, scared, wide-eyed freshman, I never imagined I would have the mental toughness, enthusiasm, and patience to become a successful RA. But I did, and I have my friends to thank for that. At the end of the year, I wrote a song specifically for my floor. I called it "Keep the Light On," symbolically meaning "Just because we're leaving each other doesn't mean we should shut each other out." There's no reason to lose the people who changed your life just because they no longer live ten feet away from you. Rosalyn told me the other day that I should be a lifetime RA. Believe me, if I could, I would.

I talked about community throughout the book. That was the second most important component of New House 5. But community led to the most important thing: friendships. The most important thing to me, anyway. My best friends right now, the people I will stay in contact with when I am long out of college, when I've got a career and family of my own, are the people I met last year. There are about a dozen of them I have become closer to than anyone else in my life, and for that alone, I am grateful that I had the chance to be an RA. Good friends don't come around all the time. You can't buy them on the internet or build them with a computer. Friendship has to be earned. And when it is, there is no better feeling in the world.

We're real people with real emotions, real feelings, real desires. It's easy to forget that, to get caught up in a fast-paced world where everything is about money, getting to the top, and leaving a good-looking corpse. For a second, throw that all out the window. I wouldn't trade the friends I made last year for anything you could offer me. Because they are the people who have been there for me, and they are the people who I will always be there for. New House 5. It's not just a floor, it's a way of life.

I've said it a hundred times. In person, in print, in my mind. But one final time, here it is: New House 5, thank you. For everything you've given me and everything you will continue to give me.

Andy Butler
12/13/04